MANSIONS
OF
DARKNESS

MANSIONS OF DARKNESS

A NOVEL OF SAINT-GERMAIN

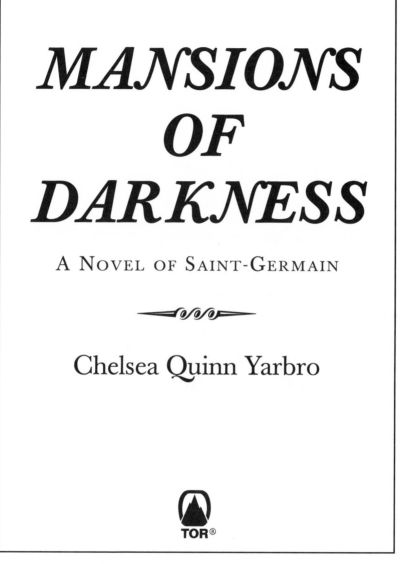

Chelsea Quinn Yarbro

TOR®

A TOM DOHERTY ASSOCIATES BOOK
NEW YORK

A Tor Book
Published by Tom Doherty Associates, Inc.
175 Fifth Avenue
New York, NY 10010

Tor Books on the World Wide Web:
http://www.tor.com

Tor® is a registered trademark of Tom Doherty Associates, Inc.

Library of Congress Cataloging-in-Publication Data

Yarbro, Chelsea Quinn
    Mansions of darkness / Chelsea Quinn Yarbro.—1st ed.
        p.   cm.
    "A Tom Doherty Associates book."
    ISBN 0-312-86382-9 (pb)
    1. Saint-Germain, comte de, d. 1784—Fiction.   2. Vampires
—Fiction.   I. Title.
PS3575.A7M36   1996
813'.54—dc20   95-52688
                                                      CIP

First hardcover edition: August 1996
First trade paperback edition: November 1997

Printed in the United States of America

0   9   8   7   6   5   4   3   2   1

For
A.H.
and about bloody time

THE VICEROYALTY OF PERU

-- 1645 --

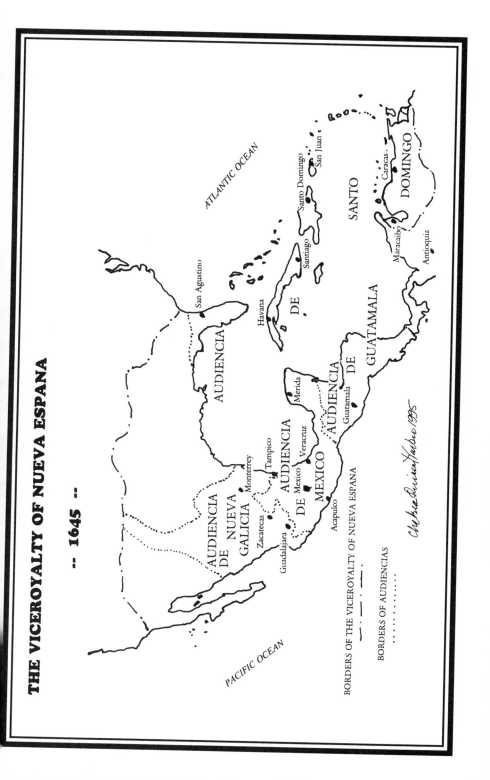

Author's Notes

In the sixteenth century, Spain established itself as the preeminent European force in North, Central, and South America, carrying on a vigorous campaign of conquest from what is now Texas and California as well as much of what is now the southern United States, to the tip of Chile. Spanish colonialism was a very different institution from English or French colonialism, and was most remarkable for its determined prohibition of the emergence of a middle class; except at a village-market trade, the upper (Spanish) class got a lock on mercantilism and land early and maintained it as part of their privilege, thus preventing any entrepreneurial advancement of the people they had conquered; they also were able to control much of the judicial and educational processes for all levels of society.

As the major colonial power in Latin America, the Spanish brought with them a formidable, magisterial bureaucracy as well as the tremendous bureaucracy of the Roman Catholic Church. Without any line drawn between Church and State, the policies and agendas of the institutions quickly became intermingled and established the climate of oppression that has not lessened significantly with the passing of time. By uniting land-holding military/administrative families with the Church, the Spanish created a bastion for themselves that is evident to this day. Between those two inexorable forces the native peoples of North and South America—many of whom had long traditions of ongoing warfare, and their own patterns of religious and military oppression—were unable to provide any prolonged or useful resistance, although from time to time there were uprisings; the ones which were the most successful were those with a leader who had strong connections to the Church-and-State.

Not only was Latin America seen as an opportunity for the Church to spread Catholicism through the New World, it was also viewed as a kind of safe dumping ground for those upper-class Spaniards who were out of step with the political and religious climate at home, and so it often happened that political liberals and radicals were set cheek-

13

by-jowl with the most rapacious and oppressive arm of the Catholic Church—the missionaries and officers of the Holy Office of the Faith otherwise known as the Inquisition. Dissidents were often kept in line through intimidation: the old do-you-have-relatives-still-living-in-the-old-country line. Most notable among these early radicals was Bartolme de las Casas, who in 1514 became a vocal supporter of the rights of the native peoples, a cause he continued to champion all his life. The New World provided a kind of social buffer zone for the Old World as well; a fair number of those who rose to prominence in the New World were younger or illegitimate sons whose exploits were welcomed half a world away. Many of these ventures would not have been acceptable closer to home. There were also rascals and opportunists from all over Europe, men determined to get ahead away from the constraints and conflicts of the Old World. Another small but important component were the adventurers, those who were eager to see something new, to open the sea-road to Japan and China, not only to make money, but to have the satisfaction of being one of the first to do it.

Prior to the catastrophic earthquake in Cuzco of 1650, there were a number of less destructive foreshocks that rocked the city from time to time; the cathedral was under repair from a previous quake when it was destroyed in 1650, so my use of one such quake is in keeping with the city at that time. Until the 1650 earthquake, many temples of the old Sacsahuaman Fortress, the Incan stronghold, were still recognizable and visited from time to time by those native people unwilling to forsake their old faith in favor of Catholicism. After 1650, the temples were in ruins and left that way.

Given the tenor of this story, it is important to be aware that in the seventeenth century, the records of Francisco de Coronado were lost and his very existence was forgotten by everyone but the various Indian peoples he visited in his extensive treks through Mexico and much of what is now the southwestern United States and, as a result, his legacy was not recognized or understood in Latin America until almost three centuries after he began his travels.

As in the case of some of the Saint-Germain books, many of the characters in this book are composites of actual historical figures, drawn more for exigencies of plot than for accuracy to specific personalities of the time, although these composites are faithful to the lives of actual people of the period. For this, I have researched as many contemporary accounts as I could find. Records of many of the colonial administrators are revealing in terms of the conduct of daily life, but tend not to contain much personal information—not surprising in a society where the Church held such records for close scrutiny. The social and political structures, however, are as careful a reproduction as I could make them, from the judicial/administrative intricacies of the Viceroyalty of Peru, to the maritime activities of the period, to the strange transmogrification of Christianity at the hands of certain groups of Yaqui people in Mexico.

And to answer a question that I have been asked many times in the last decade, a league is approximately 3.2 miles. Seven leagues was about as far as a man could comfortably walk in a day.

Thanks are due as always to Dave Nee, who continues to provide me with bibliographic information on everything from footwear to market records to military dispatch routes; to Jeanne McArthur for information on Latin American colonial institutions; to Melanie Dartmouth for access to her thesis material on religious institutions in colonial South America; to Tom Jackson for showing me his photographic essay on Spanish colonial buildings of Peru and Ecuador; to V. Y. Shaw for insights on Latin American historical politics; to Alfredo Suarez for specific sources on Yaqui traditions and the explorations of Francisco de Coronado—and with the warning that I have subsumed some of the extrapolations and theories that are as yet unincorporated into the mainstream of archeological thought. Errors in fact or historicity are mine and not any of these knowledgeable people's. Thanks are also due to the ever-helpful Beth Meacham, my long-time editor at Tor, and Greg Cox, who has taken over this cycle, with apologies for taking so long to get it done; to my attorney, Robin A. Dubner, who continues her vigilance on the Count's behalf; to Lindig Harris of Asheville, North Carolina, for her determination to get the word out; to my good friends, Kathy McDermott and Robert Bloch, both of whom died in 1994 and will not see this story, but who were such staunch supporters of the cycle; and to the Count's many fans who have been gracious enough over the years to continue their interest in this most enduring un-dead gentleman.

Berkeley, California
February, 1995

PART I

ACANNA TUPAC

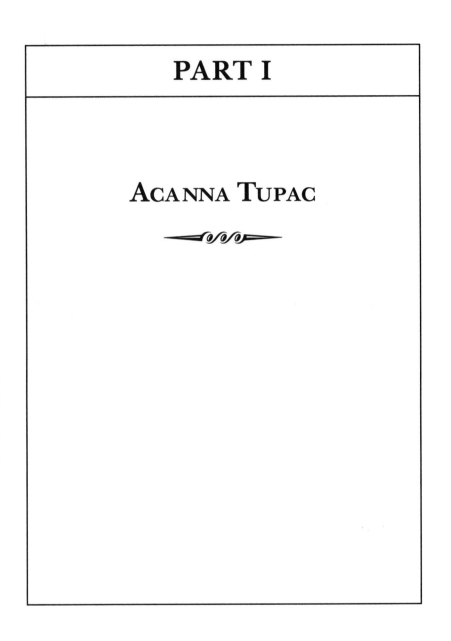

Text of a letter from Padre Andreas Hogaza y Cinta in Padova, Italia, to Don Ezequias Pannefrio y Modestez in Cuzco, Audiencia de Lima, Viceroyalty of Peru.

To my most esteemed cousin, the governmental magistrate Don Eze-
quias, my greetings and blessings from one alien land to another.
This is to introduce to you the distinguished foreign scholar, Francisco
Ragoczy, el Conde de San Germanno. I have known him for almost six
years and I recommend him to you for his erudition as well as the qual-
ity of his company. He is a most capable fellow, with a well-informed
mind that is not as hampered and hemmed as many of those we have
both known. I will describe him so that you will recognize him as the
bearer of this letter. He is a man of middle height and deep chest, with
fine features, great personal elegance with a taste for Italian clothes
though he is of an ancient Hungarian line, dark and penetrating of eye,
and eclectic of knowledge. He writes equally well with either hand. He
wears a pectoral of silver and sapphire in the form of an eclipse—a disk
with raised, displayed wings.

To be candid, I questioned his motives for venturing to Peru. He has
no need of money, being a man of great personal wealth, and I feared
that he might be seeking political advancement that would not be ac-
cessible to him in Europe. As an exile, I feared he might see Peru as a
bastion for him from which to establish his House afresh. He has assured
me, however, that he has no such ambitions, and I have allowed him to
convince me of this. He has kept no followers about him and sought no
influence with those who might assist him, and though he can afford

19

such an effort, he has made no move to gain for himself the support of the Pope or any of the reigning Houses. I take this as a good indication that he means what he says. Thus, it is my belief that his claims to want to learn from the people of that distant place before they have fully accepted Spanish ways are sincere, no matter how puzzling they may be, even to so curious a man as you are, and I am. If you come to doubt his motives, I would appreciate knowing of it, for I would then owe you a profound apology, and would need to admit to a great fault in my judgment.

He is accompanied by his manservant Rogerio, who says he is a native of Cadiz. He is in his middle years, lean and austere of demeanor; his temperament is steady and steadfast. His hair is sand-colored and his eyes blue, which makes such an assertion doubtful, and his Spanish has a cadence to it I have heard from no other. Nevertheless, he is a reliable fellow in other matters, and so it is as well to take him at his word. He reads and writes in three languages, which leads me to think he may have once been in Orders, for why else would a servant have such knowledge?

I have heard from those known to you in España that more missionaries are being sent to Cuzco with the stated intention of bringing the heathen souls of the people of that place into the Church. Although it is not a laudable thought, it has occurred to me that with things going badly for our Portuguese brethren in Japan, the Order may wish to show itself in a better light by working more in the New World than in Asia. Surely so mundane a consideration would not move the leaders of the Order to that decision. Yet while I pray daily for the salvation of the world, unless those missionaries are cut of different cloth than I remember, the heathen souls might do better to continue in their ignorance, for to be persuaded by the Holy Office for the Propagation of the Faith and San Domingo's Holy Hounds is to endanger more than the soul, I fear. In my humble opinion (and it is humble after all I have endured these last two decades) Inquisitors make poor missionaries. And my brother-Jesuits do not often manage much better, if their experience in Japan is any indication. Do not, I beg you, repeat that, for though I am no longer in España, I have no wish to give the Holy Office any more reason to suspect my devotion. How ironic it may look to those with less faith than I possess, to have a priest of an Order founded in España afraid to set foot on Spanish soil for fear of what my own religion might to do me.

Not that I have reason to suppose you would betray my confidence,

*given the many exchanges we have had in the past, and the many views
we share. You have been as banished by our family as I have, though
it was your fortune to be beyond the confines of the Church. Perhaps in
time I will be permitted to travel to the New World, too, where I may
continue my inquiries into the nature of human language. I am still
fascinated by the many ways in which the peoples of the earth express
themselves, and incidentally, in this regard, Ragoczy has been invaluable, for he commands more than two dozen tongues. Would that I did,
as well. And if I am permitted to study in the New World, I may yet have
such knowledge. For that, I will need someone to sponsor me who is willing to overlook the inquiries the Inquisitors made against me when I was
at Salamanca. I have some hope of Baccalare Omero Gianni
Tornabuoni, who shares my interests and is in a better position than I
am to promote them with the officials here, for he is a wealthy Florentine with powerful relatives who endorse his studies.*

*So, cugino mio, as they say here in Italia, I entrust to your good coun-
sel my foreign friend, and I pray that you will discover him to be as
excellent company as I have. You may benefit from his vast store of
knowledge; I know that I have. His understanding is astounding, if you
can persuade him to share it with you; he is often reticent to say much
in the company of priests, as indeed am I, in spite of the fact I am one,
and a few of our discussions have been constrained on this account. As
he has pointed out to me three years ago when I charged him with with-
holding facts from me, flames do not distinguish between loyal Catholic
and heretic, living flesh or dead; its sole task is to burn. He sails on the
ship* La Luz *from Seville for Heredia's harbor of Cartagena, via the Ca-
nary Islands, and will portage to the west, taking ship for Guayaquil.
God willing, and no pirates, he should present this to you before August.
Receive him in my name as you would myself, and accord him all the
good-will you can show a stranger. And let me know how you fare, and
what you have achieved there in those mountains.*

*With my affection and respect, and, of course, my blessings, for what
they may be worth to you, this, by my own hand.*

> *Padre Andreas Hogaza y Cinta*
> *Societá de Gesu*
> *Universitá di Padova, Italia*
> *On the 31st day of October, 1640*

1

It was a splendid afternoon for early September; spring was finally taking hold of the mountains, and flowers were everywhere, turning the slopes from green to a brightly mottled pattern of red and orange and sunset pink. From the market square to the mud-and-stone houses of the poor, to the new buildings of the Spanish, all of Cuzco was filled with color and perfume, and the promise of the ripening year.

Don Ezequias Pannefrio y Modestez tore his eyes away from the fragrant display on his balcony and gave his attention to his visitor. His servant, pausing to listen in the doorway, attracted no real attention from either man. "Yes, Conde, what may I do to be of service?" He was a mature man, of imposing stature and impeccable manners, with regular features, clever golden-brown eyes and an unexpected, quirky smile that turned his thin-lipped mouth from severe to wry in an instant; his hair was streaked with silver and cut somewhat shorter than current fashion so that it only brushed his soft, wide collar. Seated behind his writing table, he was not quite so impressive as when he was standing, but the breadth of his shoulder was still remarkable.

Francisco Ragoczy, el Conde de San Germanno, bowed slightly to the regional magistrate and said, "I regret I must impose upon the introduction of your cousin once again, but I fear it is necessary, Presidencia. I have been told I must apply to you for permission to employ natives as servants. I believe the license is called an encomienda, though I do not wish to be allotted any territory."

"As a foreigner, you would need the permission of the Corregidor in any case. For employing servants in the household, I have the authority to grant the encomienda." Don Ezequias hinted a bow.

"That is my understanding. Therefore, behold me and my petition." His quick, ironic look belied the formality of his words. Like Don Ezequias, he wore black, but unlike Don Ezequias, it suited him, as did the Italian cut of his clothes and the ruby fixed in his white silk lace-edged collar bands. A pectoral in the form of a winged disk depended from the ruby-studded silver chain around his neck.

"Ah, yes," said Don Ezequias. "Of course. I had not realized you would want to do that, or I should have issued the license before now. Your house must be almost ready to receive visitors, and servants are always required to serve one's guests." He drew a sheet of vellum toward him, then selected one of the sharpened quills and dipped it into his standish; the fragile plume seemed too small for his large hand, as did the moderate ruffles at his wrist. "These servants—how many do you think you will need?"

"Eight at first. To establish the household. If more are necessary, I will ask for them when the need arises, if that is acceptable to you," said San Germanno, his left hand resting comfortably on the hilt of his sword in the same manner as most of the Spaniards affected.

"Suppose I authorize ten?" offered Don Ezequias. "That should be sufficient to your needs, Conde, don't you think?"

"You are very understanding," said San Germanno. He watched while Don Ezequias completed the brief document and sanded the ink. "If there is some appropriate way I might show my thanks for this?"

Don Ezequias was about to say no, but then his expression changed. "Yes. I think there may be something you can do for me." He tapped his big hand twice at the edge of the page. "I will be giving a reception for the Incan nobility in ten days' time. If you would be available to attend, I would appreciate it if you would be willing to escort the daughter of Quispe Titu. Her name is Acanna Tupac, she is a woman past youth but of some importance, and most of her relatives prefer not to recognize her. In spite of this, she must be included because of her birth. It would be less of an ordeal for all of us if you would do this for me."

"Certainly," said San Germanno at once, inwardly glad for the opportunity he was being presented; then he added, "I would consider it an honor to perform that office. But it might be easier for all of us if I knew the reason she is shunned by her kinsmen."

"Ah, that is something of a difficult matter," said Don Ezequias, fingering the point of his small beard. "But I suppose it would be best to tell you." He leaned back in his chair and again let his gaze wander to the profusion of flowers on his balcony. "It is a question of family lines. She is the last of the senior branch of the royal family. We promoted the cadet branch; they were more willing to assist us than the senior was."

"Hardly surprising that they would," said San Germanno, recalling many other times when this ploy had succeeded where force of arms would not.

"I agree," said Don Ezequias, his attention still on the flowers. "Still, the woman must have a suitable escort and I would be grateful if you would do this for me. It would spare me the necessity of asking one of the Dominicans to do it, and I would rather not. Acanna Tupac would be offended."

"So might the Dominician," San Germanno remarked, and repeated with an emotion which Don Ezequias could not read, "I would be honored." He paused a moment, then went on. "Tell me more of this Acanna Tupac. Do I have her name right? If I am to be in her company, I should know more about her, so that I will not commit any gaffe while with her, or give offense to your guests."

"You have her name right, Conde." The Presidencia shrugged and began to prepare wax for his official seal on the encomienda. "I actually know very little about her, aside from her being the great-granddaughter of Quispe Tupac and the great-great granddaughter of Atahualpa Inca and his third wife Choque Suyo. Juan Enrique de Almansa Inca y Loyola explained the genealogy to me shortly after I arrived; such things are as important to these Incas as they are to Spaniards. I have met her only twice before. She keeps to her own society, in part because she has little money, and in part because the clergy have not been kind to her. She is probably nearer forty than thirty, unmarried, though whether she is a spinster or a widow, I cannot discover."

"What company does she bring with her?" asked San Germanno. "Someone of so high a birth surely does not come alone."

"Occasionally she brings another woman with her, but most often her only suite is her servants, and she does not have many of them." He dropped a blob of hot wax onto the foot of the vellum sheet, then turned his ring to fix its impression in it.

"I take it she is not well-connected, then; I would have thought with such relations she would have been better provided for. Is there not an inheritance to support her?" There was no criticism in this observation; San Germanno waited for Don Ezequias' answer with interest.

"No. She has nothing. None of the senior line have much left. My predecessors saw to that." This last was admitted grimly. "It was a successful ploy, and it suited their purposes perfectly, keeping the senior branch in obscurity while raising the cadet branch to prominence for their own uses." He stared at his fingers. "She is . . . striking, not beautiful, and most dignified."

"And such treatment rankles with you, does it not? the elevation of the cadet branch as a way to control the senior branch by removing the privileges of the senior line," said San Germanno, recalling the many times he had seen cadet relatives supplant their seniors. "You believe it is an unworthy way to gain control of the country."

"I did not say so," Don Ezequias responded promptly.

"No, you did not, but your implication was fairly clear; for what comfort it will bring you, I share your indignation," San Germanno told him, and waited.

Don Ezequias answered carefully. "If I were indignant, I would be most unwise to admit it. And so would you. Indignation on behalf of these people will benefit neither you nor them. Obispo Punto y Sello is inclined to think such opinions are heresy, and though he may be in Lima, his power reaches from the southern tip of Audiencia de Charcas to the northern-most edge of Audiencia de Nueva Galicia. All other Obispos are afraid of him. And no one—not clergy, not officials—is promoted without his approval." He inspected the impression of his seal and nodded twice before handing the license to San Germanno. "There, Conde: permission to employ up to ten natives in your household. No one will question it. If you have any interference from . . . anyone, show them this."

"Thank you," said San Germanno, taking the vellum and rolling it with care. "You have made my situation much less awkward with this single sheet." He bowed again, this time formally.

"It pleases me to have men of your calibre here in Cuzco, where one cannot be too selective if one wishes any friends at all. You improve the society more than you know. If we had more like you, and fewer of those who seek—" Don Ezequias broke off, noticing the ironic lift of San Germanno's fine brows. He cleaned the point of his quill on a small square of cotton and put it back in the stand. After a moment he added, "Too often those who come here are those who are not welcome in Europe, or those greedy for what they cannot have in the Old World. We are where all the misfits are sent. All of them. Only a few, like yourself, are here from choice that is not the product of zeal or greed."

"So I have gathered," said San Germanno, his tone level; this was not a matter he wanted to discuss, for it could be used to his detriment if Don Ezequias reported his opinions to the Church authorities in the region.

"Oh, you have no cause to fear me. Why do you think I have been sent to this remote part of the world, if not to keep from embarrassing my family? Yes, they put another face on it, as you would expect, but their intention in sending me to this place was to make certain I would have no opportunity to express my views where they would bring disgrace upon them. It is not wise to be liberal in España. The Church disapproves, and perforce so does the Crown." His lips curved, though the smile did not light his eyes. "My wife, of course, still lives in España, along with our children. I haven't seen any of them in eight years, though I have letters occasionally." This last admission was more troubling to him than the rest.

San Germanno considered his response carefully, and spoke calmly. "That is . . . unfortunate, Presidencia."

Don Ezequias shrugged with false unconcern. "They are an assurance that I will continue to behave well, meaning that I keep my opinions to myself." He indicated the window and the noisy plaza beyond. "Who is going to listen to me here, after all?"

"There are those who might," said San Germanno with a nod in the direction of the massive, dark-wood crucifix on the far wall.

"True enough; for they listen to everything, not just Confession, and report to more than the Obispo," said Don Ezequias. He rose abruptly, a good head taller than San Germanno, though this did not appear to bother el Conde. "I will have a formal invitation delivered to your house tomorrow, with all the particulars. You may send me your reply with my servant. If you have brought court dress with you, it would be appropriate for the occasion."

"Certainly," said San Germanno, stepping back from Don Ezequias' writing table and offering him a graceful bow. "You are all kindness to a stranger."

"Hardly an effort in your case, San Germanno," said Don Ezequias as el Conde left him alone in his reception room.

All through the plaza the people of Peru were selling their wares, their foodstuffs, their cloth; the cacophony was tremendous. San Germanno passed the length of market at a leisurely pace so that he could see the fruits of these people's industry and imagination. His manner was calm even when he was accosted by a dozen boys all demanding coins from him in broken Spanish, their voices strident. One or two of them held knives at the ready.

"Not today," he answered them, the authority in his voice and stance unquestionable though there was no trace of aggression about him.

The leader of the band made a single, short lunge at San Germanno, who stepped aside easily. The boy swore.

"You aren't going to stab me in the middle of the market, are you?

where the sentries can see you?" San Germanno asked lightly. "Wait for a dark alley. It's much safer."

The youths hesitated in confusion, and then one of them made an obscene gesture before he turned toward the nearest street.

A woman watching from one of the booths chuckled as the boys moved away sheepishly but with the swagger of victory in their walk. "They are fools, those youngsters, reckless fools," she said to San Germanno when the young men were gone; her Spanish was flavored with the rhythms and vowels of her native tongue. Her face was broad and had few wrinkles, though the lines bracketing her mouth revealed her age more than any other feature.

"Not fools, just youths afraid of their futures," he answered, and paused to look at the lengths of alpaca fabric she had draped over the sides of her market-stall.

"And so they might be," she replied heavily. "But they put themselves and all the rest of us in danger when they behave so, though they will not believe it. What they are doing will turn into misfortune if it is not checked. They are daring the Spanish to notice them. One day they will go too far, and someone will be killed or maimed, and then what?"

"You are to be applauded that it has not happened yet," San Germanno said as he fingered the wool, testing its hand.

She snorted. "They play at games they do not understand. For they are not games."

"You will never convince them of that," San Germanno told her, and selected a portion of fabric the color of soot. "How much?"

"Two golden reales, Señor," she answered at once, knowing the amount was outrageous.

They bargained their way down to a single golden real and two silver doña, both of them enjoying the exchange. San Germanno gave her the coins and took possession of the cloth, then continued on his way to the house he had purchased upon his arrival in Cuzco six weeks since.

It was in an unpaved street that led eventually to the abandoned Incan fortress Sacsahuaman; it was a building less than ten years old, two storeys high, with a courtyard with a large tree growing in the center. The courtyard was even now being paved in rough tiles made of Spanish clay and finished in a dull-ocher glaze. The workmen looked up from their task as San Germanno came through the stout wooden gate and paused in his walk to the main section of the house to see how they were progressing. "Save the decorated tiles for the base of the tree and the edge of the courtyard. Make sure there is a layer of earth beneath each tile," he reminded the foreman of the crew.

"If that is your wish, Patrono, it is our duty." He lowered his head in a show of submission.

"You know that it is, but you need not abase yourself because of it." He studied the man with concern. "You are not my slave, Inigo, you are a craftsman I have hired to supervise this work, and the men of your crew are craftsmen, too. Do this well, and I will be satisfied." For an instant the face of Gasparo Tuccio filled his memory, and his palazzo in Fiorenza.

Inigo looked away from him. "I do not want the priests saying I have failed to honor you, mi Patrono."

"If I do not say it, how can they? I am the one who employs you, not they, and I am satisfied with all you have done," he said with more assurance than he felt, for he was well-aware that it would take less reason than one he might provide for the priests to decide that the Peruvians had not worked with the required obsequiousness. "You have set the cross-beams in place in my ceilings, reinforced the doors and the chimneys, and now you are completing the courtyard to my specifications. Where is the error in any of that?"

"I do not know, Señor. But fault may be found in spite of what you tell me and we will have to answer for it. The priests are not men like other men, and they demand things of us that others may not," said Inigo, clearly wishing to get back to his work and end this difficult exchange. "But we will do what you have paid us to do, and we will do it well, if God will permit it."

"Amen to that. We are obeying your instructions. One double-handful of earth for every tile," San Germanno reminded him, already feeling the support of his native earth in this place.

"As you have said." Inigo touched his forehead to show his acceptance of these orders. "Another two days and we will be finished."

"You are doing well, you and your men," said San Germanno, hoping to make the workman believe him.

"The Patrono is gracious. We will strive to do his bidding." He lowered his head once more as if taking on a great burden.

"Excellent," San Germanno declared, trying to make it clear that he was satisfied with this. "I am most satisfied and grateful." He was saved the trouble of finding more assurances for Inigo by the sight of his manservant approaching from the far side of the courtyard.

"My master," said Rogerio as he approached San Germanno, pausing to bow as much as society demanded. He was wearing a long, Italian smock of a pale blue over his grey breeches and buff-colored muslin shirt; his boots were soft leather that reached to his knees. In one hand he held a ledger, two fingers marking his place in the pages. "The accounts are not yet complete, but I will present them to you if you wish to review them."

"I trust you, old friend. If you tell me the cook needs five reales for stocking the kitchen, I am sure you will attend to it." He glanced around the courtyard, his face showing little more than mild interest. "How many trunks of my native earth are left? I reckon the number at nine."

"That is correct," said Rogerio, standing aside to permit San Germanno to pass into the house ahead of him. Once out of earshot of the workers, the manservant asked, "How did you fare with the magistrate? the Presidencia?" he corrected himself. "Did he accept your petition? Will he authorize you to staff the household?"

"Yes he will, as I told you he would, and without any delays. I have a license for hiring ten servants," San Germanno declared, holding up the rolled vellum. "Behold—the encomienda, signed by the Presidencia. You may commence your interview tomorrow, if you like. We will need a kitchen staff, a groom for the horses, and a seamer to make cushions and draperies for the house for a start. Then a gardener and someone to tend the fires for the household. Nights are cold so high in the mountains." Then he handed the alpaca wool to Rogerio as well. "I will want this made into a cloak. One of those Venetian ones, with the standing collar. Use the white silk we brought for a lining."

Rogerio took the cloth and nodded to show his compliance. "It will be done, my master."

"You are always reliable, Rogerio," said San Germanno. They had reached the door to his private study, and he retrieved a large key to open the lock. As the wards turned, San Germanno glanced along the corridor, hoping that none of the workers were watching him. Quickly he swung the door open and stepped into his study.

The room was more an alchemical laboratory than a study, for although there were several hundred books in the shelves that lined the walls, the focus of the room was on two trestle tables that flanked the egg-shaped brick athanor located at the center of the room. There were a number of glass vessels set upon stands, as well as a dozen large jars sealed with wax in a variety of colors. A brass scale stood near the largest of the glass vessels, its weights lined up beside it like ranks of soldiers.

Rogerio closed the door with care and stood near it, not quite keeping guard. He indicated the high windows in the far wall. When he spoke again, it was in the Latin of Imperial Rome. "Are you certain you have not been watched?"

"No, I am not," said San Germanno bluntly in the same language. "And that causes me concern, given where we are."

"I should think so," said Rogerio. "There will be rumors enough in your household without marketplace gossip adding to it."

"True enough." San Germanno rubbed his eyes with one small, beautiful hand. He had not yet accustomed himself to the altitude of the place, or his hunger, and as a result he suffered occasionally from a slight, ill-defined headache, as he did now. He thought back more than four hundred years to his travel in Asia, and the majesty of those distant mountains, where he had faced worse than headaches. Deliberately he straightened up to the limits of his moderate height. "You think I should leave here."

"I think it might be wise," said Rogerio carefully.

"And go where? Europe is not safe, which is why we are here. Asia is caught up in wars no stranger could survive, and surely you do not want to return to Russia?" He turned around and looked directly at Rogerio. "This place is as much a haven as one of my blood will ever find, but for my native earth."

"And still the Church watches you," warned Rogerio.

"But not in the numbers as they do in Europe, and not with the same power, not yet." He touched the scales lightly, watching the balance tilt. "Make a note: I have a social obligation in ten days."

Rogerio had been with San Germanno long enough not to permit such abrupt announcements to distress him. He schooled his features to neutrality. "What obligation is that?"

"There is some sort of reception the Presidencia is giving which I am supposed to attend to provide a suitable escort for a senior descendant of the Incan ruler, a woman of middle years and no apparent fortune, more's the pity for her. I gather her presence is required but not entirely welcome." He stared at the neat array of vials on the nearer of the two trestle tables.

"A strange request," said Rogerio in a noncommittal voice.

"It is, isn't it?" San Germanno countered. "And I fear it may prove as awkward for her as it is apt to be for me." He gave a fleeting smile and went on with a trace of amusement in his tone, "Still, she may prove more interesting than Don Ezequias knows. Or so I hope."

"You hope she will tell you who among her people keeps to the old ways," Rogerio said, certain of this.

"That I do." He glanced at his manservant. "Do not worry, old friend. I will tread lightly. We may be an ocean and a continent away from the Holy Office for the Faith, but their grasp certainly reaches this far, though not with the strength they desire. I will not forget them, for her sake if not for mine." He smoothed the front of his fine black coat, his finger tracing the elaborate lacing around the buttonholes.

"Take care you do not forget that, for all of us," warned Rogerio, his face severe. "They may be few, but they are the more determined because they are few. And their presence is increasing steadily. Before long they will do all in their power to show their might in this place."

San Germanno shook his head. "You are right. And leaving now would be . . . unpleasant." He looked down at the square toe of his boot. "All those days lying in that stinking hold, weak as an infant and so ill it hurt to move. I would not care to repeat the experience soon. I will endeavor to keep your caution in mind."

Rogerio shook his head emphatically. "You think you can ignore them, my master. You are gambling on the isolation of Cuzco to provide protection. You look at these mountains and suppose that they would not be able to pursue you, let alone catch you, if they took up the chase." His blue eyes took on a metallic cast. "But this is not your native earth, and between you and it lies the Atlantic Ocean. You dare not expose yourself to their scrutiny, not with so much water between you and home."

It took San Germanno a little time to reply. "All right. I will be discreet, even in being a friend to this Acanna Tupac, if she is willing to have me be one. Will that satisfy you: I doubt I can do anything more that will not compromise me in some way in the eyes of the Spanish. If you are convinced, then write to Olivia and tell her you have delivered her message, and thank her for her concern. How like her." This time his smile lasted longer as he saw the confusion in Rogerio's blue eyes. "Well, who but Olivia would tender me such a lecture as the one you have delivered. Not content with upbraiding me herself she has tasked you with the work as well." He raised his hands in mock surrender, his dark eyes glowing with something that was not quite amusement. "Very well. I will comply with her requests and caveats."

"That I will, my master," said Rogerio, though it was obvious from the set of his countenance that he was unconvinced.

"She has more to fear in Paris than I do in Peru, but she will not believe it. She thinks I am the one among savages, and she is safe at the French court. As if she or anyone could be safe there, no matter what the Italian Cardinal tells her. She might as well be in Moscovy, for all the safety she has." With a shake of his head expressing disbelief, he crossed his arms and walked the length of his study, past the athanor and other equipment he used to make gold and jewels, past the alembics where he combined mouldy bread with other ingredients to create his sovereign remedy, to a tall candelabrum where a massive beeswax taper with three wicks stood. "There is much to learn here, and for a while, I may do it unimpeded. You and Olivia are right—I intend to make the most of this place while I am able. The people of these mountains have information that I seek, and skills I wish to acquire. The Church is not yet the uppermost power in Cuzco, and that lends me a little . . . grace." His smile at his own witticism was wry. "When that changes, I will have to be on the alert, for no matter how much a friend Don Ezequias may want to be, there are demands made on him by his family, and I will not put him to the test of making a choice."

"Are you sure of this?" Rogerio asked. "Truly?"

San Germanno regarded him in silence. "I am reasonably certain of it, yes, and that is the best I can hope for, given that this place is under Spanish rule, and their strength, as you have reminded me, is increasing every month."

"And that is the trouble, that España is the force in this place." Rogerio looked around the study meaningfully. "You dare not let any of the workmen know of what you do here. This is not Fiorenza—"

"Nor was Fiorenza Fiorenza after Savonarola came," San Germanno interjected with a trace of emotion that was not quite grief, not quite despair.

Rogerio would not be put off. "—but an outpost of the Inquisition, with the purposes of the Inquisition. There are no Artei here, no Guilds to protect them. Those men would be in danger if they knew what you do here."

"I was not planning to tell them," said San Germanno with sudden weariness.

"Just as well," said Rogerio.

"So I thought," San Germanno remarked, adding with a rueful smile, "Give me a little credit, old friend. I have had some experience in these matters." He put his hand deep into his pockets. "Break out my court dress for the reception. Make it the Hungarian fashion, so that it will be apparent to all that I am not among the Spaniards. I don't think I should wear the Order, however. It would seem too much like display."

"The Italian is handsomer," said Rogerio, "and richer."

"True," San Germanno allowed after a moment. "But the Hungarian will tell the Church more than the Italian. It will show that I have stood against the Turks in their advancement to the west, which I have, upon more than one occasion. They will not want to discredit me for that."

"Turks, Huns, Romans, Dacians, Greeks, Scythians, Hittites, and all the rest; your poor homeland has endured much." Rogerio's manner softened as he recited these peoples, many of whom were forgotten by history, but not by San Germanno.

"So much that my own people have left it long ago," San Germanno said as if he were speaking of the weather. "Yet it is my native earth, and I will defend it, no matter who comes against it." He sighed once. "I ought to understand the Incan people here better than they know."

"Will that be enough, your understanding? Will they accept you, do you think?" asked Rogerio.

San Germanno fingered his silver pectoral, outlining its raised wings and then the disk. "That remains to be seen. I will know more after the reception, when I have met those who are in power here."

"Do you think it likely?" Rogerio persisted, acutely aware of the number of times San Germanno had sought such acceptance and failed to achieve it, often at great cost to himself.

"I don't know, but I have hope, damnable hope. And because I do, I want more than acceptance: I want learning, I want to find comprehension, I want to know compassion," said San Germanno quietly, his eyes glowing with intensity. "And I want touching."

"Is that possible?" Rogerio wondered aloud. "After you have come so far and made so great an effort to isolate yourself?"

"Is that what I have done?" asked San Germanno, his handsome, irregular face sardonic.

"Isn't it?" Rogerio countered.

San Germanno's answer was given softly and his tone was distant. "I will find out after I have escorted Acanna Tupac to this reception."

Text of a letter from Frey Jeromo to Obispo Hernan Guarda.

To the most reverend and excellent Obispo Hernan Guarda, the humble greetings of your servant, in God's name.

You have asked me to tell you all that I observed during the reception of last week, given by the magistrate, Don Ezequias Pannefrio y Mod-estez, in the honor of the Peruvian nobility. I pray that I may report truly to you, and that my account finds favor in your eyes.

I arrived with four of my Brothers, at the end of siesta, and we were greeted by Don Ezequias and Don Alejandro Morena y Osma, Capitan of soldiers here. From there we were taken by the major domo to the courtyard where tables were laid for the banquet. There were eight ta-bles set, and barrels of wine were already tapped as we arrived, and many of the guests were taking their first cupfuls. As you yourself will remember, there were many fine people present, and I will not bore you with a recitation of their names, for you were introduced to all of them during the afternoon and evening. While you were in deep conversa-tion with the two Portuguese explorers, I made my way amongst the other guests who were gathered for the occasion.

It appears you are right about the French officer—he told Don Ale-jandro that he was in disfavor with the King's Guards and had thought it best to seek employment elsewhere until the scandal attached to his name should fade. Peru appealed to him for any number of reasons, which include the chance for plunder and the favors of Indian women. He is seeking a place with Don Alejandro's men, as an officer, not a reg-ular soldier. I do not know if he will get it, for at that moment, Don Ale-jandro noticed I was near and changed the subject to horseflesh.

I then listened to Padre Juan Batista Serrano y Piedrascaldas, who was deep in discussion with the men who had just arrived from Lima. He was much distressed to learn they had not brought him certain packets. He was expecting a number of books, the titles of which were not mentioned, but from his furtive inquiry I take to be those not ap-proved by the Pope. He was upset to learn he would have to wait until the next pack-train for them, or perhaps the one after that. It may be useful to search for the items mentioned when these are delivered, for even Jesuits must learn that they cannot hide heresy in these mountains.

The young nobleman from Lisboa was boasting that he had made arrangements with certain Dutch merchants, so that even if the Jesuits and the Portuguese are not permitted in Japan, he will be able to con-tinue to protect his investments there. I noticed that only four men were listening to him, and that they did not believe that such drastic arrange-ments would be necessary. The nobleman made no secret of his deal-ings, and I report them to you only because my Brothers will also re-mark upon him, I am certain, and you will wonder if the account is not in my report. Duca Roldo Simao Vila Nova de Gois has not made himself inconspicuous in the time he has been here, with his nine ships in the ports of Arica and Callao. His pride may bring him to grief before his time here is done.

I then encountered that foreigner, Ragoczy, who was in full court regalia I did not recognize, but I have since been informed was Hungarian. He had been given the task of providing an appropriate escort for Acanna Tupac, that last descendant of the old Incan line, who was a necessary guest for the occasion, though her cousin, whom the banquet honored, did not speak to her at all. Her garments were simple and she had but one jewel—a cabochon emerald set in gold—at her throat. Her features have little beauty, but she bears herself well and has the dignity that befits her years. She did not seem as displeased with his company as she has been with most Don Ezequias has assigned to her in the past, but whether that was because Ragoczy was pleasant to her, or because he told her tales of being an exile, I cannot say. If he was aware I was listening, nothing in his manner suggested it, and I lingered for some time to hear his accounts of all the various invasions his land has suffered over the decades. They live in the same quarter of the city, although Ragoczy's house is much finer than hers, and that gave them more grounds for discussion. Acanna Tupac, at Ragoczy's urging, described what the city was like in her youth, and the many legends of the place before any Spaniard came here. The manner in which Ragoczy indulged the woman was quite remarkable, given that he must have known at least half her accounts were nothing more than fables. The woman was seated with those wives in attendance, in the alcove adjacent to the courtyard, when the dinner began.

For the banquet, I was seated with the four men from Genova who are trying to buy silver ornaments from the Indians here. Their greed was so open and obvious that I did not think they presented a danger to anyone but the unwary Indians they seek to prey upon. I told them that the Incan people living in Cuzco cannot be easily fooled, and they declared they would venture into the distant valleys for the purpose of making their fortunes. What could I do but laugh at their dreams?

At the conclusion of the meal, when it was growing dark, I happened to overhear Dom Enrique Vilhao say he wanted to arrange to bring black slaves here as laborers. One of the other Portuguese said he would try to arrange it, for it has succeeded in Brazil, but warned that so long a voyage would increase the costs of the slaves, since many of them would not survive the journey from Africa. They will meet again to discuss money before entering into any agreement.

I left with my Brothers to return to our church, and we have said that we will each prepare our accounts for you without consulting among one another, so that you will be better able to judge our efforts without prejudice. If there are any particulars upon which we disagree, I pray you will examine and correct our errors to that we may serve you and Holy Mother Church in full devotion.

Frey Jeromo
Order of the Preachers of San Domingo
At Cuzco, the 17th day of September, the feast of Santa Colomba de Cordova, in the Year of Grace, 1641. By my own hand.

2

In the stifling heat, a pervasive odor of something green and rotten rose up the long slopes from the distant jungles to Cuzco. The market plaza was occupied, but those who came there moved slowly in the tremendous heat as midday siesta began. Even the donkeys and llamas had the stunned look that heat imparts. At the gates to the city, the sentries kept to their posts but with little attention to the road beyond; lethargy had taken them into its embrace.

A short while later a few of the donkeys began to bray, which set dogs to barking. This ruckus lasted for a short while, and then ended with the animals crowding as closely together as their hobbles and tethers would allow, the sweat on their flanks as much from anxiety as from heat; they carried their heads low, their long ears moving restlessly. None of them ate the hay set out for them. A few fretted, worrying at the leads that held them. Some of the dogs continued to whine.

Not quite an hour later there was a shimmer in the ground, hardly enough to notice. It faded away quickly, and then returned with a lurching jolt that set the church bells to clanging in useless warning. People wakened from their siestas with a start, some of them alarmed, many more only puzzled.

Suddenly the earth rumbled, growled, then thundered, and shook like the withers of a gigantic horse; pots fell from balconies, and many of the brick houses tilted, swayed and broke. A section of the town wall collapsed, taking the hapless sentry on guard there with it. The belltower of the Catedral folded in on itself, muffling the last tocsin of the bells with their own destruction. The Presidencia's house rocked vigorously, shedding its shutters and balconies as if in a frenzy of itching. In the market plaza, the animals broke and ran, bringing a new chaos to the sudden catastrophe. Those few people in the market plaza who had managed to get to their feet were knocked down again in the last jolt that sent another seventeen houses into heaps of fractured brick. Then the earth was still, and the sounds that remained were the laments and screams of the people and animals.

In his study, San Germanno surveyed the damage around him with dismay tempered by relief. The displaced books would be put back on their shelves, the broken glass vessels swept away and new ones made to take their places. The jugs and jars which had cracked could be emptied into other receptacles. Fortunately the athanor had not been touched by any of the falling debris, and showed no signs of damage.

"My master," cried Rogerio as he pulled the door open.

"Come inside," said San Germanno bluntly. "Are you unhurt?"

"Yes; nothing more than a bruise or two." He looked at the broken glass vessels and the books on the floor. "You are fortunate the cases did not fall over."

"Truly," said San Germanno with feeling. He did not like to think what would become of him had the wall or ceiling collapsed on him: a broken spine would be the end of him as much as fire or beheading would be.

"It will be some while before the staff can clean this," Rogerio said as he looked around.

"I will tend to it myself," San Germanno said with a direct stare at his manservant. "I will not allow an earthquake to rid me of my good sense, and permit my servants into this room, no matter how great its disarray. It would not be wise for them to know what I do here, and so I will give them no chance to speculate. And so you may inform Olivia." This last was accompanied by a chuckle that surprised both of them. "She has been through a tremor or two herself, in Rome and in Greece, and she will not think it strange that I—"

Another shaking, now more tentative, went through the mountains. The noise in the street was growing louder, a combination of shouts, screams and wails that made an eerie discord.

"If I tell her of this at all, I will reassure her, if it is possible," said Rogerio, his voice steadier than before.

San Germanno took a minute or two to inspect his study walls. "I am glad now that I had the metal braces fitted at the corners of all the doors," he remarked as he went.

"And the cross-beams as well," said Rogerio, attempting to match his master's composure. "The workmen thought you were absurd, having them installed."

"Yes." He steadied himself as a departing wriggle slithered away through the mountains. "I trust it was sufficient to keep us from serious damage?"

"I haven't been through the whole house yet," said Rogerio, his self-composure restored at last. "I will attend to that at once."

"Good," said San Germanno, and added as Rogerio reached for the doorlatch, "When you are through, bring my red chest and prepare to go out into the streets. There will be people needing our help."

Rogerio shot him a warning glance. "Do you think it wise?"

"Wise or not, it is necessary. Listen." He gestured toward the window where cries more piercing than broken glass echoed. "There are people screaming. They are in pain and distress. Do not tell me the farrier and the barber at the barracks know enough to tend to the injured, or that the good Brothers are ready to provide more than Last Rites. I cannot bear to listen to that while I have the capacity to help alleviate it."

"I will return shortly," said Rogerio, "with the red chest." He closed the door carefully behind him.

By the time Rogerio came back, San Germanno had stacked most of the fallen books on the trestle tables and swept the broken glass into the far corner of the room. He looked up as his manservant came through the door, the red chest of Roman lacquer-work strapped with broad bands of leather to his back. "How are the servants?"

"The cook was knocked on his head by a pot falling from the rack, and his assistant was burned. His scullion has pulled his shoulder badly, but not enough to need bandaging. I gave the cook a composer and bandaged the bump with the wormwood salve, to lessen the swelling and draw the bruise. The burns I treated with the Egyptian unguent. You may inspect him now or later. The scullion I gave a composer."

"And the rest? What of them?" San Germanno asked as he took his black coat from the back of the largest chair in the study, and pulled it on over his white shirt and black waistcoat.

"The groom is worried about the horses, but aside from a wrenched shoulder, he is unhurt. The two chambermaids are badly frightened, but they are not in any pain other than spiritual, and I have nothing to aid them for that malady. The stoker was knocked unconscious but has recovered himself and is expressing worry for his wife and children. I have persuaded him to remain here until we are certain the streets are passable. The gardener has a bad scrape where he fell against the tree in the courtyard, but I can detect nothing more serious. I have used an anodyne lotion on the scrape, and said that you will examine the injury this evening. The seamer fled the house as soon as the earth stopped shaking. I know nothing of his condition."

"So long as he did not take the damask for my draperies with him, I suppose I cannot complain," said San Germanno, his tone light and ironic. "Just the same, go fetch the two bolts of muslin from his workroom and bring them along." He glanced at the chest again, and said, "Never mind, old friend. I will do it." With that, he strode purposefully out of his study and went up the stairs at the end of the hall two at a time.

Rogerio had finished locking the study door and was halfway down the corridor to the courtyard when San Germanno caught up with him, a thick bolt of new muslin under each arm.

The street beyond San Germanno's stout wooden gates looked as if a gigantic and wanton child had played with the structures and smashed them in sudden, irrational frustration. Dust rose from the rubble, and screams. The house immediately opposite San Germanno's leaned at an angle so that every window was misaligned and gaping, and the door itself was jammed closed. From inside came shouts for help, appeals to the Blessed Rosa de Lima, and wails of anguish.

San Germanno made a gesture to Rogerio, handed him the two bolts of muslin, and reached for the iron ring on the gate. "Stand aside."

Rogerio moved back and watched as his master gave his enormous strength over to the task of opening the door. It was not often that he had seen San Germanno struggle with an object as he did with those gates. The muscles stood out on his neck above the bands, and his jaw clenched with the effort. But finally there was a sound like a groan of defeat and San Germanno shouted, *"Get back!"* to the people inside as he dragged the gates open, staggering a bit with his last effort.

Half the remaining wall above the gate fell in, sending an obscuring cloud of dust into the air. It took a short while for the breeze to carry it away and reveal the people it had cloaked.

The master of the house was not quite erect; he held his right arm against his chest in a protective hunch. Behind him, his wife and three children cowered, the two youngest weeping silently. Nearby, a Franciscan stood among the crouching mass of seventeen household servants, praying in a steady monotone, "*. . . Dei, ora pro nobis peccatoribus nunc et in hora mortis nostrae. Amen. Ave Maria, gratia plena, Dominus tecum, benedicta tu in mulieribus et . . .*"

San Germanno swung to the side and let the gates fall, then looked back at the people beyond the ruin of the front of the house. He bowed slightly, breathing deeply from his exertions. "God keep you, my neighbors," he said. "And give Him thanks that He has spared you today."

"How . . . " The master of the household stared at him. "The gates were jammed closed. I know they were. I have been trying to get those gates open forever." By which he meant the thirty minutes or so since the earthquake struck. "But you . . . it was as nothing. You opened them."

"But your shoulder is injured. Mine is not. And I was working with the jamb, not against it." San Germanno offered his explanation as if it were so obvious that everyone should believe it. He indicated Rogerio. "We have brought medicaments. If anyone else is injured, we will be pleased to offer what care we can."

The master of the house looked stunned. "Why would you do that?"

"Because I am able to, and you have need," answered San Germanno as levelly as he could. "Your shoulder, for example. I can give you a tincture to dull the pain, and then I could set it for you and bandage it so that it will heal. If you leave it as it is, you may lose strength in it, and sensation in your fingers, and the injury would not improve of its own inclination, as some do."

The man rubbed at his short beard with his left hand and looked at the broken wall. "Very well." It was a grudging concession on the man's part, as if accepting any help disgraced him.

San Germanno climbed over the mound of fallen bricks and bowed again. "Permit me to introduce myself. I am your neighbor, Francisco Ragoczy, el Conde de San Germanno. I do not have the honor of knowing your name."

This elaborate display of courtesy softened the man's demeanor, restoring some of his dignity as well, so that he was able to bow to the stranger with a touch of cordiality, "I am Gregorio Simeon Calderon y Mazez."

"A distinguished name, Calderon," said San Germanno, his urbane good manners exercising a steadying effect on the members of this household.

Señor Calderon y Mazez was especially grateful for it, and rose to the occasion. "You mean my cousin Pedro Calderon de la Barca, I suppose. Yes, he is one to be proud of. Thank you for such a compliment." He indicated his family without moving his arms. "My wife and children, who, mercifully, were not killed in this calamity. And Frey Amadis, who is our teacher as well as the guide for our souls." He glanced once at Rogerio. "Your servant?"

"My manservant, Rogerio. He is from Cadiz," said San Germanno, but did not add that the city was a Roman one called Gades when Rogerio lived there.

"An old family, judging from his blue eyes," said Señor Calderon y Mazez, his face expressing as much doubt as pain.

"Yes, quite old," said Rogerio, and did not expand on this. He set the muslin bolts one atop the other, then knelt down and began to unfasten the straps that held the chest in place.

Suddenly the youngest of the children broke away from his mother and came rushing over to Rogerio, his face streaked with dusty tears. He flung out his hand as Rogerio opened the upper door of the chest, demanding something for the bruise on his arm.

"No, Vives," shouted his father loudly. "You must not do this. Let him decide who is to be treated first."

"It is all right, sir. I am a father, myself," said Rogerio, knowing that his family line had vanished with the coming of the Moors to España. "I will look at this, if you will permit, my master."

"By all means; do as you think best," said San Germanno, approaching Señor Calderon y Mazez. He could see the man's fear and pain beneath his stiff formality, and for that reason, he moved very carefully, doing his best to keep from alarming him. "I want to see your arm, Señor. I am afraid it may cause you some pain, but I must have a look at it if I am to aid you."

"You said there was something for the pain—" began Señor Calderon y Mazez, then stopped himself for his unseemly display of cowardice.

"Yes, there is. And I will give it to you as soon as possible. But if I do not know the extent of your injury, I will not be able to help you as I ought. So bear with me a moment. I will not hurt you any more than I must." He did his best to smile at the man as he took his damaged arm in his small hands, and felt the shoulder with sure and gentle fingers as he moved the limb about, making note of every sign of discomfort that showed in Señor Calderon y Mazez's eyes. At last he said, "It is dislocated, but that you know. I notice that you have a break in your collarbone as well, very clean, but if it is not treated now, it will give you trouble in future."

"Are you a physician, San Germanno?" asked Señor Calderon y Mazez, suddenly suspicious.

"I have practiced that art, yes. In Egypt," he answered truthfully, though his training had begun in the Temple of Imhotep during the distant, glorious Eighteenth Dynasty and had ended there seven centuries later, when San Germanno had been worshipped as Imhotep himself. "I will not do anything that will harm you. My word on it." He indicated one of the household servants. "Please go fetch a chair. Your master will need to sit down while I treat him."

The man singled out faltered. "But . . . it could fall down," he protested, indicating the house itself.

"It could, but I suspect it will not," said San Germanno with such confidence that the man moved in spite of his dread.

Frey Amadis regarded San Germanno narrowly. "How can you tell the poor man such a lie? Do you know if the walls will stand? Have you knowledge of such things? Are you gifted with prophesy?" he demanded, affronted worth and the residue of panic making his words sharp-edged. "God will surely bring more misfortune on this household for so arrogant a statement."

Around the monk a number of the servants crossed themselves and muttered as they watched their selected comrade enter the maw of the house.

"We may be struck dead in a moment, for any cause, or none," said San Germanno with the same maddening calm. "War may come. Rivers may rise and drown us, drought may dry up the land, plague may ravage the world, mountains may erupt in fire, the earth may give way beneath our feet, but if we have faith, we must show it by accepting that we are in the hands of God, and conduct ourselves as those who trust in Him." This was what the monk would not be able to contradict without bringing questions to bear about his own calling; San Germanno had long experience with priests. He had gone to the chest and taken out a large stoneware jar. He pried the seal from the mouth of it and poured out a generous mouthful into a silver cup. This he handed to Señor Calderon y Mazez. "Drink this. It will ease the pain."

"God may intend him to suffer," said Frey Amadis, his tone raised high enough to be a challenge.

"Then the syrup of poppies will have no effect upon him, for surely He is mighty enough to remove the virtue from this little cup," said San Germanno, and watched while Calderon y Mazez drank. "In a few minutes you should feel drowsy, and a little warm. That is correct and good. A faint dreaminess will come over you, and while you are in its grasp, I will set your shoulder and the collarbone." He made a gesture of encouragement as the servant came out of the house carrying a large chair in front of him. "Very good. Set it down, if you will."

The servant put the chair where San Germanno indicated, then stepped back, but only far enough to get out of the way. He stared in fascination as San Germanno helped Señor Calderon y Mazez to sit.

Rogerio busied himself tending to the Calderon y Mazez family, taking care to block the direct sight of the children toward their father. He selected a small jar of ointment and began to use it on the scratches and cuts that were shown to him; he did not let himself listen to what he heard behind him as he stopped to tear two lengths of muslin from the bolts he and San Germanno had brought.

In spite of the syrup of poppies, what had to be done was painful, and San Germanno realized he would have to work quickly if he was going to spare Señor Calderon y Mazez any suffering at all. He watched as the glazed shine of the man's eyes became more apparent, and then he went swiftly to work.

The servant who stood watching this crossed himself as he saw San Germanno brace his knee against Señor Calderon y Mazez's chest, then pull his injured arm sharply in a swift arc. There was a popping sound, and Señor Calderon y Mazez went pale.

"That's the shoulder. Now for the collarbone," said San Germanno in his direct way. He motioned to the servant. "Tear me four strips of muslin, about as wide as your palm. Quickly." As the servant nodded and went to work, San Germanno pressed the collarbone into proper alignment, then paused to wipe the sweat from Calderon y Mazez's face. "It's just about over. As soon as I have this bandaged for you, you will be able to rest. I will leave some of the syrup of poppies for you, should you need it."

Señor Calderon y Mazez squinted at San Germanno. "You are . . . very strong."

"So it is with those of my blood," said San Germanno, and reached for the first strips of muslin to begin the task of bandaging the man's shoulder.

Within the hour everyone in the Calderon y Mazez household had been treated for their injuries. San Germanno had given a composing draught to four servants and the Señora, and the children were back in the care of their nurse.

"I think we will stay in the courtyard tonight," said Señor Calderon y Mazez, his words slurred and indistinct.

His wife agreed at once, and added, "We will burn candles to the Blessed Rosa de Lima. Perhaps she will come to our aid."

"A wise precaution, doubtless; the family will rest better," San Germanno said as he gathered up his jars and bottles and prepared to leave the house. "I will call upon you in a day or two to see how you are doing. If you have any sharp pain, send me word and I will come at once."

"I will," said Señor Calderon y Mazez sleepily, adding with an effort, "And I thank you most sincerely for what you have done."

"It is what neighbors must do for one another when there is trouble," said San Germanno. He helped secure the red lacquer chest to Rogerio's back. "May God keep you."

"And you," said Señor Calderon y Mazez.

By nightfall, San Germanno had tended more than sixty injured persons and watched another eleven die of injuries beyond his skills to mend. Most of those he treated had cuts, scrapes and bruises, but a few had sprained or broken limbs, and three were so gravely hurt that San Germanno doubted they would survive; he had done what he could to make them comfortable. He was just finishing bandaging the head of a middle-aged widow whose son had perished when a section of wall buried him; looking up from the widow, he noticed that Acanna Tupac was coming toward him in the company of her servants. He abandoned his effort to offer the stunned widow the expected phrases to assuage her grief.

"Yupanqui. Gracious royal lady," he said, using her title both in her language and Spanish; he rose enough to bow to Acanna Tupac. "What am I to have the honor of doing for you?"

She was modestly dressed, as much from necessity as from character, and she took his punctilious behavior with amusement. "You are quite the one for grandeur, aren't you? Yupanqui. Why not Nusta, if you wish to use titles? Or Coya? Or Orejon, as the Spanish call us? But wouldn't you say that these circumstances make fine manner unnecessary?"

"The Spanish do not think so," said San Germanno, getting to his feet and attempting to brush the dust and blood off his black coat. "As I am sure you have learned."

"I have learned many things about the Spanish," she said, and lowered her eyes. "Not all of them are—" She broke off and addressed him directly. "I have a servant who has been struck by a falling beam at my house. It is heavy and we haven't been able to lift it, though the servant is pinned beneath it. I am afraid to move my servant, for the whole of the ceiling is threatening to fall. But if I leave the man without any help he will surely die, for his legs are crushed and he is in terrible pain. We have given him coacca leaves to chew, but they are not enough."

"And you want me to do what, gracious lady?" San Germanno inquired, looking into eyes that were almost as dark as his, though hers were tinged with brown as his were with midnight-blue.

She made a gesture of helplessness. "I don't know," she confessed. "I suppose I want you to do something to save him. You have great gifts for saving the injured. But I don't know what that would be in this circumstance." Her confusion was the more distressing because she admitted it so readily. "I cannot simply let him bleed to death. It would be a wrong thing."

"I am almost finished here," San Germanno said, indicating Rogerio, who was busy tearing up a shirt for bandages, the muslin bolts long since exhausted. "If you are willing to wait a short while, I will come with you."

"The man is suffering." She made a gesture San Germanno had seen many of the Incan people make to keep danger away from them.

"I will do what I can, gracious lady." He regarded her steadily, his dark eyes enigmatic. "It may not be much."

"Anything is more than I have been able to do," she said, defeat coloring her voice. "We tried for an hour to move the beam, but every time we lifted it at all, more of the ceiling fell."

"It may be very difficult," said San Germanno, helping Rogerio get to his feet. "It appears we have another task to do. Bring the oil lamps with you; you need not leave any here, for they have torches. We will probably need them all, if we are to work inside a house." He knew that half a dozen of them were stored, with flint and steel for lighting them, in the red lacquer chest. He, himself, was not hampered by night, for his vision pierced the darkness easily, but he had learned over the centuries that working without light brought unwonted attention on him, and could lead to accusations of witchcraft and other nefarious deeds.

"Yes," said Acanna Tupac, pulling a woven shawl around her shoulder; now that night was coming, the day's heat vanished and the mountain chill took its place. "Light will be needed."

Rogerio did his best to banish his fatigue and trudged after San Germanno and Acanna Tupac through the devastation of Cuzco.

"My soul goes out to all of them, even the Spaniards, who have brought worse things to us than any earthquake," said Acanna Tupac as they passed the Catedral de Los Sacramentos where long lines of dead were laid out for the rites before burial. Several monks were moving among the bodies, trying to learn the identities of the corpses so that appropriate burial could be given them. "There are many dead to be found yet. The Temple of the Sun has been badly damaged on the south side, and one of the gates to the Sacsahuaman fortress has fallen in."

"It is . . . tragic," said San Germanno.

"For some," agreed the last senior heir of the Incas. "For others, it is misfortune, and for some, it is an opportunity. It is always thus when Viracocha moves." She signaled her servants to go ahead of them. "Have as much of the rubble cleared away from around Jasy as possible."

"And bring a large pot of boiled water," added San Germanno. "I will need to clean him, if he has been so badly hurt."

"Do as this man commands you," said Acanna Tupac as she noticed her servants hesitate. "He is not one of the priests. He will not use priests' magic on Jasy. He has saved many others today, and never with a cross."

"Tell me what I am to do," Rogerio said, aware that if he behaved with respect to San Germanno, the servants of this household were likely to do so as well.

"Keep near at hand. And I will need the chest open." He moved to help Rogerio get out of the straps. "Also, cloth for bandages and, if we are very lucky, splints for his legs. Otherwise . . . " He had knives and saws in the chest, if they were needed.

"See?" said Acanna Tupac. "He is no priest. He is not from España. His ways are not the smokes, candles, and mutterings of the Spanish. He will care for the wounds and leave us to minister to his soul." It was as much an order to him as a reassurance to her servants.

What would she think, San Germanno wondered, if she knew the nature of the priesthood into which he had been initiated all those centuries ago? Not the priests of Imhotep, but the war god of his own vanished people, who had given San Germanno his blood in the sacred grove on that long-ago night, before their enemies had over-run their country and made San Germanno a slave. What would a woman like Acanna Tupac, with her own people conquered, make of his past?

The front of Acanna Tupac's house had crumpled as if it had been stepped on. The small courtyard was filled with wreckage, some from the earthquake itself, some from the efforts to salvage objects from the building. The servants had cleared a path into the sagging house and were waiting anxiously. What little talk had been going on was silenced as Acanna Tupac and San Germanno, with Rogerio close behind him, approached. Little notice was given to Rogerio.

"Is Jasy conscious?" Acanna Tupac asked; she went into the house as if she were wholly unafraid.

"Not completely," said the servant who stood nearest to the stricken man. "He has tried to speak, but . . . nothing comes."

San Germanno paused at the entrance to the room where the man lay. A beam had, indeed, fallen from one end and pinned him to the floor, leaving the ceiling without the support it required.

"We have tried to lift it," said another of the servants, his manner apologetic.

"If it must be done, I will do it," said San Germanno, adding to Rogerio, "Three lamps to start with, I should think. Be careful lighting them."

"Certainly, my master," said Rogerio as he opened the red lacquer chest.

As soon as the first lamp was lit, San Germanno approached the fallen beam and the man trapped beneath. Kneeling down, he gave the man's face careful scrutiny. "You say his name is Jasy?"

"Yes," said Acanna Tupac. "He has been with me since he was seven years old. It is our tradition." There was no trace of hesitation in her words, though they were pitched somewhat higher than her usual speech.

"I will do what I can," said San Germanno, looking again at the man's pasty face. He felt the forehead and noticed that his skin was clammy to the touch. The pulse was fast and thready, his breathing too shallow to give much hope of a good recovery. San Germanno moved down toward where the beam had struck.

It was an appalling sight in a day that had already had more of them than he wished to face. A single glance told San Germanno that there would be no saving Jasy's legs, not below the knees, in any case. "I will need tourniquets, Rogerio," he said, his manner crisp and distant.

"And syrup of poppies. And the compound to staunch the bleeding. And bandages." He rose and faced Acanna Tupac. "I am sorry, gracious lady, but if he is to have any chance to live, I will have to sever his legs at the knees."

Acanna Tupac blanched, but she did not flinch at this information. "I feared it would be thus." She put her hands together in a ritual gesture of accepting her fate. "If it is the only chance, then it must be done."

"I do not know if he will survive it," San Germanno pressed on. "He is very weak and has lost much blood. If he dies—"

"He will die here if you do not try," she said sharply. "Do what you must. I will thank you for whatever comes." She turned away from him. "Jasy will decide if he is going to live or die."

"Yes," said San Germanno, and added, "It would be best if we worked alone."

"I will send the rest out. But I must remain here, to account for what you do. Or they will think you have worked magic upon him, which neither my people nor the Spanish priests would like." She made a quick gesture of apology. "If you were not a foreigner among foreigners, it would not matter, but—"

"It will be bloody," San Germanno warned her, knowing better than most the implications of what he said.

"I am prepared," said Acanna Tupac. "It is my obligation to my people to be certain that this is done properly." She then turned to the other servants and issued a few crisp orders in her own language. As they departed, she gave her attention once more to San Germanno. "They will bring you cloth for your work. And the boiled water you requested. And anything else you may request, if we have it to give. They will also pray there is no more shaking, so that your hand will be steady." She looked around, and added in a deferential manner, "If you would not disdain them, I have medicinal gums that will help his wounds to heal."

"He will need it." San Germanno offered a terse bow of approval. "And I have a tincture that will do much to prevent infection."

She regarded him in some surprise. "You will use the gum?"

"Of course. I will use whatever I can to save him, and you will know the virtues of your plants better than I. La Condessa de Chinchon is alive because she was willing to use the bark her servants gave her." He watched as Rogerio set out his tools for amputation. "Anything that will give this poor man a greater chance, I will accept."

Acanna Tupac gave him a measuring look. "You are not like the rest. And not because you come from the mountains of Hungary, wherever they may be."

"It is my age, gracious lady," he said as he unbuttoned his coat; beneath it, his shirtsleeves were rolled to the elbow. "Age brings wisdom of a sort."

"My master," Rogerio interrupted. He indicated the various instruments he had placed on a linen sheet beside the suffering Jasy.

"You're ready?" San Germanno asked, feeling a fatalistic excitement as he reached out for the linen smock Rogerio handed him; it was an emotion he neither enjoyed nor sought. He tugged the garment over his head and put all his concentration on the work that lay ahead. Over his shoulder, but without turning, he said to Acanna Tupac, "If you would get your medicinal gum, gracious lady, I will start as soon as the boiled water is brought."

She regarded him for a brief moment, then hurried away to carry out his request.

"What do you think?" asked Rogerio when Acanna Tupac was gone.

"I think that I have seen very few Indians with amputated legs," said San Germanno. "There are many with bad scars, but few amputations."

"And yet you want the gum?" Rogerio was not able to conceal his dismay. "Why?"

"Because there may be a reason that there are few amputations, and if this gum is part of it, I will want to know of it. If they have a gum that can help keep arms and legs intact—" He took the jar with syrup of poppies from the chest and measured out a portion. "See if you can get this down his throat, will you? And yes, I realize that there may be few with amputations because most of them die."

Rogerio took the measure without comment and began by moistening Jasy's lips with it, then poured a bit more rapidly until the servant sputtered and coughed. He waited and then started in again.

Three of the household servants carried in the kitchen cauldron balanced on a slab of wood. They set it down awkwardly, and left without comment.

"They are not so certain of us as their mistress," said Rogerio.

"Does that surprise you? After everything that foreigners have visited upon them?" asked San Germanno as he soaked another linen cloth in a clear liquid and rubbed his hands thoroughly with it.

Rogerio was spared the necessity of answering by Acanna Tupac's return. She handed an earthenware jar to San Germanno. "Use it all, if you must. I can replace it by noon tomorrow."

"That I will. My thanks, gracious lady," he said, and began to set the tourniquet in place so that he could begin his vital, grisly work.

Text of a letter from Dona Sevilla Luisa Violante Ruedalta y Bueyencrucijada in España to her husband, Don Ezequias Pannefrio y Modestez in Peru.

To my most esteemed and well-favored husband, the greetings and blessings from your wife on the occasion of La Navidad.

It is now almost ten years since I have seen your face, and it would seem that it will be many years more before I am to have that privilege again. Your letter of August 9th was delivered to me three weeks ago, and I was assured it had made good time from Cuzco. Whether this is so, I cannot say, as I have never made the journey you and your letters have taken. Nor does it seem that I will. I have asked my father once again to petition el Rey for permission to join you, or to send two of our children to you. But again I have been refused. El Rey considers the voyage too dangerous for us to undertake, or so I am informed by my father. Your opinions have not yet been forgotten, and el Rey does not wish to have you where you will cause any greater embarrassment to España than you have already, or so my father tells me.

Your children are doing well, or as well as they might, given the position you have placed them in. I am beginning to hope that Hernanda's vocation will prove lasting. The Sisters have said that her devotion is admirable and that she is showing herself a true child of the Church, her piety going far beyond the other girls her age. I pray daily that she will be acceptable to the Order. My father has already promised to provide her dowry, should she be called of God to be a nun.

Carlos, who is almost eleven, still does not thrive. He is bled regularly and has been physicked twice since summer, but all to no avail. On the advice of my father, he has been in the care of the Carmelites for a month now, and all their prayers and care have not brought about any change in him. I begin to think that Padre Dionisio is right, and that God is visiting His wrath on your son, as He gave His Son to ransom the sins of the world.

Gualterio has entered the army at last, and will be promoted when he is seventeen. It is understood he will not be sent to the New World, but will be put on duty on the French border, where there is fighting from time to time. He is a fine man now, and rides like an ancient god. If you were not under such suspicion, there would be fathers seeking him for their daughters now. As it is, my father is attempting to arrange a match that will not dishonor us any more. He has hopes of Almago y Figueroa's second daughter, who has a squint.

I visit Dorotea's grave every day after Mass. The statue to her is nearly completed and it will be put in place when the Resurrection is celebrated. I cannot think of her little life without weeping still. I have offered up my suffering to La Virgen, but I can find no peace. That she should die from a thorn! Padre Dionisio has said that the sins of the father are visited upon his children unto the seventh generation, and so it must be, I fear. I ask for faith, but you have robbed me of my right to faith.

Rosamunda is doing well with my aunt. Tia Juanna has taken Rosamunda into her house with the intention of preparing her for a life as a lady-in-waiting, which is the most we may reasonably hope for, given your conduct. That, in fact, may seem at first to be too much to hope for, given what you have done, but Rosamunda is so pretty and tractable that it is believed she will be accepted at court for her own sweetness of nature and winning ways. She is as pretty as she is demure and that must persuade the court that her disposition is unlike yours. However, her needlework must improve before she can aspire to such a post, and as Tia Juanna is known for her skills with embroidery, she has said she will do all in her power to pass on her knowledge to Rosamunda, so that our daughter may be assured of her future.

It is my father's wish, and it is seconded by Padre Dionisio, that I return to his house and sell your house for the maintenance of your family. I have decided on this course, and I thank God that my father did not disown me as so many others might have, but has continued to regard me as his daughter in spite of everything you have done to disgrace me. My brother Rodrigo does not share my father's understanding nature, and has forbidden his children to have any dealings with me and my children, which I must accept no matter how unfair his condemnation may be to our innocent children. Padre Dionisio will accompany us, so that he will be able to guide me. I know I am fortunate to find so compassionate a Confessor. He will help me atone for all the ills we have been sent as a result of your folly.

May God keep you, my husband, and be more merciful to you than He has been to me. And I will try again next autumn to ask el Rey if any of your family might be permitted to travel to visit you.

In my humble duty to you, and by the good hand of Padre Dionisio,
this brings the affection and devotion of your distant wife.

X
the sign of Dona Sevilla Luisa Violante
wife of Don Ezequias Pannefrio y Modestez
At La Navidad, in the Year of Grace 1641

3

"It has come to my understanding," said Don Ezequias at last reaching
the point of his visit as he strode around the courtyard of San Germanno's house, the clear, midday light making his grey-threaded hair
shine like a metal helmet, "that you have formed a friendship with
Acanna Tupac."

San Germanno stood unmoving by the tree in the center. "Am I not
supposed to, Presidencia? Is there some error in this?" The question was
light and asked without any hidden ire or fear. "I had not been aware
that was the case. It was my impression that she has little company to
keep her entertained or informed, and she seeks both. When you
asked me to escort her, I assumed it would be acceptable to befriend
her as well. She has need of friends." He fingered the silver-and-black-
sapphire pectoral that hung from a ruby-studded silver collar.

"So she has, so she has," said Don Ezequias heavily. He cleared his
throat and continued, "Again I tell you, it is her family seniority that
makes it very . . . difficult for many of the people here to do more than
acknowledge her existence. She is an embarrassment to the cadet
branch of the family, for all we have given them Spanish titles and our
favor." He stopped by the wheelbarrow where the last of the tile repairs were being made. "There are so many more places in need of
work to make them habitable again. Another strong shaking could raze
the city." He tapped the wheelbarrow. "It is my understanding that
when Pizarro came here, the Indians had never seen a wheel. They
did everything with levers and pullies, but had no wheels."

"In steep mountains, wheels are not always an advantage," San Germanno observed. "Levers and pullies are."

Don Ezequias nodded, his eyes somewhat distracted. "You're right. No doubt." He resumed his pacing. "I have been told by . . . certain authorities, my superiors, in fact, that it is thought likely that Acanna Tupac . . . " He fell silent and his pacing resumed.

"What is thought likely about Acanna Tupac? And who thinks it? Don Alejandro Morena y Osma? Or perhaps Duca Roldo Vila Nova de Gois? Both of them would profit at her expense, wouldn't they?" asked San Germanno when Don Ezequias did not go on. He saw from the quick frown that marred his guest's face that Don Ezequias was not happy about the reason for his visit. "You might as well tell me, so that it will not rankle with you. Then, once you have said what you must, we may talk as friends." He managed a suggestion of a smile by way of encouragement.

"This is not a fitting way to treat a stranger who has done no harm. I am vexed that I should have to undertake this mission at all," Don Ezequias admitted, his big hands knotted together.

"I can see that," said San Germanno. "All the more reason to tell me now, before you become too upset by it to wish to remain here." He bowed, and added, "I will understand that you do whatever it is you must do because you are compelled to, not because you wish to."

"It is thought that she might have some information, information that is urgently wanted," said Don Ezequias, his words crisp and hissing, "on the location of various of the hidden Incan cities." He came toward San Germanno at once, his hands up in protest. "I do not think such places exist, and I have said so. It is likely that there are villages we know nothing of, and their legends have been enlarged upon until there is no recognizing the original place. But there are others who do not agree." His brow darkened. "There are men who think that all the wealth of Atahualpa has not yet been discovered, and that anyone with any knowledge of the location of such wealth should be made to reveal it."

"You do not see it that way? You do not want such treasures found?" San Germanno watched him, his features revealing little of his thoughts.

"How can I, when I think the places are legends?" He was not able to laugh. "I have been told, however, that I am expected to make all reasonable attempts—"

"Reasonable according to whom?" interrupted San Germanno.

"The Crown, or so I am informed." He shook his head in condemnation. "How can anyone think that the Indians would leave treasure behind anywhere, for us to find? If I were one of them, I would take care to put my valuables where no one could find them. And that would not be a hidden, fabled city," he went on, growing irritated again, "where any adventurer would happen across it, but in one of the high peaks, or in a gorge where rope ladders are needed." He stopped still and folded his arms. "Still, I have to ask. Has Acanna Tupac said anything about a hidden city? Or buried treasure? Tell me no and we will forget this altogether."

"Actually," said San Germanno in a quiet, precise tone, "she has." He was rewarded with a sharp look from Don Ezequias, which he met with a growing smile. "She has said much the same thing about it as you have just now, that the unknown places are unknown for good reason—they are small and obscure, in locations that are hard to reach. These places, because of their sites are assumed to be hidden on purpose, or so many Spanish think. And she is losing patience with those who refuse to believe her when she tells them otherwise. She has tried to explain these things many times, all without success. It is difficult for her to convince the foreigners that she knows her lands and people better than they do." He touched his short, perfectly groomed beard. "I do not suppose this is information your superiors will want to hear, but it is what I have been told."

Don Ezequias made a gesture to show he had done his duty. "What more can they expect?"

"Why, they expect their dreams to be realized," said San Germanno lightly, though with underlying grimness. "They expect this strange land to yield up wealth and power and good reputation and honor and adulation and adoration and all the rest of the things they fear they have missed before. Listen to them when they talk. Every word is stuffed full of their desires. They have fancies they have made real in their minds, and do not wish to be deprived of them. They suppose that so long as they are masters here, they will achieve what they seek."

"Sangre de Dios," exclaimed Don Ezequias, beginning to pace once more. "If you are so . . . so persuaded of the perfidy of the Spaniards here, why do you remain?"

"Because of the Indians, these last Incan people, of course," San Germanno replied, his smile this time as swift as it was sad.

"But . . . why?" asked Don Ezequias, too perplexed to be offended. "What are they to you?"

"They are . . . " He faltered and began again. "They are part of a vanishing nation, as my nation has vanished. They have knowledge that is worth saving. And *they* are worth saving." His face was more expressive than he realized; he went on. "I hoped to learn from these people before all they know is passed off as legends and superstition."

"Because they are like you are?" suggested Don Ezequias.

"Yes," he answered simply, and then shook off his burgeoning despair. "Not that all the foreigners are here to exploit the land and its people; I have found good men here—such as yourself. Most of you are kept in cadet positions yourselves." Again he bowed, but now it was informal, with a touch of amusement in it.

"You need not say that; that I am a good man," Don Ezequias protested with sincere intention. "I require no flattery."

"I am not offering any; I say it because it is true, Presidencia. You were sent here to save your family embarrassment for your humanity and your learning. You have not described it that way, I know, but I know enough of España to recognize that any taint of humanism turns one into a dangerous, radical person, who cannot be trusted to know how to behave properly, or to support the ambitions the Crown and the Church have in the New World. You have reason and compassion, a very inappropriate combination in España." San Germanno strode toward Don Ezequias, the westering sun making auburn highlights in his dark hair.

"You sound like a Protestant," said Don Ezequias in a failed attempt at humor. "A dangerous one, as well."

San Germanno gave him a swift, serious answer. "I am no Protestant, nor Catholic."

Don Ezequias stared in astonishment. "Then what—"

"Nor Orthodox Christian, though much of my country is, where the Ottomites have not conquered. Nor am I a Jew. Some have called those of my blood pagan, though I would not, for we take life from blood, as good Christians do, and for the same purpose." He had no intention of revealing any more of his religious convictions, for Don Ezequias' sake as well as his own; he shrugged. "From time to time I attend Mass, to avoid any unpleasant speculations."

"But you do not take Communion," said Don Ezequias, adding uncomfortably, "It is in the reports the monks give me."

"As I have said, I take Communion in my own way," said San Germanno quietly, "and hold it sacred: believe this."

"Do not tell me about it—it's probably heretical," said Don Ezequias. He stopped pacing once again. "In fact, why do you tell me any of this?"

"Because we both are in need of an ally," said San Germanno without preamble. "Because in this remote place there is hardly anyone who is inquisitive without also being avaricious or zealous. But that is not the case with you. You have dared to think your own thoughts. To me this is an admirable thing, worthy of respect; I suppose you might enjoy discussions with me as I would with you, if there is no interference from the Church or her agents, or tacit observation from your superiors. I have no reason to reveal anything you say to me, because it would only add to the suspicions in which I am already held, and would benefit neither of us."

"You mean more heresy," Don Ezequias accused, but with curiosity.

"I suppose some would think so," said San Germanno candidly. "It does not seem so to me. But I do not accept the Church as the ultimate authority in such matters, which is heresy in itself, I assume." He looked closely at his guest, aware that Don Ezequias was deeply troubled by his most recent assignment. "So your superiors want you to find treasure for them, do they?"

Don Ezequias sighed. "Yes. They do." This time his stride was long and slow, as if he tugged an invisible burden behind him. "They expect me to discover what Pizarro himself could not find."

"And you are supposed to speak to everyone here whom the Indians might confide in? You are to learn what they are being told, in confidence? What do you offer them for this? gold? Or security from God's Hounds?" San Germanno pursued, knowing he was right. "Or do you seek to find those who are willing to force the Indians to speak."

"That is the way of it, yes." Don Ezequias was growing nervous once more, his big hands clenching. "You are not the only one I have spoken to today, nor are you the last." The admission made him angry, more with himself than anyone else.

"What have you been told thus far?" San Germanno asked.

"Duca Roldo Vila Nova de Gois was the last. He has three Dutchmen visiting him, making arrangements regarding Japan, anticipating the need for their help." He looked up at the branches of the tree. "I told him what was wanted, asking if he had heard anything I should report to my superiors, and one of the Dutchmen became most inquisitive. He is eager to make his fortune, and if Japan proves impossible, he may become one of those who venture far into the jungles to find the lost cities." He made no effort to conceal the disgust he felt.

"And he was not the only one," said San Germanno with unhappy certainty. "And now that it appears the government wants the treasure,

the number of men searching for it will treble in a month. You are re-
lying on avarice, not on curiosity, to give purpose to the searches. For
a short time, it may be to your advantage to do this, but that advantage cannot last." He had seen this madness before, and always it had
brought devastation in its wake.

"No; on that we agree, but we are against the grain. In fact, Dom
Enrique Vilhao has suggested that we bring black slaves here to do the
work of finding the treasures, for being African, they are more able to
endure the heat of the jungle, as they have shown in Brazil. All we
need do is reap the rewards of their labor." He slammed his fist into
his palm. "He is determined to bring blacks here, if only to profit from
their sale. He has applied to the Crown for their encomiendas; the Corregidores support his petition."

"And you have opposed this," said San Germanno.

"Most emphatically. Until now, with the Corregidores endorsing it,
what can I do? They are my superiors," he confessed. "Now he has also
enlisted the support of Obispo Guarda, because so many Spaniards
have perished from the heat and pestilence of the jungles. Not long
ago it was feared we might have to abandon our explorations there,
because none of the men we sent could endure the conditions more
than a few months, and the journeys anticipated might well last a year.
But now it is thought that blacks might be the answer, for no one ex-
pects Spaniards to labor in that green oven, given how many of them
have died in the attempt."

"Do the Corregidores know this? Have they been made aware of Dom
Enrique's intentions?" asked San Germanno. "Have you told them what
Dom Enrique's goal is?"

He shook his head miserably. "No. I have already protested too many
things; to stand against Dom Enrique would be tantamount to throwing myself on the Church for mercy." His eyes were shining with tears
of frustration and disgust. "I have done all that I may. I cannot disobey
my orders, but I know they are folly."

San Germanno approached Don Ezequias. "And have you said so?"

He nodded several times. "Yes. Oh, yes. As much as I dared. Dom
Enrique has said he will only bring Africans who are slaves already in
Africa, so there will be no danger of an uprising among them. I have
warned them that they are creating a greater problem than we have
had before. The Incan people are not willing to fight us now, but if we
start to plunder their lands this way we may have a rebellion that could
lead to slaughter. In these mountains, troops could not arrive from Lima

in time to aid us or be revenged on our behalf. And I do not think the Africans would defend us." He opened his hands to show his efforts had not been heeded. "The Obispo does not think that the people, coming newly to Christianity, would lash out at those who have saved their souls. The orders stand."

"And so you must visit all the foreigners here in Cuzco, to ask them about hidden cities and buried treasure they may have heard of from the Indians, to show that you do not oppose the work of the Crown or the Church," said San Germanno, sharing Don Ezequias' dismay.

"I must not fail in my duty," said Don Ezequias, then his voice grew hushed with fear and shame. "If Maria Cusi Huarcay had only revealed where the gold mines of Usanbi were! Or the quicksilver mines at Vilcabamba. There was so much hope that we would find them at last. Since this has not happened, it falls to me to discover the lost mines, or to aid those who can. They—the Corregidores and the Obispos—have expected me to do more in this regard than I have. My efforts have not satisfied my superiors, who have made their discontent known. They fear I am coming to champion the Incas instead of the Faith. The Secular Arm has indicated that they might want to question me if I do not show myself eager to do this work." He lowered his eyes. "If I did not have a family, I might find the courage to resist the Inquisitors, but as it is, I dare not."

"How can the Secular Arm make a claim upon you for not finding treasure? Isn't that beyond their authority to mandate? Why should they instigate a Process against you for resisting the sin of greed? I was not aware that it was the Inquisition's work to gather up worldly goods," said San Germanno, making no attempt to conceal his contempt.

"It is not for worldly goods—" said Don Ezequias.

"Truly?" San Germanno interjected.

"—but the concern that the pagan religion of the Indians has corrupted me and blighted my faith," said Don Ezequias. "It was already in question when I was sent here."

"How can finding treasure change that?" asked San Germanno, anticipating the answer.

"It would prove my dedication to Holy Church and to the Crown." He could not bring himself to meet San Germanno's dark, compelling eyes.

"In other words, by bribery," said San Germanno curtly. He was familiar with this sophistry; he had seen it develop and flourish for more than four hundred years. "So you will do as they ask, and greedy men will try to find what is not there. Many Spaniards and countless Indians will perish, but the Inquisition will remain."

"That may be a possibility, once the Catedral is repaired and Obispo Guarda returns," Don Ezequias said quietly. "While he is gone, I am not quite so strictly watched. Which is why I must demonstrate zeal now, so that it will not be assumed that I support the Church only when it is present."

"Isn't that a bit convoluted?" suggested San Germanno.

"I fear it is not, not with all I have learned in the last few years," said Don Ezequias. "But—"

"But," San Germanno agreed with asperity, "you have a wife and children who are hostage in España, if only they knew it. And if you do not do all that is asked of you, your family will suffer for it, and hold you accountable." He gave an impatient gesture. "Well, what have you decided to do? Beyond talking to all foreigners here in Cuzco?"

Don Ezequias hitched his shoulders. "I will await the guidance of my superiors, as I must."

"And what then?" San Germanno asked, surprisingly gently.

"I don't know," Don Ezequias admitted.

"When the time comes, it may be difficult to act," San Germanno told him, recalling the many times in the past he had waited just a bit too long and had been compelled to deal with the results of his hesitation; he wanted to spare Don Ezequias that if he could. "It may be best if you move first."

"It may be," Don Ezequias allowed. He touched the crucifix that hung from his collar of office along with the Order of the Golden Fleece. "And I do not say you are wrong. But—"

San Germanno saw the apprehension in Don Ezequias' eyes and knew the man feared for his family. "But you do not want to precipitate any—"

"That is it exactly," said Don Ezequias, deliberately cutting him off in case he should say something too frightening. "I want to keep as quiet about this as I may. It would be very bad for me and some others if information on my decisions were to reach certain persons. If it is seen that I am taking matters into my own hands in a way that is not liked, my wife would curse me more than she does already." He looked directly as San Germanno. "If you speak of this to your Confessor . . . "

When Don Ezequias ran out of words, San Germanno said, very quietly, "I have no Confessor, and well you know it. And I will not acquire one so that I may use the Confessional as a bartering-place, so much information about you for so much favor for me." He paused a moment, weighing his thoughts. "Your Christ chased the money-lenders from the Temple, as I recall. I doubt He'd approve of Confessional bargaining."

Don Ezequias cracked a single laugh. "Don't let the Inquisitors hear you say that: they would take it as certain proof of heresy."

"They would not like having their true lights shown, would they," said San Germanno, relieved that Don Ezequias was no longer sinking into despondency, or anticipating ruin in his life. "No, they would not," he went on, answering for his guest, aware that in that single exchange, he had thrown in his lot with Don Ezequias. He hoped he had made a wise decision, and that this remote location would protect them from the dangers that filled court life in España. "As if you did not have enough demanding your attention, with so much of the city waiting for supplies in order to rebuild, they now expect you to leave the work undone and find treasure, not for Cuzco, but for Madrid and Rome."

"Does this trouble you? Do you expect the Church and Crown to endorse your assessments? After what you have said, what is left that could be more damning?" asked Don Ezequias sharply; he had seen something in San Germanno's visage that had renewed his worry.

Inwardly San Germanno reviewed the many things that would put him into danger from the Church which Don Ezequias knew nothing of, though he said, "Nothing that has bearing on you." Then, in order to account for his reticence, he said, "I was remembering your cousin in Padova, and how he came there."

"Ah. Yes, I suppose you know the story. His book was seized and burned, of course, and had he not been well-regarded by the Jesuits, he would never have made it out of España. As it was, it was a near thing." Don Ezequias looked around the courtyard as if he expected to find spies listening to them. "You knew him in Padova. Have you read the book? I have. I have a copy of it. Hidden." The last was almost a whisper.

"Yes, I have read it, and I agree with his thesis, that the increase of the realms of knowledge diminishes the realms of faith, for the benefit of both knowledge and faith, and that both are part of the glory of God, and that to condemn knowledge because it is contrary to doctrine is to embrace ignorance, which is the source of all superstition." San Germanno made a gesture of dismissal. "All but the most untutored would accept such notions, and welcome them, or it seems to me. But not to the good clergy of España."

"Sadly, no, not to them," said Don Ezequias. "And I cannot but worry for my cousin's safety. Though, being here, my hands are tied if I try to act on his behalf."

"He is much respected in Padova. The Italians are not so alarmed by heresy as the Spanish are," San Germanno said; he did not add that he thought Don Ezequias' hands were well-tied here in Peru as well as in Europe.

At this Don Ezequias began to pace once more. "It was not always so. A century ago, the Church was assured of the triumph of right-eousness, and believed that they would see an end to heresy. There was hope that with our conquest would come the salvation of the world. When the Conquistadores set foot in the New World, they did so with confidence in God and their cause, and with the might of the Church to aid them. It was seen as a sign from God when these inno-cents of the New World welcomed our faith. Now, it is feared that the Devil has marshalled his forces and has risen afresh in a thousand places, so that all the efforts of the Secular Arm cannot keep pace with the spread of heresy."

"Perhaps," San Germanno suggested gently, "that is because the Church is mistaken about heresy."

Free-thinking as Don Ezequias was, this notion shocked him. He blinked as he came to an abrupt halt. "How can anyone suppose that?" he demanded.

San Germanno hastened to lessen the impact of what he had said. "Consider, Don Ezequias: you did not waken one day and say to your-self 'Today I am going to entertain heretical ideas.' No. You had many hours of questions and doubts that grew from your desire for faith, and the conclusions you reached from your questions were not those the Dominicans and Jesuits and Augustinians and Franciscans approved, and so you were regarded as a potential heretic. You permitted your-self to become educated, not merely instructed. You have widened your view of all things. It is ever thus with those whose minds are restless and inquisitive. Why should you think yourself unique among your fellow-men? aside from the exhortations of the monks and priests, who condemn you as much for being the only one as for the nature of your doubts?"

"But surely the continuing strength of the Church in the face of heresy must mean something." He looked around quickly. "If the questions of heretics were right and the Church wrong, would not the heretics prevail?"

San Germanno chuckled with little mirth. "Ask those the Church considers heretics if they think of themselves as heretics and you would receive some startling answers." How adamantly the Church had stood against heresy, and how much the definition of heresy had changed since San Germanno had first encountered it, more than thirteen hundred years ago. He recalled with a sudden, intense ache the loss of those of his blood, burned at Lyon, in 1159, for the heresy of not being properly dead, and for living as their nature demanded. Two vampires and a ghoul consigned to the stake because their lives were not the lives the Church endorsed, and their love required them to embrace humanity before religion. The flames had certainly ended that dispute to the satisfaction of the Church, and to the despair of Csimenae.

"You have faced such admonitions yourself, haven't you? The sort the monks and priests give? They have pursued you, haven't you?" asked Don Ezequias shrewdly. "It is in your eyes, Conde. Any man who has seen what you have seen must answer the Church, or the Church will not be secure."

"Anyone who has land conquered by the Turks, and has lived to flee them, has been scrutinized," said San Germanno, accurately as far as it went. "There is a feeling among some of the more strict churchmen that once the Turks have your land, Mahamot has your soul."

"But surely you defended your native land?" exclaimed Don Ezequias. "And everyone must know it."

"Yes; I did," San Germanno answered, thinking of the many times he had done so over the centuries, and against so many foes.

"And so you endured a double hardship," said Don Ezequias, sympathy apparent in the tone of his voice and the lines of his face. "The loss of your place in the world, and the doubt of your religion."

San Germanno gave a slight shrug. "As you do. You are sent here where you can do no harm, as the Church reckons it, and you are kept from your family, to ensure you will not cause any further embarrassment. And I would think that here they are certain your education will be curtailed, for they have no understanding of the desire for knowledge. I can see it burns in you like thirst in the desert. It will be satisfied, no matter what the cost." He clapped his hands, and was pleased when Rogerio answered the summons promptly. "Be good enough to open a bottle of the French Côtes du Rhone and bring a goblet for my guest."

"At once, my master," said Rogerio, bowing before he hurried away into the depths of the house.

"That is hardly necessary . . . " Don Ezequias protested, all the while looking very pleased.

"I do not offer from necessity, my friend," said San Germanno, returning to the shade of the tree in the center of the courtyard; the sun was becoming enervating, despite his native earth lining the soles and heels of his boots.

Don Ezequias began the formal protestations, only to have San Germanno lift a hand to silence him. "But it is not suitable to accept such a gesture from a stranger on so brief an acquaintance, Conde."

"Don Ezequias," said San Germanno, "surely here, in these mountains, with the ruins of the Incas at the ends of the streets and España more than half a world away, you need not stand on the ceremony of the Spanish court, or use the forms of good society where there is so little society to choose from. I have hoped to find someone willing to discuss ideas, for surely we may have ideas in this place you would not entertain in España. I have nothing to gain from such conversations but the pleasure of testing ideas, and I thought you might also enjoy such debate in this far-away place. Just as we may have friends who would not be accessible to us, or . . . desirable in España." He hesitated slightly, changing the pitch of his voice. "Does not our shared foreignness in these mountains make us comrades in this place, if not our mutual penchant for heresy? We are both a very long way from our native earth." His smile was wry, hardly more than a lift of the corners of his mouth, but he could see Don Ezequias consider his answer, and knew he had won.

"If you make the offer from fellow-feeling and not from courtesy"— he gave the word its proper meaning of court conduct—"then there is no reason not to indulge. As a token of missing Europe, if nothing else." His stiffness was fading as he spoke; his posture grew less rigid and his features relaxed. "I would welcome a French wine, dreadful as such an admission may be. My family has vineyards, and in fifty years of our cellars, I have not tasted one vintage to equal the French."

"That would please the French, if only because it confirms their opinions," said San Germanno. "I have a small winery there, and when I came to Peru, I brought a few bottles of the best years with me." He did not add that he had owned the land for more than five centuries.

Now Don Ezequias permitted himself the luxury of laughter. "Yes, it is true. The French always wish to hear the best of themselves. They expect praise and envy. It is their nature." He squinted up at the sun. "How odd, to be thinking of such differences this far away from Europe."

Privately, San Germanno was convinced all nations wished to think the best of themselves, but that every nation had a different conception of what *best* was. He said only, "Yes, at such distances these issues grow less acute."

"Do you suppose there could be any point far enough away that the differences will vanish completely?" asked Don Ezequias, his words coming quickly, as if he feared what the answer might be.

"It may be possible, when history has forgotten them," said San Germanno, with such utter loneliness that he forced himself to make light of his abrupt desolation of spirit. "For when a thing is forgotten, so are the questions around it."

"Is forgetfulness the only way?" asked Don Ezequias, astonished by the change he had seen in San Germanno.

El Conde was spared having to answer by the return of his manservant, bearing a tray on which stood an opened bottle of wine and a single silver goblet. "A buen' hora," he said to Rogerio, and took a moment to read the label on the bottle before indicating that Rogerio should present it to Don Ezequias.

"But are you not enjoying this with me?" protested Don Ezequias as he took the goblet but did not lift the bottle from the tray. "So excellent a vintage, surely you will drink it with me?"

"Alas no; I do not drink wine," said San Germanno. "Fill his goblet, Rogerio."

This was done at once, Rogerio handling the bottle with expertise and just enough flourish that Don Ezequias would be impressed. He then went to stand in the arch of the door leading into the house, not quite out of sight or earshot, waiting to be summoned again.

Don Ezequias sipped the wine and gave a slow nod of approval. "Very fine, Conde."

"Thank you," said San Germanno. "Please enjoy it."

"I am certain I will. So rare a vintage is a treasure in this place. Possibly too much of a temptation," he added as he took a longer second sip. "Splendid as this is, it would not be fitting for me to drink too much. It would be regarded as a sign of indulgence, of laxness, and an abuse of your hospitality. I will limit myself to this single goblet, and intend no slight upon your generosity. My thanks are as genuine as if I finished the whole bottle." He put his free hand to his chest over the Golden Fleece and regarded San Germanno thoughtfully, after a covert glance in Rogerio's direction. "Do you anticipate remaining here long, Conde? You have said nothing of such plans."

San Germanno answered with a slight smile. "I do not expect to leave at any time soon. That is why I have purchased my house and employed servants, with the encomienda you issued to me. Circumstances may change, however—"

"For a man with opinions like yours, the future can be uncertain," Don Ezequias agreed, gloom coming over him like a shadow.

"The future is always uncertain, no matter who you are. 'Di doman' non c'e certezza,' " he quoted in Italian, recalling, too, how true it was for Laurenzo, who wrote the words and had died before his time, his blood diseased beyond any healing even San Germanno could offer.

"A melancholy lyric," said Don Ezequias appreciatively. "How did you come to learn it?"

The question was so bland that San Germanno was at once cautious. "I learned it from a Florentine friend, some while ago," he answered, satisfied he had again told the truth, though not the whole of it, for his friend had died on the eighth day of April in 1492.

"Ah." Don Ezequias made a sign of understanding. "Yes. They still quote de'Medici in Firenze, I have been told."

So his reticence had been wise, thought San Germanno; Don Ezequias had recognized the poem. "My friend did."

"A most remarkable family, the de'Medicis, to accomplish so much for Toscana and Firenze," said Don Ezequias with a measuring look in his eyes. "In España they would have not fared as well as they have in Italy and France, given their wealth and their worldliness."

"Probably not," San Germanno said, thinking that the cadet branch of the family which now led it was of a different bent than the senior branch had been.

"Still, they have done much; to go from being merchants and bankers to being royalty in less than two hundred years is remarkable advancement." Don Ezequias saw something in San Germanno's face that made him hesitate. "You don't agree? What makes you question this?"

"Nothing," said San Germanno shortly, who recalled that Laurenzo wanted no title beyond that of citizen of la Repubblica Fiorenzana. It had taken his cousin to bring titles into the family, after Laurenzo was dead and his family exiled.

"Your face says otherwise," Don Ezequias remarked, sipping his wine.

"I was . . . thinking about the turns of fate visited on the de'Medicis. From charcoal burners to spice merchants to bankers to exiles to Gran' Ducche in Toscana. And all, as you say, in a short period of time. Less than four hundred years from the first of them to the present. Not that their fortunes have been always bright, or will remain so." This last he added as he thought of the late Queen of France, Catherine de'Medici, who had begun in triumph and ended in defeat, and Pope Clement VII, whose reign had been marked by upheaval.

"Nor were the fortunes of Borja y Lara family without question, once they went to Rome," said Don Ezequias, doing his best to soften his condemnation of the Italians.

"Ah, but the Borgias brought much of their misfortunes on themselves," said San Germanno, using the Italianate version of the family name.

"So the Italians say." Don Ezequias was half-done with his wine now, and he looked down into the goblet. He gave San Germanno a measuring look, but not an unfriendly one. "How strange that an exile from the Carpathians should know so much about these families."

San Germanno sensed the direction Don Ezequias was taking their discussion, and made a gesture of dismissal. "When one is—as you point out I am—an exile, it is prudent to learn all that one may of those who have offered him refuge. Don't you think?"

"It depends somewhat on whom the hosts are," said Don Ezequias, his expression changing as he looked around the courtyard. "For instance, it is not wise to know too much about the Indians here. It is looked upon as unsuitable, or audacious. Such knowledge could lead to unwelcome questions."

At that, San Germanno made an ironic bow. "I will keep your . . . admonition in mind, Don Ezequias."

"Por favor," said Don Ezequias said, and finished the wine.

Text of a letter from Obispo Hernan Guarda to Obispo Melchior Puente y Sello.

> *To my esteemed Brother in Christ and His Church, Su Excelencia, my blessing, prayers, high regard, and respectful greetings from my current place in Lima.*
>
> *It distresses me more than I can express here that I have had to leave*

my own Bishopric in Cuzco and avail myself of your gracious hospitality for so long, all because the earthquake ruined my quarters and much of el Catedral de Los Sacramentos. It is most kind of you to continue to grant me and my staff the quarters you have provided, but it is not fitting for us to remain here as long as we have. Had we more money for the repairs, and were more of the churches in Cuzco in good repair since that terrible event, I would not have to be the burden I fear I have become to you. It is not what I would wish to have to do. Daily I pray that God will spare the city another such disaster until we have rebuilt and shored up the city and our buildings within it. But God may not be willing to stay His hand if His servants continue to neglect His houses.

What is most distressing of all is that with a reduced presence of the Church in Cuzco, the hold we have on the souls of the pagan peoples of these mountains cannot but be lessened. The old ways are still strong among them, especially in the villages, and if we are seen to abandon them at a time of trouble, they will not so readily take us back when we return. I left under protest, and with the assumption that monks would be sent quickly to fill the gap left when the earthquake caused our churches and residences to collapse.

To give weight to my concerns, I have learned that recently some of those Indians who have not fully accepted the Church as their salvation have been saying that the gods of the Indians have beaten the God of the Robed Ones. It troubles me that some now think us vanquished, driven from the field by the ancient powers of the mountains, and I cannot find it in my heart to disagree, not entirely. In vain have I appealed to España for our Orders to send more monks and priests, though I know that any loss of faith on the part of the Indians will be laid at my door because Cuzco is my Bishopric. It must not be seen that we can be driven out by a shaking of the earth, any more than a clap of thunder will send us running. We must do our utmost to hold those souls we have brought to Holy Mother Church, and to gather the rest into the Good Shepherd's fold, as well, which cannot be done while I and my priests remain here in Lima, availing ourselves of your gracious hospitality.

I beseech you, in the name of the Church we both serve, to help me and the rest of my clergy to return to Cuzco, to rebuild Los Sacramentos and establish our churches once again as the center of activity in the city. I am wholly convinced that if we do not take such measures at once that there will be more resistance when we finally are given leave to return. It is a terrible thing to see so many of these good Indians suf-

fering for want of the ministrations they have every right to expect from us. It is impossible to judge how much damage they will have sustained by the time we are granted the permission I have so constantly sought. As the buildings of Cuzco were wrecked by the earthquake, so the souls of Cuzco's people will be blighted for lack of the rites and sacraments of the Church, and that blight can only grow worse with the passage of time.

As you have observed yourself, there are many things we must learn from these Indians, to add to the glory of their conversions. The Vilcabamba silver mines are not producing as they did once. Your intention of discovering the wealth of the old rulers and presenting it to the Church is a most laudable one, but I do not think it can go forward while Cuzco is in such a state. To enforce your desire, we must have clergy present, and stout walls to guard all that is given to the Church. At this time, none of these things are possible.

Therefore, as equals, let us work together to persuade the Church to take action to end the sad neglect which has been visited on all of Cuzco, so that we may once again restore the faith and the confidence of the people which we had begun to enjoy before the earthquake. The longer we are absent, the less credence the people will give us. It is already autumn, and if we do not plan now, spring will arrive and we will not be prepared for our undertakings. Let us devote a portion of our time this winter to make ready for our work at Cuzco.

May God guide your meditations on this and all things, may His angels guard and protect you, may the spirit of charity and humility grace you in all things, and may no sin stain your life. With the love of all that is Christian and the abhorrence of all that is not, I sign myself your brother in Christ's name,

Hernan Sigismundo Bernal Guarda
Obispo, Los Sacramentos, Cuzco
On the 25th day of April, the feast of San Marcos el Evangelista, the Year of Grace 1642, at Lima

4

A cutting wind drove through the mountains and into the streets of Cuzco, coming from the south-southwest with ocean gales to power it. The day was darkened by clouds as much as the time of year, for it was less than a week since the June Solstice, and the days were just beginning to be noticeably longer. There was as yet no other promise of spring as the afternoon dipped toward night, with snow promised in the sheets of clouds riding the wind like sails.

In the garrison barracks, soldiers whiled away the time with drinking and dicing. A few, who had to face guard duty, kept near to the hearth, drinking hot wine and eating the spicy sausages that were offered by the four native cooks who tended to their food. The room smelled of smoke, wine, garlic, sweat, cooked meat, hot metal, wet wool, and leather. Those who had no such duty facing them were variously occupied cleaning their weapons, oiling their boots against the wet, playing cards, or dicing.

To the side of the main room, Don Alejandro Morena y Osma had opened the door of his quarters to take advantage of the warmth of the barracks and to keep an eye on the men; soldiers never endured long enclosure well.

At the rear of the room, somewhat isolated from the others, half a dozen visitors sat with the four sergeants who lived in the barracks. They huddled around a square plank table, their cloaks still over their shoulders to minimize the chill from the wind outside.

"I say we should go to her house and confront her. The Presidencia won't be able to interfere, not against me," declared Dom Enrique Vilhao, his impatience translated into anger. "What's the point of waiting for her to come to the authorities?"

"We don't want complaints made against us," said Gerben Deykenwaard, whose Spanish was very good in everything but rhythm. "You are here with higher position than we Dutch have."

"I can arrange that this does not happen," said Dom Enrique. "It will take little to make certain we are not questioned or disturbed."

"This is excellent," said Deykenwaard. "I would not like to be brought before the magistrate for what I wish to do."

"Don Ezequias is in no position to deny us anything," Dom Enrique told them with cynical satisfaction. "He has been discredited already. They sent him here to put him out of harm's way. If he shows himself on the side of the Incan people, he will be removed from his post here and they will find some remote place in the jungles to be Presidencia where no one will have to deal with him except the monks who will bury him in six months after he is sent there."

"You are so confident?" asked van Zwolle, who had lost an eye and two fingers in a shipboard brawl a decade ago and had developed a predatory caution since that time. In his thirty-one years he had been twice to Japan, once to China, and had rounded both the Horn and the Cape of Good Hope. He had survived a shipwreck and the attack of pirates; he despised all forms of cowardice.

"I have written to my brother, who confirms this for me. The Presidencia dare not keep us from doing as we wish, not without great personal risk. He will not dare to bring another cause for condemnation upon himself. Do you think he would protect Dona Acanna if in doing so, he would be disgraced afresh?" Dom Enrique preened as he announced this, reveling in the power it demonstrated. "If we go to the woman, we will not have to answer to anyone for what we do."

Deykenwaard ran his tongue over his lips suggestively. "Is she too old, do you think? They say she is nearing forty. Women past thirty-five care not much for men in their beds, or so I've been told."

"We can find out," suggested one of the sergeants, making an obscene gesture with his hands. The other men laughed, a few of them chiming in descriptions of what could be done to the Incan woman.

"Not that I would touch one," added Lazaro Escaso, whose voice was permanently hoarse from long hours of shouting orders at soldiers.

"They put you into the army here because you don't want to touch *any* woman," scoffed Martin Vigaracimos, who had been born in Peru to a Capitan and his Indian woman almost twenty years before; between the army and his illegitimacy, he had turned bitter early.

Escaso, older than most of the men at the table, made a gesture for silence.

So did Dom Enrique. "We'd best not do anything too bad. The Presidencia would do nothing to us, but the Church would, if they decided we had not behaved honorably. She is a woman of station, not just an Indian female in the street. We would have to answer for it."

This was a sobering notion and all of the men around the table faltered at that grim reminder.

"But Obispo Guarda is still in Lima," said Diego Herrero, the youngest of the sergeants, a twenty-two-year-old who had been in Peru for six years. He had taken two Indian women as wives and had fathered eight children so far, three of whom were still alive. "What can the Church do with half the priests and monks away in Lima, begging for a new Catedral?"

"They like Lima better in any case," added Vigaracimos. "There's more power in Lima."

A few of the men took up this tone, pleased that they had found something to fire their ambitions.

Escaso glared at the rest. "If you don't hold your tongues, they will know what we plan to do, all the way in Lima."

Deykenwaard made a gesture of disdain.

Dom Enrique scratched his elegant beard and gazed thoughtfully at a vacant place in the air. "Yes, you have something there, Herrero. The Church is weaker here than usual, which can only serve our work. As long as the Catedral is a ruin, we have nothing to fear from the Church. There are not enough priests here to take up her cause, if she could persuade them of the justice of her claim. Not that she would go to the priests, not a woman of her birth. And it could be that we could prevail upon her to keep silent. Surely we can persuade her to say nothing, for if she did, she would disgrace herself completely. The Presidencia would not have to pay attention to a ruined woman, which she would have to confess to being if she complained of us. And the Obispo, if he were here, would not allow her into his presence."

"And we would have the location of the gold," said van Zwolle. "That would be worth a few *Aves* from our Confessors." He put his clenched hands on the table. "Maria Cusi Huarcay was willing to say where the mines were. Why should this woman be any different? We could go tonight. Why should we wait for the officers go get wind of our plans? Anyone who is at this table might decide to protect himself by speaking to the magistrate or his Confessor, and then where would we be?" He glowered at the rest. "If we go now, no one will have the chance to betray us, and will share in our guilt, if there is guilt to be shared."

The rest exchanged uneasy glances. "I hadn't thought we would . . . " said Diego Herrero. "It would be wiser to find a servant to let us in. As it is, we will have to break down a door, and this—"

"We have sergeants here," said van Zwolle, indicating the four men. "They can say they are carrying out their orders. Sandoval and Carillo can stand guard, to keep away anyone approaching the house until we are inside it. And Olleros can watch the barracks here, to be sure no one follows us. Escaso can guard our backs for us. No reason to use the authority of Dom Enrique here. It would only draw attention to our errand." His laughter was a roar without humor. "From whom have we the most to fear?" he asked, and answered before anyone spoke. "From one another, of course. All the more reason to act promptly, so that we will not lose sight of our purpose. Delay can only serve to undermine our determination. We will have to make our best efforts now, to be certain that we have surprise as well as numbers on our side."

"You are said to be a cautious man," observed Dom Enrique with a touch of alarm.

"And I am," said van Zwolle firmly. "It is less prudent to wait than to act. That proves me cautious."

On the far side of the vast hall two half-drunken soldiers got into a noisy dispute over dice, each damning the other in slurred voices. A number of their companions separated them and did their best to calm the pair, without much success. As one of them was escorted out into the wind, a chill whipped through the room, driving the men before it toward the fire.

Deykenwaard gestured to those around the table to lean forward, creating more privacy. "We could do it when the guard changes. It won't be long. No one will notice if we leave with the sergeants." He looked directly at Dom Enrique. "Is this what you want of us?"

"It is," said Dom Enrique. "It is definitely what will serve us. Van Zwolle is right—the sooner we do this, the less chance we have of being discovered." He looked down at the irregular grain of the table. "When we have what we need, it would be best if the woman did not . . . complain."

Sandoval and Olleros signaled for a pitcher of hot wine. "We will need it," said Olleros, rubbing his hands together, but whether against the cold or in anticipation of their success it was impossible to tell.

Van Zwolle showed his teeth. "We will do what is best, as soon as she tells us what we want to know."

One of the servants set down a pitcher of hot wine and retreated as quickly as he could.

"Good," said Dom Enrique with a slow, satisfied smile. "Let us drink to our success."

"And to our not getting caught," said Deykenwaard, lifting his metal goblet with verve, as if his plans were already realized.

"That is part of our success," said Dom Enrique, as if this should be obvious.

"Whatever we drink to, let it be now," said Escaso.

As the others joined in drinking, Herrero said, "It would be better to meet near her house. We should not all go there together, because the men standing watch could make note of us, and report later."

Dom Enrique endorsed this. "Yes. Once we are outside, we must appear to be going our separate ways toward our houses and our beds. We will go by twos and threes toward Sacsahuaman fortress, and gather at the rear of her house. Be careful not to alert the servants."

"Why should we not?" asked van Zwolle, spitting with contempt.

"Because they might send word to the Presidencia that there is trouble, and you know what that could mean," said Dom Enrique with a display of patience that made van Zwolle want to smash his handsome, sneering face.

Van Zwolle gestured for silence. "The guards are getting ready to change. We ought to be ready to leave."

"Just so," said Dom Enrique, getting to his feet, stretching and faking a yawn. "In such weather it is tempting to seek one's own hearth once the sun is down." He tugged his cloak about his shoulders more closely. "Hasta luego, amigos," he told the men around the table.

"Not too luego," said Deykenwaard sotto voce, then added, "Good night to you, Dom Enrique."

Van Zwolle lurched to his feet and dragged his justaucorps closed, taking care to button it. "May God favor our enterprise," he said, and started toward the door, Herrero following behind him.

"I will escort you to your inn," Herrero offered to account for his leaving the place. "Two men on the street after dark are safer than one."

As the others straggled out, they all flinched as the wind plucked at them with frigid fingers. In a matter of minutes they were all away from the barracks, going by various routes in the direction of the Sacsahuaman fortress and Acanna Tupac's house.

Dom Enrique was the next-to-last to arrive at the rear entrance to the modest house where Acanna Tupac lived. He looked around in the shadows, not making any special effort to stay out of sight himself. "As soon as Maldonado gets here, we will be ready to— Ah. There you are."

Matteo Maldonado patted his hip. "I stopped to get my other pistol. We may have a need of it."

"Knives are better," said van Zwolle. "Knives don't make noise."

"True," agreed Dom Enrique. "But pistols are more frightening, and there is much to be said for fright."

Lazaro Escaso pulled out a small pistol and held it up. "We will be safe using pistols. No one will hear this one with the wind so high. If shooting must be done, I will do it."

The men all laughed confidently, but not too loudly; they did not notice the gate at the rear of the kitchen garden swing open, and a figure no larger than an eight-year-old child slip through, or hear the rasp of the bolt fixed behind him.

"Who's to go first?" asked Dom Enrique, looking about him at his companions. "What about you, Herrero. You are young and a soldier. The servants will not question you if you demand admission."

Diego Herrero stared around in dismay, not ready to make himself obvious. "Do you think it is wise? They would report to the Presidencia that a soldier came with companions. It might make it easy for Don Ezequias to have charges made against us."

Dom Enrique nodded once, acknowledging the strength of Herrero's argument. "Well, it will have to be one of us, Sandoval or Olleros or Carillo, I suppose. They will have to open the door for a sergeant." He rested his gloved hand on the hilt of his sword. "They will not refuse me entrance, will they?"

"Probably not," said van Zwolle, and offered the Portuguese nobleman a lavish bow. "Lead the way."

"I think it would be better," said Olleros quietly, "if Dom Enrique summons the servants. He is a nobleman. No servant will turn him away."

Carillo thrust out his jaw. "They will admit me. I have rank."

"Not graciously," said Olleros. "We don't want them expecting the worst from the beginning. Too much could go wrong."

"Perhaps it should be Dom Enrique, after all," said Carillo.

"That's so," said Herrero, relieved to have escaped that duty.

Don Alejandro wandered out of his quarters to look over the men in the barracks. Satisfied, he went back through the door, still leaving it open.

"It is better someone of position, not a soldier," said Escaso. "There is no one in the streets to see us. No one will know we are bound for the same place if we are careful. Once there, the servants will receive Dom Enrique more kindly than any of us. They do not trust soldiers here."

"Well enough," said Dom Enrique, nodding his satisfaction. He put his poignard back in its sheath under his cloak and strode up to the gate, testing the bolt; he was not surprised to discover it was in place. He looked about for the bell and tugged its pull energetically, making as much noise with it as he could.

A few minutes later the cook pulled open the gate, a cleaver in one hand, a lantern in the other; he gave Dom Enrique no chance to speak. "It is late. What do you—" Then he saw the finery of Dom Enrique, lowered his weapon, and bowed. "Señor. I did not know . . . "

Dom Enrique enjoyed the obeisance offered him, and let the man remain bent over for a short while before saying, "Forgive the lateness of the hour, and my arriving in this manner, but my companions and I wish to speak to your mistress, Acanna Tupac. It is pressing business and cannot wait."

The cook looked up in confusion. "The house is not open tonight. She has no guests. It is not appropriate."

"I think she will see us," said Dom Enrique. "There are important matters, *private* matters we have to discuss with her." He held up a golden real for the cook, who stared at it in amazement. "It is necessary that our visit remain secret. You take my meaning, don't you."

The cook nodded, held fascinated by the coin: it was more money than he earned in six months, and this high-born caller was offering it to him. "It shall be as you ask." And with that, he took the coin, pulled open the gate and admitted the men into the kitchen garden, holding the lantern so that the men could find their way through the rows of vegetables.

Deykenwaard took care to close the gate and set the bolt so that they would not be disturbed.

Once inside the kitchen, the cook stared at the new arrivals and for the first time doubted the wisdom of admitting them, for some of those with Dom Enrique were rough men, scarred and pugnacious. He drew back, not knowing what to do. "I . . . I will have someone . . . send word to . . . "

"Tell us where she is," said Dom Enrique with such cold courtesy that the cook had to resist the urge to flee. "We will announce ourselves. You need not bother yourself with us any more."

"But, Señores," protested the cook in a last attempt at preserving the household, "she is alone. None of her women are with her. It would not be fitting . . . "

Van Zwolle spat. "Tell us where she is, meon, or you will have no use for that real."

Though he was trembling so much his teeth chattered, the cook held his ground. "It isn't fitting." He lifted his chin as if he hoped one of them would strike him and absolve him of his cowardice.

Herrero drew his poignard. "I can make him tell us," he offered, his breath coming a little faster than before.

"Yes," said Deykenwaard, his eyes brightening.

But Dom Enrique shook his head. "Why should we provide the woman with proof of our presence? Tie the fool up and gag him, but do not hurt him. We'll find her ourselves. The house isn't that big, and we know she isn't in the reception rooms, not if she is not receiving tonight."

"Yes, gag him," added van Zwolle. "We do not want him shouting for help."

Herrero looked for a suitable gag and settled on the cook's apron. He fixed this in place while Carillo took a length of hemp and secured the cook's hands around one end support of the drying racks near the hearth; the supports were pillars made of rough stone.

"Try to stay where you are," recommended Sandoval with an angry chuckle as he patted the cook on the head.

"Leave him alone," said Dom Enrique, motioning the men to draw their swords. "There are other servants to be dealt with. Try not to kill them." This last warning was stern enough to hold the attention of his companions. "Try not to kill her, either. There would be questions to answer. The woman has standing in the city; el Presidencia would not like it."

Carillo stifled a hoot of laughter as he stepped into the hall that led to the dining room. They were off to a very good start. He was beginning to enjoy himself. He liked nothing so much as intimidating those with no power to strike back at him, for it made him feel mighty as el Rey himself. His stride became a swagger as he continued through the house.

There were a few other servants in the house, that much was certain, but they were nowhere to be seen. It was typical of servants to be cowardly. Van Zwolle did not think it was a bad sign that they kept their distance, for it seemed to him that no matter what they did, it would be best if there were few or no witnesses.

"It would be best if we do not go into her private rooms," said Herrero. "The Presidencia would not overlook such an insult."

"Then we must lure her out," said van Zwolle, his manner suddenly quite stern. "If she will not come readily, we must persuade her."

"But how?" asked Carillo, hoping the plan would be one he would like.

"We will cause damage. She will not permit it to continue. She is not wealthy, and the loss of her things would be a hardship for her." Van Zwolle looked about the corridor, and indicated a large pottery urn at the entrance to the withdrawing room. "That will break if we kick it over."

"So it would," said Carillo with awakening enthusiasm. "And it would be loud enough to get her attention."

Escaso chuckled. "And there are masks on the wall of the room. We could smash them. That would rouse her." He was about to step through into the chamber when a cool voice interrupted them.

"I regret, gentlemen, I was not able to welcome you to my house. Had you come to the front instead of the back, and had you treated my servants with proper regard, I would have received you with courtesy." Acanna Tupac came out of the shadows, holding a Scottish sporting snaphance pistol in one hand and an Italian rapier in the other. "As it is, I must greet you as robbers."

The men faltered, but only for an instant. Then Escaso started toward her, unholy delight in his eyes. "You are not prepared to fire on us."

There were mutters of agreement from his companions. "We're here on Spanish business," said Herrero.

"You will learn how prepared I am if you come near me, no matter whose business you may be on," she said calmly. "You are not the first to come here in this manner, with the same goals you have. None of them have found what you seek." She cocked her head in the direction of the rest of the darkened room. "Five of my servants are with me, and they, too, are armed."

Dom Enrique looked at her with contempt. "How can you think that your people would dare to attack us? This man is a Dutch Capitan. I am a nobleman of Portugal. You are only—"

"The legitimate heir of the rightful ruler of Peru, the descendant of gods," she said coolly, no sign of fear in her stance or her voice. "I am descended directly from Atahualpa Inca and Choque Suyo, through Quispe Tupac. My heritage is better than any of yours."

Van Zwolle exchanged uneasy glances with Carillo. He despised these natives who thought their lineage had any comparison to the royal lines of Europe. "You are one of a fallen race, woman. And we are the ones who conquered you."

"I am not conquered," she told them with such calm that the men became uneasy. "And you are here with the intention of harming me. I heard everything you said."

Escaso moved carefully; he wanted to be able to reach her without mishap.

"Tell your man to stop trying to reach me," said Acanna Tupac quietly. "I will be forced to have one of my servants shoot him with a dart. A poison dart." She added the last with satisfaction.

"Hold," said Dom Enrique, doing his best to control the anger that welled in him, filling his mind with the blackest, most deadly images he had ever encountered.

"Very good," said Acanna Tupac. "I hope you will put down your weapons before you depart. I will see they are given to the Presidencia, who will have them returned to you."

This was the least acceptable thing she had said, for it would be a tacit admission of guilt, and all the men knew it. "We will keep our weapons in their sheaths," said van Zwolle, resentment turning this offer into a growl.

"I think not," said Acanna Tupac, unimpressed. "I have listened to such promises before, and lived to regret my trust." She said something in her own language, then added to the Europeans in Spanish, "The hour grows late and I fear your visit must end. My servants will escort you out the front of the house once you have put your weapons aside."

"I regret, woman, that we cannot do this," said Carillo with such relish that those with him felt encouraged for the first time since they had encountered Acanna Tupac. "You will do as we say, or you and your servants will suffer for it."

Escaso reached for the oil lamps that gave a faint, golden illumination to the hallway. He pinched out the flame on first one, and then another, and another.

"I regret it, too," said Acanna Tupac, and stepped sideways into the shadows. An instant later a dart the size of a bee flew through the air and into Sandoval's upper arm.

The last of the lamps were put out; now both sides of the door were without light.

Sandoval felt the dart strike, sinking into flesh and muscle. The Spaniard howled and clutched his shoulder; his sword fell noisily to his feet.

A second dart whizzed, and missed Carillo's ear by less than a finger's width. He heard it thud into the wall behind him.

Maldonado rested his hand on the hilt of his pistol, getting ready to shoot.

There was a moment of silence, perhaps as long as two heartbeats, and then someone shouted and figures rushed together in the darkness.

The first one to scream was Sandoval; a cudgel struck him hard in the back of the legs and sent him toppling into the side of the door. He swore loudly and obscenely, and was rewarded with a shout of triumph from one of the men with him as a blow against Acanna Tupac's servants struck home.

Now there were scuffles in the corridor and the room beyond. Scrabbling hands and feet beat a tattoo with the scrape of steel to accompany it. A relentless pounding of bodies and weapons that was as confusing as it was terrifying. Moans and cries answered hard strikes with weapons; the air was alive with menace.

A scuffle broke out as two of the servants tripped over Sandoval's sword; one of them screamed in dread while the other lashed out with his stone-tipped flail, striking nothing more than the frame of the door.

Acanna Tupac kept at the head of her little household force. She was afraid to use her pistol for fear of hurting one of her own servants. But she had felt the blade of her rapier strike into flesh and glance off bone once, and was attempting to do the same again when she heard a sound at the back of the house and saw the wavering light of torches.

Deykenwaard muttered and started toward the brightness, promising to chop the insolent natives to bits. His oath congealed on his lips as he caught sight of the black-clad foreigner coming toward them.

An instant later crisp, firm steps were heard making their way from the kitchen toward the main part of the house; the battle faltered.

"Gracious lady," called out San Germanno in Spanish, "I received your message. Is all well with you?"

It took Acanna Tupac a short while to master herself. "It is," she answered as she heard his steps approaching. Now torchlight shone in the corridor, filling it with huge, wavering shadows.

Dom Enrique realized now that he was about to be discovered by someone who could make a complaint against him, and he attempted an escape. He took his sword, and holding it at the ready, he prepared to run at the newcomer.

San Germanno lifted the odd-looking pistol he held and fired it, not once but twice. The report was soft, hardly more than a dropped candlestick. "There are four more darts, all ready to be fired," he said with a great show of courtesy. "And I have been told my aim is excellent."

Dom Enrique held his hand to his neck where the two little darts were lodged immediately above the soft fold of his collar. He cursed comprehensively, his voice growing fainter with each syllable.

Escaso looked around him, trying to mask his desperation with bravado. "We can fight past him. We're not all badly hurt. He is only one man."

"But you forget the lady's servants. Not all of them are hurt," San Germanno said, his manner still unruffled, his unusual pistol held uncompromisingly. "I think it would be best if you made your apologies and left. At once."

Carillo, who was trying not to whimper, stared hard at Dom Enrique. "What is wrong with him?" he demanded. "Is he dead? Is he going to die."

"In time," San Germanno answered. "As we all must. But not now. The darts are tipped with a powerful soporific. If one strikes you, you will wake sometime late tomorrow with a throbbing head and a terrible thirst. And perhaps a little wisdom to temper your discomfort. Otherwise you will be unhurt." He nodded toward Dom Enrique. "Two of you should be able to carry him out."

"I say we fight our way," said van Zwolle. "He cannot defeat all of us, and the servants will not dare to—"

San Germanno put the end of the torch he carried in a wall sconce and bowed to van Zwolle. "Capitan, at your service, since you insist."

This calm acceptance of van Zwolle's challenge took the others aback. A few of them attempted to gather their courage for a rush on the foreigner, but were distracted by a sharp sound close at hand. A whisper went among them as Acanna Tupac came into the torchlight, her servants behind her. For the greater part of a minute all was silent. Then Escaso offered a mock salute to the Incan woman. "You have the advantage, woman. Another time you will not."

"Another time may be long in coming," said San Germanno at his most genial as he indicated the way to the front of the house. "Especially since the Coya will be better guarded in future."

Herrero was nursing a bad bruise to his hip, but he had helped to sling Dom Enrique between himself and Maldonado, who was favoring his left wrist which he feared was broken. The Portuguese nobleman was now so deeply asleep that he was limp, his head lolling like a man newly dead.

As the band of fortune-seekers straggled out of the house and across the courtyard to the bolted front gate, the servants gathered to watch them leave. They were silent as the Europeans stumbled into the street, offering no sign of the victory they had just won.

When the bolt was once more set in place, Acanna Tupac gave orders that she was to have the lamps lit in her reception room at once. "I must talk with you, San Germanno," she said to the man in black who stood beside her.

"Of course, gracious lady." He bowed as he prepared to holster his pistol in his sword-belt.

She stopped him. "I want to see that." She held out her hand for the weapon.

He laid it carefully on her hand. "Hold it gently. It fires very easily," he warned her.

"But what is it?" she asked, turning the weapon carefully to examine it. "I have not seen one before, I think."

"No, you probably have not," he agreed. "It was made originally for shooting at targets. It is ingenious in its way. The mechanism revolves so that the barrels are brought into line with the lock. It does not fire very far, but in this instance, I thought it would be preferable to a more . . . traditional weapon, as much for its silence as for its results. My servant, who is watching the street to discourage those men from returning, has a German carbine as well as a rapier."

"A clever solution," Acanna Tupac said, examining the pistol as closely as the uneven torchlight would allow. "May I see it again? In better light?"

"Of course," said San Germanno. He accepted the pistol back from her and then looked closely at her, noticing how the stern set of her features was giving way to the aftermath of danger. The corners of her mouth were trembling now, and her face was turning pale. "You need to sit down, gracious lady."

Her hands fluttered and she looked at him fleetingly. "I must . . . see to my servants first."

"Rogerio will do that directly, as soon as the whole of the grounds are secure again," San Germanno told her, and came to her side. He could hear her heartbeats, too fast and without much strength. "You are in need of something warm to drink, as well as a chance to get off your feet." He knew from long experience that she could collapse suddenly now that her immediate hazard was gone.

"But some of my servants are injured," she protested in a small voice. "It is my duty to see them cared for."

"All the more reason to leave them to Rogerio, who can give his full attention to their plight." He had got her to the door of her house and now stepped inside in order to usher her to her reception room. "I am certain no one will think the less of you for permitting me to tend to you." He would not stay long, he reminded himself, so that Acanna Tupac would not have her reputation compromised.

"But—"

He turned and looked down at her, his dark eyes penetrating in the gloom; his voice was low without being hushed. "Acanna Tupac, allow me to do this for you: I ask you. It would cause me great chagrin if you have been harmed and I have done nothing to alleviate your hurts."

"And if I do not allow it, you will insist, I suppose," she answered, taking secret relief from his insistence.

"I am not so churlish," he said, his voice smooth as the black silk of his camisa, "nor are you so recalcitrant."

She did her best to laugh, made a hash of it, and capitulated, allowing him to aid her as far as her withdrawing room. Much as she did not want to admit it, she was more at ease because of his presence than she was with only her servants around her. If any of the men who invaded her house returned, she was certain San Germanno would make short work of them and would not have to account to Don Ezequias afterward. As she sank down in her best chair, she said, "I am now going to have to be grateful to you, I suppose."

"If it is what you wish, then by all means," said San Germanno. "I do not expect it from you." He saw that two of the servants had brought candles, and he nodded his approval. "It was very wise of your servants to send Jasy to me. Matters might not have gone so well if he had not alerted me to what was going on here."

"He is a good servant, Jasy," said Acanna Tupac. "I am pleased to have him." She did what she could to keep erect in the chair, but her efforts failed, and she slumped. "I . . . what has come . . . "

San Germanno was at her side at once. "Gracious lady, do not put yourself in such travail." He looked around, hoping one of the servants would help. "Where is your body-servant? You should have your stays loosened."

She made a gallant attempt to straighten up once more. "You will not touch my stays."

"Of course not," he said at once. "But one of the reasons you are short of breath is that your stays are too tight."

"Then," Acanna Tupac said, doing her best to stand, "I will go up to her."

San Germanno put his small hand on her shoulder, hardly more than the weight of a leaf, but enough to keep her where she was. "It would be better if she came to you. It would not do to have you swooning on the stairs."

Acanna Tupac stared at him. "I would never—"

"Then stay here, and have your women do for you." He took her hand and kissed it, noting that her pulse was still very fast but not as thready as it had been at first. "Rest, gracious lady. As soon as your women come, I will leave you to their care. When I have reached my house, I will send a tincture to you that will ease you. Take it with hot water and retire at once." He had already remained with her longer than was proper.

She nodded. "You are a wise friend. I will do as you tell me."

"I would say circumspect," he replied to her compliment. "And I will spare you the necessity of accounting for my presence beyond a few more minutes."

One of the servants approached San Germanno. "Your man has checked all the entrances to the gardens and the house and he says all is closed and locked now. We have set men to watch them through the night. Your servant will be expected and admitted upon his arrival."

"Excellent," San Germanno approved, as much for Acanna Tupac's peace of mind as for his own satisfaction.

Acanna Tupac put her hand on his sleeve. "You will come tomorrow, Conde. I must speak with—"

He bowed, as much to keep her from squandering her strength on conduct as to keep himself from awkwardness. "Tomorrow, gracious lady. At noon, if that suits your purposes?"

"Yes," she answered.

"The women have come down," said the servant nearest the door, and stood aside for the two middle-aged women who served Acanna Tupac.

"Then it is time I was gone," said San Germanno; he kissed Acanna Tupac's hand once more, then withdrew from the room as if leaving the presence of royalty.

Text of a letter from San Germanno's manservant Rogerio to Atta Olivia Clemens, written in the Latin of Imperial Rome.

To my master's oldest and most enduring friend, greetings from these mountains on the far side of the world.

I have taken the liberty of sending this to you at Paris, for no information has accompanied the cargo you sent that you have returned to Roma. Therefore I will assume you are still working on behalf of the Italian Cardinal Mazarini. Given that Louis XIII remains in failing health, the fortunes of the Cardinal must be uncertain, and with that, your own position.

Your shipment of trunks of Transylvanian earth finally were delivered here ten days ago. It was wise of you to stipulate that ten of them were to remain in the warehouse at Lima-Callao against any sudden need for departure. While I hope such foresight will not be necessary, it is best to have it and not need it than to need it and not have it. My thanks to you for your planning.

To answer the questions you so carefully did not ask about Sanct' Germain, I will tell you that he remains steadily himself, and I know you recognize the style: cordial, helpful, intelligent, distant. He is unfailingly polite, more reserved than the Spanish, and yet for someone who is twice a stranger here, he is received well. He has sought no enemies, though a few have declared themselves. As far as I am aware, no one suspects his true nature and account for all his apparent eccentricities by remembering he is an exile from the Hungarian mountains, as unlike the Spanish in his way as are the peoples of the New World. He has made no continuing alliances of blood here, saying it is not safe. But it was not safe in Rome, or in Tunis, or in Saxony, or in Leon, or in Florence, or in Moscow, or in Antwerp, or a hundred other places, but he achieved it. I admit I am perplexed by his continuing reticence, for if he is apprehended during one of his ventures, the consequences would be immediate and potentially fatal. The Church is strong enough here to demand the flames for those of his blood.

Not that you and I are apt to change him. He will persuade himself in time, if only because he is alone here. Eventually the dreaming complicity of the women of mixed race he has visited in the night will not be sufficient for him, no matter how he clings to the determination that they will be. I will continue to urge him when he permits it, but I know it will take more than my recommendation to break his isolation.

There are a few hopeful signs. In the last year it has become known that he is an alchemist and that the potions he makes can cure illnesses and diminish pain. Many of the people of this city who hold him in high regard for this also feel a degree of suspicion about him. Thus far, the chief magistrate, the Presidencia, has made my master his friend and silenced the most scandalous talk, for the present. As long as Don Ezequias continues his acceptance of Sanct' Germain, Sanct' Germain will be able to move about in this remote society without too much limitation, providing none of the clergy distrust him. This friendship with Don Ezequias is an association I hope will continue while we remain here, for all our sakes.

Yes, I think your offer to ship chests of Sanct' Germain's native earth to Nobre de Dios, Cartagna, Guatamala, Vera Cruz, and Santo Domingo is a good one, and I tell you now that Sanct' Germain will be grateful for your planning. Let me know to which establishments you have sent the trunks, and should it become necessary, I will be able to secure the trunks for him. It might also be wise to send a few trunks to Buenos Aires, though given the state of smuggling there, who can tell how long they will remain where you shipped them.

Until I see you again, this letter must carry my utmost respect and continuing high regard to you.

Rogerian
At Cuzco in Upper Peru, Viceroyality of Peru, by my own hand on the 17th day of July, 1642

5

Obispo Melchior Puente y Sello arrived in Cuzco at midafternoon on a glorious August day as spring was bursting forth throughout the mountains; all the vestiges of winter had faded and the entire Andean range simmered with burgeoning life. The Bishop was riding a pale grey mule, his regalia shining in the brilliant light, the monks flanking and following him more drab beside his splendor. The trek up from Lima had been more arduous than he had anticipated, and he was as irritable as he was glad that the trip was over. As he came through the city gates to the cheers of the people, he muttered to Padre Gustavo that he hoped someone could take the pain from his saddle sores before he had to undertake the return journey.

Presidencia Don Ezequias Pannefrio y Modestez and Capitan Don

Alejandro Morena y Osma met the Obispo at the gates of Cuzco, stand-ing at the head of a gathering of local dignitaries, including a few of the cadet Incan nobles. Don Ezequias, and all the rest, were in court dress, with sashes and Orders on full display. As Presidencia, Don Ezequias knelt to Obispo Puente y Sello and kissed his episcopal ring, saying as he did, "You are most welcome in Cuzco, Excelencia. The people rejoice that you have come to see their city."

Obispo Puente y Sello glared at the top of Don Ezequias' head; he was in no mood for what passed for ceremony in this place, and was not prepared to endure it with good grace. The journey up the moun-tains had exhausted him; he felt thick of thought and vaguely sleepy; his skin was pink and shiny. He blessed the Presidencia in an off-handed way, then made a more general blessing in the direction of the gathered officials. "Where are my clergy?" he asked as he finished.

Don Ezequias got to his feet. "They are at Los Sacramentos. They wanted you to see the Catedral, so that you will understand their con-stant petition for repairs. Obispo Herman Guarda has not been able to—"

"I am aware of Obispo Guarda's efforts," Obispo Puente y Sello in-terrupted, and sighed. He would have to remain in the saddle a bit longer. He would offer up his aches during Vespers. "Show me where they are."

Don Ezequias indicated the street leading to the Catedral, and gave a signal to those with him to follow after the Obispo's party. He stepped out briskly, not wanting to give Obispo Puente y Sello any cause to complain of him. "As you see," he called out over his shoulder as he led the way, "many buildings were damaged, but there have been re-pairs made on most of them. Sadly, a portion of the east wall of the Catedral gave way and the roof—"

"—is no longer safe, and the walls are not stable. Yes, I have heard it all," Obispo Puente y Sello finished for him. He was familiar with the situation by now and made no apology for his abruptness.

"Truly," said Don Ezequias, thinking they were not off to a good be-ginning. He tried another tack. "I had the honor to meet you when I first arrived at Lima, some years ago. Su Excelencia gave me an audi-ence of more than an hour, and prepared documents for me to take with me when I came here. I was struck then by Su Excelencia's affa-bility and Christian humility. It was graciously done, and I appreciate how generous you were for a newcomer to—"

Obispo Puente y Sello rolled his eyes upward. "It is what is expected,

Don Ezequias. No man coming to a position like yours could prevail without the official support of the Church, and no man may remain in such a position without my endorsement." His warning was plain; he could not keep the smugness out of his voice. "If I had not given you my license, you would have had no authority, no matter what el Rey said." He relished his power. That he, a legitimized bastard son, shunted off to the backside of the world, could have such hold over the properly born hidalgos who were given posts here in the Viceroyalty of Peru! He had sent Don Ezequias to Cuzco and would not allow him any promotion, not as long as he was in power. It was one of the privileges of his office that delighted him entirely.

"Very true, Excelencia," said Don Ezequias with stiff deference. "And it is a lesson that is not easily forgot, once learned."

"Not unlike family obligations," Obispo Puente y Sello said pointedly, wanting to make the most of his opportunity.

"As you say." Don Ezequias conceded.

There was a short silence before Obispo Puente y Sello spoke again. "We understand each other tolerably well, Don Ezequias." How good it was to make the Presidencia squirm. He did his best not to grin, although the corners of his mouth quirked up.

Don Ezequias led the rest of the way in silence, his thoughts roiling with unpleasant reflections and a few realizations he did not want to face. Now he wished he had asked San Germanno to be part of the celebration, for he wanted the stranger's assessment of the Obispo's motives. He also would have liked to cause Puente y Sello some distress in return for what he had received. Perhaps that evening, when the great banquet was to be held, he would be able to seek out San Germanno and discover how he viewed the events of today. Unhappy speculation occupied his mind the rest of the way to the Catedral. "This is Los Sacramentos, Su Excelencia," he said as the damaged building loomed ahead. "Your servants in Christ wait to receive you."

At the front of the Catedral a large party of monks stood, Franciscans and Passionists being the most numerous, although Trinitarians and Dominicans were among them, as well. In the doorway the priests were waiting, all vested for Mass, with the sacred vessels in their hands.

Frey Martin, who was forty-four and looked sixty, doddered forward and knelt at the hooves of Obispo Puente y Sello's mule. "May God and His Angels be with you in every thought and action, Su Excelencia. We pray every day that God may show Su Excelencia honor and the bounty of His Favor. May Jesus grant you the joys of salvation and the Holy Spirit bestow the charism upon you. May Neustra Señora protect you from all harm. May San Cristobal guide your steps in your travels, may San Bernardo keep you from—"

"Yes, yes," said Obispo Puente y Sello, blessing the old monk impatiently. "You wanted me to see the Catedral, did you not?" He motioned for the leader of his armed escort to come and help him dismount. As the Capitan moved with alacrity to comply, Frey Martin was thrust aside and fell back, uttering a single cry of protest.

Don Ezequias hurriedly bent to help the fallen monk. "Are you all right, Frey Martin?" he asked as he held out his hand.

Frey Martin had clapped one bony hand to the back of his head; his rheumy eyes were dazed. "I think . . . It is very strange."

"Doubtless," said Don Ezequias, trying to get the old man on his feet again before the Obispo set foot on the earth of Cuzco.

"I—" He was trying to roll to his side, or so Don Ezequias thought, when the monk began to tremble. His eyes rolled up in his head and a thin line of foam came from his mouth as his body twitched, then convulsed.

Horrified, Don Ezequias stopped still, afraid to do anything more. He could not make his arm move to cross himself against the sight. If only San Germanno were here, he thought as if he were observing this all from a great distance. He would have something that would stop Frey Martin's visitation.

Obispo Puente y Sello had just dismounted, and was about to send his Capitan away, when he saw the old monk. He crossed himself at once and stepped back. It was a very bad thing, this kind of visitation, and as he looked at the gathered clergy, he saw revulsion and dismay in their demeanor, and heard their muttered supplications to God. Somehow he had to turn this to his advantage or face the loathing of all faithful Christians in the city. He reached for his crozier and held it up. "God reminds us that as He shakes this old man, so He shakes the very earth. We are as nothing in His hands." It was weak, but it was enough.

The priests in the door of the Catedral hurried forward, holding out the monstrance and the aspergilium, preparing to minister to their stricken comrade.

"No," said Obispo Puente y Sello. "Leave him."

"But Excelencia," protested one of the priests, "if we do nothing, he may die."

"So he may," agreed Obispo Puente y Sello, doing all he could to conceal his revulsion while looking down at Frey Martin, and thinking quickly. "God often takes the life of His messenger; the truth of this is in Scripture. It is the cost of knowing the presence of God, and doing His Will. For it is clear that this monk has become a herald of what is coming. It is a sign from God that this place may yet be shaken again." He pointed to Frey Martin, who was within the shadow of the damaged Catedral. "Look at where he lies. The Catedral is before us all, and this old man is filled with palsy. Who cannot see the Hand of God in this? Who are we to scorn God's mercy in sending us this warning." The harsh look he gave all the clergy stopped them in their rush to Frey Martin, and sent them hurrying back to the door of Los Sacramentos.

Don Ezequias wanted to think of some reason to protest, to explain the sudden attack as the misfortune of age, but the words would not come. If he questioned the Obispo, it could be counted against him by the Corregidores, and that would blight his position in the world more than it was blighted already. Feeling an emotion he dared not recognize as shame he turned away from the pathetic form of Frey Martin, but not before he noticed that the foam on the old monk's mouth was foaming red: the old man had bitten his tongue.

As he entered the Catedral, Obispo Puente y Sello knelt and recited a blessing on the place, taking satisfaction in the monks and priests who gathered around him. "It will be necessary to exorcise the site before a new building is erected," he declared once his prayers were ended. "Given all that has transpired in this place, we must presume that the forces of darkness have claimed it for their own."

"Exorcism?" Padre Orin inquired, made bold by astonishment. "There was no deviltry here; the Hand of God touched these—" He was about to go on, but faltered under the Obispo's cold gaze.

Obispo Puente y Sello regarded Padre Orin with narrowed eyes. When he spoke, there was deep suspicion in each word. "The whole building—your Catedral—is about to collapse and you do not see the Devil's work in it?" He would have liked to castigate all the clergy for the incident but held off, in case he could use this lapse to greater advantage at another time.

Padre Orin made a gesture of helplessness, doing his best to return to the Obispo's good graces. "From time to time there are shakings in these mountains. There are ancient accounts of them in the writings of the Incas who supported Pizarro."

"And you believe these writings? You do not think that the Devil was here before we brought God to them?" Obispo Puente y Sello challenged. "You see many of the old Indian buildings still intact while this Catedral is about to fall in on itself, and you say there is no deviltry here, no need for exorcism?"

Two of the other priests exchanged uneasy looks: it did not appear that Obispo Puente y Sello would endorse reconstruction in the way they had hoped he might. "If it is what God wills," murmured one, inwardly cursing Obispo Guarda for not coming back to Los Sacramentos with Obispo Puente y Sello, to plead for the restoration of the building. He was unaware that Obispo Guarda had been forbidden to come to Cuzco until Obispo Puente y Sello had left. They only knew their petitions would not be deemed important without Obispo Guarda to enforce their requests, for within the Church, Obispos, legitimate or not, were superiors to monks and priests, no matter how well-born.

"As you see, the vault is cracked, and the beams are not on true," one of the monks said to the Obispo, his face creased with his efforts at being ingratiating. He stared at the altar as if something devilish had just appeared there. "After the earthquake, the crucifix fell."

"Yes, the vault is cracked, and the wall is precarious," said the Obispo, trying to make a degree of concern come into his voice, but without success. He got to his feet and made a hasty survey of the place. "It is not a safe thing to be here."

"It must be repaired," said the monk with fervor.

"Either that or pulled down and another built in its place." He preferred the latter notion, though it meant that Obispo Guarda would be in Lima for another year at least. Yet he could not have the Catedral fall; the Indians would take it as a sign, he was certain of it. He did not like being in the Catedral, but there was no way for him to leave hurriedly without revealing the depth of his fear of the place.

"It can be rebuilt," said Frey Jeremias, his voice echoing strangely on the leaning stones.

"It would be a bad thing for the natives to see us demolish this Catedral when their own monuments continue to stand," Frey Diego said, and attempted to drive his point home without offering the Obispo more disrespect. "It would give many of them an excuse to turn away from the Church, claiming their old gods had vanquished God Almighty and His Church."

"And if the building is damaged again, what would they say?" Obispo Puente y Sello ventured. "You fear what the natives may think now, with this damage: if they should see another earthquake destroy the building, their gods would be held in great awe and reverence, wouldn't they?" He made a gesture toward the vault once more. "Look at that. Do not tell me that another earthquake would not bring it down."

"But—" Frey Jeremias began.

"No, I do not want to hear about it. I want this building taken down, stone by stone, and those stones used to build a new Catedral, a grander Catedral. That way all will know that our God cannot be defeated by movements in the earth. We will select the site and consecrate the ground while we are here." There, he congratulated himself inwardly. He had reached a decision without having to listen to hours of whining from that coward Obispo Guarda. He started toward the door, eager to be out of the place.

Frey Diego was shocked. "You cannot mean to do this, Su Excelencia."

"And why not?" Obispo Puente y Sello demanded from the half-open doorway. It would not do, he reminded himself, to be seen fleeing the Catedral, not if he wanted the thing to be built again. "Surely this city deserves a grander Catedral than this one? Your new Catedral will be larger, more appropriate to the Bishopric of Cuzco than this one has been. You want the Church to show her power, don't you? Or are you catering to ignorant pagan peoples, who do not like their idols desecrated? Once it is seen that the Church will not be thwarted by ancient superstitions, we will improve our standing with the natives of Peru." He had raised his voice so that he would be heard for some distance; he had no intention of arguing with any of his underlings, let alone in public.

"But Su Excelencia—" Frey Diego began.

"I assign you a penance for the sin of disobedience. You are to beg your supper for two weeks and speak only then and in Confession for that time." Satisfied that he had silenced all opposition, Obispo Puente y Sello went back to where his mule was being held. He noticed that the old monk suffering convulsions had been carried from the plaza and the monks and priests had arranged themselves once more according to their ranks. "The old Frey . . . is he being cared for?" the Obispo asked, more because it was expected of him than from genuine concern.

"He is," said Padre Cornejo, making himself spokesman for the gathering of clergy.

"He was taken to the foreign alchemist's house," volunteered Frey

Alejandro, ducking his head to show his humility, as well as his awe of Obispo Puente y Sello.

"Foreign alchemist?" repeated Obispo Puente y Sello, his indignation lifting his voice half an octave. "What foreign alchemist? How dare an alchemist treat a monk?"

"He—el Conde de San Germanno—has ministered to many of us. He is known to cure those who seek him out," said Padre Cornejo. "He has great skills, and has thanked God for them. Even some of the natives here have come to him." He looked around uneasily, afraid he had over-stepped himself.

"Surely he has not treated them as well?" Obispo Puente y Sello demanded, affronted. "What can have possessed Guarda to allow it? Or Don Ezequias, for that matter?" He used the word *possessed* with deliberate, delicious malice.

"He has been allowed to treat anyone who comes to him," said Padre Orin, speaking timorously but with resolution. "And we honor him for it, for practicing charity and healing the sick, as approved by Our Lord."

It was something he could hold against Don Ezequias, having a godless alchemist care for good Christians: there might well be an occasion when such knowledge would be useful. Obispo Puente y Sello fixed the young priest with a hard stare, trying to place him. He decided Padre Orin must be the ardent one who had so greatly embarrassed the Church at Zaragosa that it was thought he would do better ministering to a less susceptible flock. He made a note to remember the young man's sharp features. "Charity is one thing," he said, his rebuke deliberately cutting, "aiding the enemy is something else entirely. It is the sin of Judas. He may save you, this alchemist, only that he may save *them,* those who spurn salvation. Take care you do not defend the enemies of Christ because the Devil knows how to make himself good company."

To Obispo Puente y Sello's surprise, there was a general murmur of dismay and alarm. Frey Juan burst out, "I was taken with a rotting sore, and San Germanno saved me when no one else was able. Surely this is doing God's work."

"Do not be so certain, for therein lies your destruction. The Devil is a subtle adversary," warned Obispo Puente y Sello, growing tired of all the commotion. He had heard about this San Germanno and his misgivings about the foreigner grew keener. "Learn to distinguish true salvation from the lies of Satan, or you will become one of the many who have succumbed to his lures." He swung around so that he could see the whole of his audience. "In a place like this, you will find temptation in many forms. Most of them will not be terrible. What temptation would it be if all the devils of Hell came, burning, around you? No, it is in treachery and seduction that the Devil himself makes a pleasant companion, one who aids you in little matters and corrupts you with this aid. It is only a little thing to take the bribe offered by a widow to the majordomo of a large household, or the sergeant of recruits, wanting to see her children, isn't it, a gesture that is easily made. But it suborns the will, and the next time it will be difficult to refuse another pleasant request. Thus we are turned from the path God has made for us to the ruination of Satan." He was satisfied to see shock on many faces. No doubt matters had become lax in Cuzco and he would have to be more attentive than he anticipated in dealing with the people here.

A few of the clergy exchanged thoughtful glances, and Padre Orin flushed a deeper shade of olive and his mouth set in a stern line.

It was a hesitant and careful Presidencia who moved to lessen the volatility of the moment. He went and dropped onto his knee before Obispo Puente y Sello once again. "You need not make your decision regarding the Catedral now. You have only just arrived and have not had the time you might need to make a decision that would please the Church and the people of Cuzco alike." He kissed the ring Obispo Puente y Sello offered him before he rose. "There is a parade to be given in your honor in the central plaza. If you will permit us to escort you, it will begin."

The Obispo sighed, a mixture of aggravation and satisfaction. "Of course." He would listen to all the petitioners, and in the end, he would have the old Catedral taken down and a new one built up. That was already settled in his mind. It was the most prudent thing to do, and it would strengthen the hold of the Church in Cuzco. He would also avail himself of this chance to meet men of vision in the region, who were not content to accept those few baubles and other items given up by the Indians thus far. There were said to be treasures—whole cities of gold and silver—still hidden in the high valleys and deep forests of these mountains. He wanted the Church to have it all, for by right, the Church was entitled to it.

"Obispo?" whispered Frey Jorge, not quite daring to touch the sleeve of his august charge. "The mule is waiting."

Obispo Puente y Sello looked around abruptly and sighed as he put his foot into Frey Jorge's clasped hands. "I expect all of you to accompany me; let my churchmen escort me, and the rest may come after as your rank requires," he announced grandly, and gave the signal to begin the procession away from this place. He was becoming uneasy, wondering if the ground was going to shift under his feet in defiance of the Church he represented. "I will watch the parade with all of you and then the presentation will begin."

"It is to be expected," said Padre Orin, just loudly enough to have the priests beside him hear and nod.

Obispo Puente y Sello felt his joints protest his return to the saddle; his back ached from his pelvis to his skull and every step his mount took jarred through him with the force of carpenters' sledges. He clung to the saddle and set his expression to suit his state of mind.

The procession moved off once more, going slowly and straggling toward the central plaza where a viewing stand had been constructed the day before. Don Ezequias walked immediately behind the clergy this time, aware that this was what Obispo Puente y Sello expected, though it was an affront to him and his position, and was, he realized, intended to be. It had been bad enough, relegated to leading the Obispo's mount, but to be ordered to walk behind the monks was an assertion of position Don Ezequias had rarely encountered in all his time in Peru.

Along the way, Spanish and criollo women leaned out of the upper windows of houses and waved their lace mantillas at Obispo Puente y Sello, or threw flowers down to him. Servants standing in the gateways of houses dropped to their knees and uncovered their heads as the churchman went past. As they neared the barracks, the soldiers set up a cheer and a few of them fired their carbines in celebration.

At the end of the central plaza, a number of local dignitaries and other distinguished persons flocked to join the throng. They fell in behind Don Ezequias, a few of them looking disgruntled to have the clergy a favored escort. Dom Enrique made a point of praying as he walked, knowing that it would be noticed and commented upon later, when he expected to have time with Obispo Puente y Sello.

There was some confusion when the procession reached the viewing stand, and it took a short while to arrange the seating in a way that was generally satisfactory. A few of the monks were displaced from their seats by hidalgos, and a few of the lesser personages had to give up their seats to priests, but in half an hour all was in readiness and the trumpet sounded for the parade.

"The soldiers are in need of more weapons," said Capitan Salazar to

Padre Orin, doing his best to be heard over the commotion. "Perhaps you could mention it to el Obispo for us?"

Padre Orin had no wish to put himself at any greater disadvantage than he was already, but he could not bring himself to tell Capitan Salazar that he lacked influence with Obispo Puente y Sello, so he said, "If the opportunity presents itself."

"Because we need guns, you know, and ammunition," Capitan Salazar persisted. "If there should be an uprising among the natives, we would not be able to defend ourselves or the Spaniards here for more than a day or two. And we could not get word to Lima in that time, could we?"

"Very likely not," said Padre Orin, wishing he had a good reason to move away from the Capitan.

Another bray of trumpets brought the mounted soldiers up to the stands. All saluted and then uncovered their heads for the Obispo's blessings. It was a short while before this was finished and a number of the horses grew restive; two of them whinnied in impatience, earning a ferocious scowl from Obispo Puente.

Don Ezequias was seated at the end of the stand, a place of diminished favor but great convenience; when the parade was half-finished, he rose and offered his formal excuses to Obispo Puente y Sello, explaining that he had arrangements to attend to for the presentation which was to follow.

Obispo Puente y Sello waved him away, enjoying his privilege of deciding who would remain and who would depart. In Lima he had to be far more accommodating than he was here. He was beginning to understand Obispo Guarda's affection for the place. Had he not occupied his episcopal seat at Lima, he might strive for Cuzco, for the satisfaction he could achieve in the position.

By the time the parade was over, the sun had slipped down the sky toward the distant and unseen ocean. Watchmen were sent out early on their rounds to light the torches so that the streets had no chance to fall into darkness before the festivities of the evening got underway.

At the magisterial palace a great banquet had been laid out, and the foods offered were the rarest and most unusual dishes that could be made in this part of the Viceroyalty of Peru. Some of the dishes were European—the young spit-roasted pig with chestnuts, raisins, onions, and walnuts for stuffing was one such—but more were the unique dishes of the region—spangled fish from Lago de Langui y Layo cooked in layers of fragrant leaves was much favored. Wine brought from Spain was served by the barrel, and the evening became raucous as time went by.

Dom Enrique, not nearly so drunk as he appeared, finally saw his chance, and bowed unsteadily to Obispo Puente y Sello. "God guide you, Obispo," he said, taking pains to slur his words.

"And you, my son," said Obispo Puente y Sello automatically. He knew the look of ambitious younger sons, and recognized the man before him as one of that neglected, ambitious brotherhood. "May your efforts in this world be rewarded."

"Amen to that," said Dom Enrique with feeling, and took another mouthful of wine, to be convincing.

Concealing his intense boredom, Obispo Puente y Sello said, "What troubles you, my son."

"Su Excelencia," Dom Enrique said, determined to take advantage of this opportunity to gain the Obispo's full attention. He plunged in with reckless enthusiasm. "I have wondered why it is that we have not been permitted to claim all the wealth of the Incas for the glory of God?"

Obispo Puente y Sello regarded him with a stare that neither conveyed nor denied interest. "It was my understanding that this has been done. That when the Incas came to the Church, they brought their treasure with them, as gifts."

"Some did, some did," said Dom Enrique. "But not all." He waited, trying to read the Obispo's closed countenance.

"Those are rumors for the credulous," said Obispo Puente y Sello, without the conviction he knew he was supposed to display; he was as familiar with the tales as anyone, and they burned in his imagination with the malign yellow brilliance of sulphur.

He abandoned his pretense of inebriation. "In Lima, perhaps, but not here. In Cuzco, where there are living descendants of Atahualpa who have not aligned themselves with the Church, it is known that they have secrets—"

"How is it known, if they are secret?" interrupted the Obispo. He was growing more fascinated with every word.

"It is known because from time to time one of these former nobles will convert at last, and reveal the whereabouts of hidden cities and tombs." Dom Enrique leaned forward, his mouth all but brushing Obispo Puente y Sello's ear. "There is a woman here in Cuzco who is one of the last of the old nobility. She has not yet revealed what she knows, claiming that she knows nothing. But that is a lie."

"Who claims it is a lie?" Obispo Puente y Sello asked quietly.

"The Indians in the marketplace. They revere her and guard her. Some of them say that she is their true leader." His smile was vulpine. "Their true leader? A woman?" The Obispo dismissed the notion with a flick of his hand. "Not even these natives would repose such trust in a woman."

"Not if there were men of equal position, no they would not. But those men are gone. She alone remains. And she has all the weaknesses of womankind." He giggled, the first indication he did not have the degree of self-control he thought he had.

"Surely men have tried to seduce her before now," said Obispo Puente y Sello, no longer fascinated by what Dom Enrique told him.

"Yes, and as far as is known, without success." He paused. "But offer her knowledge, the gift of the serpent, and she may well give knowledge back." He smiled slowly. "Her world is these mountains. She knows of the greater world only what she hears. If she were to be given permission to travel, not just to Lima, or throughout the New World, but to España, she may be willing to tell us what she knows."

"Why should she be granted approval for such travel?" asked Obispo Puente y Sello. "You say she has some reputation here. What would be the use of permitting her to expand it?" He had often heard just such propositions put forth, and he had learned how to turn them away without mishap.

"Once she is away from here, from Peru, from the New World, what would she be but an Indian woman, an oddity? And if the Dominicans should decide to inquire into her faith, it would be an easy matter, would it not, for her to end her life in the hands of the Church? Where she would be an excellent example to her countrymen?" Dom Enrique was grinning now, tremendously pleased with his assumption and his cleverness.

Obispo Puente y Sello favored Dom Enrique with a nod of understanding, and then did his utmost to make himself plain to the young Portuguese. "If she were to be sent away and not treated well, it would dishonor España and the Church, for no host should defame a guest. That is the first flaw in your scheme. If the Holy Office were to question her, there would be an outcry against it that would turn her from . . . to use your word, an oddity, to a martyr. And then every monk and priest in the New World would be in danger. That is the second flaw in your scheme." He sensed he was about to be interrupted and held up his hand to prevent that. "Listen to me, you foolish puppy. If you suppose this woman, who is neither a girl nor a fool, is not inwardly alert to plans of this nature, you deceive yourself. To think otherwise is the mark of a man without keenness of reason. That is the third, and most damning, flaw in your scheme." He motioned Dom Enrique back from him.

Chagrin and wrath warred within Dom Enrique. Chagrin prevailed, and he shook his head in confusion, deciding that perhaps he had had too much to drink. He stumbled back toward where his friend Capitan Mauricio Ayala y Carbajal was seated at a small table, picking the last of the meat off a chicken-breast. "He won't listen to me."

Capitan Ayala y Carbajal nodded once and went on licking his fingers. His wide collar had spatters of grease on it, and his mustaches shone.

"I said he won't listen to me," Dom Enrique repeated, sounding ill-used now, and petulant.

"He's tired. And everyone is asking him for something," said Capitan Ayala y Carbajal. He was bored of the evening already; he knew almost everyone in the room and had little to say to them. "Van Zwolle is waiting for us."

"Not yet," said Dom Enrique, gesturing for silence. "And not so loud."

"I told him we wouldn't be long," Capitan Ayala y Carbajal went on as if he had not heard. "He and Vigaracimos have someone they want us to meet." He picked up the chicken bones and made a last attempt at cleaning them.

"We've heard that before," said Dom Enrique. He glanced around the room and said, "She isn't here tonight."

"Who isn't here?" The question was muffled by his food.

"Acanna Tupac." He laughed once and reached for his goblet where he had put it down before he went to speak with Obispo Puente y Sello. "They don't want to cause the Church any awkwardness, I suppose."

"Over a woman of her age and station?" Capitan Ayala y Carbajal would have chuckled had he not been chewing. "Not likely."

"But Don Ezequias makes a point of inviting her to official functions," said Dom Enrique.

"You don't see that foreigner San Germanno here, either, do you?" Capitan Ayala y Carbajal took a long swig of wine and rose from his seat. "All the people here want something from the Obispo or from the Church, or the Church wants something from them."

"But you would expect to have her here, wouldn't you?" Dom Enrique persisted. "Don't tell me she wants nothing from the Church."

"I think that is just what she wants—nothing." He stretched. "Well, if you have no reason to linger, let us join van Zwolle and Vigaracimos. They are expecting us. It isn't wise to keep them waiting. We are eager to know more of your cousin's husband." He hooked his thumbs into his wide sash. "We can learn something useful if we . . . " The movement of his hands toward the door completed his thoughts.

Dom Enrique finished the wine and glared at Capitan Ayala y Carbajal. "This person we are to meet—who is he?"

"Someone who is close to Acanna Tupac, or so I was told. Someone who might be able to discover what you could not frighten out of her." This last was said with mild disgust. He continued with modified contempt in his voice. "You should leave such things to those of us who know how. You have not served our purposes with your inept attack. She is alerted now, and will not capitulate as we hoped."

"If the foreigner had not come, she would have told us," said Dom Enrique, his mouth sullen.

"Perhaps. From what I was told, however, she was more than prepared to fight you. You permitted her to defeat you, to make you flee. And that was stupid." He scooped up his gloves and again indicated the door. "Leave the Obispo to these sycophants. We can accomplish nothing here. All they want to do is dicker about the Catedral. We have better things to do."

"Yes, we do. Many better things, thanks be to God or some—" Dom Enrique conceded, setting his goblet aside and following Capitan Ayala y Carbajal out into the street and the festivities of the night.

Text of a letter from Frey Jeromo to Obispo Hernan Guarda in Lima.

To the most reverend and excellent Obispo Hernan Guarda, the greetings of your devoted servant in Christ from your city of Cuzco, Audiencia de Lima, Viceroyalty of Peru.

This is being carried by Frey Justino who accompanies Obispo Puente y Sello on his return to Lima. He has given his vow to me that this will reach no one's hands but yours, so that you will have my account without Obispo Puente y Sello interjecting his views on the matter.

Obispo Puente y Sello was in Cuzco for eighteen days, and during that time proposed to have the Catedral partly taken down, and a new one, larger than before, erected on the same place. This decision has been endorsed by most of the monks and priests in Cuzco with the exceptions of Frey Anselmo at Santa Inez and Padre Matienzo at San Esteban. They have expressed fear for what would happen if another severe earthquake should come, and both believe that the foundation of the Catedral is not strong enough. But we are assured that rebuilding is possible.

There were nine formal receptions for Obispo Puente y Sello, and all of them were attended by as many as could procure invitations to them. When the Obispo visited the churches, he was met with throngs of people come to see and hear him and to receive his blessing. It was a most demanding schedule. Frey Justino said that most nights the Obispo did not keep midnight vigil due to his exhaustion. I do not question this, for all the clergy of Cuzco were left worn out by this visit.

It was Obispo Puente y Sello's stated wish that we continue to assist those searching for Incan silver and gold, and to that end, he has spoken often with the Corregidor of the Audiencia, Don Vicente. He did not speak to any of the Incan people who were still allied with the old ways, but entertained only those who have embraced the Spanish and the Church, to demonstrate his determination to see the last of the old ways gone from Peru. Many of those who have come to Cuzco for the purpose of searching for riches have welcomed his license. While he does not believe all the tales of lost cities filled with treasure, he is convinced that not all the caches of the Indians have been found, and that there must be many mines left that would yield up their riches to us. This was greeted most favorably by those who have come here to make such a search. They now have nothing to stop them from plundering villages on the expectation of finding gold, silver, jewels, mines, or any other valuable things. And although I seek to glorify the Church and God with the tribute of those who have converted, I do not like to see the victory achieved by men of this stamp.

Don Ezequias has attempted to modify this general permission at exploitation, but he can do little in the face of Obispo Puente y Sello's and the Corregidor's support of these ventures. He has made it be known that if any word of slaughter or torture of natives reaches his ears, he will use the garrison to protect the Indians. I suppose the Corregidores will put an end to his folly as soon as they are informed of it; in the meantime, I am certain that the soldiers know better than to guard Indians from Europeans.

Among the Europeans, I have again to single out Francisco Ragoczy, el Conde de San Germanno. He has made a reputation for himself treating the sick, as you are aware. It appears that his reputation is growing beyond Cuzco. It is said he has cured rotten wounds and has treated

*putrid lungs, and that most of his patients have recovered. This causes
me alarm, for it is not known in whose name he saves these people, or
through what arts. Alchemy is not explanation enough for what this
man has done. Too many of the clergy in this place regard him as a God-
send, and praise him without knowing how he succeeds when others
would surely fail. I, myself, have watched him tend to Frey Martin when
a visitation was upon him, and have seen Frey Martin restored to himself without harm. While I believe that this was a true recovery, I am
much afraid that Frey Martin may be drawn away from his faith in God
to the worship of those medicaments or revere San Germanno himself.
Such a seduction cannot be tolerated, nor can it be ignored, for it es-
tablishes a precedent that may do much harm in future. You must return as soon as possible and put this foreigner to the test. All of the religious in Cuzco pray for your return.*

*There are rumors that more soldiers are to be sent to the garrison, but
we have heard such rumors before. If it is true, it is welcome, for in these
mountains armies could be swallowed up and never found again. If it
is not true, I beseech Su Excelencia to request them, and to be firm in
your demands.*

*It is now time for Mass. I ask God to return you to us soon, and to re-
store His Catedral to its full glory. May that day come quickly, with His
grace and your presence. With my devotion to you and Holy Mother
Church, by my own hand.*

*Frey Jeromo
Order of the Preachers of San Domingo
At Cuzco, the 31st day of August, in the Year of Grace 1642*

6

A gentle mizzle of rain came from clouds made pale by the full moon
behind them. The roads were no longer swathes of mud but had not
yet developed plumes of dust; the mountains looked brightly polished.
Wind coming off the distant peaks bore a lingering edge of ice in its
breath, sharpening the wet. By morning the roads would be drenched
for perhaps the last time before the height of summer, but for now the

evening was chilly but not cold, and the wreckage of Sacsahuaman glistened.

Acanna Tupac did not need to see to stop at the entrance to the Temple of the Sun. She indicated the gaping door, a denser darkness than the night around her. "It isn't safe to go in. The earthquakes have seen to that. They are as relentless as the Spanish, in their way. This place will probably fall the next time the mountains tremble, and no one will build it again." She looked saddened by her own words. "A pity you cannot see it."

"I see it," he said, for the night did little to hamper his sight. "As it is, not as it was: you can do that."

She accepted this in silence. After a short while she put her hand on his, to get his attention. "How does it happen you are interested in these places?"

"I am interested," said San Germanno, his easy words underlaid with intensity, "because I want to know what was here before it is completely gone. I want a sense of what is being lost. So many things have been lost, over the centuries, and we cannot recall them. Here there is a chance—a small one, but a chance—to save something, if only through knowledge of what was. If it is possible, I want to understand it." He looked down at her from the shelter of his mente's raised hood. "You're sure you're not cold?"

"When you are my age, you are always cold. In this place, all the world is cold. I am used to the cold." She tapped her woven hat and the engulfing alpaca-wool cloak she wore. "This is enough." For a another unspecified time she stared into the Temple of the Sun, unaware of the eloquent yearning in her eyes. "Never in my life have they worshipped the sun here." Then she made herself stand straighter and move away from the entrance to the massive building. "They say our gods will leave us when the Temple falls. They tell us that they will return to the depths of the ocean and the highest place in the sky, and will not hear us when we call to them. Most of them have already begun to retreat."

"And you?" said San Germanno, his face hard to read, his well-modulated voice gentle, persuasive. "How does it seem to you, Acanna Tupac?"

"I think the gods left when Pizarro came and Atahualpa Inca died, for he made himself a Christian so that he would rise from the dead. He thought Christ would enter him and save him." The words were

flat but spoken a few notes higher than usual. "He did not. They stran-
gled him. His body rotted."

"The Spanish do not readily accept strangers," said San Germanno
with more feeling than he knew.

"I am told it is far worse in España than here," said Acanna Tupac,
and shook her head at the notion of it.

"Yes," said San Germanno.

"Which is why you are in Peru," she finished for him.

"One of the reasons. There are other places to go in the world. To
see this place while it can be seen is one of them." San Germanno nodded and walked beside her in silence for some little distance along the
south wall of the Temple. "You tell me that Jasy has improved."

She looked at him through the darkness as if she had forgot he was
with her, or he was on the far side of a great chasm. "Oh." She nodded. "He manages better than before, much better than when he first
left his bed. The legs you brought him may serve, after all, now that
he has had time to use them, and the supports you have made for him.
He does not always think he was done a kindness in living, as you
might expect. But those times are not often, though he complains of
the ache he has from them, and his lack of strength, but he would do
that in any case."

They had reached a stone wall most of which was still intact. San
Germanno paused beside it. "If I could have saved his own legs for
him, I would have. It was not possible."

"I know that," she said simply and directly. "And I am grateful. You
have done more than my people or the Spaniards would have done.
Jasy will be grateful, too, in time. When he realizes how he would have
to live if you had not made these for him."

"Perhaps," said San Germanno, knowing it was foolish to anticipate
gratitude for such service. "The Guarda will be making rounds shortly."
He offered her his arm for support as she started away from this end
of the Temple of the Sun across the uneven and slippery paving stones
which were uncertain footing in the day; on this night San Germanno
was pleased that his eyes were not hampered by the fitful scraps of
moonlight. When his hood fell back, tugged by a fitful wind, he made
no move to replace it.

"The god of the sun is Inti. He is honored with the mocha." She gave
an odd kiss to her palm and lifted her hand into the air. "This is not to
honor the night, but the day in its absence."

"And urge it to return," San Germanno ventured, having some sense of the workings of this religion. "You worshipped Inti here."

"Not as they used to, not as he should be worshipped, with pomp and ceremony, not hurried rituals without celebration. But, yes, I have worshipped Inti. Here, and throughout the city. You can find his face carved in stone in many places, though the Black Robes defaced many of them, calling them the faces of demons." She looked around her as if she could see all the ruins as the fine buildings they once were, though most had fallen before she had been born.

There were a vast number of questions he wanted to ask her, to learn what her life had been when she was young, when the Spanish had not completed their domination of Peru. But such questions were dangerous, and her answers would be doubly so; he kept them to himself, and was content to walk companionably beside her in the night.

"There has long been a legend among my people," she said a little later as they prepared to leave the abandoned city. "It was taught that fair strangers would come from far away, with the power of life and death in their hands, and all who were unworthy would fall before them, while those who lived would be their servants. It has been told since the beginning of time. Every child knows it. When Atahualpa Inca befriended and welcomed Pizarro, many thought the legend had been fulfilled, and made themselves the allies of the Spaniards."

"Ah?" said San Germanno, and risked asking, "And what do you think, gracious lady?"

"I think that my people are the servants of the Spaniards, those of us who are still alive, and that the prediction has little to do with it, but to soften the weight of the yoke we now bear. For the Spanish have done more than conquer us. In the years since they came, many of my people have died from ills that have never touched us before, infections we had never seen. Surely this is the teaching of the legend, that we would not survive the coming of those with fair hair. Thousands died of the Spots in the first twenty years after the Spanish came." She stared up at the raveling clouds, unaware or uncaring of the light rain on her face.

"Spots," said San Germanno, thinking that it must have been smallpox. "And the Spaniards died as well."

"Very few. The monks said that the Spots were an illness of children in España, and most of the children in España survive it, though a few are blinded or left crippled by it. That was not the case here. It attacked us all, parents and children alike, and killed many." She paused once, her face impassive, though her hand dug into his arm with talon-like ferocity, and her eyes were hard as the eyes of raptors hunting. "It preyed upon us. Those whom it did not kill were blinded or deafened, or crippled, like those few Spanish children. Many went off into the mountains to die, unwilling to live as beggars. Some who survived the disease were dead within a year of their recovery, all their strength used up."

"I know this disease." San Germanno had treated it for nearly three thousand years, and all the other ravages of nature and humankind.

"So do we," Acanna Tupac told him bitterly. "I had sisters and a brother, when I was young. The Spots claimed them all, and our mother as well." She stopped as they reached the edge of the Spanish city. "It was the end for my father. He lived, but he was not alive."

San Germanno touched her hand. "Acanna Tupac, I know your sorrow. I understand it: believe this." He did not resume walking but stood beside her, letting the misty rain settle on his caped Hungarian mente and his hair, turning the dark, loose waves to curls. "My homeland was over-run by conquerors long ago, when I was a young man." There had been many conquests after that over the centuries, but for him, the coming of the horsemen from the eastern plains beyond the Carpathians had been the most destructive of all. "My father was killed and my mother taken as a concubine by the conquerors, as were my sisters. They made me and my two brothers their slaves, and they did their best to kill me, after I had won a battle for them." He and his men were supposed to lose, and all of them had known it. "I wanted to save my soldiers: I was the oldest son, and marked by our god as his own." The scars of his execution were the last marks left on his flesh, and they were formidable, stretching from the base of his ribs to the rise of his pubic bone; the faces of his brothers and sisters were only the faintest memories, but the scars were constant.

"But you are free now," she said, her bitterness colored with a wistful envy.

"Am I." He regarded her kindly. "It seems so."

"But you do not think so," said Acanna Tupac, her expression sharp as she regarded him.

"Not entirely, no," he admitted, his enigmatic gaze fixed on the middle distance and spanning millennia. "There was a price for my . . . freedom . . . and it is not yet paid."

She studied him from the tail of her eye. "You are not like the others who have come here."

"Gracious lady, I am not Spanish," he said.

"It is more than that, for you are not like the Dutch or the English, either, and they have been in Cuzco." She held his arm more tightly as they stepped off the flagging and into the slick muddy street.

"No I am not any of those," he agreed with an expression that was as equivocal as it was fleeting. He sighed once. "Though my servant is from Cadiz. We are both strangers here." How long that had been the case he dared not tell her.

"But why have you befriended me?" she asked him, determined to have an answer from him.

"I was under the impression that it was *you* who had befriended *me,*" he said, pausing to smile at her.

"Don Ezequias threw us together, but you were not content to escort me and say farewell at the end of the evening. Most pale ones do so, to keep from earning the disapproval of the Black Robes. You did not set me away from you because of who I am. Before I met you, this happened only when something was wanted from me, and I was certain you were one such. But that is not the case. Or it has not yet been." Her apprehension tightened the last words to a whisper.

"But I do want something from you, Acanna Tupac." The words were calm enough to hold her attention. He was silent for a dozen steps, and then said, "Few of my blood remain, and they are scattered about the world as if driven by strong winds. Even when we seek to remain in a place, circumstances drive us on. Everywhere we go, we are . . . separate from all around us. None of us stay long in a single place."

"If I were an exile, as you are, I suppose I would do the same." She looked directly at him, forcing him to stop and meet her eyes.

"It is possible," he allowed, keeping his voice neutral.

"For it is less painful to be among strangers and move often than to see one's line and people die out." She nodded, continuing with sad bitterness, "Oh, yes. I understand that. Though my line has not been slaughtered in battle as some have been, or . . . No. The clever Spanish have chosen the surer way, though it takes longer: elevate the lesser nobles and marry into their families. In three generations, they have made Spanish and Inca so mingled that only a few of us are left who have no direct links to our invaders, as I do not, though most of our cousins do. To rise against the Spanish would mean to rise against blood relatives. In another generation—" She resumed walking, going more slowly over the treacherous surface, her hand on his arm. "They will not have much longer to wait. When I am dead, there will be only one left who is not at least one quarter Spanish, and he lives in so remote a place that he is thought to be a legend by most of our people. He may not survive me. He is our last true High Priest, and he is not robust in nature. He will not live much longer. Then the religion will end. When he is gone, I may not want to remain behind."

"That is unfortunate," said San Germanno, with the odd sense that he was providing her some comfort in spite of her sorrow. "But it is preferable to outright slaughter, is it not?"

She sighed. "I suppose it is, but some of the Spanish do not agree."

"You would not expect them to, would you?" he asked, leaning a bit closer to her. "They are the ones who have claimed their prize, and you must not tell them that gold and silver are not all that is valuable here."

She looked at him in some surprise. "What do you mean?" she asked, her manner becoming guarded. Now, she supposed, she would learn what it was he was seeking and she braced herself for his demand.

"Why, that your people and your lives are the real treasures," he said, knowing that she would not entirely agree.

"Most of those left are nothing but ignorant farmers, not the people who made us great. They have despoiled our blood as much as our land," she said flatly. "Our nobles have married Spaniards in their hurry to preserve their position, and they do not know how much they have lost in saving themselves." She sighed, and looked up into the darkness. "They wanted me to marry, but I refused."

"And it was allowed?" San Germanno asked, curious what her answer might be.

"I said I had been married, promised as a child, and would remain true to my husband, on an oath of blood. Even the Spaniards respected that." She looked over her shoulder as a night-bird cried. "That is thought to be an omen of pleasure." As she said it, she wondered what had possessed her to speak this aloud.

"Is it." He stopped her and looked into her face, the night not hampering his vision significantly. His scrutiny was compelling without being unkind, evoking, not demanding. When he spoke again, his voice was deeper, and his dark eyes fixed on hers as if he were a magnet and she the pole—a star she had never seen and thought to be mythic. "And would you want it to be? such an omen?"

She returned his look with the beginning of alarm; she stood very straight, her hand on the dagger she wore in her belt. "If you do anything, Señor Conde, I will tell the good Padres and you will be—"

"I meant nothing you would dislike," he said quietly, taking a step back from her. "You say you are alone, and I know what it is to be alone. I am not the last of my blood, but I am the last of my line, of my people, as are you. I know how bitter it is to see one's own vanish from the earth. I know how the loneliness of being the last can wear at your . . . soul as water wears at rock." His loss had happened more than thirty-five centuries ago, but he still felt the keenness of it as he felt the slice of the wind. He resumed walking, going no slower and no faster than before. "I have hoped there could be trust between us. I have hoped this would lessen the barriers between us, as friends, if nothing else."

"There are worse fates than being alone," she said, not convinced at the moment that this was so.

"True enough," he said, his manners unfailingly polite.

She regarded him narrowly, searching for subterfuge or mockery and finding only kindness. "San Germanno, you are an enigma."

"Yes," he agreed.

When he offered nothing more, she went on, "Yes. And I cannot keep from wondering: you have helped me for no reason I can understand." She ended this with a lift in tone, making it more a question than she had intended, encouraging him to explain himself.

"Yes," he said.

They had reached the street leading to her house, and the path was growing slippery once again; she skidded as she stepped from stone to stone. She took his arm more firmly to keep from losing her footing, and was relieved that he did not use this as an excuse to put his hands on her, or to attempt to foist his gallantries upon her. Still, she could not keep from asking, "You have not yet said . . . What is it you want of me, San Germanno?"

"Yes, gracious lady. And I will tell you." He said it in the same steady way he had spoken before, but there was something in his voice now, a promise she had never heard, and the smile in his compelling eyes reached a part of her she had thought inviolate.

This time when she stopped, she was not so afraid. She stood nearer to him than she had, and made herself look directly at him as she asked, "What is it you want, San Germanno?"

"Why, you, Acanna Tupac," he answered tranquilly. "That is what I want, to know all of you, if you will let me."

She shook her head as she moved a few steps away from him, her regret more apparent than she knew; her response was filled with reproach, and an emotion she did not realize was grief. "I thought you understood: I will never marry."

"I do not believe I asked that of you," he answered, evincing no upset at her stern tone. "It would serve neither of us to marry, if what Don Ezequias has told me about marriage taxes on foreigners is true." It was not the money he begrudged, but the relentless invasion of his affairs the Church would make in the name of preserving the Spanish hegemony in Peru.

She considered this, her expression unreadable as she struggled to assess this, and nodded. "I am not a loose woman, to hold my honor in such contempt. I will not disgrace myself for anyone, not you, not one of my people, not for the Spaniards," she said, but with less heat than she felt, for there was nothing in his manner that suggested he meant her any compromise.

"I do not believe I asked that of you, either," he told her as they reached the door leading to her courtyard.

"No, you did not," she said, trying to be offended as she reached for the pull that would ring the bell and bring one of her servants to answer the door. "What *did* you ask of me, if not the things I have supposed?" She was curious enough to ask the question, but hesitated to ring the bell.

He touched her face with the back of his fingers, his dark eyes fixed on hers. "I asked you for a great gift, Acanna Tupac. If you wish to give it, I will accept it with profound joy."

She shivered, but not because of the wind in the night, or the thickening mist that would be rain before morning. Although she was still a bit frightened, she was far more fascinated. She studied him. "What is this gift?" she asked, so softly he had to bend nearer to make out the words.

"I have told you already." His mouth touched hers lightly, hardly more than the pressure of a feather, but its impact went through her like a twig of lightning, stopping the breath in her throat. He continued, his words low and musical. "I seek you, Acanna Tupac: all of you. If you are willing to let me touch you, I will try to be deserving of your trust, and value you. If you will allow me, I will welcome all that transpires between us and honor you for it: not as a trophy, or a conquest, as a gift." The torch by the door showed his features in its fitful, sputtering light, the illumination so unsteady that it was impossible for her to read his face.

She pulled on the bell-rope so hastily that they both could hear the clang in a distant part of the house. Embarrassed by her own action, Acanna Tupac released the rope, and the bell rang again, the second tocsin louder than the first. Now she felt her face grow hot, and she turned away from him with an incoherent farewell. It was not that he wanted her, she realized, but that he was able to speak of it so . . . clearly, with such generosity. It was all she could do to frame an inadequate response. "Another time, perhaps, or . . . " she mumbled, marshalling all her courage in order to face him, expecting to be upbraided for her indecision.

"As you wish," he said, unperturbed by her confusion. "You have no reason to fear me, gracious lady." He moved away from her as he heard footsteps in the patio beyond the door. "I will call upon you tomorrow, if you will permit."

She stared at him, her thoughts in disorder; she had not anticipated such acquiescence from him, nor such affection. "Is that all?"

He bowed slightly, elegantly, and spoke with kindness. "What more should there be? Would you welcome importunities?"

"A Spaniard might not worry about such things. But you are not Spanish." She spoke more forcefully. "You say . . . such things as you have said to me, and then you ask if you may call tomorrow?"

His smile was as gentle as it was ironic. "I have told you already I want nothing you do not want to give. And it would serve no purpose for either of us to have you uncertain of your mind. I am willing to wait until you are certain. To know you against your desires is not to know you at all, and it would set your heart against me. What would be the joy in that, for you or for me? No, Acanna Tupac. I would have to be a greater fool than I am to require you to accommodate me." Again he touched her cheek lightly, lightly. "That will be true, whatever you want to give."

On the other side of the door the bolt was being drawn back, and a voice called out, "In a moment, Señora. The hinge is stiff, because of the damp."

He bowed to her. "Tomorrow, Acanna Tupac?"

She was about to step through the door, into the safety of her patio, when she paused and held out her hand to him. "If it is what you want," she heard herself say, "you may come in."

He took her hand, but lingered in the open doorway, concern at the back of his dark eyes. "Is this what you want?"

She regarded him with exasperation and surprise. "As you say, we are the last of our peoples. No matter what else we may do, we may understand that in each other." She looked directly at him. "I would like you to come into my house, San Germanno, if nothing more."

He accepted this without reluctance. "Very well," he said, and let the servant secure the door behind him.

The enormity of what she had done rushed in upon her and she shivered, looking about her enclosed garden as if she thought spies lurked there. "A moment, San Germanno." She rounded on her servant and dismissed him brusquely. "You have done your task. I will manage the rest." But her turbulent emotions did not depart as readily as her servant did; she stood, trembling, near the door into her house.

"Would you rather I left? You may tell me so and I will leave until you ask me to come to you again." He took two steps back from her, his smile sad. "You need not decide now: Acanna Tupac? I will do nothing to displease you, gracious lady. You have only to tell me what you wish me to do, tonight, tomorrow, or any time you want to designate."

"Any time?" She reached out to his hand, her fingers cold on his.

"Well? Shall I go?" San Germanno asked softly as he watched her. He could feel the beat of her pulse from where he waited, an arm's length from her.

"No," she said. "I want you to remain." She sighed impatiently, her dissatisfaction with herself fueling her annoyance. "I want you to remain, and I want to have this pleasure you offer. And I do not know why."

"Because you are curious," he said in the deep, serene tone she had heard for the first time that night. "Because you are tired of being alone. Because it is late and the night is cold. Because you have ceased to fear me as an enemy. Because you would like an ally. Because I am not Spanish. Because you have been circumspect too long, and have grown weary of its demands. Because you want to learn if it is possible for a European to understand what is taking place here in Peru, within your soul." He made these suggestions calmly, giving none more emphasis than another, allowing her to respond without apprehension.

"Yes," she said, her acknowledgement making her light-headed. "All of those things. And more." She stared at him, wishing there was more light in her courtyard. "I do not know what that will be," she warned him.

"Then we will have much to discover," said San Germanno. He did not come any nearer, but there was about him a compelling aura that was as real as the water on her face. "You have only to tell me, Acanna Tupac."

"Tell you what?" she asked, held by the glow of his dark eyes. She had never before been so aware of another person, let alone a foreigner. Nothing about him was insignificant to her, and her thoughts were caught up in every nuance of him, which was starting to frighten her.

"Whatever you want me to know about you," he said, and came a step closer. "There is nothing I do not want to know."

"You cannot be certain of that," she said, her sorrow sharp within her.

"But I can," he told her, all the solace in the world in his words.

Her attempt at laughter was not quite what she hoped it would be, and she concealed her emotions by striking out. "Then why do you have to ask? You are a European. You are in a position to demand."

He turned away from her, and when he spoke, his voice was distant and ancient in a way she had never encountered before. It was as if he had gone leagues and eons away from her. "Those of us who have had our homes and our lives ground to dust under the heels of conquerors know better than to demand. We know to the core of our hearts what the cost of such demands are." He gave her his full attention once again, and the whole of his compassion. "I will not make demands of you, now or ever. Tell me what you wish me to know because you wish me to know it. I will accept what you give me. Or tell me nothing, as you like."

Whatever had come over him, she knew to the marrow of her bones that she understood it, and by her understanding she shared in part of it; she held out her hand to him, saying the first words that came to her tongue. "It is a hard thing, to be the last. For all they say that life is sweet, being the last is a bitter thing." The depth of her loneliness appalled her, as if she had not comprehended its extent before. She felt his fingers enfold hers, and she was no longer as isolated as she had been for so many, long years.

"Even when there are those of my blood still in the world, yes, it is hard to be last of my line." There was a forlorn note in his voice now, something so far beyond grief that Acanna Tupac had the eerie impression she stood at the top of a deep gorge where a cold wind blew. "It is not the same."

"San Germanno, how long have you been the last of your line?" she asked, seeing something in his countenance she had not noticed before.

He closed the distance between them. "You would not believe me if I told you," he whispered as he took her face in his hands and kissed her.

This was not like his first kiss, a swift and feather-soft pressure of his mouth over hers, but a revelation; this was immediate, evocative, and disturbing without being frightening; his arms enfolded her without confining her; his small hands had strength she had not realized he possessed. Acanna Tupac had never felt her lips soften and yield as they did now, as if she, herself, were melting, a sensation that was much more pleasantly persuasive than she had thought it could be. Her hat slid back on her head, unheeded. She clung to him as if she were afraid of falling, finding in his unexpected power a solace she had not known until then she sought; when he began to release her, she held on more tightly, unwilling to be separated by so much as a handsbreadth from him, as if to be apart from him would leave her vulnerable to all the secret terrors of her soul.

He drew her close and held her for some time, untroubled by her silent tears. Only when her breathing became regular once more did he take a step back, but no further than the distance needed to be able to look directly into her eyes once more. "Gracious lady, you honor me."

"Honor?" Acanna Tupac was amazed. "I should not weep. That is for children and cowards. What sort of woman weeps for such things, but one unable to face her fate without cringing." She was angry with herself for giving way as she had and it was tempting to take it out on him. A few curt phrases formed in her mind, but she could not make herself speak them aloud.

He said nothing for a short while, and then: "Tears are . . . high tribute," he said, with utter conviction, and the aching sense of his loss of them.

She wanted then to have his arms close around her again, but she was ashamed to admit it. To her astonishment, he sensed this; he embraced her even as she attempted to protest. "You don't need . . . There is no reason to . . . "

"There is comfort," he whispered. "For both of us."

"Comfort?" she repeated as if the notion had never occurred to her. "How can there be—"

Now he put his finger on her lips. "It isn't a thing that can be spoken," he said, so gently that she feared she would weep once more. "There are no words for it, gracious lady."

Few things had caused her such inner consternation as his esteem did; she shifted in his arms as if she wanted to break free of him even as she grasped his shoulders more tightly. A sensation like vertigo went through her, and then a quick, hard trembling. She shoved her head against his neck to continue her illusion of resistance while maintaining her contact with him; she did not dare to look at him. She swore by her gods, and did not know why.

San Germanno made no attempt to stop her outburst; he did not cajole her or try to soothe her, or to dismiss her response. He held her while her emotions racked her, making no protest when she wished perdition upon him for ending her isolation. Finally he lifted the brim of her hat and kissed her a third time, very gently, very long. "It is never easy, gracious lady."

Acanna Tupac was shocked afresh. He had answered the very thought that had shaken her: *was it always so difficult?* She did not know what to say to him, and found a strange consolation in the assumption that he knew her mind well enough not to have to be told. She caught his hand in her own. "I don't know what . . . I hadn't realized what was . . . " Again her turmoil seized her.

"You owe me nothing, Acanna Tupac. Not gratitude nor explanation, nor any other thing. It would not be possible for you to have such a debt to me. What we have can be a bond, if you will accept it, but not a debt." He regarded her steadily. "That does not mean I do not seek you, for I do."

How could he speak so calmly? she wondered. What was it within him that kept him from being afraid? She laced her fingers through his and tried to smile at him. "Why should you do that?"

He was not troubled by her question. "You have sense and courage and strength. You have comprehension of matters that bother you, and you are able to face what you see. You are sagacious without loss of your humanity." He paused to allow her to think over all he had said. "And you have warmth and beauty in you. I would be a fool not to seek you."

Much as she disliked the impulse that drove her, she asked, "And the treasure I am said to have? What of that?"

His chuckle was as reassuring as it was unexpected. "I have two chests full of jewels in my house, the quality of the stones is excellent. Their worth is beyond easy reckoning. I will gladly tell you where they are hidden if it will ease your mind." He put his free hand over the one she held. "I have no need of your wealth, Acanna Tupac. And it would be reckless to attempt to gain it, since I am not Spanish."

She cocked her head to the side, looking at him from under the brim of her hat. "And what are you, San Germanno? Since you are not Spanish?"

"My people are gone from Europe, and have been for . . . many years. Those of my blood who lived in Italy were called Etruscans," he said, thinking that by the time the Etruscans came around the arm of the Adriatic from the Carpathians, he had been in the Temple of Imhotep for three centuries.

"Your people . . . you were their king, then?" There was just enough skepticism in her voice to hold his attention. "So many who have come to Peru were once kings."

"I have told you already, gracious lady: my father was, though his name is forgotten." He could say this without rancor; he could hardly recall his father's face after all this time. "His lands have been held by many nations since he . . . died. Just at present, the Turks and the Hungarians are fighting over it, as countless others have before this time."

"I have heard of the Turks. Most of the Catholics hate and fear them," said Acanna Tupac, taking refuge in this safe subject, and glad that nothing could be said now that would intrude on her fragilely restored separateness.

"They have a different religion and their way of life is unlike the way of life of most Europeans. Of course the Catholics hate and fear them, especially Spanish Catholics, who lived under Moorish rule for centuries. It is to be expected they would fear Moors and Turks. And you." His eyes grew more compelling. "As they have hated and feared you," he said quietly. "They have conquered you as a means of ending their fear."

The illusion of distance ended abruptly; Acanna Tupac shook her head in a vain effort to shield herself from San Germanno's encompassing empathy. "That was long ago, when there were fewer of them and more of us," she admitted as she pulled at his hand. "And they have horses and guns."

"And wheels," said San Germanno, making no protest to the mauling of his hand. "Though they admire your bridges."

"Our bridges helped them to conquer us," said Acanna Tupac with sudden bitterness, dropping his hand and pacing away from him. "Our bridges were our downfall. If we had cut them down when Atahualpa ruled, the Spaniards would never have reached Cuzco."

"Perhaps not quickly, but eventually they would have come. Once they knew of this place, they would have found a way to reach it. Greed

would drive them," said San Germanno, his certainty filling his voice
with sadness. "You could not have held them off forever, no matter
what your High Priest may tell you."

"The guns and the horses and the wheels would be enough, you
think?" she asked, her stride lenghthening.

"Yes, and so do you," he said without apology for his bluntness.
"What had you to oppose them that would have endured against
horses and wheels and guns? You are not blinded by wishes as so many
others are. You have clarity of mind, little as you want it, gracious lady."

"And you hold that in high regard?" She rounded on him. "A clear
mind in a woman? And one such as I? How can you? What can you
find praiseworthy in such necessary defeat?"

His answer was calm to the point of angering her. "The profligate
wasting of lives on lost causes has appalled me for . . . most of my life.
When lives are held more valuable than Pyrrhic victories, I cannot help
but respect those who do not insist on ruination as well as conquest."

"I do not know what a Pyrrhic victory is," she told him suspiciously.

"It is a victory more costly than a defeat," San Germanno told her.

She considered this and nodded. "And you think that had we cut
down our bridges, it would have been a Pyrrhic victory for my people? You think we would still have lost?" The question was an accusation.

"Yes," he answered without distress. "Because you would have. The
Spaniards would have oppressed and enslaved all your people once
they held the land, and with guns, there is no doubt they would hold
the land, and exact a terrible price for your resistance." He had not
moved and seemed content to have her prowl around him.

"You have seen this happen, have you? You know what the Spanish planned to do here?" She stopped and glared at him. "You knew
their ways, before they came here. And you gave no warning."

"What warning could I give? When Pizarro was befriending
Atahualpa, I was—" He stopped, realizing what he had said. He saw
her standing very still, three strides away from him, her eyes wide with
astonishment and recognition. He decided to continue. "When Pizarro
was taking Atahualpa's side against his brother, I was selling spices and
changing money in Venice."

"That was more than a hundred years ago," she said, trying to sound
incredulous and not succeeding.

"More than one hundred ten years, I believe," he said, and waited,
the light rain gathering on the hood of his mente.

The silence in the patio was heightened by the nearly inaudible spatter of water as the drops grew larger and their density increased. At last Acanna Tupac was able to speak. "How is it you were alive then?"

"It is the nature of those of my blood to have . . . long lives," he said, reassured to be telling at least a portion of the truth.

"But more than a hundred years—" She did not know how to continue with words. She came to his side once more and laid her hand on his arm. "You do not look so old."

"And I am . . . somewhat older than that," San Germanno said, and was startled as he felt her arm go around his waist.

"Then I am not a hag to you," she said, a trace of smugness in her manner. "You are not distressed at my wrinkles."

"No, you are not a hag," he promised her, and turned enough to be able to hold her again. "Is that what bothered you?"

She shrugged. "A woman my age without position and fortune does not often have suitors, and those who come courting want more than a nighttime companion, or a mother for his children." Her smile was provocative as she leaned against him, no longer put off by his pursuit.

San Germanno could not conceal his satisfaction and relief at her change toward him. "And you are not offended to be the object of the attentions of one as ancient as I am?" He was half-teasing, half-pleading, the sense of her as potent as brandy and opium fumes. "I do not repulse you?"

She was amazed at the question. "You? I—" For an answer she encouraged him to kiss her once more.

He opened her lips with his own in response to her quickening need; her mouth was softer than before. Now that she was growing ready for him, his ardor fired. He was as eager as she to explore her body, and began by the way he moved his hands on her clothes as she pressed closer to him.

"Come inside," she urged him, trying to move toward the inner door without breaking her contact with him. "It will be better."

He allowed her to decide how they would reach her apartments on the second floor of her house. As they went, he kept his arm about her, holding her as near to him as he could without impeding their progress through the dark hall and up the narrow stairs. As they reached her door, she slipped away from him. "Acanna Tupac," he said.

"I must dismiss my body-servant," she whispered to him. "I will not be an instant longer than necessary." And with that she went through the door, calling out softly to the woman whose job it was to dress and undress her, "I want you to hurry, Nacia."

San Germanno moved back into the deepest shadows so that he would not be seen by the 'tirewoman when she left for her own room. As he listened, he imagined what was being done, and wished he had the chance to attend to Acanna Tupac himself; he would remove her garments with care, reveling in each new opportunity offered, taking delight in all he discovered. There would be time for that, later, when she was certain she could trust him. For now, he was willing to wait.

Nacia left the room hastily, calling back a promise to present herself not long after dawn. She had a vast shawl bundled around her, and she was huddled against the chill as she made her way down the stairs. She did not notice Acanna Tupac's door open again, or see the neat, dark-clad figure enter.

Acanna Tupac was in a long shift of pale muslin, her face pale but composed. She raised her arms as San Germanno came up to her, locking her fingers behind his neck. "If you leave now, I think I will die."

"Do you," he murmured as he gathered her in his arms again, relishing the promise of her flesh.

"And I depend upon you to keep me alive." It was a confession more startling to her than to him. She felt as awkward as a girl, as determined as an avalanche.

"And I." He held her while her turmoil quieted, then began at her brow to lavish kisses on her, light, coaxing kisses that soothed and roused her at once. "Acanna Tupac," he murmured as he unfastened the lacing of her shift, "you have nothing to fear from me, but if you fear, tell me. I do not want to cause you distress."

She stared at him, astonished he had known the anxiety that had possessed her even as her flesh yearned toward his touch. "I . . . I am not afraid."

His swift smile revealed he knew otherwise, but he asked her, "How long will we be undisturbed?" Before she could answer, he stopped her words with his lips. This time his kiss began slowly, deepening until she was shaken to the roots of her being as his hands slowly, miraculously, inexorably ignited her body, ardor and tenderness in everything he did. Some while later, as she cast her nightrail aside, he repeated, "How long?" worried now about nothing but interruption.

"We have until dawn," she exclaimed victoriously when she had caught her breath, and gave herself over to the delicious frenzy he had already roused in her. She opened herself to learning passion from him, finding more in her fulfilled surrender than she had ever known she possessed.

Text of a letter from the Franciscan missionary Frey Pascual, in Cuzco, Audiencia de Lima, Viceroyalty of Peru, to his mission superior in Toledo, España.

In the Name of the Father, the Son, and the Holy Spirit, Amen.

Thanks be to God we are arrived here in safety at last. It is my greatest delight to write to tell you that I and my fifteen Brothers in Christ and San Francisco de Assisi have completed our journey and are now at la Catedral de Los Sacramentos, which has been much damaged by an earthquake not more than three years ago, though not so severely as the old priory, which we are now endeavoring to repair. We will remain here working to rebuild Los Sacramentos until Obispo Hernan Sigismundo Bernal Guarda gives us our assignments with the pagan peoples of this wild country, at which time I will inform you of our various destinations, so that our Brothers in España may give us strength through our prayers.

Five of the monks who traveled with us are now at the Universidad de Lima and have no doubt sent you word from that place, so you will have their accounts to judge this by, and by extension, to assess the rest of my account. We spent a month there before coming into the mountains, and we learned much from those pious and wise monks and priests who teach there and know this country of old. Of all those giving instructions the most valued information came from Padre Enrique Antonio Llorez, who has been here for more than forty years, which the fate of many of those whose illegitimacy makes it unwise for them to live too near their families, or to advance too high in the Church. He is very well-versed in the ways of the people of the country, though I cannot judge the quality of his knowledge yet. He has gathered together what he purports to be accounts of the pagans' activities and histories.

Already we are hearing great tales of the undiscovered wealth of Atahualpa, the last reigning Incan King, and his lost cities of gold which remain hidden from us. Even in Lima there was talk of these places, but it is here in Cuzco that the air is buzzing with whispers about these hidden treasure cities. One city in particular is sought, a place called Choquerquirau, which is said to contain riches beyond reckoning, the last treasury of the Incan Kings. I know that it is our duty to bring this wealth, if it exists, to the Church for the Glory of God, and I am pledged to that task. Some of the Christians here declare that they believe these cities are nothing more than phantoms, tales of long-vanished days given more treasure with each retelling, but I am not as sanguine as some of these, for I find all accounts of this nature suspect. I believe that there are indeed riches untold held by these native people, and I intend to see them in the hands of the Church Triumphant, so that our work in the world of pagans may continue and increase. It is God's Will that we claim the gold and silver of these mountains, as it is God's Will that the pagans come to the True Faith.

Most adamant among the skeptics, at least in regard to hidden treasure, in this city is the Presidencia, Don Ezequias Mateo José Gregorio Andreas Pannefrio y Modestez, a distant cousin of Frey Rafael's, who has been here for twenty years and who claims he has never known of a single discovery of any hidden or lost city in the last century. He does not trust the accounts made before that time. Don Ezequias comes from Salamanca, and his family is well-known and high-ranked there, though his own reputation is not quite so untarnished as the greater part of his family's. I have listened to his claims and I am willing to believe that for all his protestations to the contrary, he is hoping to find treasure for himself, and make his fortune without presenting the bounty of his enterprise to the Church or the Crown, much as certain bold and unscrupulous pirates have done on the sea. I am certain this man, and those who are often in his company, bears watching, for he is inclined to be indulgent of the pagans here; for that reason, among many, I suspect he may not be as dedicated to Holy Church as a Spanish official in his position ought to be, which cannot help but trouble me, and many of my Brothers as well.

There are many Europeans here whose motives for coming into the mountains of Peru do not seem worthy of our great purpose in this place. So many of them are seeking fortunes from the natives that I can feel sympathy for them in their plight. There are many who eschew the company of Europeans altogether. I have made it a point to avoid men of this stamp, myself, but I cannot help but encounter them from time to time. It is a sad truth that when one is isolated from the world as this city is, that one must make the best of the company provided, no matter how questionable that company may be. In such a place, there is no opportunity to select those who will know you. I have soon to endure an evening with the cousins of the Incan King: these men have been our allies, and have supported our presence here, but they are not as selective in their guests as I would wish, for my soul's sake, and it will be a trial to pass four hours with such men as must be present. Not that I have yet made the acquaintance of any of them; however my recent arrival will not long serve as an excuse to absent myself from these functions much longer. So I must resign myself to the company of heretics, exploiters, thieves, adventurers, bastards, and alchemists, the flotsam of the Old World that has washed ashore here in the New. My service demands that I make accommodation to all exigencies I encounter, and I will do it. I will offer up any humiliation I may experience for the redemption of sinners everywhere, in accordance with my vows to the Order.

In this remote place, and with such restrictions as are given to me now, I am reminded of the eloquent and inspiring admonition of Padre Jesús Joaquin Sanchez y Molino, who spoke to us as we left España, regarding the pagan souls here—mansions of darkness, locked in the pagan errors and sins, which we, as Christians, are mandated by our Savior to turn to mansions of light, through His Mercy and Word. It is a task that fires my soul with zeal. How privileged I am to be part of those bringing light into darkness. How my entire being yearns to build those mansions of light, to banish all darkness from the people who have so long been denied the joy of salvation and the company of the Saints in the presence of God. What more glorious task can any devout Christians aspire to than this one? Let me renew my vow to you to do all that body and soul may do to bring this mandate to triumphant fruition.

With my prayers and my most humble duty to you, our founder San Francisco, and our Order, I ask your blessing on this autumn morning, the 16th day of May, and the Feast of Saint Brendan the Voyager, and Saint Honorius of Amiens, in the Lord's Year 1643, in the Viceroyalty of Peru, Audiencia de Lima, in the city of Cuzco, at Los Sacramentos.

Frey Pascual
(Don Carlos Martin Roberto Maria Filipe
Puno y Zapatillero)

7

Padre Eugenio Bocan was known for his thoroughness and his attention to detail. Had he been wholly Spanish, his intelligence might well
have advanced him far in the Church, but being the illegitimate son of
a Spanish officer and his native woman, he had attained his post as
secretary to the Corregidor Don Vicente Angel Luis Jorge Yniguez y
Nievereos, third son of the Conde de Zaragosa. Padre Bocan was thirty-
two, spoke six languages and was regarded as the real authority in Don
Vicente's office; known to be incorruptible his reputation for fair judg-
ments was unsurpassed. He met the stare of the two men seated across
the table from him with cultivated neutrality. "I do not know how I can
assist you, Señores."

"We were told the Corregidor would have to agree to . . . provide a
. . . what is the license called, van Zwolle?" asked Dom Enrique, who
knew the answer perfectly well.

"An encomienda," the Dutchman supplied, his impatience making
him brusque with the priest.

"Yes," said Dom Enrique, doing his best to be ingratiating to make
up for van Zwolle's rudeness. "We need an encomienda."

"You come from Cuzco; you should obtain the encomienda from
Don Ezequias," said Padre Bocan, all but dismissing them. "You have
wasted your time in coming here, it would seem."

"He has referred us to you," said Dom Enrique, his jaw set.

Padre Bocan smiled frostily. "You mean he has refused you, and you
wish to have his decision reviewed by higher authority."

Van Zwolle glowered at this suggestion, but did not dispute it. "He
was not willing to hear our petition because we are not Spanish."

"Is that the reason he gave?" asked Padre Bocan, his voice edged
with disdain, for he was well-aware that one of the most frequently
voiced criticisms of Don Ezequias was his too-ready accommodations
of foreigners.

"Not precisely," said Dom Enrique before van Zwolle could speak.
"He has reservations about our purpose, or so he claimed."

Van Zwolle shot him a vitriolic look, and added, "He has not issued many encomiendas in the last three years. He claims it would invite trouble with the native people, who are required to supply labor."

"And do you think he might have reason for such concerns?" asked Padre Bocan, letting his sarcasm color his question more than he properly should. "Cuzco is off in the mountains, isn't it? And the Incan people are all around the city. If they should decide to cut it off from Lima and the rest of the Viceroyalty, they could. Create another Audiencia. And if we know of the danger here, most certainly Don Ezequias does, and more keenly. I doubt we could get enough men-at-arms there in time to prevent a siege and slaughter, particularly if the Incan peoples cut down their bridges, as they have threatened to do in the past." He cleared his throat. "I believe Don Ezequias to be a prudent man, of sound judgment where his duties are defined. His other lapses do not appear to influence him unduly in this regard, so I will not change his orders to you. You have come here in vain. There will be no encomienda." He did not add that he had already decided to inform Don Ezequias of this attempt to circumvent his decision.

"We must have the encomienda, Padre. We cannot do the things we wish to do without it," said Dom Enrique, sounding like a petulant child. "We will not be able to carry out our plans if our petition is denied."

"That may be, but you will not have one from me," Padre Bocan informed the two with stern purpose.

Van Zwolle glared at Padre Bocan and shook his head once. "It is useless to keep this up, Dom Enrique." He plucked at the young nobleman's padded sleeve.

"I want the encomienda," said Dom Enrique, all appearance of accommodation and good manners vanishing. "Inform Don Vicente I expect to be given one."

"I fear that will not be possible," said Padre Bocan, showing no distress at Dom Enrique's threatening manner. "Don Vicente leaves the issuing of encomiendas to me. It is my decision, and I have made it."

"Then you will have to reconsider; keep the petition. You will need it later," said Dom Enrique, making no apology for the obvious hostility in his voice. "I have the money, if that is your fear. And I will give a generous donation to your Order."

"It has nothing to do with money, or with rank, to save you your next argument," said Padre Bocan with ill-disguised contempt for Dom Enrique. "And your belief that it does reveals to me more surely the reasons I was correct in refusing the encomienda, as well as convinc-

ing me that Don Ezequias was unquestionably prudent in his unwill-
ingness to issue you one."

"You will regret this," promised Dom Enrique. "You will. Don Vicente will see to it as soon as I speak to him." He had a sly look on
his face as he stood back from the priest's writing table. "You will give
me the encomienda before tomorrow is finished and you will provide
me your apology for your behavior before the year is over, and I will
be gratified to receive it."

"That may be," said Padre Bocan in a tone that implied the opposite. "God give you a good day, and favor your endeavors." This last
was by rote and wholly lacking in any sincerity.

The Portuguese turned his back on the priest and signaled to his
Dutch companion. "Come. It is useless to remain with so unreasonable
a clerk. We have intruded on this fellow too long." With no leave-
taking, he strode out the door, van Zwolle in his wake.

They reached the street quickly, and only then did they pause. "What
the devil do you mean, putting the priest's back up like that?" demanded
van Zwolle, gesturing back toward the gate to the courtyard of the Residencia.

"Do not let it bother you, van Zwolle," Dom Enrique recommended.
"Our options are not yet exhausted." His smile was more a display of
teeth than mirth. "I think I know where we can find Don Vicente."

"And be refused again?" van Zwolle asked angrily. "You will not content yourself until you get us both exiled."

The street was a busy place, far more crowded than any place in
Cuzco. There were carriages and sedan chairs as well as carts, barrows,
wagons, and horsemen making their way along the dusty paving stones,
their passing stirring up miniature tornados of dust. The noise was
enough to make conversation difficult, and as neither man wished to
shout their business to the world, they started down the way, looking
for somewhere they could talk.

"I doubt my cousin's husband would do that, for any number of reasons," said Dom Enrique, his smile precariously close to a smirk. He
saw the recognition dawn on the face of his companion, and nodded
in satisfaction. "Yes. What I told you is true: my cousin Alma is the wife
of Don Vicente and she will support my petition with him, if I ask her
to do it. She has always been very fond of me, and she helps me when
she can. A word or two to her and we will prosper. If there is no more
direct way to accomplish what we want. So it hardly matters what the
priest decides, don't you see?" He indicated a number of stalls set up

to sell food, and said, "Let us have something to drink while we decide how best to go about this next stage."

They had reached a stall selling sweetened chocolate, the steam from the deep pot making the air itself tasty. Two mugs of the strong, fragrant beverage were purchased for five copper reales and drunk at plank tables set out for those wishing to consume their chocolate while it was hot. The day was becoming quite warm, and the sun was like a weight in the sky. A few of the stall-keepers were closing in anticipation of the approaching hours of siesta.

"We do not need her help yet. I will save that for our last resort, when we have exhausted all other means. There is another ploy that may be more successful that we will attempt first. You see, I know where we may find Don Vicente," said Dom Enrique in a spirit of nasty amusement. "I recall his habits from my last visit."

"And where might that be?" asked van Zwolle, pulling the brim of his hat down to shield his face from the sun.

"I will take you there shortly. I have asked his coachman about him, last time I was in Lima, and I paid him well for his answer and his silence." He chuckled as he set his mug down. "My cousin's husband will not be expecting me to call upon him during his entertainment."

"Is it wise to do it at all?" asked van Zwolle.

"Certainly," said Dom Enrique. "The priest has made it necessary. If he had agreed to do as I requested, I would not have to do this, but—" He shrugged and took another long draught of the chocolate.

"Do you think your relationship is enough to persuade him to help you?" asked van Zwolle, beginning to think he had not been wise to throw in his lot with the discontented young Portuguese.

"If the request is handled correctly, it should succeed quite well," said Dom Enrique, his secretive enjoyment betraying his certainty of accomplishment.

Much as van Zwolle wanted their venture to prosper, he did not want to deal with the Spaniards in too underhanded a way—the Spanish were known to have little humor about those failing to observe their laws, and their concept of punishment was known to be severe. "I have no desire to be thrown out of the New World," he warned Dom Enrique.

"No chance of that, so long as you keep with me," said Dom Enrique with a wink. "I know how to manage this, little as you may think it."

"And what way is that, pray?" Van Zwolle was in no mood to play with high-ranking Spaniards, even those with Portuguese in-laws. He set down his mug so firmly that the sound of it was loud enough to attract the attention of the porters lingering by the chocolate-seller's stall.

"Careful; you'll alert them," teased Dom Enrique.

"Alert whom?" demanded van Zwolle testily, glancing around in spite of his wish not to: it made him appear guilty, and that was a dangerous thing to do in this place, where spies were as plentiful as monks.

"Those set to watch these streets, who report to the Residencia and the Catedral," said Dom Enrique calmly. "They will want to know what has brought you such agitation of spirits that you act in so . . . anxious a way. They will note your nervous conduct and report it if you continue."

"I have done nothing," said van Zwolle abruptly. "And I will not remain here to have you toy with me in this—"

Dom Enrique motioned him to be quiet. "It will not be long. You have to be patient for a short while, and then you must come with me on my errand. Once this is accomplished, if you are not satisfied with what I have secured for us, you may be on your way with your money in your purse and my good wishes to speed you."

Although he did not wholly trust Dom Enrique, van Zwolle's curiosity was piqued enough to keep him at his place on the bench. He narrowed his eyes as he filled his pipe with tobacco and set it smoldering with a spark from the flint-and-steel he carried. The smoke wreathed his head, and he stared into it as if it held a message for him. At last he finished his chocolate and said, "I will remain, for the time being."

Dom Enrique smiled. "A good thing." He glanced up at the sun. "Siesta shortly. Good." He seemed content to enjoy the sunshine until the heat of midday shut down the public life of the city.

"When do we go to see this relative of yours?" asked van Zwolle a short while later.

"When siesta begins," said Dom Enrique, no trace of awkwardness or avoidance in his outward conduct. "I know where he goes at siesta."

"Home," said van Zwolle, satisfied now that they would have a chance to plead their case away from the formality of the Residencia.

"In a manner of speaking," said Dom Enrique with a wicked little smile. He bent over his mug, amusement still shaping his features, and said nothing for almost half an hour, until the stall-keepers began to close up their flaps for siesta. Then he rose, stretched and spat, then signaled to van Zwolle. "Are you ready?"

Van Zwolle shrugged as he got to his feet and tapped out the ash in the bowl of his pipe. "Why not?"

Dom Enrique laughed once, and started off down the street, going away from the grander residences toward the warren of streets leading down to the waterfront, passing through a part of the city where the buildings were solid, older, and showed prosperity without grandeur. "Come on, van Zwolle. It would be foolish to be late."

There was a great deal of jostling bustle on the street as the people of Lima hurried for their homes. Once or twice Dom Enrique and van Zwolle had to step out of the way of carriages bound for houses higher up the hill, and once an ox-cart blocked their way while the drayer argued with a barrow-man over right-of-way. But soon these inconveniences were over, and the two found they were almost the only two men remaining on the street that echoed with the sound of closing shutters.

"Where are we going?" asked van Zwolle, beginning to feel anxious. He did not like wandering about on unfamiliar streets.

"Down this way." He pointed negligently. "There is a cul-de-sac toward the end of this block." He indicated the well-kept buildings around them with their impartial, whitewashed walls that revealed nothing of what would be found inside them: with shutters closed for siesta, they were as forbidding as fortresses or prisons. "In it there are three houses, not unlike these. We want the one in the middle, with the rose-trellis gate." Dom Enrique achieved another smile. "No one will mind if we are a bit late. It is more prudent to arrive when not too many are watching. I know Don Vicente would prefer it that way."

"You're certain of that?" challenged van Zwolle, who was beginning to worry that Dom Enrique had been leading him on about the Corregidor of the Audiencia de Lima, Don Vicente. It was all well and good to claim influence, but another thing to demonstrate it, particularly when their petition went directly against the stated policy of the Presidencia de Cuzco. "How can you be so confident. Why should the Corregidor overturn the Presidencia's decision? Don Ezequias may have alerted Don Vicente about this. It has been a long time since you visited him last."

"But I can be sure. Absolutely. I've been here before." He indicated the entrance to the cul-de-sac. "Just there. You see?"

Van Zwolle admitted grudgingly that he did. He stared in admiration at the large, wrought-iron gate that revealed a lovely patio and courtyard where lavish, flowering plants climbed the walls of the courtyard and the house with splendid indifference. He watched as Dom Enrique reached for the bell-rope and pulled.

"Ah, Señor, it is an honor," said the half-native, middle-aged servant who came in answer to the summons, his smile practiced to the point of being meaningless. His hairless face and soft body were as telling as his high voice that he was a eunuch. "Welcome to La Casa della Toda Hermosa." He bowed before he unlocked the gate.

"I said I knew where we would find the Corregidor." Dom Enrique swung around to van Zwolle, showed him a snide curl of his lip, and once again regarded the servant. "Thank you, Matteo. It is good to see you again, after all these months. You look well. I trust Don Vicente is here?"

"That he is, that he is," said Matteo, precariously close to groveling before the young Portuguese nobleman. "He is just sitting down to a repast with Luisa, Serafina and Cirilo. Your interruption would not yet be importune."

"Very good," said Dom Enrique, handing Matteo a silver coin and signaling van Zwolle to follow him.

"My friend and I would like to see him, if you will tell him we are here? Or it might be better if I announce myself." Dom Enrique coughed delicately. "No reason for you to bother him. And when we are finished talking with him, we would like to have the chance to . . . lie down ourselves."

"I will arrange it," said Matteo. "Would you like separate accommodation or to share?"

"Separate, I think, this time," said Dom Enrique, strolling toward the carved-and-strapped doors of the two-story house. "Is Ofelia busy this afternoon?"

"I don't think so. She was not half an hour ago, and there have not been many arrivals since then. I will arrange it, if you wish," said Matteo as another silver coin disappeared into the wide sash around his waist. He turned to van Zwolle, bowing without such courtesy as he showed Dom Enrique. "And what is your pleasure? We have women, young ones, old ones, and girls who have not been touched by a man before, though they are the most expensive and unless your tastes run that way, they can be disappointing. And we have boys so pretty your heart will break." He bowed to the Dutchman, his smile as fixed as if it had been painted in place.

"I . . . " van Zwolle faltered, thinking of the cost of a place like this.

"I will pay for what you want, van Zwolle, as soon as we finish our

business," said Dom Enrique, his voice amused. "When we have con-
cluded arrangements with my cousin's husband, you can tell Matteo
what you want then." He snapped his fingers at the servant. "Where is
Don Vicente?"

"In the Camara Rosa. You know the way? It is his preferred place."
This was more of a statement than a question.

"Third door on the left," said Dom Enrique, lengthening his stride.
He paid no heed to the decoration of the house, or to the few servants,
who were all women, and all dressed in little more than corsets and
petticoats.

Van Zwolle followed after, but had to keep from staring, for the main
entry was a magnificent expanse of Flemish carpets, French paintings,
Spanish furniture, and Roman statues, many of them covered in gilt,
showing naked men and women in a variety of postures that made van
Zwolle's thighs ache to look at even as they stirred his lust. He had
never seen such a casual display of decadent sexuality, or carnal possibilities. Surely living men and women did not tangle themselves into
such positions, he thought. And if they did, to what purpose? The act
was a simple one. Any man could subdue a woman. It rarely took more
than a dozen blows and she would accommodate any demand. The
air was heavy with the scent of flowers and cloves. From some room
on the floor above came the sound of a viol and masculine laughter.

The knock Dom Enrique gave the third door on the left was nothing more than a pro forma tap with his knuckles. "Vicente?" he said,
flinging open the door. "It's Enrique."

The Corregidor, a man tending to portliness and past his youth, was
seated at a low table, his ropilla draped over the back of his chair so
that his arms embroidered on the hanging sleeves could hardly be seen.
His inner casaque, of fine, white Egyptian cotton, was unbuttoned
down to his waist, where the ties at the top of his Venetian pantalones
were visible. Beside him a young woman in a loose garment of gathered saffron-colored cotton all but reclined for the purpose of ex-
posing her breasts to the Corregidor. On Don Vicente's right was a
remarkably beautiful young man with a discontented mouth, dressed
in what appeared to be page's clothes, but looser than the usual cut.
Next to him, a serving girl of hardly more than twelve was standing in
her corset and petticoats, a tray of fruit in her hands. She had been
about to set this down when the door swung open.

"Enrique," said Don Vicente, hardly pleased at such an interruption.
"This is a surprise. I did not know you were in Lima." He was obvi-

ously eager for an explanation so that he could resume his amusements.

"Arrived last evening. It was too late to visit you and my cousin, so I decided to wait until a more auspicious time, when I knew we could have our discussion in a . . . discreet setting. It would be more prudent to discuss matters in private. I went first to your office, more than an hour ago, at the approved time for such petitions as I have. But you were not . . . " He ambled into the room, reaching for one of the low benches as he approached the table. "I'm sorry to disturb you in this way, but that idiot you employ as a secretary made it necessary," he went on, taking a melon slice from the tray the girl carried.

"Padre Bocan? What has he to do with this?" asked Don Vicente sharply.

"He is the cause I have had to seek you out in this . . . inconvenient way," said Dom Enrique as if it were an apology.

From another part of the house came a sudden scream. The two women with Don Vicente exchanged looks, and the young man lost his faintly insolent expression for a moment.

"Oh, my . . . associate and I went to him to purchase an encomienda, and he refused to issue one." He spoke as if this were nothing more than a petty annoyance, too insignificant to discuss. "I decided it was most reasonable to come to you directly than try to persuade that . . . fellow of his misapprehension. He was not willing to honor the request we made, though we made it most reasonably."

"An encomienda?" repeated Don Vicente, doing his best to appear unflustered.

"Yes. We want to—" he began, watching while the girl set down her tray and signaled to the young man to unfasten her corset. "—explore certain areas around Cuzco, areas rumored to have hidden caches of treasure. We believe we may be able to lay our hands on an Incan treasure map. With an encomienda we can act. For the sake of the Crown and the Church, of course," he added without undue concern.

Don Vicente smiled and stretched out a hand to caress his nearest companion. "I begin to understand," he said.

"I am sorry if my request comes at an inconvenient time, but my cousin is undoubtedly laid down upon her bed for the afternoon, I thought we might tend to this without delay." Dom Enrique offered another of his ready smiles.

"You had planned to visit your cousin?" said Don Vicente, doing his inadequate best to maintain his aplomb.

"If I am detained here for any length of time, I fear it would be inexcusably rude of me not to; you know how touchy she can be about the niceties—she is your wife," said Dom Enrique, managing to look chagrined.

"So that is the game, is it?" He shrugged, saying, "And if I agree to your request, and the encomienda is available, signed and sealed, by this evening, what then?" Don Vicente made no effort to hide his cynicism, or his capitulation. "Will you then have to visit my wife?"

Dom Enrique considered his answer. "I don't think so," he said, glancing once at van Zwolle. "We would have to be about the business of Church and Crown, and it would not be respectful to linger here, no matter how the ties of family might—"

But Don Vicente was not enjoying the game, and was not willing to prolong it for Dom Enrique's amusement. "The Crown would also mean the Corregidor, would it not? And surely you are not thinking I will do this for amusement. My position is part of this business you wish to pursue once you obtain the encomienda, that is?"

"Most certainly. I am not about to take ship for España to hand over whatever treasure we find," he went on, pausing to chew on the melon slice. "I leave that to you, since you are Corregidor here."

"Naturally," said Don Vicente. His hand moved over the older woman's breast as impersonally as if he were inspecting a horse. "How diligent you are on behalf of the Spanish Crown, and you Portuguese."

Dom Enrique would not be insulted. "I am, I am," he said with what might have been genuine conviction. "The King of Portugal has done nothing to gain my appreciation, and half my relatives are married to Spanish nobility, which influences me to the favor of España. The King of Portugal cannot help me in the Viceroyalty of Peru, no matter which Audiencia, in any case, can he? The King of España may do so, through you. If you will provide the encomienda."

"And you would assume I would benefit, as well?" said Don Vicente, doing his best to sound surprised at such an offer.

"Naturally, as well you should," said Dom Enrique. "You would be the one making such a venture possible, and it would be suitable for you to claim some part of our discovery as your reward." His smile was predatory.

"I should not listen to you, Dom Enrique, you are proposing something offensive to my honor. Don Ezequias will protest, you may be certain of it," said Don Vicente, trying to muster a sense of outrage at this proposal, but failing to do more than appear irritated. "But if I do not, you will have to stay in Lima, won't you? And if you are in Lima, you will have to attend my wife."

"Yes. Nothing else would be acceptable in the eyes of our family." He did his best to mask the smugness that filled him. "And you would prefer that I show the initiative that was the reason I came here." He had finished his melon, and now licked his fingers, making sure all the juice was gone.

"If it would mean you would return to Cuzco promptly, it would please me," said Don Vicente, sounding tired.

"All that is lacking is the encomienda that would grant us land and laborers. Padre Bocan would not give us one because Don Ezequias would not. We spoke of this to him, and he claimed it was not possible. You know what difficulties these sticklers create for themselves. It is a matter of Don Ezequias' past behavior that bring me to you. I know he is thought to be a sensible man, but that is not the case. He has shown favor to foreigners, but refused to issue one to me." The anger he felt was shown more in the line of his mouth than in the tone of his voice. "There is a foreign alchemist, who claims to be a Conde, who has received two encomiendas from Don Ezequias while I cannot procure one. This is not fitting."

There was another scream, this one longer and more genuinely terrified. Van Zwolle shifted from one foot to the other; he studied the young servant in the petticoat and corsets with growing interest. It pleased him to see her shrink under the power of his eyes on her.

Don Vicente sighed. "Must you have the encomienda today?" he asked after watching his wife's cousin for a short while in measuring silence.

"Not immediately, not today, no," said Dom Enrique, his conduct excessively civil. "But tomorrow I would have to make my bow to my cousin, unless it would be time for us to depart for Cuzco again. Then my license would make it imperative that I not linger here. I would then do little more than have a note carried around to her, explaining that my departure could not be delayed. I would not mention your role in my leaving, so that she could not hold you responsible for my absence."

"Of course," said Don Vicente. "I will have the encomienda prepared for you by nightfall. Just inform me of the terms so that I may be specific; you would not want to be authorized for the wrong task, would you? If you will come to the Residencia, I will order Padre Bocan to have it ready before supper." He indicated the woman in the open, saffron-colored shift; she preened for him with a desperation he sought as much as he desired her flesh. "Lovely, isn't she? Such skin and such eyes! And so willing, as most of these half-breeds are. It is the wildness of their nature that makes them wanton." As he spoke, he resumed his caresses in a lazy, detached way, smiling as the woman squirmed in response.

"Quite tempting," said Dom Enrique in a measured tone.

"And if you didn't pay her, what then? Do you think she'd spread her legs so willingly?" asked van Zwolle, wishing he might take Don Vicente's place, for then the woman would know what a real man could do to her. This effete Spanish hidalgo was as refined as a tapestry, and as exciting, requiring, as it appeared he did, more than one woman to stimulate him.

"Your friend is a boor," said Don Vicente to Dom Enrique, hardly deigning to notice the Dutchman.

"That he is, but he is stout of heart and fixed of purpose, and in Cuzco, his lacks are not as obvious as they are here," said Dom Enrique, and winked over his shoulder at van Zwolle.

Don Vicente made an impatient gesture with his free hand. "What are the terms of this encomienda you seek?" He wanted to resume his pleasures and this interruption was becoming tedious.

"I left them with Padre Bocan. He will have them still, I would wager; he does not throw such things away from what you have told me the last time I was here," said Dom Enrique in a careless way. "If you will tell him of your decision, he will provide you with all you need to know to endorse the encomienda."

"I will inquire when I return there, later this afternoon. When I am finished here," he added pointedly.

This time Dom Enrique was willing to take the hint, satisfied that he would shortly obtain the thing he sought. He prepared to depart, rising and bowing in superior form. "I am most truly grateful to you, Corregidor of the Audiencia de Lima and husband-of-my-cousin, and I would like to assure you that you will have no occasion to regret the assistance you have given me and my associate in our venture. In a year or two, you may well thank me for what you have gained."

Don Vicente motioned the intruders to the door. "If I do not have such reason, I will not endure it alone. I am not doing this solely to gain your silence, Dom Enrique, but because I will not tolerate your profiting without due acknowledgment to the Crown," he warned them as they stepped into the hall and closed the door.

Dom Enrique chuckled. "What do you think will happen now? With those?" He nodded to the door.

Van Zwolle shrugged, feeling awkward. He was a simple man, and liked his dealings with women direct and uncomplicated.

Dom Enrique had no such constraints. "He will have the women excite him, and then, while they use each other, he will take the young man." He grinned at van Zwolle's expression, showing equal cupidity and disgust. "I've watched him. There are peepholes in all the rooms, and everyone is observed, or so Matteo tells me. I paid to see how my cousin's husband amuses himself. Unless his tastes have changed in the last eight months, I know how he is gratified. Sometimes he has the women take the young man while he uses the boy's mouth. The Church would not approve and my cousin would demand a separation if she knew any of this. I have not spoken, of course, because Don Vicente would be no use to me if I did." He turned away from the door. "Who can condemn him, taking what amusement he can in this boring place? And married to Alma as well! If this is what makes his position tolerable, then why should the Church—" He stopped as another scream went through the house.

"That is allowed?" asked van Zwolle, not entirely sure what he meant.

"This house provides many things," said Dom Enrique as he moved away from the Camara Rosa. "And not all tastes are as . . . delicate as Don Vicente's." He saw that Matteo was approaching them. He drew out two golden coins. "My friend and I are at your disposal now."

Matteo made the coins disappear with his usual finesse. "Ofelia is waiting for you, in the room above with the yellow door. For the rest of the afternoon she is yours. She has brought the things you liked the last time you were here." He held up an admonitory hand. "And do not give her money if she pleases you. It is her work to do that, and this house pays for her living."

"Of course. But perhaps you will let me send her a gift, later?" It was a standard courtesy for men of his rank.

"So long as it is not jewels or money, you may. A bottle of scent is always welcome," said Matteo, then looked to van Zwolle. "What can this house provide for you?"

Van Zwolle recalled the screams and answered slowly, "I like women who resist me. There is no sport if they do not fight."

"Certainly not," Matteo agreed, though it was evident that he had no personal experience of this. "Do you wish to conquer or to confine as well? We can provide a bed with strong fittings so that you may secure your woman there."

"I—" Van Zwolle had been about to say no, but the thought of tying a woman down and then doing all his imagination could conjure up filled him with need of an intensity he had not often known. "That would be . . . interesting," he made himself say, hoping that Matteo would not realize how excited he had become.

"The woman—a beginner or experienced?" asked Matteo as if enquiring about sauce for a main dish.

"I . . . I don't know," said van Zwolle, afraid of what he sought.

"Then let me suggest that you let me choose for you?" said Matteo pleasantly. "I think there is a woman you would find suitable. I think I know what you are looking for, and which of our women will best please you." He paused while another scream clawed the air. "It is the Prior," he said by way of excuse. "He despises women for compromising his chastity, and when his blood rises, he makes the women pay for turning him from his vows." He shook his head. "He whips himself as well as the women."

"Um," said van Zwolle, nodding several times. He was finding it difficult to converse, and Matteo took mercy on him.

"Go up the stairs and take the blue door. Chavella will be with you shortly." He patted van Zwolle on the arm. "Be patient a little longer."

Van Zwolle did as he was told, feeling all his flesh pull into his groin so that moving was an effort. By the time he reached the room with the blue door his temples were pounding and his skin was feverish. As he stripped off his clothes, he heard another scream and at the sound, he felt himself at one with the Prior. It would be a good thing to feel a woman under him again. It might be better if he tied her, made her his captive, but that would take time. His need was too immediate for that. Later, when he had spent, he would make her feel her perfidy for his lust. He relished the vengeance he would wreak on the woman who dared to rouse him, to fill his thoughts with visions of breasts and thighs, distracting him from his purpose, while he had dedicated himself to the acquisition of treasure.

"Señor?" The woman was still young—not more than sixteen or

seventeen at most—and she was in the kind of shift the woman with Don Vicente had been wearing.

With a snarl of rage he was on her.

Text of a letter from Padre Molino y Gallegos, written by Frey Jeromo.

To the hidalgo, Gregorio Simeon Calderon y Mazez living in Cuzco, respectful greetings on behalf of the Most Holy Roman Catholic Church, from Padre Molino y Gallegos, by the hand of his scribe, Frey Jeromo.

This is to make inquiry into the affairs of your neighbor, the foreigner, Francisco Ragoczy, el Conde de San Germanno, for it has come to the attention of the Preachers of San Domingo that this foreigner may be involved in many unholy things, and for the protection of your souls, you would do well to tell what you know of the man and his household, including his manservant, who has been reported as being as much a danger to the community as his master is thought to be.

It is altogether fitting that you should report all you have observed this man doing, for only then can you be assured of your own salvation. If the man has done all that we suppose he has, it is essential that he be questioned and detained for the judgment of the Church. In the New World, surely we must be diligent in stamping out all forms of heresy wherever the vile plant takes hold. It would not redound to our credit if the false religions of the pagans should flourish now that we have brought them the truth of God. We are told that light has shown upon those who have walked in darkness. How terrible it would be if that darkness should come again.

That is why we must ask you to do this thing that you may find distasteful. But such scruples will not serve you well in his case. You have been seduced by the seeming quality of this foreigner. For through your innocence, and courteous intentions, a fiend may be allowed to ravage abroad. It is said that San Germanno has been a good neighbor to many, but in whose name has he done the deeds that have earned him your praise and good opinion? To what end has he given you salves for your injuries, or tinctures for your sick? It is known that the Devil may assume the appearance of virtue, the better to lure Christians to Hell.

We urge you to keep watch on this man, make note of those who visit him, and those he visits. If anything appears to be inappropriate, make note of that as well, and do not excuse his actions because he is from Hungary. As you know, the demons who follow the ways of Islam rule in his mountains, and his claims to have fought them may be nothing

*more than a clever ruse. None of us are in a position to verify his as-
sertions, beyond the patent of arms that may or may not be his. In fact,
it is thought that it may be that he is not Hungarian at all, but of some
blood not Christian of any sort, Catholic or Orthodox, by which presence we are all contaminated and our souls at peril, and from whom
we must diligently guard ourselves or endanger the Grace conferred
upon us by God Himself. All that you learn of this supposed Conde, you
are to report to the Church, with any corroboration you may have to
hand, or the accounts of other witnesses to his action. You must also
watch his manservant, for though the fellow says he is a native of Cadiz,
I have rarely seen a man with light hair and blue eyes from that city,
and we cannot be any more sure of him than we are of his master. Say
nothing to the Presidencia, Don Ezequias, for it is probable that San
Germanno has already persuaded him that Cuzco has nothing to fear,
and Don Ezequias is lax enough in his practices to believe this.*

*Know that your diligence will be remembered in our prayers, and that
all intelligence you provide will bring you the favorable attention of
Obispo Hernan Guarda, and the thanks of the Pope himself. With our
gratitude for your devotion to Holy Church, and in the Name of Our
Lord, on this seventh day of November, 1643, with my hope for the salvation of all sinners and the triumph of Our Lord.*

Frey Jeromo
The Order of the Preachers of San Domingo
For Padre Molino y Gallegos
At Cuzco

8

In the wavering torchlight the procession looked too insubstantial to
be made up of ordinary men; rather they were the spirits their garments
and masks indicated they were. The leaders of the two ranks of Incan
men wore face-covering headdresses and cloaks that made them
appear to be fantastic visions paying homage to the dead, the em-
bodiment of all the ancient gods of the Incas. Those who reached the
opening to the tomb lowered their staves and groveled in respect to

the man being laid to rest in the flank of this towering mountain, their movements slow and dignified. The procession parted to receive the company of priests bearing the body of their leader to his grave. All those watching averted their eyes as the platform carrying the dead High Priest passed by them. The distance between the Women's Watch, where Acanna Tupac stood with San Germanno, and the procession was not great, but the steepness of the valley walls made it seem greater than it was.

"No one who is not Incan has seen this before, and only women should stand here," said Acanna Tupac, her voice soft with emotion and concern. She was dressed in ceremonial finery for the occasion, though her face had no trace of paint upon it under her mask, as the priests had. She turned to San Germanno, distress making her voice sharp. "You are the first who is not one of us to see a High Priest buried. If the people here knew of it, they would think the ceremony defiled. Had his wife been alive, you would not be permitted to stand with me, but our laws say no noblewoman may be left alone here, so . . . In other times, there would have been gongs and chants, but we cannot risk those now."

He answered her quietly, beginning with a respectful bow. "You have brought me to this place before, Acanna Tupac. I respected your secrecy then, and I will do so now. When you wanted to speak to the High Priest, we came here. You permitted me to escort you; I hoped it was because you trusted me, as I hope you trust me now." He realized she needed more from him than the reminder of this time together. "And a ceremony need not be noisy to be sincere. Often there is more respect in silence." The High Priest had not been so old a man that his death was regarded as completely natural, and his death was seen as an omen of terrible things to come. These obsequies were a hard reminder to the Incan people that their world was uncertain, and their place in it no longer defined as it had once been. The loss of their High Priest was one more terrible blow to them, another sign of coming ruin. San Germanno knew their devastation of old: he remembered another High Priest on another night, more than thirty-seven hundred years ago, when he had been made into what he was. The grove had been very dark and when he cut his hands in offering, his blood was steaming. That night still lived in his memory, and would until the true death claimed him. The isolation she felt bore in upon him, fueled by his own loneliness, and his knowledge of the brevity of life. He laid his hand on his companion's shoulder once again, and spoke very softly.

"Perhaps the Chinese are right: dying is in bad taste."

Acanna Tupac pointed to the end of the procession as if she had not been listening. "There. Between the trees. They are coming. You can see the offerings now." It was still some distance away as it wound along the line of the ridge into the saddle near the crest of the mountain where Choqquerquirau lay, hidden from any but those above it. "I may not come any nearer than this. The laws were very strict at one time, but we cannot be so careful now. I may observe this with a single escort. And you should not be here at all, Ragoczy. This is not for strangers."

"How does it happen that you are willing to have me with you, then?" There was no challenge in his tone; he had wanted an answer to this question since she had asked for his company.

"I am not supposed to be alone here, and I would be alone, but for you. All the women who might attend me are the wives of Spaniards and cannot . . . " She looked away into the distance, then spoke directly to him. "You, too, are alone. And since you are not like the priests of the Spanish, who want to destroy all of this, you are helpful to me, and I am glad of your presence. The High Priest would not like it, but that no longer matters. You will not take our gold and silver, you will not desecrate our graves and our altars, and you will not reveal this location." She spoke with great weariness.

"Ah, but the Spanish will, you fear, because theirs is a holy cause," was San Germanno's ironic rejoinder.

"So they continue to tell me as they try to wrest information from me, for the good of my soul," she said, making a gesture of condemnation which only he could see. "But you are as much a stranger to them as you are to me, which gives me reason to hope that I might not lose all, or not while I live." Her attention went back to the procession and the soft, rhythmic march of the mourners.

"Acanna Tupac, I grieve with you." As San Germanno watched, he saw distress in many of those who lined the way of the cortège; their grief and dread were not the display of ritual, but deeply felt emotions that found expression in these ancient, fading ways. He had seen that look many times before, in many places. These people were bereft of more than an important man, they had lost the last direct link with the old priesthood and all it represented. The few remaining men with a claim to the position of High Priest were not of pure blood and many had been instructed in the ways of the Church as well as the religion of their ancestors. Not one of them would be acceptable to the Incan people to take the High Priest's place, for none were thought to be without Spanish taint, and therefore unable to speak with the gods.

Once the body was placed within the tomb, the four sacrifices that would guard the High Priest's rest were brought forward; San Germanno had to steel himself against the killings—three animals and a wide-eyed young man in full ceremonial armor of hammered gold. How could their slaughter honor the dead man? he wondered, appalled at what he knew would be done. Over many centuries, San Germanno had come to regard such wanton offerings as a profligacy that bordered on obscenity; it was painful for him to watch.

A jaguar, carried from far down in the eastern jungles was the first animal to die, and then a white llama, followed by a huge Andean condor. Last was the young man, who fell without a sound; it was a good omen, indicating that the tomb would remain hidden and unprofaned. Unbidden, San Germanno found the symbols of the four evangelists coming to mind: a winged lion for Marco, a winged ox for Lucas, an eagle for Juan, and a winged man for Matteo. The sacrifices seemed eerily familiar.

"Why do you watch from here? There is another platform just at the entrance to the tomb. I would have thought you would stand there. Is there a reason you do not?" San Germanno asked when the sacrifices had been taken into the tomb. He found her separation from the rest of the ceremony troubling. "You are the legitimate descendant of Atahualpa Inca and his son Quispe Titu. It is your blood and traditions that are honored. Must you remain so much apart from—"

"I am a woman, and this is the Women's Watch," she said with a sigh, moving away from him on the platform, her eyes serious beneath the elaborate mask-and-head-dress the occasion demanded. "And we do not change our old ways—especially now—to permit me or any woman nearer to the grave of the High Priest than you and I now stand. If I were to go down even one stair, I would meet the same fate you would, should you try to go nearer. Coyao Paucar would have another sacrifice to protect him." She regarded him thoughtfully once more. "This troubles you. Why?"

He framed his answer carefully, matching her tone. "It is so . . . short-sighted to keep away women for no reason other than their female-ness—especially now—when there are so few of the true line left. Your blood is more truly you than your body, which constantly changes while your blood does not."

"But the ancestors have said—" she began, shocked at his remark.

"Half of those ancestors were female or there would be no Incan line." He waited to hear her protest and was relieved when she did not.

After a considerable silence, she came to stand next to him again, her large eyes somber and wide behind her mask; he felt her shiver as she touched him, and he wished he could be allowed to embrace her. "Surely you understand why I mourn, and why I want to honor our ways. It will be gone so soon, all this. You say you, too, come from mountains where your foes now rule. None of this is strange to you."

"No, it isn't." He cast his mind back to the haven in the bow of the Carpathians where he had been born so long ago. How many times he had returned there, each time more a stranger than the most recent conquerors; he feared the same would be true of this place in a century or two, when the Spanish had taken hold. He covered his thoughtful silence saying, "But the mountains of my homeland are nothing compared to these mountains."

She smiled at him with naïve pride. "We have heard this before, that these mountains around us are unlike any other mountains in the world."

"True enough," said San Germanno, and added, "though there are mountains as high, they are not so endlessly green or—"

"As high?" she scoffed, though there was a glint of curiosity in her eyes. "Where are there any mountains so high as these?"

"In Asia, almost halfway around the world from here." He did his best to offer her no insult. "I crossed them once, and was stranded in Tu-Bo-Te, the Land of Snows, for all of winter. Your mountains are not so forbidding as those of Asia, but I believe they hold more secrets."

"The Land of Snows," Acanna Tupac repeated distantly. "In Asia. It sounds like a place in a fable."

"There is truth in that, yes. For many it is a fable: distant, remote, its people rarely seen beyond its borders. The people to the north and south of them regard them with awe and puzzlement. Their customs are unlike the customs of their neighbors and their religion, while similar to those of China and India, is filled with their own rites as well. Most of the world does not know of the Land of Snows and would not believe any reports of it. The mountains are high, and many think they cannot be crossed, and that no one can live in their snows." He knew this from his own travels through Tu-Bo-Te, more than four hundred years ago, when he had fled the advancing might of Jenghiz Khan. San Germanno gave her time to think about this. "Your home, this place, is becoming the stuff of fable, now that the Europeans have been here. All manner of things will be told of these mountains and your people."

"Do the Black Robe priests think that?" she asked sharply. "They have decided so much for us in the last years, it would seem they seek the same thing you mention—to turn us into legends."

San Germanno shook his head. "Alas, I fear you are right. They are not willing to permit you to be as you are. They are certain they can improve your welfare by compelling you to share their faith."

Acanna Tupac spat. "Then they should be content to have us as legends, then, and make their fables from our dreams." The torchlight etched the lines of her face in deep relief. "We must be silent now."

"Because of the Spanish?" he asked, glancing in the direction of the road.

"Because of the dead," she told him.

He accepted her instruction, and watched while the younger acolytes sang the praises of their departed master; it was a weird, ululating cry that carried to the high peaks around them. When they had completed this disquieting salute, the mourners set up a great, wailing shout, the two combining in echoes so that the mountains themselves seemed to weep. Then the torches were extinguished all at the same instant, and the blackness of the ancient, deserted city of Choqquerquirau was all around them, engulfing them in its darkness.

"The mourners will keep watch here all night," said Acanna Tupac in a whisper. "I cannot remain with them."

"Why not?" asked San Germanno, his voice as low as hers. "You are of the true blood. I should think they would want you here."

"It would be seen as an indication that the true royal line was ended," she answered, with hardness in her words. "Though that is already certain. They want to believe that it will not end with me."

He could say nothing to deny this. He laid his hand on her shoulder and looked down into her eyes. "Then say what we must do."

She covered his hand with her own. "I should leave now."

"All right, as you—" He broke off. "If I may come with you."

"Oh, yes, San Germanno," she exclaimed softly, and held his hand tightly. "I do not want to be alone tonight, not after this." She glanced in the direction of the tomb.

He followed her gaze with his own. "I did not know so many would come." He had feared she would be more alone for this occasion than she was, not only because it was dangerous, but because the dead man was the last High Priest. "This is a sign of courage as much as faith.

With the Spanish everywhere, and the Church, I thought most would stay away. The Black Robes would not approve of what is happening here."

"It was important to all of them that they come, as a final gesture," said Acanna Tupac. "Our land is changing, turning from the old ways, and without the High Priest to guide them, they will forget all— Before the Spanish came, the High Priest's mummy would have been given a place of honor, remaining among his people with all those who came before him; with the Black Robes here, we have had to bury our great ones as the Nazca did. For many of these faithful people, this will be the last time they witness such a burial." She looked at him. "Will it not?"

"Very likely," he said, not wanting to speak the words aloud, and knowing that for her sake, he must. "In ten years, many of your people will not want to take the chance of earning the disapproval of the Spanish by defying their ways. In twenty, some will forget the importance of the ceremonies. After that, only a few will keep the old ways alive, and they will be hounded by their own people as well as the Spanish." He saw the sorrow in her eyes. "Would you prefer I lie to you, Acanna Tupac? Tell you tales that would not convince a child? If you want that of me, tell—"

She stood very straight. "No."

"Then pardon my answer." He reached for her other hand and discovered it was cold. "How much longer must you stay here? You're freezing."

"As I have told you, it is time I was gone, but no one has yet decided . . . what is next to be done," she said, sounding very tired. "Perhaps the omen is fixed already, and nothing we do will change it. There is no tradition in this, in what we have done tonight. Those ways are . . . gone." She seemed to call herself to order. "The men are supposed to carry me, as they have carried all the descendants of the True Inca, but . . . "

"But the Spanish might notice, and that would not benefit any of you, given the price they could exact for what you have done here," San Germanno finished for her. "Well, you may ride pillion behind me, if that is not too shocking an offer. My horse can carry us both." He was able to sound slightly amused, though the importance of his invitation was not lost to either of them.

"The High Priest would not have allowed it," said Acanna Tupac in a measured way, her eyes shining in the frame of the mask.

"If the High Priest were here to decide, there would be no reason for you to ask," San Germanno reminded her, his calm returning. "Let me do this for you."

"And you can protect me, if it comes to a fight; that is your meaning, isn't it? You can make it possible for me to return to Cuzco without any more danger than an ordinary traveler encounters on the road. You are afraid that I might be set upon if I go, borne as I am entitled to be borne, on the shoulders of my people." There was a touch of anger in her tone, and her shivering was more marked now.

"It is a factor, yes," he said, unwilling to be drawn into a dispute to keep her from feeling too much in his debt. "Most Spaniards believe all Incas, even those who live in hovels and have only two chickens to their names, have caches of gold here in these peaks, and they are not above waylaying you to claim what they think you have."

She broke away from him, her face averted in shame. "Not only Spaniards."

"No. Not only Spaniards," he said as gently as he could.

Her eyes glazed with tears, making the mask she wore look jeweled. She swung away from him, her long cloak whispering. She could say nothing while she concentrated on regaining her composure; she refused to disgrace herself by crying. When she was certain she had stopped all temptation to weep, she turned back to San Germanno. "All right. I will ride with you."

He smiled at her, wanting to end the pain he knew had fixed itself in her vitals. "Good." With a gesture to their surroundings, he went on, "Who will take your ceremonial dress? Or do you keep it with you?"

She lifted the mask from her head. "In old days, this would be burned in tribute to the High Priest, along with the staves the rest of the priests carry. But we cannot risk a fire here now, for it might bring the Spanish." She held the mask against her, giving herself an enormous second face beneath her own. "I will take it with me, in case it is needed again." What that need would be she could not imagine, but she took comfort in holding the mask, as if it contained her memories as well as her faith. "Eventually I will decide what to do with it." Her sorrow made her words blur.

"As you wish," he said, holding his hand out to her again, and doing his best to conceal his concern as he felt her gelid fingers in his. He had left the grey gelding some little distance from their vantage point, in the shelter of a brushy copse; he hoped that no one had stolen the animal while the burial ceremony was in progress, for the long walk back to Cuzco did not appeal to him on this night.

"Why do you do this for me, San Germanno? You have done more than any foreigner and have asked less. Why? What do you seek?" Acanna Tupac asked once they were off the Women's Watch and had passed the first group of guards at the foot of the platform.

"You cannot do it for yourself, not without risk." He said it directly enough, with no sign of the apprehension he felt for her, and all the rest attending the burial of the High Priest. He wondered if any of the mourners gathered near the Women's Watch were listening to them. "And I dislike having to worry about you when I can do something to help." It was a portion of the truth, enough that he knew she would believe him.

She tightened her grip on his hand. "I am more grateful than you can know."

He stopped then, and faced her. "I am not interested in your gratitude. That is something you may be certain I do not seek." It came out more harshly than he had intended, and he saw shock in her countenance; he modified his manner at once, hoping to recapture the comfort they shared. His voice deepened, and his expression changed, his dark eyes holding hers compellingly. "I ask nothing of you, Acanna Tupac. I have not come with you to earn anything."

Her demeanor changed as she listened to him; she drew in on herself. "That is not easy to believe, foreigner."

"Nonetheless it is true," he promised her.

"How can I be certain?" she asked, and sensed his despair at her question. Although it was incorrect, she leaned against him, her face turned into his shoulder, the mask pressing against his body. "I am not worthy of your devotion," she whispered.

"What has that to do with anything?" he asked, deliberately lightening his voice. "I do not love you as the result of a contest, or to claim you as a prize: I love you because you are who you are. There is no other reason, and there can be none. What I do for you is how my love manifests itself, I swear by all the forgotten gods." He touched her hair, wanting to offer her solace, and to assuage his own sense of helplessness.

"How can you say this to me?" she asked, her trembling now having little to do with the cold.

"I say it because it is true, as true as blood may be." There was power in his whisper, and a deep note that filled her with passion.

"May the gods protect me," she said, but did not tell him from what.

"If you need their protection, I hope they will," said San Germanno with strong emotion. He would have drawn her more closely into his arms, but hesitated, caution holding him back as he remembered where they were.

A cough sounded not far from them, and one of the guards watching the approach to the road stepped out of the shadows. "Gracious lady," he said to Acanna Tupac, doing his best to ignore San Germanno.

"I am well. You need not fear for me," she said, showing a hauteur worthy of the most noble Spanish woman.

The man made a show of respect and stood aside to permit Acanna Tupac and her foreigner to pass. He knew better than to show curiosity about San Germanno, for that could bring questions none of them wanted to answer.

By the time they reached his horse, there were a number of people climbing the slopes behind them, most preparing to return to villages in the mountains, a few of them going toward the same road San Germanno would take, toward the high, swinging bridge over the chasm carved by a river roaring far below.

The grey accepted the second rider, and made his steps with extra care to compensate for the weight, as if he knew that a slip or a stumble with two riding would be far more hazardous for himself as well as the two on him. His hooves made firm reports on the road.

"He is a good horse, from a good line, with a sensible disposition. You need that in these mountains, on these roads," San Germanno said to Acanna Tupac as they made their way down the narrow road toward the bridge. "If you don't shift, or kick him, he will carry us safely."

Acanna Tupac had never ridden a horse—she had only twice been on a burro, and for the most part avoided riding in carriages when she could, so she was not able to repose the same confidence in the grey gelding San Germanno did. "We are so high off the ground," she said, to account for her stiffness as she sat behind him, arms around his waist in rigid grip.

"Andalusian horses are sure-footed," he said to her, in the hope of lessening her fright. "His breed is an old one, and he comes from superior stock, and from a stud farm of fine reputation." The gelding had been one of a dozen horses he had purchased from his oldest and most treasured friend, Atta Olivia Clemens at her stud farm near Rome before going to Spain, and taking ship to the New World. "If you are afraid, he will sense it, and grow frightened himself."

"As you say," she murmured, to inform him she heard him.

They went a fair distance—perhaps a league or more—in silence.

The night enveloped the mountains in darkness, and that leant a majesty to the hour and the isolation. When they reached the swinging bridge, San Germanno dismounted and led his nervous horse across, fighting his own rising sense of vertigo from being suspended so far above swift-running water. Although the gap the bridge crossed was narrow, the distance from one end to the other seemed to be endless. The massive cables creaked and sighed like a ship sailing in a storm as they crossed, the sounds swallowed up in the vastness of the place. Only when they had reached the far side of the gorge did Acanna Tupac speak. "It is sacred, this bridge."

"It is an accomplishment, surely," said San Germanno with sincerity as he got back into the saddle and patted the gelding's neck to calm him. He recalled the bridges of Rome, and the low Russian river crossings, under water or snow in the long winter, but still in place for spring and summer, the thaw flood running above the bridges without washing them away. Nothing he had seen in all his wandering was like the high, suspended bridges he found here in Peru: even those in far-off China and Tibet, while astonishing, were less impressive.

"It is sacred," she repeated. "It is given to the gods, to thank them for their mountains."

He offered no observations on this information as he kept his eyes on the narrow track ahead, listening as intently as he watched, for he had the uneasy feeling that they were being observed, although by whom or for what purpose, he did not know; it was folly to speculate on the person or motive, for he could not be sure it was Acanna Tupac or himself who was the target of this scrutiny. The prickly sensation remained with him for more than four leagues.

When at last they reached the road leading back to Cuzco, more than two hours later, he turned as much as the saddle would permit. "Have courage. It is less than an hour now."

"Good," she murmured.

"You will need sleep," he said; for the last hour he had felt her slump against his back as fatigue took hold of her.

"And you, as well," she replied, making an effort to be more alert.

"Perhaps," he allowed, not wanting to tell her how little sleep those of his blood required.

She made an effort to talk with him in order to keep herself awake. "You have never said much about your family, though you inquire much about mine. Why is that?"

He gave her what he had come to regard as his usual response.

"Those of my blood are scattered over the earth, and our numbers are few," he answered, and after a brief hesitation, went on, "My . . . wife died many years ago, far away." Though it had been more than half a century since Xenya Yvgeneivna had been buried in that little church-yard seven or eight leagues beyond Nizhkovo on the road between Moscovy and Novo-Kholmogory, the memory of it was as painful and persistent as a half-healed wound. "I wanted to save her, and could not." He had been able to kill the man who had murdered her, but there was little consolation in that thought.

"You have a wife?" Acanna Tupac said with shock: of the many se-crets she knew San Germanno had locked in his soul, this was not one she had anticipated, for he had always been forthcoming with her.

"I *had* a wife." A long distance ahead of them he could see the bulk of Sacsahuaman fortress at the side of Cuzco; it pleased him to know this journey would be over shortly. "She died . . . was killed . . . dur-ing a . . . raid by . . . armed men." Though these were soldiers, Guards from Spaso-Kamenny, they had been acting on false authority and San Germanno did not want to dignify their actions in any way. "One of the men was trying to kill me. She stopped him. He killed her for it." He felt Acanna Tupac's arm tighten around him. "I did not want her to die."

"Were these armed men Spanish?" Acanna Tupac asked through set teeth.

"No, gracious lady, they were not." He tried to picture those wild lancer Guards as they came into the merchants' camp, demanding his arrest. Only the face of the man who had cut Xenya down with a shashka remained etched in his thoughts. "They were Rus."

"Rus? I do not know these men," she said slowly.

"From Russia. It is a vast, cold land, lying far to the east and north of España." He found he was caught up in his memories. "Our mar-riage was arranged, commanded, in fact, by the ruler of the country."

"He was not your ruler," Acanna Tupac said cannily, curious in spite of the sudden stab of jealousy that went through her.

"No, he was not." He felt her consternation and explained. "I was there representing another ruler and it was the desire of Ivan, the Rus-sian ruler, to . . . to bind me to his country. He did it by marrying me to one of the women of his court."

"As the Spanish have married Incas," said Acanna Tupac with a trace of her bitterness sharpening her words.

"Something like it, yes." It was a vast simplification, he knew. "It was a matter of policy, and loyalties. The ruler I was representing had been my countryman." Istvan Bathory had left Transylvania to assume the Polish throne, and it was as King of Poland he had ordered San Germanno to Moscovy.

"Before your people fell?" asked Acanna Tupac, fully wakened now.

It took all of his skill to give her an answer that was true without revealing too much. "We fought the same enemies."

"Was this before or after you sold spices? In Venice?" She was gratified to recall the name of the city, though what she had been told of it seemed far more the stuff of legends than anything she knew about Peru; tales of the distant past were nothing compared to the accounts she had heard of places in Europe.

He answered her with genuine relief. "After."

"Venice is the city in the sea, isn't it?" she pursued. "I have heard tales about it. They say it is wealthy and beautiful, floating there in the waves."

He accepted the digression as a welcome mitigation of her growing misery. "Actually, it is built on a group of islands. Originally her people settled there for the same reason many of your people have left the coast and taken refuge in the mountains—to escape a better-armed foe," he said, and for the rest of the ride back into Cuzco, regaled her with accounts of the legendary Adriatic city and its glorious, scandalous history. By the time he had recounted the life of the fabulously old Doge Enrico Dandolo—"He commanded the Venetians in battle when he was over eighty and blind; he led the advance himself. All his children were dead by then, and most of his grandchildren, but he was vigorous and as hale as many a man of fifty would like to be"—they passed through the ruined gates of the Sacsahuaman fortress and made their way into the dark streets of Cuzco.

When they arrived at her house at last, she had reached that state of fatigue where sleep is difficult to achieve, when the body has tuned itself to resolute wakefulness and will not easily succumb to rest. She ordered her servants to see to San Germanno's horse, and for once made no effort to conceal their attachment. As she climbed the stairs to the second floor, she regarded him over her shoulder. "The household knows everything anyway. What is the point in deceiving them?"

"They are your servants. How you deal with them is your decision, Acanna Tupac." He saw that she was not satisfied with his comment, and added as he climbed the last few steps to stand beside her, "I do not presume to know how you expect your servants to conduct themselves in regard to you. Being a foreigner, I cannot anticipate the things you would take as given, nor would I try to do so. That is why I will say nothing about what you decide."

"You think they might betray me?" she demanded, a little more loudly than was prudent.

"I think you are a woman alone in a city where you are not among allies," he answered very softly, and reached for her hand. He touched the ceremonial mask she carried instead, and for a disconcerting moment he felt the wood as if it were skin. Then he found her fingers. The relief he experienced from her living flesh disquieted him, reminding him of the brevity of all life. "And I think you want more from your life than an end to loneliness."

She looked down at him, something of his emotions having communicated itself to her. "What is it? San Germanno?"

"Nothing," he said with a quick shake of his head. "Nothing that has any bearing on either of us." He came up beside her and wrapped his arms about her. "There is not much left of the night."

"Probably not," she agreed, her pulse starting to race in spite of her desire to be calm in his presence.

"And you are tired." His lips brushed her brow, hardly a kiss at all.

"So must you be," she said, willing to lean against him.

For an answer he covered her mouth with his own, wishing he could imbue her with a portion of his strength and stamina. He could feel her exhaustion in every fiber of her body, and much as he longed to know her passion again, he realized what she needed most from him was sleep. After a moment he moved back and smoothed her hair away from her brow. "This evening, gracious lady," he promised her, his voice low and gentle. "This evening when both of us are eager, we will take pleasure together. Then there will be time for us to enjoy all we do, to savor what we can give to one another. For now, it is better that you rest."

"And you?" She was astonished to hear how forlorn she sounded. "What will you do?"

He knew what she sought better than she did; he took her face in his hands. "I will lie beside you, if you like."

"To guard me?" she demanded.

"To be with you," he amended softly, his enigmatic gaze as steady as his touch. "If you need guarding, then I will do it."

"Is that all?" Her attempt to provoke him did not succeed.

"For now. Later, when it is what you want, we will do other things."

The promise in his voice was unmistakable, and his desire stirred in answer to hers.

"Will you want . . . what you have not yet sought? Are you waiting until I demand what I said I would not?" she asked, her apprehension mixed with surprise at his continuing deference. All she had been told of men said that eventually they would claim possession of women's bodies, fixing them with male flesh, claiming them by right of conquest. In spite of her longing for him, she drew back from the haven of his embrace. "This can never happen. You will not master me. I will not permit you to compromise me, San Germanno."

"No. I said I would not, that I cannot." His compelling eyes met hers. "I am no conqueror, Acanna Tupac: believe this."

She considered him, his respect for her, his passion, and his honor, and finally gave a single decisive nod, aware at last that her desire for him was as real as his for her. "Then come with me, San Germanno," she said, taking his hand and leading him to her bedchamber. As they walked together, her gratitude began to change to trust at last, and though neither of them knew it then, her lingering doubts fell away and her infatuation deepened into something far more complex.

Text of letter from Ragoczy Sanct' Germain Franciscus to Atta Olivia Clemens. Written in the Latin of Imperial Rome.

To my dearest, most treasured Olivia, my greetings from this strange and distant place.

Only recently have we been told that the French King is dead and that his heir is nothing more than a child. The news was a long time in coming, or you would have heard from me sooner, so close as you are to Paris and that Italian Cardinal.

You said in the last letter I had from you that you were being pursued by a dashing young man and that you were in doubt as to what to do. You, of all people, to doubt. I hope with all my heart that he is capable of knowing you and loving you, and that you have that joy and consolation to aid you through the danger of court life. I do not doubt your skills, your good sense, or your intelligence; I am worried about the intrigues that must surround the court with Louis dead. Have a care, Olivia, for my sake if not your own.

You inquired about this place: I wish I could tell you of the things I have seen here, but there are so few words to describe the way in which these people live, or the ferocity the Spaniards have in their determina-

tion to extinguish that way of life, for sadly, these people are rich in gold, and the Crown and the Church covet it.

Not since Egypt, long before I knew you, have I seen so much gold, and so much of it squandered on burial tokens. They struggle to bring the gold from the earth so they can return it to the ground along with a corpse. The richness of the tombs in these mountains beggars the imagination. I have been told that there are priests and monarchs buried encased in gold, on catafalques of gold, with golden attendants to watch them through eternity. That does not mean the people are rich: they are much the same as the rest of the world, most of the people are peasants and farmers and artisans, ordinary humanity, in fact. But their dead are glorious.

Not since I crossed from China to India through the Land of Snows have I encountered mountains like these. They are more enormous than anything Europe can boast: only in Asia have they any rivals. To stand so high, on ancient roads, which until the Spaniards came never knew the wheel, and see the peaks rising high above is an experience few have been fortunate enough to have. Were it not for the ongoing war between the people here and the Spanish, I would recommend you come to see this for yourself, but not if you have to join the massacre, as I fear it is fast becoming.

I write this to Paris, certain that Mazarini has not yet released you. With all that has happened, he must have more need of you now than before, when he was detained in Roma. I have yet to meet this second cousin of his, though I have been told he is in the New World. But the New World is a vast place, Olivia, and who can tell if his path will ever cross mine?

It is late and the courier leaves at dawn. I will hand this to him before he retires so that it will come to you now; the next courier will not arrive for more than a month, and by the time the journey is made over land and across the sea, whatever news I can send to you will be musty.

Perhaps that is why I have gone on so long; I wish there to be something of merit in this letter beyond my concern and my love for you. If there is not, then the concern and the love must suffice.

Sanct' Germain
(his seal, the eclipse)
By my own hand, on the 11th day of March, 1644

9

At thirty-eight, Obispo Hernan Sigismundo Bernal Guarda was becoming an old man; his hair had turned silver before he was thirty, there were deep lines cut into his lean, aristocratic features, and his vision blurred when he held a page at less than arm's length. His constant resentment at his lack of promotion because of his illegitimacy rankled within him, crabbing his back and his nature at the same time, making him suspicious of his assistants, haughty with strangers, and imperious with his congregation. He spent many long hours wishing—for he dared not pray for what he should already possess—God would provide him with humility, but it had not happened yet, and he still had regularly to confess the sins of envy and pride. Today his head was pounding in rhythm with the mallets and hammers of the monks working on Los Sacramentos where he was spending his afternoon reviewing the records of the newly arrived men from España.

"Frey Rafael!" he shouted as he reached the limits of his tolerance. "Come here at once! And order that pounding stopped! It is unendurable." He knew all the monks could hear him, and he wanted to see how swiftly they would comply with his orders.

All noise of construction halted abruptly; the sound of tools being set down filled the echo.

The temporary head of the builders working on Los Sacramentos came at once, his hood thrown back, and his face ruddy, glistening with sweat. "Mi Señor," he said respectfully, his accent revealing more distinguished connections than Obispo Guarda possessed.

"Why have I no reports on the Europeans in Cuzco? They should be ready by now. This is the third time I have had to ask about them. That speaks of laxness, and a failure of obedience. Why must I require you to submit these things when you know already that it is your duty to bring me such reports? You are answerable to your Order, not to your House; I should not have to remind you. It is vexing when you fail to do as you are instructed." It was oddly pleasant to take the well-born Franciscan to task, and he made full use of the opportunity. "I have noticed a growing slothfulness in your community, Frey Rafael, a lack of dedication, and this causes me great distress."

Frey Rafael lowered his eyes. "Tell me my error and I will confess it." He clasped his hands over the wooden rosary which hung from his hemp belt.

"Your error is that you are not as vigilant as you must be, especially in this place, where so much is at stake. How can you permit yourself to be so lax, and not realize how close you are to sin? You forget the great purpose for which we are sent here. If you permit any of your men to become inattentive in his duties, you will soon have a community that is more secular than the most worldly soldiers will ever be, and you will bring disgrace on your House, your Order, and España." He relished the misery he read in Frey Rafael's eyes. "And you will disgrace God," he added, driving the last and most devastating blow with determination.

"I . . . I have no excuse," said Frey Rafael, sinking to his knees beside the writing table, his head bowed over his hands. "We have had much to do here, but it is not enough to . . . " His words straggled off.

"Yes, and well you might say so," Obispo Guarda said, not quite gloating at how quickly he had brought Frey Rafael—the hidalgo—literally to his knees. "We have a most important mission here in Peru and throughout the New World; if we fail here, now, how will we answer when the Last Judgment comes?" He stared at the monk with an expression compounded of pity and loathing. "Frey Jeromo is not so faint-hearted in his dedication to our work here as you are. Why is that?"

"Tell me what penance to perform and I will do it with a glad heart," said Frey Rafael, his eagerness showing in a hasty motion of his hand that caused half a dozen rosary beads to slip through his fingers.

"Yes," said Obispo Guarda again, trying to settle on some activity that would shame Frey Rafael enough to satisfy the Obispo. "Since we are lacking in records on Europeans currently living here, I want you to spend the next forty days watching one foreigner each day, from dawn until twilight, unless the one being watched is not yet within his own doors when twilight comes, in which case you will observe him until he returns to his house, no matter what hour that may be. If you do not do this diligently, I will have to recommend your reassignment. In addition to following these men, you will make note of who visits these foreigners, when, and for what purpose. It is essential that the duration of visits be noted as well as the visitors themselves." He touched his fingertips together as if in prayer, but actually in contemplation of the embarrassment this would bring on Frey Rafael. "You will report to me every Sunday after la Misa, with a full account of all you have seen and heard—"

"That may offend some of those you set me to watch," said Frey Rafael, the color fading from his face as he realized what was being demanded of him. "There are nobles of España who know the foreigners, and who will defend their friends and associates. We must respect the authority of the Presidencia, as they are entitled to do. It has been approved at the highest levels. In so remote a place, to do otherwise than obey this law could bring odium and disapproval on monks, and disgrace to the Church."

"So it may," said Obispo Guarda. "But better to offend a few men than to give offense to God and His work. Don't you think?" He added this last in order to force Frey Rafael into compliance. His door, badly hung, began to swing open on its own weight.

Frey Rafael crossed himself, and did his best not to appear shocked by what was being asked of him. In the short time he had worked with Obispo Guarda, he had come to recognize the signs of frustrated ambition; he was still discovering how deeply Obispo Guarda felt his plight. He decided against saying anything now, certain that Obispo Guarda would seize on it for more criticism. It was not his place to question the Obispo, especially this Obispo. Cautiously he got to his feet, hoping he would not be subjected to another rebuke.

"Good; very good." Obispo Guarda looked distractedly at the door, the renewed pounding beyond it again inflicting itself upon him. He put his hands to his head and pressed his eyes closed as if this double shutting out would quiet the noise.

Watching the Obispo narrowly, Frey Rafael once again thought about the rumor that had circulated about the man: that his mother had been a novice at a convent who had eloped with a young hidalgo and was abandoned by him when she became pregnant. If it was true, it was a curse on his blood twice-over, and a scandal neither family could ever forget or put aside. To Frey Rafael it sounded like the stuff of Italian romances, but it was possible, he supposed. God knew—he crossed himself—there were debauched hidalgos as well as corrupt foreigners, if half the whispers one heard were true. He did not venture to speak, for fear of adding to the Obispo's discomfort and his own chagrin.

At last Obispo Guarda raised his head and opened his eyes. "Tell me, Frey Rafael, how much longer will they be at that infernal clamor?"

"It should be summer, Obispo Guarda, but alas, it is not. They will work until the rains come, which will be soon, and then they will labor indoors, if the roof holds." He managed an encouraging look, to show that the monks were industrious. "They are making good progress."

Obispo Guarda sighed, longing just then for the mountains around Toledo where he had spent his childhood. He motioned Frey Rafael to rise. "I suppose it is wrong to think badly of this place because the seasons are upside-down. God has made them so." He shook his head several times as if the motion would set the world to rights for him. "But there are times when I think it most peculiar to celebrate the Misa de la Navidad at the height of summer, and la Pascua at the beginning of autumn. It smacks of heresy."

"It is strange, mi Obispo," said Frey Rafael, choosing what he hoped was a safe response. "But the world here is strange."

"Or worse," muttered the Obispo, his reflections darkening as he dwelt on the many dissatisfactions he had found in Peru, dissatisfactions that could not be remedied here or anywhere. He looked out at Los Sacramentos, and could not but dream for a proper restoration of the Catedral, commensurate with his rank and mission, and a means to compensate for his lack of advancement. He directed his attention to the cracked walls of his office. "How do you think this place will fare in the winter? With so much still to be done, will the weather not undo much of the work?" He had heard others make this complaint and could not hide his apprehensions.

"We will do better this year than last; the roof will be fully repaired in another month if the rains hold off." He spoke quickly, trying to find something to tell Obispo Guarda the irascible bishop would like to hear.

"And if there is not another earthquake," said Obispo Guarda fatalistically. He crossed himself as an afterthought. "I have been told that such things happen often here."

"We pray daily there will not be another," said Frey Rafael at once. "Every night we ask la Virgen to protect us and pray for our safety in this place." He crossed himself and again touched his rosary. "The native people tell us that such bad earthquakes do not happen more often than once or twice a century."

"So they tell us!" scoffed the Obispo, and took a more somber posture. "We must pray that such another earthquake will not be visited upon us again for as long as Los Sacramentos stands," he said to Frey Rafael as if to imbue the monk with his commitment. "I will address the community at supper, so that we may prepare for such an eventuality." He stared down at the open book on the table before him; his expression was supremely blank.

"Mi Obispo," said Frey Rafael quietly, "do you require anything more of me at this time? For if you do not, I should return to my work, to aid my Brothers. There is still much work to be done."

"Of course, of course," said Obispo Guarda, waving the hidalgo-monk away with a gesture that might have been a blessing. He remained in his chair, listening to the sounds of industry and hating them. It would have pleased him to find a punishment for the monks that would bring them the same keen sense of futility that filled him every day. He realized that as much as he might accomplish in this place, it would never be sufficient to return him to Europe in glory, or to advance him beyond the rank he had already achieved.

His unpleasant reverie was interrupted by a short scream and an ominous, gourd-like thud. He raised his head, his attention arrested by what he had just heard as all sounds of industry stopped and the babble of voices grew louder and more shrill, and one of the monks began to recite prayers in a fast, high chant. Sighing, Obispo Guarda got to his feet and went to the door, peering into the gloom beyond only to see a number of monks and laborers gathered around a supine figure. "What is the matter here?" he demanded as he stumped up to the knot of men.

"He fell," said the nearest monk. "From up there." He pointed to a beam above them. Then he crossed himself and pointed to the worker. "He may be dead."

"Dead?" repeated Obispo Guarda as if the word were unfamiliar to him. "God saves all those who work on this building, and takes them to His bosom in Paradise," he declared, coming near to the workman. "How bad is it?"

"He will need help," said the leader of the workmen. "His heart still beats, but it is very fast and—"

Obispo Guarda raised his hand. "Where is the physician who attends this place?"

There was an uneasy exchange of glances, and finally Frey Rafael said, "The physician sent from Cuzco died some months ago. We have asked the foreign Conde de San Germanno to tend to our sick and injured."

"San Germanno? The Presidencia's friend? The foreigner? The one they say is the lover of Acanna Tupac?" His scowl deepened with each question, and at last he drew himself fully upright. "It is a transgression to use the offices of such a man."

"But, mi Obispo, if there is no one else . . . " Frey Domingo protested hesitantly.

"No one else? What do you mean! How is it we have no physician here? Why was no word sent to Lima? Why have we not been informed of this?" Obispo Guarda was working himself up into another splendid display of temper and, without knowing it, relishing the experience. "How can we be expected to do what God asks of us if we cannot have the support we need?"

The injured man moaned; half the monks echoed the sound in sympathy for the worker's plight.

"We did send word," said Frey Rafael, hoping he did not appear to be defying the bishop. "Twice. Nothing has been done."

Obispo Guarda's ire grew: that this should happen and he not be informed! His face went from ruddy to white as he counted up the affronts Lima had given him. "Is there another physician we can send for?" His voice was dangerously soft, a poisonous sweet offered to his monks.

"There is one . . . for the soldiers," said the gangly Frey Esteban. "But he is a drunkard and he keeps three women in his house."

Now Obispo Guarda was ready to curse, and would have had he been alone. He folded his hands, gripping so tightly that his knuckles were white. "No other?"

"Not who can tend this man, no," said Frey Rafael with as much courage as he possessed. "If he is not to die in agony," he went on, kneeling down beside the fallen worker, "then have San Germanno brought here at once. He may be able to . . . to treat the worker in some way. They say he's given a crippled man new legs. He might know the means to . . . keep him alive. Otherwise, we might as well begin the Requiem and have it done with."

"How can you say this?" Obispo Guarda railed. "What devils have taken your soul, that you should do this? Better this man should die than he be left to the care of the Godless sinners of the world." He paced away from the whimpering man, and turned back. He knew if he did not do something to help the laborer none of the others would continue their work. It was a realization that aggravated him, but he strove to conceal this as he returned to the workers and monks gathered around the man. "Well, he cannot be left here. Have him carried into the vestry." At least then he would be out of the way.

But at the first insignificant change in his position, the worker let out such a wail as the damned must make falling into the fires of Hell. All those who had tried to move him released him and moved back.

"He . . . I don't think we should . . . " the leader of the workmen said, ducking his head in anticipation of blows and rebukes. "He is . . . You see how he is, Excelencia."

"They say San Germanno was able to save one of Acanna Tupac's servants whose legs were crushed." Frey Domingo looked directly at Obispo Guarda. "They say the man lived because of San Germanno."

"I can reach his house quickly," Frey Barnabas volunteered. "For God's Mercy, mi Obispo, let me bring him."

The man on the floor was pale as wax and his hands spasmed as those around him watched, aghast. There was a small halo of blood spreading on the stone floor, though there was no sign of spurting.

"Excelencia, *please.*" Frey Barnabas almost dropped to his knees in supplication. "For the sake of these good men, so they will know that the Church values their labors on her behalf."

It was all of a piece, and Obispo Guarda knew it. He was thwarted at every turn. He was about to refuse when it occurred to him that the worker's death—and surely he would die—would be blamed upon him unless he had another, more likely man to blame for it. He pretended to be lost in thought while he considered the possibilities. When he looked up from his folded hands, he saw he had the full attention of everyone but the injured man. "All right. God often sends strange tools to work His bidding. Very well, Frey Barnabas. Fetch this San Germanno." With that, he swung around and went back to his study, aware that this decision would be the main topic of conversation until the foreigner arrived.

Not more than a quarter of an hour had passed—the time marked by regular, thin screams and the susurrus of prayers—when the door of the Catedral was thrown open, and the sudden surge of voices summoned Obispo Guarda from his study: San Germanno had arrived.

"God bless and keep you," said Obispo Guarda to the neat stranger in black clothing of Hungarian fashion, the dolman closed with ruby clasps and laced in silver. Though he was almost a head shorter than the bishop, San Germanno had the stance and manner of a much taller man. Perplexed, the bishop extended his ring, and was mildly surprised when San Germanno knelt to kiss it.

"Amen," he said as he rose. "I understand there has been an accident," he went on in a pragmatic way. "My manservant will be here shortly with all my medicaments. I would like to see the man before I attempt any treatment of him."

"I fear he is more in need of last rites than any medicines you may provide," said Obispo Guarda, taking this opportunity to take the mea-

sure of the foreigner. He disliked what he saw, certain of hidden insolence in San Germanno's respectful comportment, hearing disdain
in his well-modulated voice.

"Let me see him, if you will," said San Germanno, moving to do this
as he spoke. His concentration was so immediate and complete that
his dark eyes seemed to glow. "So. His hands have been shaking this
way since he fell?"

"Yes, Señor Conde," said Frey Luis.

The monks and workers carefully gave him room, but remained near
enough to watch him.

After a cursory examination of the injured worker, San Germanno
asked, "What is this man's name?"

"Manco," said the leader of the workers. "Manco Ignacio."

"Thank you," San Germanno said, then addressed the supine man.
"Manco. Can you hear me? Manco?"

The man continued to moan but gave no other indication he was
aware of anything happening around him.

San Germanno's fine brows drew together and the line of his mouth
grew stern. "Has he been moved?" he asked.

The leader of the workmen answered. "The Obispo ordered it, but
when we tried he . . . he—"

"I see," San Germanno said. He found the pulse at Manco's neck and
measured it. "Much too fast," he said, more aware than ever that the
chances of keeping the man alive were slim. He made himself speak
briskly. "He is not going to improve with a pulse so fast. This is not a
good indication. And no fever," he added as he put his hand on
Manco's forehead. "Not yet."

"That is good, isn't it?" the leader of the workmen asked anxiously.

San Germanno did not answer. Gently he lifted one eyelid and studied what he saw. "The white is red. He is bleeding."

"From the wounds on his back and his head," said the leader of the
workmen. "After such a fall, I expect nothing less. At least there isn't
much blood."

"But it is in the eyes," said San Germanno remotely, rocking back
onto his heels. "Has he bled from his ears?"

"No," said Frey Domingo, who was kneeling on the other side of
Manco. "But, as you see, there is bleeding in his mouth. Not much, and
it is from the teeth." He indicated the thread of blood at the edge of
Manco's lips. "You can see where he has bitten himself. The teeth are
through the gum just here."

"That is something, at least; it could be much worse," San Germanno said under his breath, knowing that if Manco was bleeding from the ears he was beyond help. He hoped that Rogerio would arrive quickly, for he knew that minutes would count with Manco. He set his mind to tending to him as best he could without his chest of medicaments. "After such a fall, he should have a blanket over him."

"The day is warm, Señor," Frey Domingo pointed out.

"Not for Manco," San Germanno countered. "With injuries, it is as if one is plunged into ice. He will have to be kept as warm as he would be if there were snow on the ground. If he becomes cold, he will die and nothing I, or the Saints can do will change it." He rose and went to the bishop, who was watching this from his study door. "I am afraid the workman has injured his spine. I do not know how badly. There are undoubtedly other injuries as well, although I cannot determine their extent." Just speaking those words gave San Germanno a moment of vertigo: breaking his spine was as deadly to him as anyone. "No hurt to the spine is good."

Frey Emerico went off in search of a blanket for Manco as the rest continued to stare down at the injured worker.

"What can you do?" asked Obispo Guarda with an ill-concealed look of achievement.

"I am not sure yet. My manservant has my medicaments. If it is possible for Manco to recover—"

"Manco?" Obispo Guarda interrupted.

"The man you wish me to treat," San Germanno said, pausing slightly as he realized that the bishop did not know the name. "If he can recover, we will know it by this time tomorrow."

Obispo Guarda once again felt ill-used. "Will he have to lie there until then? Here, on sacred ground? When he is so—"

"It would be best. If he is as badly hurt as I suspect he is, any attempt to move him will kill him," San Germanno answered bluntly.

Obispo Guarda glowered at the black-clad interloper. "I must suppose you know what you are talking about," he allowed grudgingly. "But I do not want him in this building one instant longer than is necessary. His suffering is an offense to God."

"I share your concern," San Germanno said dryly, and went on as if they were in accord. "He cannot be cared for as he should be in this place. And I have no doubt he is an intrusion; you will not get much work done while he lies here. As soon as I am sure it is safe, I will move him. Until it is safe, however, he must lie here; I will see to his welfare," he promised the bishop.

The sound of the door opening again caught the attention of all those attending Manco.

"Ah. That is Rogerio," said San Germanno, making a sign to his manservant who had come into the Catedral carrying an antique red lacquer chest strapped across his back. "With my supplies. In good time. I can begin to try to help this worker. If you will permit, Excelencia?"

"I will leave you to your task. Since I can do nothing more here, I am going to pray," said Obispo Guarda, wanting to have his study door between him and Manco.

"Thank you, Excelencia," said San Germanno with a graceful bow that only served to make Obispo Guarda dislike him the more.

Rogerio was unbuckling the straps that held the chest in place on his back as San Germanno came up to him. "I brought the tubing for his throat; I thought you might need it, my master."

"You anticipate superbly, old friend; yes, that and the topical ointment will be needed once I have a better understanding of his hurts; by what I see now, the damage is extensive," San Germanno told him as he went to open the chest; he knew that all he said was being noted, and not entirely by those who wished him well. He swung open the doors revealing a number of stoneware jars and glass vials as well as a rank of small drawers, each one labeled in faded Latin. San Germanno took three of the stoneware vessels from the chest and used his small dagger to peel the wax off the stoppers. "I will want to have this heated, I think, with spirits. The man is too cold; we must warm him if he is to live."

"I am certain the workers will let us use their fire, my master," said Rogerio with a significant glance at their leader who hovered near Manco, doing his best not to dither with worry. "The fire is lit already, and tended. They must want the man to improve, and surely if we need it—"

"What is your name, good worker?" asked San Germanno, knowing he would have the man's attention if he could use his name.

"It is Gaspar, Señor," said the leader of the workmen, ducking his head.

"Gaspar," repeated San Germanno, his mind suddenly back in Fiorenza with another builder with the same name—Gasparo Tucchio, who had helped to build his palazzo there a century and half ago. San Germanno blinked and forced himself to concentrate on this Gaspar. "Will you let us use your fire, Gaspar?"

"Certainly, certainly, we want to help Manco," said Gaspar, a bit too hastily, as if to make up for his previous inaction. "It is through that door, where they are making beams. We have our carving tools there as well." He did his utmost to smile and was unable to make it work. "Do you think there is any chance?"

"I think he may recover," he said carefully, and made his voice level as he went on, "but for the sake of his soul, I would ask for Extreme Unction, just in case he does not respond." San Germanno looked over at Frey Rafael. "Will you send for a priest, to perform the rite?"

"Yes," he said, grateful to be doing something at last. "At once."

San Germanno watched him scurry away, and shook his head once before asking Rogerio to bring him his measuring glass. "I want you to mix this with spirits of wine and then heat it enough to warm him. Test it with your fingers."

"Very well," said Rogerio. He waited while San Germanno prepared the medicament in an alabaster cup, then took it to the workmen's fire.

"Will he be cured?" asked Frey Emerico, approaching quickly, his sandals slapping, a rough blanket clasped in his hands. "I have prayed with every step I've taken."

"It is possible," said San Germanno as he took the blanket and spread it over the worker. "But it may not be likely. He has lain here for more than half an hour, and his breathing is no better." He sighed, aware that if Manco could recover, he would be damaged in more than his spine. "The longer his breathing does not ease, the more likely he will die."

The bluntness of this assertion shocked those gathered around Manco. A few of them made the sign to ward off evil; the monks crossed themselves.

From the other side of his study door, which was carefully ajar, Obispo Guarda smiled as he heard this.

"What can we do?" asked one of the workmen. "He is my cousin. I must do something." He looked directly at San Germanno.

"The blanket will help," said Frey Emerico, his tone going up at the end of his statement, making it more a question than the assertion he had intended.

"Yes, it should," said San Germanno. "If he can be helped."

Again, those watching Manco crossed themselves and Obispo Guarda nodded his satisfaction.

San Germanno checked the man's eyes again and did not like what he saw. He returned to his red lacquer chest and opened it, taking out a vial of clear liquid which he brought back to Manco, where, with great care, he tipped two drops into the man's eyes, then closed the lids once more. "That may help," he said by way of explanation, although he was beginning to doubt anything would save Manco.

Rogerio came back, a steaming cup in his gloved hand. "Here, my master. It is hot but will not burn his tongue or lips," he said, giving the vessel to San Germanno with the admonition to hold it with care.

San Germanno nodded once and opened Manco's mouth enough to permit him to dribble a little of the liquid into it. Aside from a slight cough, there was no response from Manco, and his cousin, watching this, drew back from him.

"He still isn't breathing right," said Rogerio in Latin as he studied the worker with unruffled calm. "Will you be able to get the tubing into his mouth?"

"No," said San Germanno. "Not if he will not swallow." He kept up his ministrations for a short time, then rose again, motioning to Rogerio to step aside with him. "Nothing."

"Yes, my master," said Rogerio, continuing in the language of Greece three thousand years before. "It appears even your blood cannot save him." He switched back to Latin. "What would you like me to do?"

San Germanno frowned. "I wish the priest would arrive. I suspect that Obispo Guarda would like an excuse to blame me for the man dying without proper Christian ceremony, and I have no wish to be his scapegoat." He sighed once, rubbing the back of his neck just above the little pleated ruff he wore. "I could ask the bishop to do the rite himself, but it wouldn't be wise, I suspect. He wants no part of this work."

"No; he is not happy that these men are working in his Catedral," agreed Rogerio, glancing up as the door once again opened and Frey Rafael hurried in, Padre Correa, muttering, in tow.

"Does he live still?" asked Frey Rafael anxiously, rushing to Manco's side.

Gaspar shrugged and whispered something to Frey Rafael.

"Good Padre," said San Germanno at once, going to the priest and kneeling for a blessing. "I have tried to revive him, but I fear I am challenging God in my presumption." He saw the look in the eyes of the monks as they came nearer again. "When God has his mark on a man, only the sin of Pride attempts to stay His will."

From his vantage place by his study door, Obispo Guarda heard this with stark disapproval, thinking the rebuke was knowingly directed at him, for he could not but suppose that this arrogant foreigner knew of the many slights the bishop had endured and was taking advantage of this opportunity to add to them. It was enough to endure the hidden contempt of his fellow-clerics, but when someone like this San Germanno offered such an affront, Obispo Guarda could not deceive himself: he was of little value to the Church and none at all to the Crown. He felt the hot thrill of wrath spread through him, and sin though it was, he welcomed it as an old and trusted friend, reliable in any predicament.

The priest, angular and short-sighted, absently made the Sign in San Germanno's direction, saying, "That is true." He peered into the shadows, hoping to see Obispo Guarda, but could not. "I will do what I am mandated to do," he announced as if expecting dispute.

"And God reward you for your compassion," San Germanno said to urge him to get on with it. As he spoke the words he felt an eerie certainty that they would return to haunt him: it was a sensation he had experienced before, in Poland when he had first confronted Father Pogner; outside Baghdad where the caravan leader had claimed to have been set upon by thieves; in Rome when Led Arashnur had goaded him into an unwise show of strength; and long before that, in Thebes, when Denin Manhipy had hankered for advancement. All the weight of those moments came back to him as he felt more than saw Obispo Guarda's eyes in the shadows.

As the priest prepared to minister to the dying man, Rogerio came to his master's side, saying in a low voice, "I fear there will be trouble, my master." He cocked his chin in the direction of Obispo Guarda's study.

"And I," he admitted, wishing it were not so.

Text of a letter to Acanna Tupac from Dom Enrique Vilhao. Written in Spanish with a Latin translation appended.

To the woman Acanna Tupac, residing at Cuzco and calling herself the descendant of Atahualpa Inca, the greetings of Dom Enrique Vilhao of Portugal.

On the authority of the encomienda granted me by Corregidor Don Vicente Angel Luis Jorge Yniguez y Nieviereos I am claiming the labor of seven of your servants, such labor to begin the morning after you receive this notice. This is fully within the rights granted by the encomienda, and any resistance to these orders will be construed as willful violation of an official declaration. You are to provide these servants

*clothing and footwear for their labors, a cape against wind and rain,
and sufficient food for three days. Should you fail to do any of these
things, I am authorized to fine you at the rate set out by the Corregidor,
of six gold reales per servant per day they do not work due to your failure to observe these stipulations.*

*Consult Don Ezequias if you like, and have him review the terms of
our grant. There is nothing wrong in asking his advice, or in informing
him of your decision, since it must pass his review in any case. You will
discover the Presidencia is bound by the ruling of the Corregidor to demand your compliance with the terms laid out above. Of course, if you
cannot deliver the servants we require, you may purchase their exemp-
tions for the sum of six hundred reales each, or the equivalent in silver.
Or you could sign over your mines to us at once and keep your servants
for as long as you live, for knowledge of such mines would more than compensate us for the trouble of having to round up other Spanish-speaking
laborers. You could order those who feel an alliance with you and your
House to take the place of your servants, but they would have to speak
Spanish, and many of the Indians of this region refuse to learn it.*

*I await your laborers at the northern gate tomorrow at sunrise. Do
not make it necessary for me to prosecute my claims, Madama, for that
would lead to unpleasantness for both of us, which I am sure you do
not wish any more than I do. Let me urge you to comply readily, for such
cooperation will be regarded with favor when it is reported in Lima to
the Corregidor, and may benefit you in time to come.*

*Any effort to subvert this license or to interfere with what we are
doing will not be tolerated, and you will be made to answer for it. Do
me the honor of recognizing my sincerity in this, as in all things.*

*Dom Enrique Vilhao
On the 4th day of May, 1644*

10

"I suppose there is nothing you can do," San Germanno said as he faced
Don Ezequias across his writing table; in his hand he held the letter
from Dom Enrique. He was in mente and dolman again, both silver-

edged black, and on a ruby-studded silver chain his black sapphire eclipse device hung, matching the signet ring on his right hand.

Outside the first autumn rain was falling, making the light shattered and milky by turns as the morning sun fought a retreating action against the advancing clouds.

Don Ezequias shook his head slowly. "No. My hands are tied. I cannot gainsay the Corregidor without the aid of Obispo Guarda." He took his cup of wine and sipped.

"And have you told Acanna Tupac about this? Does she know how Dom Enrique accomplished it?" San Germanno leaned forward so that his left hand rested on the surface of the writing table. "He makes no mention of it here, as you can see."

Don Ezequias tapped the proffered letter with two fingers. The minute shake of his head might have been because of his ruff. "When he approached me about this, I refused him. That should have been the end of it. He clearly decided to take his petition elsewhere, to Lima. I did not realize he was so purposeful." The sorrow and disgust he felt were on his face. "It is a despicable thing Dom Enrique has done, and not only in regard to Acanna Tupac. He has also slapped my face."

San Germanno said nothing, knowing he could offer no sympathy for what the Presidencia felt, though he had experienced the same intense chagrin many times in his long, long life. He directed his gaze toward the rain on the windows as he folded the letter and thrust it back into his dolman, then he rested his hand on the hilt of his sword, waiting, at ease, with no indication of impatience in his stance.

After a while, Don Ezequias sighed. "It galls me to admit it, San Germanno, but I do not like being treated in this way, with my authority traduced and my position denigrated. Being sent here was supposed to be humiliation enough, but this—If I had it within my power to demand apology from Dom Enrique and that Dutch scoundrel, I would. But, of course, it is not within my power." He had been rolling a length of sealing wax between his fingers, but now set it aside as if seeking greater distractions.

"Have you heard anything from Don Vicente?" asked San Germanno, knowing the answer before it came.

"Only through Dom Enrique, who carried a memorandum from the Corregidor reiterating the terms of the encomienda." He shrugged as if to relieve tension rather than express indifference. "That Portuguese wastrel has outmaneuvered me at every turn. I am at a loss to know how to deal with him."

The response San Germanno gave him was oblique. "You know, when I was much younger than I am now, I had occasion to encounter a very perplexing and difficult young man, one who sought to abuse the kindness of everyone around him, from his family to his friends to his servants. He did this without shame and without any attempt to disguise his actions, and no indication that he had the least notion that what he was doing was unacceptable. He was well enough placed in the world that few dared to complain of him to the justices. When he finally was punished for raping the niece of his oldest friend, he was outraged that he should be so unfairly condemned. He strove to blame everyone but himself for his guilt." That had been in Aix-la-Chappell, when Charles-le-Magne was trying to establish some semblance of government. The episode had brought attention to the Emperor's demand for laws of conduct as well as laws of property.

"What happened to him?" Don Ezequias asked, uncertain of what San Germanno was saying to him.

"He was blinded and castrated." He recalled the wretched state of the offender when the law was through with him. "He died three years later, taken by the pox." He did not add that had he not taken pity on the wretched, debauched young man, he would not have lasted three days.

"And?" Don Ezequias prompted.

Again San Germanno provided an indirect response. "The young man thought no one noticed his venality, for he supposed everyone was as corrupt as he, that all advancement beyond position of birth was the result of chicanery. For him the world was made up of fools, masters, and reprobates. When it proved otherwise, he was outraged, thinking those he had taken advantage of had deliberately betrayed him, although he had never scrupled to betray them." He went to the window and stared out into the rain. "There may be similarities between that man—his name was Boves—and the Portuguese Dom."

"And this Boves, did he come to understand his crimes, his improbity?" asked Don Ezequias, his manner slightly distracted, as if his thoughts were elsewhere.

"He came to know they were crimes," said San Germanno quietly; light from the window made the black sapphire glow.

"Was that enough?" Don Ezequias studied his foreign friend.

"It was all he achieved," was San Germanno's oblique answer.

Don Ezequias considered this answer for a short while, and at last said, "How is it that you may wear black like a Spaniard and still look so foreign?"

"My clothing?" San Germanno, aware that was not the issue; a cold tremor went through him. "My device?" He indicated the silver pectoral.

"In part, in part," said Don Ezequias, tapping his fingers together thoughtfully. "But I think you could be in full court dress, with gregas and ropilla, and I would still know you for a stranger." He took a deep breath, and then plunged on. "You are unlike the rest of us in Cuzco."

San Germanno did not want to be so obvious as to change the subject as abruptly as Don Ezequias had, but he did not want to dwell on the matter much longer; he knew the questions that could arise from such scrutiny, and he sought to avoid them. "My features are not Spanish," he remarked in an off-handed manner.

"No, they are not. Nor are they noticeably Italian, or German, or French." He regarded San Germanno with a narrowed eye. "What are you?"

"My people come from the Carpathians, Don Ezequias, just as I have told you," he answered truthfully. "There is fighting in my homeland as we speak."

"Fighting with the Ottomites?" he said, concealing his suspicions.

"Yes," San Germanno said in a neutral voice.

"Peru is a long way from your homeland," Don Ezequias pursued, although his remarks were no longer courteous.

"As we have agreed before," said San Germanno, as if unaware of this lapse in conduct. When the Presidencia remained silent, he said, "You seek to know something. Why not ask me directly?"

Don Ezequias took a deep breath and pushed back from his writing table. "Very well," he declared as he paced down the chamber, his head lowered in concentration and chagrin; he disliked his inquiry more than he could express. "I know you say you have no desire to found a dynasty here, but you are the lover of Acanna Tupac. It is generally acknowledged that she is well-disposed toward you. You must know that there are rumors you intend to marry her and establish a new House in one of the lost cities."

"Who says this?" asked San Germanno, somewhat more sharply than he had intended; he watched Don Ezequias closely.

He coughed once. "That is what the rumors say."

"Rumors," San Germanno said distantly. "Let me set your mind at ease. I have no intentions of making myself ruler here or anywhere in the world. Had I wanted that, I might have had it in many places before now, and with less difficulty, for no matter what the rumors say, this is not the place I would choose to remain for the rest of my life." His tone was level and his words crisp, but there was something in his dark eyes that made Don Ezequias hate himself for his doubts. "No, my friend, I will not attempt to make this place native earth for me; were it possible I still would not do it." He at last turned directly to Don Ezequias. "I am here to learn what I can of the Incas before they are gone: nothing more. I have no granted authority in this place, I do not need wealth, I do not seek advancement, or dynasties. You may tell whomever has been asking questions that you have had my answer. Frey Jeromo will learn of it, without doubt." This last was ironic, the words delivered with a slight bow.

"Frey Jeromo," said the Presidencia, as if the monk's very name was sour.

"No doubt, since there are rumors, he is interested. He is interested in all my affairs, or so it appears. I am told he has made inquiries about me," San Germanno told him, wondering if saying so much was wise.

"I will look into it," said Don Ezequias somewhat grimly. "To make such an inquiry without my consent is beyond his office. It will give me great satisfaction to tell him he is exceeding his authority in this. I would be pleased if, for once, my position would not be compromised," he admitted, then he changed the subject as he took his place at the writing table once again. "I have had another letter from my wife."

"Ah?" San Germanno said, accepting this without comment.

"She wrote to tell me that Carlos, our youngest child, died in January. He was never truly well, and neither she nor I had much hope for him." He went back to his writing table and looked down at the pages laid out at one corner. "Actually, her Confessor wrote. She does not know how. The Sisters taught her prayers and needlework, to keep her from sin."

"In your situation, that may be a disadvantage," San Germanno suggested. "But if she could read and write for herself, wouldn't her correspondence still be supervised? I thought it was required that all letters leaving España be reviewed."

"At least it would be in her handwriting, a part of her." He made a gesture of futility. "I have been trying to think of how to reply." His expression was impassive but his eyes were troubled. "I do not know what to say to her."

"I am sorry to hear about your son," said San Germanno carefully, trying to fathom what Don Ezequias wanted to tell him.

The Presidencia nodded. "It is the worst of this predicament," he exclaimed suddenly. "If I were certain that my wife truly holds me in the contempt her letters claim she does, then I have nothing left in España. But it is possible that the Confessor, knowing of my beliefs, is not willing to relay my wife's concern to me, and substitutes his own rancor for hers. It is maddening, not knowing."

"And there is no way for you to find out?" San Germanno asked, already certain of the answer.

"No. I considered once enlisting a messenger, but that would have put the messenger in danger if my wife is truly so wholly against me as her letters declare. If she is not, then she would be in danger if she gave the messenger an answer that the Church could discover." He sighed once. "They send many of us here, to the New World. Those of us who embarrass our families or disagree with the Church. But we must come alone. Many have made second families here, and forgot their wives and children in España. But I . . . I cannot make myself forsake my wife. It would be a desertion worse than the one forced upon us. If she is still loyal to me, she has been compelled to live under scrutiny every hour of her life, and I would be beneath contempt if I did not remain loyal to her."

"That assumes, as you say, that she is being coerced by her Confessor," San Germanno pointed out, continuing in a circumspect way, "And what if the sentiments claimed in her letters are genuine?"

"I would only confirm her worst judgment of me if I were to behave as so many others have done, and put her and our children behind me." He slapped at the top of the table. "It is a terrible thing when a man puts his family away from him without regard for what they will endure because of him."

"Do you speak of others, or yourself, Don Ezequias?" asked San Germanno, aware of the complicated situation he addressed.

"In this instance of myself," said Don Ezequias. "Though there are many others to serve as examples." He sat down and stared at the tabletop as if discerning wonders in the grain of the wood. "What have I done to her?"

"Surely she is not without means," said San Germanno, surprised at the force of the Presidencia's emotion.

"As to that, her family is wealthy, and they will not let her want for anything," he said. "But she is like a prisoner, with the Church on the one side and her brothers on the other. No matter her feelings toward me, I cannot convince myself that she has not been put into an untenable position. And our children are forever the children of a disgraced father." He rubbed at his chin, then smoothed his short beard. "They have given me this post to punish me, and to remind me that I cannot go far enough to escape my shame."

"What shame was that?" San Germanno asked carefully.

Don Ezequias shook his head decisively. "No. It is not fitting for me to discuss it. But I cannot blame my wife if she does despise me, given what I have done. I know the Church will not forget it." He folded his arms. "And now this. Don Vicente has seen fit to countermand my orders. Oh, it is his right. As Corregidor, his authority exceeds mine. I know it. But how it offends me to have him do this to me."

"You mean issuing the encomienda to Dom Enrique?" San Germanno inquired calmly, wanting to follow Don Ezequias' argument.

It was as if an inner door closed, quietly but firmly. "Oh, that, and other matters," said Don Ezequias remotely, nodding once to dismiss the entire matter. "Pray tell Acanna Tupac that the encomienda was not of my doing, and that I regret she has been imposed upon so unjustly. But there is nothing I can do to modify the terms of the license. I can offer her nothing but my consolation for the misfortune she has suffered." He cocked his head toward the door, a tacit suggestion to San Germanno to leave.

"I will convey your message." If San Germanno was affronted by this abrupt change in Don Ezequias, he did not reveal it. "I thank you for receiving me on her behalf." With that, he turned and went to the door, pausing there to give a departing nod of the head.

"San Germanno," said Don Ezequias in a distant voice, "Acanna Tupac has many enemies. They may become yours as well."

San Germanno gave a sardonic chuckle. "I was worried that my enemies might become hers." With that he let himself out of the room.

As he made his way back to his house, San Germanno pondered the interview he had just had with Don Ezequias. He was certain that the Presidencia was suffering from the slight he had been given by Dom Enrique and the Corregidor. It was also evident that he was troubled about his family in España. But he feared there was something more, a deep malaise that had tinged their entire exchange with apprehension.

As he attempted to assess his position, deliberately using his intellect instead of his emotions to define it, his conclusions provided him few reasons for optimism; his thoughts did not shake off the gathering sense of hazard that had clung, miasma-like, to everything he attempted, nor could he bring himself to believe that he was imagining risk where none existed, nor could he convince himself that it was his foreignness that led him to misinterpret the things he perceived. The reception offered him upon his arrival at his house did little to dispel his growing anxiety: Rogerio was in the patio, his usually impassive demeanor showing worry and strain. Touching his lips with a raised finger, he motioned San Germanno aside as he closed the outer gate, saying in an undervoice, "Someone is waiting to see you. From an outlying village. We must talk before that."

San Germanno had known Rogerio for more than fifteen hundred years and realized at once that it was not the visitor who troubled him but something beyond the caller's identity, something that struck Rogerio as dangerous. "Well?" he asked, waiting while Rogerio composed himself.

When Rogerio spoke, he used the ancient, lost language of San Germanno's homeland. "Three of the servants left this morning, in spite of your encomienda. They regretted that they had to go. They regard you as a good master, but they do not believe it is safe to work for you. They would not say whether or not anyone had instructed them to leave, only that they had decided it was for the best. I gave them their wages when they would not be persuaded to remain. I tried to discover what had caused them such fear, but I, like you, am a foreigner. This much they would admit; they are afraid of the monks who keep watch on this house. One of them told me he had been questioned by two of them about the supposed cures you have achieved."

San Germanno felt as if a cold wind blew over him. "What did they hope to learn, these watchers? Were you able to find out?"

"No. He was too frightened to tell me more than that, and said he should not have told me so much but that he wanted to warn you. He felt he owed you that much for your fairness as a master." He glanced over his shoulder, then resumed more hastily. "The man who is here now wants your help."

"What sort of help?" San Germanno asked in the same tongue, although he already knew the answer.

"There are villagers injured. A rock-slide has buried a part of his village and destroyed many of the dwellings. He has heard you can save those who are beyond hope. He came to you because of what you have done for others." Rogerio paused. "It was to be expected, my master."

"I suppose you are right, old friend," said San Germanno, suddenly weary. "But how can I turn them away? It is not just that I *can* help some of them—a few in any case, but in doing it, I gain a little protection. The people of this country have little reason to welcome Europeans. They may distrust me now, but if I did not provide what aid I can, they would vilify me." His dark eyes fixed in the middle distance. "And that would lead to . . . complications."

Rogerio gave a single, knowing nod. "Among the people this may be so. From what I have been told, the monks have asked the most about the cures. They—"

"There are more Incans in these mountains than monks," San Germanno reminded him wryly.

"The monks are more dangerous than the people, and the people know it," Rogerio countered.

"The monks themselves asked for my help, not so long ago," said San Germanno dryly. "Little as they wanted to." His expression grew remote. "I was not able to save the man."

Rogerio made an exasperated sound. "The word in the marketplace is that you did not wish to save the man, that you deliberately withheld treatment because the man was doing holy work. It is believed you permitted him to die to shame the Church." He gestured again. "Not everyone thinks it was a bad thing, the monk dying."

"Manco was not a monk, he was a carpenter," San Germanno reminded him. "You saw him."

"According to the rumors, he was. The rumors have it that you deliberately failed to aid a monk because you are a servant of the Devil. There is talk that you sped his death because of the elixir you gave him." Rogerio's pale blue eyes shifted restlessly. "The man waiting for you has been told you will save his village because they are not servants of the Black Robes."

"But a servant of the Devil: the man's back was broken, and his skull. No one could have saved him, God or Devil," San Germanno murmured, an ironic light in his dark eyes. He moved toward the door into the house, saying, "Make sure my visitor has something to eat and drink while I get my things."

Rogerio had long experience of San Germanno and so was not surprised at this decision. He nodded assent and was about to go to the kitchen to get bread, meat, and wine for the visitor when he could not help but ask, "My master, why take the risk?"

San Germanno paused halfway through his door, and looked back at Rogerio. "There is little enough I can do for Acanna Tupac, and most of that could have unwanted consequences for us both. And I know she would aid her people if it were in her power. At least I can do this for her without making her situation worse." With that he continued on his way to the study where he kept his alchemical supplies.

Not quite an hour later, San Germanno appeared in his reception room. He had changed into serviceable Hungarian riding clothes of embossed black leather, and he carried a black cloak of alpaca wool over his arm. He regarded his visitor with curiosity and in silence.

The man was middle-aged, not tall but burly, like the trunk of a tree, with big shoulders and massive arms. His close-cropped brown hair was shot with grey, and his neat beard was entirely white. He wore native clothing but for the dented metal breastplate and scuffed, old-fashioned military boots, mud still caked around the heels. He was just finishing his meal, elbows braced on the table, using his knife to slice off a wedge of hard cheese, when San Germanno's soft footfall made him look up sharply. He smiled with his teeth, his hand still on his knife, his hazel eyes alert. "You're San Germanno?" he asked warily.

"I am," he answered.

"You don't look Spanish," said the visitor, leaning back in his chair once more. His Spanish was utilitarian, flavored with another European tongue.

"Nor do you," said San Germanno, waiting, leaving the challenge unanswered.

The man recovered himself quickly. "Ah. I am Toulon, Gerard Toulon, once of Artois, former sergeant, former novice Trinitarian. Now just a man with a family in a village the Spanish call Agua Pura." He took a large bite of bread, followed it with a swig of wine and went on in French as he chewed, "I hope you understand me." When San Germanno nodded, he went on. "The trouble is in Agua Pura. The place gets its name from a glacier half a league up the slope from the village. The water comes right off the ice." He swallowed and had more cheese. "The people have trouble with mud-slides. The hillside is always wet. They put up rock walls to hold it, and plant trees, but occasionally it gives way. Then we have rocks as well as mud."

"Hardly surprising," said San Germanno, trying to decide how much of the genial manner was bluff and how much was genuine.

"True. This last one was particularly bad. Even our herb woman was lost in it." He sucked his fingers one at a time, and then brushed them together to be rid of any remaining crumbs. "We need help."

"And you came to me." San Germanno contemplated Toulon's face. "May I ask why?"

"They said you helped the people, that you serve Acanna Tupac," he answered simply, and then ducked his head ingratiatingly. "They say you are not like the monks and priests, using the misfortune of the people to put them under obligation to them, and requiring service in exchange for aid. I thought you might be willing to come with me. I know the weather is closing in, but if we do not have some help, half the village will be lost, if not now, during the winter, for without houses to protect us—"

"I will order mules saddled. Unless you have one of your own?" San Germanno replied. He took up a small bell and rang it once.

"A burro." He opened his hands to indicate that he, and the people of Agua Pura, were poor. "And a llama, to carry supplies."

"We will use them both," said San Germanno, his manner crisp. "I will order my manservant to ready them. How far away is this village?"

"Ten leagues, and high. There is a path, of sorts, but not a road." He pointed off to the north-northeast corner of the ceiling, to enlarge on what he said. "It took me very nearly two days to get here." He became suddenly cautious. "Not many people know about the place."

"Enough do, if it has a Spanish name," San Germanno pointed out, and stared at him while Toulon thought it over. "I have nothing to gain from you, Toulon. You sought me out. I am willing to help you."

"You seem rich enough," said Toulon skeptically.

"I seem many things," San Germanno said in a measured way. "Choose if you are going to take me to your village."

Rogerio appeared in the door. "My master?"

"Have two mules saddled, and pack provisions for . . . five days." That would be sufficient to calm any doubts Toulon might have. "My medicaments are ready to go."

"You will not want me to come with you?" Rogerio asked.

"I think not this time, though I will, doubtless, wish you with me often. I need someone here to run the household, and to keep . . . " San Germanno said, a quick lift of the corners of his mouth conveying a secondary message: with the servants leaving, he needed someone to guard the premises.

"Very well," Rogerio said, and withdrew.

San Germanno swung around to Toulon. "All will be ready to depart shortly. Have you made up your mind yet?"

The other man glanced around the room once. "How do I know you will not take advantage of us, once you have reached us? How can I be certain you will not demand money and goods. And women. Or servants."

"You have only my word." This was said so levelly that it brought Toulon up short.

"Well," he said, blustering, "if you are a gentleman, I need no more."

"You will have to take my word on that as well," San Germanno said. He waited, standing very still, while Toulon decided.

The man shoved his hands under the edge of the breastplate. "As, I suppose, you will have to rely on me to show you the way." He sighed, disengaged his hands and bowed slightly. "What is the payment you demand."

"No payment," said San Germanno. "I will do this on behalf of the Yupanqui," deliberately using the Incan honorific.

"Not Orejon?" asked Toulon with mild surprise, using the Spanish title for Incan noblewomen. "You've got a taste for the Inca, do you?"

"In a manner of speaking," said San Germanno, offering Toulon no encouragement to inquire further. He changed the subject and went on briskly, "If we are to reach your village by tomorrow evening, we had best leave quickly or wait until the morning. From what you say, that would not be prudent. We have another five hours of daylight, which is not very long. We do not want to waste them."

Toulon became suddenly earnest. "No, we do not. I have been two days getting here, and we will be two days getting back . . . It is necessary that we make haste." His diligence rang falsely on San Germanno's ears, but Toulon did not notice the swift, skeptical glance he was given.

"My mules are fresh and I am rested. If the need is as urgent as you tell me, and you are up to the pace, we can press on. You are the one who may require sleep. If it will serve the purposes of Agua Pura, I will ride through the night with you. That should put us there by midday tomorrow, barring storms." He watched Toulon narrowly, searching for any sign of hesitation or duplicity.

This time Toulon's response was quick and to the point. "I would not ask it for myself, but one of my children was injured. If you will do this, I will remember you in my prayers all my life."

Now San Germanno realized what bothered him in Toulon: the man was like a dog who had been beaten by his master and was ready to fawn or bite in an instant. "You will need water and wine for the journey. Meat and cheese, and bread. And nosebags for the mules. Perhaps one for the burro as well."

"Excellent," said Toulon, beaming energetically. "As soon as the animals are ready, let us depart."

"And I will order lanthorns for us, for the night," said San Germanno, because it was expected, not because he needed the additional light; his eyes were little troubled by darkness.

Again Toulon was cautious. "Best just to follow the burro home," he said. "There are robbers. They could use the light to find us."

"They could use the sound of the hooves, as well," San Germanno pointed out, puzzled by this caveat.

"But they would not find us as easily, not on those slopes, with the echoes. We will only be vulnerable once, on the bridge, but it isn't very wide. Nothing like some of the great ones. The men of Agua Pura guard it day and night." He glanced back at the remains of his meal. "If we have food, and the animals do not grow over-tired, I will ride until I am knit with the saddle."

San Germanno chuckled. "No mule will travel over-tired," he said. "Horses, yes, but never a mule."

"True enough," said Toulon as if agreeing on a shared secret. He slapped at his breastplate. "Saw enough of mules when I was soldiering. Brutes, every one of them."

"Do you think so." San Germanno regarded Toulon steadily until the other man made a nervous shrug. "I have a few notes to write. If you will permit me a few minutes to do it, I will be at your disposal." With these polite words, he turned away and went directly to his study, unlocking the door with care, and setting the bolt in place again once he was inside.

Pulling out two sheets of good vellum, he laid them before him, then secured two quills which he trimmed quickly and meticulously. At last he took out his ink-cake and moistened it, then rubbed a small quantity of ink. Once he was satisfied with the consistency of it, he took a quill in each hand and penned two notes at once, his right and left hands moving with equal ease. He sanded both sheets, shook them, and folded them, and sealed them with his eclipse device before summoning Rogerio to him.

"You are going," said Rogerio without inflection.

"Of course." He handed the two letters to his manservant.

With a small gesture of philosophical resignation, Rogerio said, "I've packed two bags of native earth on the cantel of your saddle. I've made them look like food packages, the same as Toulon's, which are on the cantel of his saddle."

"Resourceful as always," San Germanno approved.

Rogerio permitted himself a fleeting moment of satisfaction. "You will need more than earth to sustain you while you are gone."

"I know; I know," San Germanno said with patience. "I will manage. If nothing else, there is the burro. It should be enough for the time I am gone." Then he touched the letters he had given Rogerio. "If you will be good enough to deliver these for me before evening? Oh, don't scowl, old friend. You know how the rumors would fly if both of us should absent ourselves from this city. And I depend upon you to see that this house is protected in my absence."

Rogerio used the letters to tap the palm of his left hand. "And Acanna Tupac? What shall I tell her?"

"As much as you think is wise, and guard her for me," San Germanno answered at once. Then he relented and gave Rogerio a swift, rueful smile. "You may be right, and this is nothing but a gesture of folly, but . . . " For a finish, he shrugged.

"And you will return when?" Rogerio did his best to conceal his apprehension.

San Germanno put his hand on Rogerio's shoulder. "I should be back in week if there is no snow." Again he smiled fleetingly. "You might pray for me—that there is no snow," he suggested. "At Los Sacramentos."

Recognizing the tactic for what it was, Rogerio nodded assent. "Every day, my master. Until you return."

This time San Germanno's expression held no trace of amusement. "If I am delayed, prepare to leave here. If you think it wise, depart for the coast. I will look for you in Guayaquil."

"Not Callao?" Rogerio was mildly surprised at San Germanno's choice of a more distant port.

"No. They will look for me in Lima and Callao if they search for me at all. Quito is a safer city and Guayaquil a safer port." He paused a moment. "I trust your judgment, Rogerio. Do as you think best and I will have no complaint."

There were many things Rogerio might have said, but his only response was, "Travel safely, my master."

Text of two letters written simultaneously by Francisco Ragoczy el Conde de San Germanno to el Presidencia Don Ezequias Pannefrio y Modestez and Capitan Don Alejandro Morena y Osma.

My dear Presidencia/My dear Capitan,

I have been called away by a man named Toulon to the village of Agua Pura, ten leagues distant from Cuzco, where I am told there has been a landslide, and many villagers there are hurt. I will not be gone more than a week if the weather holds, and not more than two weeks if it does not.

Should I fail to return, or to send word of my situation, my manservant will know what to do: I rely on his good judgment implicitly. He will not approach you if he is not obliged to; he has a notarized copy of my instructions and will present them to you upon demand. He also has my Will and is authorized to carry my worldly goods to those of my blood still living in Europe. I tell you this in order to forestall any delays in settling matters, should such settlement become necessary.

My house and stable, and all contents not claimed under the specific terms of my Will by my heirs is to become the property of Acanna Tupac unconditionally. I rely on you as a gentleman of honor to see that my instructions are carried out if I am unable to return to Cuzco, no matter what the reason may be for my detention or absence.

With my gratitude and prayers for your just rewards on earth as well as before God, I commend myself to your wisdom, by my own hand on the 10th day of June, 1644.

I remain
With utmost sincerity,
Francisco Ragoczy,
el Conde de San Germanno
(his sigil, the eclipse)

11

Van Zwolle was smirking as he sauntered through the reception room of Acanna Tupac's house, his long cloak dripping from the rain outside and leaving a trail of wool-scented drizzle to mark his passage, and although these things infuriated her, she found it less demeaning than the exaggerated bow Dom Enrique offered her as he came up to her.

"Gracious, gracious lady," said Dom Enrique in a commiserating manner, returning his hat to his head and shaking out the capes of his cloak, "I regret we must impose upon you once again."

Acanna Tupac stood very straight, her face registering none of the panic she fought so resolutely. She motioned Jasy away from the room, and was relieved when he obeyed without speaking.

"I understand your good friend el Conde de San Germanno is not in Cuzco this week. Left four days since, it's said. Something about doing more of his tiresome charitous work for villagers some distance from here, according to the rumors. And now the rains have come, so he will not return as smartly as he went, I'll wager. And his reputation! Every villager from here to Quito will seek him out in times of trouble once it is learned he is so . . . Christian a fellow." Dom Enrique relished the threat his words implied; he wanted the woman to fear him at last.

"So I have been informed," said Acanna Tupac, making herself speak with a hauteur she did not truly possess.

"Yes. And it would seem, given the weather," he went on, strolling over to the wall where four ceremonial masks hung, "that he is not expected back for at least two more days or more." He sighed in an exaggerated way. "You must feel his absence keenly. Being as you are so much in his company."

"He is a good friend to me," she said steadily. It was useless to wish for him to walk through her door now, and she upbraided herself mentally for her hope it would happen. She waited for whatever outrage these men would commit, knowing it was futile to scream.

Van Zwolle had picked up a vase, an old one with many traditional designs on its gentle upward curve. He ran his hands over it as if the clay were flesh, then deliberately dropped it, stepping back as it cracked and shattered. "Clumsy of me," he muttered without conviction.

Acanna Tupac knew van Zwolle was goading her, seeking to break down her reserve and her courage; she was determined not to respond as he wished. "My houseman will clean it up."

"Good thing to have, dependable servants," said Dom Enrique, satisfied that he had taken all but three of hers. He scuffed at the broken clay with the toe of his boot. "As we have discovered in dealing with those of yours granted us in the terms of our encomienda. If your servants were not quite so dedicated to you, this call would not be necessary. But then, I am certain you would not wish any of them to suffer on your behalf, would you? Of course not. Therefore, there are, sadly, a few more things we require of you." He rounded on her, his fashionable façade slipping. "And you will do as we require."

She made herself not flinch, and managed not to speak. Her pulse hammered in her temples and she had a moment's fear she might faint, or forget herself enough to rush at the two men and try to hurt them. It was as tempting as it was foolish, she knew, for such an attack would serve only to justify their barbarity.

Deprived of the pleasure of her asking him what he wanted, and the joy of his resultant refusal to tell her, Dom Enrique became annoyed, though he strove to maintain an appearance of good comportment. "We do not want to harm you. Understand that. And we will only if you drive us to it." He stroked her jaw with one finger. "You have not been cooperative with us, Acanna Tupac. In spite of our willingness to ac-commodate you. We have shown you respect and you have answered our respect with contempt. You have withheld things from us. You have information we must have before we undertake our explorations."

Van Zwolle dropped another piece of pottery.

"You must forgive my associate. He is a brute," Dom Enrique said with a slow, sly smile. "If he becomes infuriated by your constant un-willingness to . . . to assist us, I might not be able to contain him. That is the trouble with brutes. They cannot be contained."

Acanna Tupac made no answer, knowing whatever she might say would provide the two men with an excuse for further indignities. She wanted to bolt for the door, or sound an alarm. Perhaps, she hoped, Jasy would do it for her.

"We do not want to cause you any more dismay than we already have done," Dom Enrique went on, his face schooled to an expression of concern, though his eyes glittered in anticipation of the humiliation he would visit upon her. "It would cause me great personal dissatis-faction to know it had been necessary to try to—ah—persuade you more energetically."

"She knows where the treasure city is. They're told as a matter of course, those of royal blood. She has been there, too. They took her when she came of age, you may be sure of that," said van Zwolle, sounding petulant at having been deprived of this opportunity himself. He had taken one of the ceremonial masks from the wall and was hold-ing it negligently in his hands.

"Of course she knows where it is," said Dom Enrique, as if instruct-ing a truculent student. "But be reasonable. It is the most precious se-cret of her people. And I would not expect her to tell us at once. That would demean her." He swung around to face her once more. "Wouldn't it? Demean you?"

She hoped her eyes revealed her disdain instead of her fear.

"Very proud, these Incas. They have been under the cloak of España for a century and more, and still they suppose they may defy us." Without warning he slapped her, the blow so unexpected that she was unable to avoid it, or to keep from staggering when it struck. As Acanna Tupac struggled to regain her composure, Dom Enrique came up to her and seized the front of her garments, shouting into her face, "You will not trifle with us! We are masters here!"

"The gold isn't doing you any good," said van Zwolle, his face set with sulking. "You have no way to get it for yourself, or you would have done so long ago. If you tell us, we might share some of it with you." He fingered the ceremonial mask and then flung it against the wall, chuckling with satisfaction as it smashed.

"Stop that!" Dom Enrique bellowed at van Zwolle. "There is a man newly arrived in Mexico who will pay well for masks like these. He has connections to the Church and to Roman nobility through the Colonnas. He is determined to make his fortune in the New World, according to what de Gois told me. He can and will buy these." That last boast was more for Acanna Tupac's sake than van Zwolle's. "We will make what we can from the masks." He indicated that van Zwolle should gather them together. "Get a large sack, so the feathers will not break."

"The sacks must be in the kitchen," said van Zwolle, and went in search of one.

Left alone with Acanna Tupac, Dom Enrique studied her in silence for a short while, then said, as if resuming a conversation, "You know, when we were in Lima, I saw what van Zwolle did to a whore there. You wouldn't think to look at him that he could use his fists so harmfully. It cost me twice the usual amount to get us out of the house. He enjoys beating women, you see. The whore lost an eye because of him." He came to a tall table and slung his leg over it, attempting to appear casual. "You would not want to ire him, gracious lady. Yupanqui is how to say it, isn't it?" When she did not speak, he repeated the question very softly but with great menace.

Flatly: "Yes."

"And you think that title should protect you, don't you?" He made no effort to soften the threat in his posture. "You think you deserve the same regard we might give a Chinaman or a Greek. Look around you! You think that the Europeans who have come here ought to re-spect a band of gold-hoarding savages who haven't invented their own wheel?" He leaned forward. "You listen to me, old woman. You will tell us what we want to know, or you may be certain you will regret it for the remainder of your life, which will be as short or as long as I desire it shall be. Van Zwolle will not permit you to stand between us and the things we seek."

"Van Zwolle will not? Or you?" She offered the challenge. "He is your slave, your dog, moving at your command." She spat and met Dom Enrique's glower without any indication of her fear showing in her out-ward demeanor.

"And if he is," said Dom Enrique, doing his best to contain his tem-per, "you are ill-advised to anger me. I can make your time with us as unpleasant as necessary."

Had Jasy left the house, she wondered. And if he had, where had he gone? Don Ezequias would have to send someone to help, but who, and when? The Church would do nothing to assist her, but Jasy was aware of that, or so she hoped. "I cannot tell you what I do not know," she insisted.

"Fair enough, gracious lady. But you will forgive me if I do not take your word for it?" His smile had become mocking, his handsome, reg-ular features a leer.

"You will do as you must do." She was sorry now she had left her little dagger next to her bed. Next time she would not be so careless. There was supposed to be a pistol in the pantry, but she doubted she could reach it in time to stop these two men.

"And so will you," said Dom Enrique. "What a tiresome necessity. You insist on suffering, which is a development none of us want. Why should you risk certain injury and possible death for the sake of pro-tecting a people who would not do the same for you?"

She recognized the trap in the question at once, and said, "I have nothing to do with any of these things." Her face was impassive. "You are the one making demands on me and my people, not I."

Dom Enrique's scowl was eloquent of his dissatisfaction. "Tell me what I want to know, and you may live, unharmed, if it suits me. I will not reveal where the information came from. Your people will still re-spect you." The polished courtesy vanished utterly. "Remain silent and I will have van Zwolle break your feet and your hands to begin with, then your legs, then your arms. You will be unable to hold yourself up with crutches, or to drag yourself on a cart. And you will be helpless, because a broken foot is never strong again, and hands do not mend straight. Then your ribs will be next, and if you do not drown in your own blood, I may be merciful and have him break your skull."

"How good you are," she marveled, unable to keep from answering his threat.

His quick and mirthless laughter showed his sense of victory. "Yes. And if you will be wise, we will none of us have to be imposed upon."

Van Zwolle reappeared with a hempen sack in his hand. "This is large enough, I think, to hold them all. And I have brought rags to wrap the masks as well, so they will not be broken." He waited for Dom Enrique's approval before he reached for the most elaborate of the masks, handling it with unusual care as he enveloped it in a ragged length of linen. "Some of the feathers will be broken. I can't help that."

Dom Enrique studied van Zwolle in silence for several minutes, then said, "I don't know what value you place on these things, gracious lady, but surely they are worth less than your life. They are merely *things,* objects of beauty, certainly, but without life. Surely they are more easily given up than your blood."

For an instant Acanna Tupac recalled her last night with San Germanno, and could not forget the soft, low words he had spoken as she fell asleep: "I can give you nothing that is not already yours, in your blood, of your blood." How much comfort she had taken from his promise then, and how little she minded the blood that sealed it. But Dom Enrique's purposes were not those of San Germanno.

Van Zwolle was wrapping a second mask, the first making an ill-defined lump in the sack. His attention was on his task, not on the door, and so he dropped what he held as Jasy forced his way into the room, a German carbine in his hand at the ready.

"What the Devil?" exclaimed Dom Enrique, his face flushing with wrath as he swung around on Acanna Tupac's servant.

"That is where you will go if you harm the Nusta," he announced, his voice loud enough to carry throughout the house.

"And what happens once you fire?" asked Dom Enrique, regaining his composure almost at once. "By the time you have readied your next shot, your Yupanqui will be dead on the floor. Shoot me and van Zwolle will kill her. Shoot him and I will." He started to laugh.

Another voice cut this short. "Jasy did not come alone," said Rogerio in his usual self-composed attitude, coming into the room, a harquebus raised and pointed directly at Dom Enrique. His cloak was spangled with rain, but he took no notice of it. "Neither you nor your associate, Dom Enrique, have the advantage now. It would be best if you would leave. At once." He cocked his head toward the door.

"You would not shoot me," Dom Enrique declared, his head lifted in pride and defiance. "I am a nobleman. You wouldn't dare to shoot."

"Do you care to put that to the test?" Rogerio asked politely, as if seeking to be of service. "My master has charged me with the safety of this lady, and I will obey him to my last breath." There was nothing of the dramatic in this simple declaration, and for that reason it was the more believable.

Dom Enrique looked from Jasy to Rogerio, judging the likelihood of either servant taking action against them; then he glanced once at Acanna Tupac. "There will be another time, Orejon, when we will resume our negotiations," he promised her as he motioned to van Zwolle to follow him.

"Leave the sack," Rogerio reminded them in a gentle tone. "You do not want to be reported as thieves."

"Put it down," Dom Enrique snarled at van Zwolle, who reluctantly complied.

"We will provide you escort to the gate, to assure ourselves of your safety," Rogerio said, taking care to herd the two men toward the doors before they had time to recover themselves and strike back. As they crossed the wet patio to the gate, Rogerio added, "Just as I know there are those who watch the house of my master, so there are those who watch this house as well, and you would be ill-advised to forget it." With that he lifted the heavy latch and indicated the street beyond. "Those called to testify would not support your cause."

"Testify?" exclaimed van Zwolle, grabbing up the sack in defiance.

"Monks!" Dom Enrique jeered, and gave a dramatic toss of his head. "They would not speak against any hidalgo."

"Monks are not the only ones who watch. That sack will be reported. Her people guard her as well, and they know you do not mean to befriend her," Rogerio said courteously as he swung the gate closed in their faces, then turned back to look at Jasy, lowering his voice so that the two men outside could not overhear him. "With so many of the servants gone from this house, more watchers will be needed if Acanna Tupac is not to suffer this fate again."

Jasy nodded his understanding. "I will tell them in the marketplace that she is without a guard. The matter will be taken care of." He watched his footing with care, clutching his cane in one hand and clinging to his carbine with the other.

"Very good," Rogerio approved, knowing that Jasy would tend to the matter before nightfall. He put his hand on the latch once more, to satisfy himself it was secure, then turned back across the damp patio toward the front door of the house. "I thank you for coming to me, Jasy."

"Who else should I fetch but your master or you?" Jasy countered, making his way behind Rogerio. "The Black Robes would do nothing, the Guarda would side with Dom Enrique, if I were fool enough to bring them. And Don Ezequias is sitting for court today." He sighed once. "Besides, you and your master know the gracious lady and have stood by her before. I knew you would come if I asked it."

As Rogerio held the door for Jasy to enter, he said, "I am grateful for your decision, however you reached it."

"Your master has been a . . . good friend to the gracious lady. To all of us; I hoped you would come in his stead," he added conscientiously. "I suspect I would be dead now if not for him. As would the Yupanqui." He made a motion with his cane. "It may not be right for them to do as they do, but I will not deny them their happiness."

This avowal did not cause any remarkable change in Rogerio, who nodded once as much to acknowledge he had heard as to agree. "In times like these," he began, and then changed the subject. "The gracious lady will want to have something to eat, I suppose."

Jasy recognized this for the command it was. "I will tend to it. Since the Portuguese Dom took the other servants, the two of us who remain are doing the work of all. Neither of us cooks well." It was not quite an apology but more than an explanation.

Rogerio watched Jasy make his way down the hall toward the kitchen. He realized he ought to try to find staff to replace those who had been taken away. San Germanno would probably expect it of him. But that would mean more spies in Acanna Tupac's household, of that he was certain. Leaving her without sufficient staff invited other episodes like the one that had just ended. Spies or intruders—which were a more acceptable risk? Disliking the various notions that intruded into his thoughts, he returned to the reception chamber to find Acanna Tupac kneeling to gather up as much as she could salvage of the broken mask. Although his first impulse was to take over the work for her, he realized at once his help would not be welcome at this instance.

"There are others upstairs, of greater value." She spoke as if they had been discussing the matter for some time. "I should not have displayed these, I suppose, but I wanted to see them."

Rogerio at last removed his cloak and set his harquebus down on the wide table beneath the masks. "They are yours, gracious lady. And this is your house. Where else might they be displayed so well?"

"I have cared for them badly," she announced.

"Why? Because you showed them honor which others abused? Do you blame a man set upon by thieves because his horse is well-bred and his saddle is new?" His tone was diffident; his light-blue eyes were acute. He rubbed his face to get the last of the rain off it. "You did not know what those two men would do."

"But I knew that there were those who would not stop them doing it, those who would encourage them, or would do it themselves," she said, her self-condemnation thickening her words. As she removed the wrapped mask from the sack, she felt tears on her face, and that horrified her. To bring more shame upon herself, she accused herself inwardly.

"You did not ask them to do these things," Rogerio reminded her.

"No, but I let them know it could be done, by having the masks and the pottery out to be seen," she said, her hands clenching into fists.

"Instead of burying them in a hole, where they would quickly fall to ruin?" Rogerio shook his head, coming nearer to where she knelt "Then you would be doing the Vandals work for them."

She put her hands up in partial surrender. "That isn't—"

"Gracious lady, there are always those in the world who cannot endure to have beauty around them. When the beauty is foreign, it is the more unendurable." He bowed slightly and extended his hand to her. "Come. Jasy will do that for you."

"Jasy! Good, faithful Jasy." She wiped her eyes impatiently. "I am grateful to him for all he has done. He is loyal." She permitted Rogerio to escort her to her favorite chair, and huddled into it as soon as she felt the leather at her back. "And I am grateful to you, Rogerio."

"My master said I was to guard you," he responded, his voice almost completely uninflected.

"And I thank him for that, for giving you the task," she said, continuing with as much curiosity as circumspection, "But my true thanks are for you; you came when you were needed. San Germanno could not be certain of that, could he? You might be called to work against Spaniards. He has told me you are from Cadiz."

"A very long time ago. And I know what a crime is, even when Spaniards commit them," he said apologetically, not adding that he had left the Spanish-Roman city of Gades in the Year of the Four Caesars, and had not returned until his children's children were long dead. "I have been about the world with my master since then. I owe him far more than I will ever owe to the land of España."

To her chagrin, she was unable to stop weeping, though she managed to shed her tears without sobbing, which would have been intolerable. "You . . . you have been far? How far?" she asked, hoping his answer would distract her.

"Yes, we have gone many, many leagues, and for many, many years. Both of us." He bowed again slightly, and walked across the floor to the hearth, preparing to add more wood to the fire. The ground on which he trod was becoming dangerous, but refusing to speak with her could be more dangerous than answers. Rogerio hoped that Acanna Tupac would not guess too much.

"Tell me . . . what it was like." She continued to wipe her face dry as she listened. "Traveling so far, and with such a master."

"From the first?" he asked, preparing his answers quickly.

"Yes. And about his Rus wife," she added, and did not notice the startled look Rogerio gave her before he began.

Rogerio stared at the opposite wall, though his faded-blue eyes were held by visions long past. "We met in Rome," he said simply. "I had . . . another master at the time, who had used me cruelly, then abandoned me." In more than fifteen hundred years, he had not forgot the terrible moments under the stands of the Flavian Circus, when, with burned feet and hands, broken ribs and a cracked skull, he was certain he would die, the victim of the denizens who lived in the structure. "A man named Vardos was trying to kill me. Sanct' Germain stopped him, took me from danger, and brought me back to life." He meant the last quite literally, but trusted Acanna Tupac would understand it as metaphor.

"How did you come to be in Rome at all?" Acanna Tupac was finding it hard to concentrate on what Rogerio was saying, a constant, nagging dread of van Zwolle and Dom Enrique holding precedence in her thoughts, and her battle with tears continuing.

"There had been famine, and in its wake, disease. There was no work to be had, and no food. I had a few skills beyond farming. I could read and write and had been trained to keep financial records for the local market. I decided to become a bondsman in order to keep my family fed. I was well-paid for the bond, so that my wife and children would not end up beggars. The holder of my bond took me to Rome, although he said initially he would not take me out of España." He looked over his shoulder as Jasy brought bread and bean-paste into the reception room.

"I will bring wine directly," Jasy promised, using his cane to keep balanced as he lowered the tray onto the table. He left the room almost at once.

"An excellent man," Rogerio observed.

"He is. Now," said Acanna Tupac bluntly. "It took injury and San Germanno to make him so." She was already spooning out bean-paste onto a flat round of bread.

Rogerio was not surprised to hear the condemnation in her voice; there had been too many disappointments in her life for her to trust easily. "No one could make him something he was not able to be," Rogerio pointed out diffidently.

"So your master told me," she said, her tone sharp. "And while it may be true, the injury was necessary for it to develop." She noticed her hands were shaking and she put the round of bread down without eating.

Rogerio noticed this as well, and said, "After Rome, San Germanno traveled to the East, to Persia and beyond." He cleared his throat, trying to find a way to condense all the events into an apparently reasonable span of years. "I went with him, as I have gone with him on most of his travels."

"Most?" asked Acanna Tupac, encouraging Rogerio to continue.

"There have been a few times when . . . circumstances separated us, and may do so again." He shuddered at his memories, at the nearly two years he had searched for San Germanno when he had been missing in Saxony, or the six years San Germanno vanished from Tunis; Rogerio had finally found him again, enslaved in Moorish España, or the five long years in Poland—

Something of his thoughts must have been reflected on his face, for Acanna Tupac leaned forward. "What is it?"

It was unusual for Rogerio to be caught off-guard, and he did what he could to maintain his composure. "Certain events were more harrowing than others; the recollection of them is not pleasant," he said.

"Is that all? And you will say nothing more?" asked Acanna Tupac when Rogerio did not elaborate. "You tell me that and expect me to accept it? to bow my head and inquire no further?"

Rogerio was spared the necessity of answering quickly by Jasy's return with the unwelcome news that van Zwolle had smashed all the wine bottles. "There're only two bottles left," said Jasy, his eyes focused away from Acanna Tupac so that he would not have to see the distress he caused her. "And they're left because they're on the bottom of the pile, and the other bottles cushioned them. I've opened one of them. I'll bring you a cup shortly. They took the chicha." The Incan drink from fermented corn had become popular with many Europeans, and was easily turned into cash or amusement. "All four casques of it." With a gesture of commiseration, he turned and made his way back down the corridor.

Acanna Tupac sat very still. Then she said quietly, "I would curse them had they not already cursed themselves."

"They will bring themselves down, soon or late," Rogerio agreed without adding that he feared a great many others would suffer because of it.

"What loathsome vermin they are," Acanna Tupac said, her tone still hushed. "I wonder that the Spanish can tolerate them."

"The Spanish cannot tolerate them," said Rogerio, remembering a remark San Germanno had made. "That is why Dom Enrique and van Zwolle are in the New World and not the Old." He glanced at the broken pottery and mask fragments intermixed on the floor. "Men of their cut would not hesitate to smash anything. They do not care what it is, or where, if only they can have the satisfaction of destroying it. The Spanish—in fact, the whole Christian world—would rather they smash Peru than Europe."

"Is there not a war in Europe now?" Acanna Tupac asked, wanting to make sense of what she was hearing. "Men speak of it, shaking their heads."

"Yes, there is war in Europe. Between Christians," said Rogerio. From time to time he had thought there could never be peace in Europe, and had told San Germanno as much.

"Wars spawn men like van Zwolle and Dom Enrique," she told him, speaking her thoughts aloud. "Had Pizarro not come here in a time of war, he might not have conquered as readily as he did. Your master claims otherwise, and says that the conquest would have been much bloodier, but I am not convinced. If we had had no war among brothers, we might have held the Spanish off."

"Yes. War creates scavengers. Of all sorts." He could remember more of them than he liked to recall.

"And they are wished upon us, to do the work of the hidalgos," she finished for him. "What a fortunate thing that they do not have to soil their hands, that they have borlas such as these to do this work for them." She saw he did not understand her meaning. "Borlas," she repeated, indicating the short fringe on her shawl.

At that, Rogerio smiled slightly and said, "Fortunate for them, gracious lady, not for you."

She made a ritual gesture indicating an injustice had been permitted. "I am not safe here, in my country, with my people. I am a . . . a fugitive." She crossed her arms and grabbed her elbows as if to hold herself erect. "Nothing your master can do will change that, as I know he wants to. And any attempt to change it would place him in greater danger than he is now."

"No, he cannot change what is happening here, to you and all the rest," said Rogerio. "As he is aware." Admitting the last felt almost like a betrayal, but Rogerio spoke with conviction, hearing San Germanno's voice in his words.

Jasy brought in a goblet all but filled with wine. The scent of it was sharp, a reminder of its newness. "I will clean this up shortly."

"When you can," said Acanna Tupac, who did not want to add her temper to the burdens Jasy carried. She took a careful sip of the wine, pursed her lips at its greenness and set the goblet down. Her weeping had finally stopped and she was relieved not to have such disgrace to deal with.

"Gracious lady," said Rogerio after a few minutes of silence. "My master is known to be away from Cuzco now. Everyone knows he is away." He went on in a delicate way as if picking his steps over ice. "There can be no gossip about your doing this. No one will fault you if you decide to do as I suggest. Why not make use of his house in his absence. No," he went on, seeing her forbidding expression, "do not refuse until you consider the situation, gracious lady. I am certain if he were here, he would offer it to you, and take a room with the Presidencia, so that no idle tongues could wag. If your servants and my master's servants are numbered together, you may be fully guarded day and night."

"How do you mean?" asked Acanna Tupac, sitting very rigidly.

"I mean only that you cannot be kept safe here. Those men will return, and they may bring more of their kind with them." He walked around the room, indicating some of the valuable objects still remaining there.

"Don Ezequias . . . " she began, her words fading before she could complete her protestation.

"Don Ezequias is one man, and his soldiers answer to Don Alejandro before they answer to the Presidencia. I would not rely on those men if I were you, gracious lady." He did not apologize for his suspicions.

"But it isn't fitting. I do not want to be driven out of my house by creatures not worthy to touch my shadow." She lifted her chin as much in defiance as pride. "This is the one place I have said I would not leave."

"That may be, but attempts have been made to drive you out before now and it would be folly to think it will not happen again," he said. "I will arrange for a duenna, if you wish. My master would not expect you to be at his house without a chaperone."

She studied Rogerio's reserved features. "Do you really think that?" she asked archly. "At my age, and in my state, that I would need someone to protect my chastity?"

"I think if it was what you wanted he would do it," answered Rogerio quietly.

Her laughter was short and sad. "I thought you were not so blind as you seemed."

"If I have seemed blind," said Rogerio, hardly showing any surprise at this accusation, "I apologize."

Making a hasty gesture, Acanna Tupac looked around her reception room, trying to see it through eyes like van Zwolle's: what was worth looting, what could safely be smashed. "I do not know what to tell you, Rogerio," she said slowly a short while later. "I dislike being run out of my house; it offends me to think about it, and yet I cannot think of any way to remain here safely, as you have warned me. Staying here with nothing but three servants is folly. This house is mine, little as others respect that, and it has been a bastion for me. Now, without servants enough, it is a burden. But to go from it, frightened away by such men—" She gave a hard sigh, her face turning downward. "Still, you are probably right: they will return, or men like them. So I suppose I must consider accepting the invitation you have made, and hope that my people will not be too much offended by my accepting it, which I will have to do in the end, or something like it. Whether your master or the Presidencia opens his doors will make small difference to my people. It will be thought a bad sign by many of them, that I have had to seek refuge in the house of a foreigner, that no Inca could be found who could protect me." This last was accompanied by a deepening scowl. "I should need no one's protection."

"Better to have it than another visit from Dom Enrique, or one of the others like him," said Rogerio, a slight frown on his impassive features. Reluctantly he said, "My master has seen much of beauty destroyed, and every time, it has left a mark on his soul. But the scars he wears there for the loss of those he has . . . has loved, are far deeper than the rest." He came closer to Acanna Tupac, but not a step nearer than respect allowed. "To lose a house is a dreadful thing: to lose life is much worse."

She heard him out without comment, sipping at the wine in silence. Finally, with the goblet half-empty, she set it aside. "This is what San Germanno means when he tells me he is bound to me, isn't it?"

"In part, it is," said Rogerio quietly.

Acanna Tupac nodded once, decisively. "I'll tell Jasy to crate my things. Old Gemica can put my clothing in chests. Jasy will bring them to San Germanno's house. And he will not have to bother cleaning this." She indicated the broken wood and pottery on the floor. As she rose, she looked around the room, her eyes enormous as if to take in every detail of the room and fix it in her memory for all time.

"I am grateful for your decision," said Rogerio, knowing that San Germanno would have said the same thing.

"My servants will come to San Germanno's house this evening. Once this house is closed and locked." She did her best to say this steadily, but at the end, a quaver crept into her voice.

Rogerio sensed her distress, and did what he could to alleviate it. "Come, gracious lady. There is no reason to linger. I will convey your instructions to your servants once you are within my master's walls."

"No, there is no reason to stay," she said forlornly as she permitted him to escort her out of her reception room, along the corridor to the entrance, and from there out into the last of the rain.

Text of a letter from Frey Jeromo to Obispo Hernan Guarda.

In the name of Father, Son, and Holy Spirit, Amen, and the blessings of God be upon you, Su Excelencia, and may He guide you in wisdom for all of your days.

In accordance with the duties you have been gracious enough to grant me, I have maintained the watch you required upon the house of the foreigner Ragoczy. I have received two accounts from his neighbors in regard to his activities and I have made copies which accompany this report, the better for you to evaluate the danger this man represents.

As you are aware, the Incan noblewoman, Acanna Tupac, has been a guest in his house for more than a week, having taken refuge there just a single day before her house burned to the ground, which unfortunate event has made her continued residence necessary, for there is no other house for her to occupy with propriety. Not that the current arrangement meets with any standards of propriety, for it surely does not. And while receiving those in need is a charitable act, it is also suspect, for it is said that the two of them—Ragoczy and Acanna Tupac— are more than host and guest since his return four days ago from his purported errand to the village of Agua Pura. It is true that Sor Maria della Cruz has become a guest in the house as well, to serve as duenna for Acanna Tupac. Sor Maria is noted for her piety, and she is well-connected to the Loyolas as well as the Incan royalty, which is supposed to satisfy any who question the arrangement. But among the servants it is said that Sor Maria is an old woman who does not hear well and sees less, and would excuse an Incan noble anything. It is reported that Acanna Tupac and Ragoczy are often closeted together for a considerable amount of time, and no one to supervise them.

It is all very well to rely on the honor of noblemen, but I, for one, am not convinced that Ragoczy is Conde of anything, least of all San Germanno. It is no difficult thing to claim nobility where no man may question it. He may well be nothing more than a Hungarian adventurer taking advantage of the hospitality for which all Spaniards are famous. I recommend that inquiries be made through the appropriate channels to discover if this San Germanno truly exists in Hungary and if Ragoczy is in any way connected with it. It may be that he has some claim from the wrong side of the blanket.

The complaint that has been lodged against Dom Enrique Vilhao and his associate van Zwolle must surely be more vigorously questioned, for the claims that a nobleman of Portugal would so conduct himself as the complaint alleges are beyond possibility. Nor, I am convinced, would such a man as Dom Enrique permit any associate of his to behave as the Incan woman says he did. If Don Ezequias insists on acting upon the complaint, it would seem only fitting to give strenuous opposition to any punishment meted out by the Presidencia.

It may be advisable to conduct a thorough search of Ragoczy's house, for if monks search, they may better understand what they discover there than Don Alejandro's men would. Men who practice such arts as Ragoczy is said to must be dealt with most discreetly, since they draw on powers that are not of this world and forbidden by Heaven to faithful Christians. From what the neighbors report, there are things done within the walls of Ragoczy's house that no Godly man would tolerate, and which serve only to advance Ragoczy in the eyes of men, the better to bring damnation to those who are seduced by him. The cures he has wrought, if cures they are, may have been at the cost of the souls of those he treated. We must proceed carefully if we intend to discover the extent of his perfidy. For if it is true that this Hungarian is sworn to serve Satan as we serve God, then we must act quickly to remove his presence from our city and our lives. We have had few public burnings, but if this Ragoczy is as corrupt as I have come to believe he is, he may be one to serve as an example for all those who turn from the Redeemer and take the path into eternal darkness. I pray that salvation may come to Ragoczy before such an hour, but if it is to be, then we must bow our heads to God's will and rid ourselves of this contamination.

With all humility I pray my efforts will serve you in your glorious purpose, mi Obispo, advancing your work in God's cause in this place of benighted souls, and to that end I submit these words and myself to your use, and defer in this as in all things, to your judgment.

Deo gratias,
Frey Jeromo
The Preacher of San Domingo
The 21st day of June, in the Year of Grace 1644, by my own hand

12

Cold moonlight filled the northwest-facing chamber that had been set aside for Acanna Tupac's use, a light that limned the figures it touched and made the darkness vaster. San Germanno lay atop the coverlet, his black silken camisa his only protection against the chill. For the greater part of an hour, he had remained still, but now he was aware of the increasing receptivity in the woman beside him. Gently he drew the sleeping Acanna Tupac more close to him, his arm around her shoulder supporting her. He could just see the place on her throat where his lips had been. They had lain together since he had come to the apartment not long after midnight, to share her rapture and guard her slumber. After an hour of passionate intimacy, she was content to rest in his embrace. His dark eyes contemplated her face; he was filled with a welling sorrow at what he had discovered: he was losing her.

She moved, adjusting her fit against him, a faint smile passing over her face like a shadow. Her fingers brushed his silken camisa at the open neck, then his skin.

"Acanna Tupac?" he whispered.

Her voice was muzzy with sleep. "San Germanno?" Her eyelids fluttered but did not open, her movements slow, languorous.

"I am here," he said softly.

Her murmur was indistinct, yet her attitude was more alert as she grew more wakeful. The hand inside his camisa began to caress him in an idle, tantalizing way.

"It is wonderful, your touch." San Germanno let himself relish these ministrations for a short time, then caught her hand in his own, saying, "You recall what I told you three days ago, Acanna Tupac?"

She opened her eyes and looked directly at him. "You mean the warning about becoming one of your blood?" She ran the tip of her tongue over her upper lip in delicious anticipation.

He regarded her somberly. "Yes."

"I remember," she assured him in a more attentive way; she stretched a little, her body arching with the effort. "Unless my spine is broken, or my head struck off, or I burn, I will become like you upon my death, for having been your lover for as long as I have, and known you for what you are. That is what you told me, isn't it?"

"And this does not trouble you?" he asked, looking deeply into her eyes, and as he did, he discovered something within her that twisted cruelly as a knife in his vitals.

"No. It does not trouble me," she said steadily. "I fear nothing of what you have told me of those of your blood, for we have tales of those like you in our . . . fables they call them now. No, you do not frighten me; we Incas venerate our dead. Others frighten me, but not you. Next to what the Spanish have done to us, what can one vampire achieve?" Under his penetrating gaze she faltered. "You . . . you can love me twice in a night, can't you?"

This request startled and saddened him at once, for it served to confirm his knowledge that she was no longer bound to him as he was to her. A millennium ago he would have resented this; now he treasured the brevity of their passion all the more for its evanescence. "Yes. If that is what you want," he said, his voice low and musical.

"It is," she told him. "I want to be lost in you, to vanish. Just for now

I want to forget everything but what you give to me."

"I give you nothing but my love." His voice was as warm and caressing as his hands and eyes. "The rest is yours."

"You call it forth," she said. "You touch me where no other can reach, to the limits of my being." She fingered the silk of his camisa. "Touch me there now."

"Very well." He smiled down at her, his soul aching for her. "But do not forget the risk you run, now that you are past the point of change."

"That I will be like you when I die, if my spine is not broken, or I burn." She said it dutifully enough, but could not meet his penetrating eyes. "It doesn't matter, San Germanno. Truly, it doesn't matter."

"But it must," he said with some urgency, trying to quiet his own sense of futility, of impending loss. "You will have to make certain plans—"

"I have made what plans I need: I know what I must do," she said in a tone that brooked no further discussion. "Not now, San Germanno." By which she meant not ever.

He longed to find out what she had decided, and at the same instant dreaded what it would be, for once admitted, there would be no revocation of their parting, no calling her back from where she had banished herself. And their parting was imminent; her blood was eloquent with it. He perceived his loss of her in every word she spoke, in the weight of her touch, the rhythm of her breathing: he had offered her his life and she had chosen death. With the forlorn hope that he might rekindle her determination to survive along with her voluptuousness, he used all his understanding and all his will to summon up his strength to give her. His small, beautiful hands made a quest of her body, with a haste that seemed apart from him, though sharing his purpose to awaken what joy he could. To quell his precipitously rising dismay at his actions, he tangled his hand in her hair and drew her into a long, slow kiss that encompassed all his desire and all his compassion for her, endowing her with his tenderness in recompense for all she had endured as his esurience increased, driven by her ardor and despair. Even as he felt her need for him increase, he realized his entreaty was in vain. She was slipping away from him; this time she was not only sharing his love, she was saying good-bye.

As she broke their kiss she felt her resolve begin to weaken. "San Germanno. San Germanno. You make me wish for impossible things." She chided him gently, her finger tracing the line of his brow to the tail of his eye, then down his cheek to his jaw.

"What things are those?" he asked.

"Oh, things I know will not happen—cannot happen." Now her finger outlined his mouth, and she settled herself on the right side of his deep chest, as if she had changed her mind and wanted to sleep. "The past cannot return."

When she said nothing more, he kissed her forehead, and in a half-voice told her, "Acanna Tupac, what can I do."

"You've done more than I have any hope of—" She stopped, shivering at a sudden inward chill; she moved more closely against him. A thousand years before he would have asked what it was that made her tremble, but he had come to know that such answers were hard-won and rarely worth the animosity they evoked, so he stroked her hair, holding her, and let her decide what she would reveal. Finally she clung to him, saying, "You can do nothing, San Germanno."

It was the one answer he feared and it went through him like ice. His embrace did not falter and his tenderness remained constant, but within him, the earth gaped. "I can love you," he said quietly after a short while. "If that is what you still want from me."

At this, there was a change in her. She clasped her hands behind his neck and whispered, "Oh, yes, please do that."

Finally certain beyond all cavil that this was the last time he would know her passion, he devoted himself to exciting her profoundest responses. His small hands moved over her shoulders unhurriedly, lingering where she showed an increase in arousal, tempting her to greater pleasure. Only when her breathing had deepened did he slide the sheet back and begin to caress her breasts, using his mouth and tongue to add to and enhance what his hands accomplished, creating a celebration of her body and sweetly ravishing her senses. The emotions he had held at bay welled up in him with her desire, making him protective of her at the same time he was filled with desolation; he began to mourn her loss while he embraced her.

"San Germanno," she sighed, and put her hands over his. "You need not take so long if you would rather not."

He kissed her hands. "We have time, and I would rather," he said softly, and bent to kiss her mouth. His ministrations went on, growing in intensity but not speed. He lavished her body with every mode of gratification he could achieve, his delight in her the more poignant for his understanding that there would be no more nights with her, no rapture. The conviction that this was their last time together leant a force to their passion that could not be found otherwise, and sweet or bitter, it defined their love-making. This night would have to serve for all those they might have had; he sought her joyous delirium, his hands and lips discovering the very heart of her need so that his fervor met her fully awakened senses with reciprocity, reaching beyond sympathy to an intimacy so encompassing it held them both in its spell. All her flesh resonated to his nearness; his presence alone evoked her frenzy. It was an encounter made luminous with their shared yearning. With every touch, every exploration, he felt her quiver from her own elation and the finality of it all. Under his tantalization her body responded like an instrument of many voices; he devoted himself to satisfying her, bringing her twice to fulfillment before he put his mouth to her throat to share her glorious abandon and only true freedom which in other things so eluded her.

When Acanna Tupac was herself again she smiled up at San Germanno, her eyes wistful. "I did not realize before . . . "

He kissed her mouth again, lightly, lightly, and said in a deep, gentle tone, "It is all I can give you." The admission stung but he did not flinch from it. "If there is more you want—"

"And I thank you for it more than you will ever know," she said in a sudden ferocious rush. It was suddenly too difficult to face him, to see the expression in his fathomless eyes. She moved away from him then, retreating to the edge of the bed, lying with her back to him as if to make her spine a barricade against his tenderness.

He propped himself on his elbow, the deep folds of black silk gathering around his arm. "Is it what I am?" he asked her when the silence became taut.

"No. It is what *I* am," she said in a small voice.

He had nothing to counter this, but said, "What you are is part of me."

"Through the blood," she said with a slight nod.

"Yes. It is the essential part of you." He touched her shoulder and felt her shrug his hand away. "Acanna Tupac . . . "

"It will be light soon," she said, unable to find sterner words to send him away. "The servants will know."

"Servants always know, light or no light, no matter how careful you may be," said San Germanno with a touch of sardonic amusement. In a single easy movement he sat up. "But I will go."

In spite of her determination not to, she reached for his hand, catching it in hers as he started toward the dressing room door with its hidden connection to his own apartments. "San Germanno?"

He looked down at her. "Gracious lady?"

"There is a map. In my long cloak. You may need it." She tightened her hand on his. "Take it with you when you leave or destroy it. Do not let the Spanish have it. Give me your word."

"I will," he promised her.

Impulsively she kissed his hand. "I wish your love were enough."

It was difficult for him to answer. "And I." If only he had not lost the capacity to weep! His throat tightened and his dark eyes burned. He bent to kiss her one last time, but she motioned him away.

"No. Let this be enough." She moved to allow him to leave her bed.

The cold that went through him had little to do with that of the night. "If that is what you want of me."

"You had best go." As he reached the door, she added, "I cannot be as alone as you are."

There were a number of phrases that came to his mind, phrases of conciliation, of mitigation, of rebuke, but he spoke none of them aloud. He bowed his acquiescence to her in the Italian fashion, then left.

She lay still for some time as the moonlight faded into the pale violet of a winter's dawn; she thought of nothing at all, all her attention on the fleeting ecstasy she had had with San Germanno; already he seemed to be a distant memory. As the chamber grew brighter, she sighed once, murmured a few words to the old gods, and put herself to the task of getting ready: what she had to do now required all her concentration. Gemica had been sent to visit her family, so that Acanna Tupac would be able to do this alone. For this she would have no servant to assist her; it was a thing she must do for herself, a private ritual from a century ago, intended to fortify her spirit and define her purpose. The Spanish would not understand the significance of her actions today, but the Inca people would—that would have to be sufficient. There were a number of traditional phrases she knew to recite before she began, the prayers reserved for the dying. When the invocation was finished, she went to the ewer and basin set out for her and began to wash herself, starting with her feet and ending with her face. By the time she was done she was naked and shivering.

Next she anointed herself with oils from a small earthenware jar; the scent was sharp, pungent and acrid at once, and grew stronger as the heat of her body warmed it. The process was not a swift one and it took some time before she was ready to pull the long, pale alpaca shift over her, ending the goose-flesh and bringing welcome warmth.

She rubbed at her arms vigorously, encouraging them to sustain the heat she had awakened. When she was more comfortable, she took a loamy powder from a vial and sprinkled a little of it over her shoulders, reciting words that she had been taught almost four decades ago. Now that she was preparing herself, she felt amazingly calm; her whole being was at peace in her self-imposed condemnation. This was what she feared she would not be able to do, but now that she had started, the rite continued of its own volition. She went to the largest of the chests containing her clothes and opened it, reverently removing a shift and cloak of gorgeous feathers, so wonderfully iridescent that they seemed magical: they were her funereal vestments.

It took her the greater part of an hour to don these fabulous garments, for there was a ceremony to perform at every stage; she kept to it meticulously, reciting the prayers steadily as they became necessary. Her purpose gave her strength when she encountered resistance within herself, inspiring her to go on. "It will not be long; the hours go quickly," she vowed to the air. "When the sun drops behind the highest mountain and the shadow reaches the bridge over the Apurimac to Choqquerquirau, it will be time." In spite of herself she trembled, and then admonished herself for her cowardice.

Toward mid-morning, as she recited the old texts of homage to Viracocha, who ruled earthquakes and gorges, she was interrupted by one of San Germanno's servants, a woman of middle years who worked in the kitchen and garden. "You have eaten nothing, Yupanqui," she said as she stood in the doorway, her face showing concern; she recognized the feather garments.

"I am not hungry," Acanna Tupac replied.

"Shall I prepare a meal for you?" asked Leilla.

"No, though it is kind of you to offer." She would be gone shortly, in any case, and it was senseless to prepare a meal for her now. "Do not bother."

This was more than Leilla could bear. She twisted the sash of the apron she wore and said, "If you are ill, the master will take care of you, gracious lady. He has great skill. Let me send for him. Please."

"I am not ill, Leilla," said Acanna Tupac, rather more curtly than she had intended; she repeated, "I am not hungry."

Fearing that this denial only confirmed her worst suspicions, Leilla backed out of the room and went to the locked door of San Germanno's study. She rapped on it twice before her summons was answered. "I regret having to disturb you, master," she said to him, making a little bow to show respect. Glancing at his face she thought she had never seen him look so tired—or was it worn, and not tired?

"You would not do so capriciously," San Germanno said as he came out of his study into the corridor, very grand in Hungarian dolman and mente of heavy black silk edged in red, with a collar of silver and rubies supporting his device, the eclipse, worked in silver and a rare black moonstone. "Something must be wrong."

Now that she faced him, she struggled to put words to her apprehensions. "I do not know if . . . nothing may be . . . I have not to . . . There is no reason . . . But it is the Yupanqui," she blurted out at last.

San Germanno gave her his full attention, his fine brows drawn together in concentration and worry. "What about Acanna Tupac?"

Having spoken so hurriedly, Leilla did not know how to continue; it would not be appropriate or fitting to complain of Acanna Tupac to San Germanno, for that would bring disgrace to the Yupanqui. She made an ineffective motion with her hands. "She does not want to eat." As she said this, she fully expected her master to dismiss the matter with a few words of reassurance, so she was doubly alarmed when she saw his frown deepen.

"When did you speak to her?" he asked, his words rapping out like hard rain.

"Not long ago. I went to her chamber, since she has not left it." Again she hesitated, hoping her growing anxiety was uncalled-for. She was not certain she ought to mention the ceremonial garments Acanna Tupac had donned.

"Is she unwell?" San Germanno asked, suddenly fearing she might have done herself harm.

"No," Leilla answered, her tone sufficiently dubious that San Germanno was more alarmed than before.

"Then what is it?" San Germanno prompted, concealing his increasing apprehension as best he could.

The words tumbled out of her. "She is dressed for death, for sacrifice."

"Sacrifice," he echoed: a sacrifice meant that he had not realized the extent of her despair. Acanna Tupac was not going to leave Cuzco, she was preparing to make an example of herself: everything he had experienced of her made him certain of this.

"And she doesn't want to eat." It sounded feeble now that she said this aloud.

San Germanno nodded twice, becoming more convinced of her intentions with every breath. "Did she say anything else?"

"Only that she isn't ill," said Leilla. "She seemed pale to me."

It was not so long ago—less than two centuries—since Demetrice had had such a look to her, San Germanno remembered, not needing to see Acanna Tupac's face to recognize her purpose: it was now only a question of what she intended to do and how soon she would do it. He realized that Leilla was expecting something more from him. "Should I speak with her? Would that help?" It was more a question to himself than to the servant, but she answered it.

"If she will not come down after siesta, it might be best if you would," she said, her eyes lowered so as not to offend him.

He was about to agree to this but could not rid himself of the urgency which now possessed him. "I will speak with her now."

"Oh, dear," Leilla fretted, although relieved that something would be done. "Do not say I told you of her . . . condition, will you, Señor, please? It would vex her to know I have done this."

"If that is what you wish, I will not," said San Germanno, feeling a rush of sympathy for this servant faced with such an awkward predicament. "I will explain myself in another way." He drew a key from the wallet hanging from his vest, stepped further into the corridor, and locked the door to his study.

Just as Leilla knocked on San Germanno's study door, Acanna Tupac took the ritual headdress out of the chest where Jasy had packed it. The elaborate mask with its stylized bird face stared sightlessly back at her, the caverns of its eyes as ominous as the sockets of a skull, the gaudy plumage rising above the mask magnificent to see, a reminder of the ineffable in life, beyond life. Rainbow colors streamed around the bird face, making it look capable of flight. Acanna Tupac performed a ritual reverence to the mask, then took it, drawing a drab canvas cloak about her finery as she hurried out of the chamber, bound for the back of the house and the servants' door. As she went, she hoped that no one would try to stop her. She would not be willing to explain her choice to Jasy or the others if they challenged her departure; it was time to be gone.

San Germanno reached her chamber shortly after Acanna Tupac had left it. He called her name twice, although he knew it was useless; she was gone—he realized it with the same certainty as he understood the principles of mathematics, and felt it with the same intensity that he experienced the pull of his native earth. He saw that one of the ceremonial headdresses was missing, which served to confirm his conviction. She was gone and would not return. He had failed to restore her

desire to live; Acanna Tupac was lost to him, to his blood. The stark-
ness of that realization gripped him like a viper's jaws. Abruptly he flung
himself out of the room and started down the rear stairs of his house,
following the path she must have taken. His chase might be futile, but
he could not keep from making the attempt to find her. He hoped she
had not yet left his property; if she had he would have to be more public in his actions.

As he reached the kitchen, he called out several sharp orders, and
in a moment was surrounded by the servants of the household as well
as the three remaining servants of Acanna Tupac. "The Yupanqui is
missing, and so is one of her feather head-dresses," he told them, making no effort to soften the blow of this announcement.

"Missing?" said Leilla breathlessly, her hand going to her throat.
"How can she be missing?"

"She must have left this house immediately after you spoke with her,
and I must suppose it was of her own volition," San Germanno told Leilla,
doing his best not to make the statement an accusation. "Did she give
you any indication of what she was doing, or where she was going?"

"She only said she did not want a meal," Leilla said, tears standing
in her eyes. "She wasn't hungry."

"Or so she claimed," said Jasy, a rebuke in his tone as he looked at
the other servants, as if Acanna Tupac's departure had been engineered
by them.

"Did anyone see her leave?" asked San Germanno, knowing the answer.

There was a ragged chorus of denials.

"Is there some festival or holy day she would observe today? Would
she wear a headdress for such an occasion?" Rogerio suggested, doing
his best to preserve a calm demeanor.

"There are festivals every day," said Gemica, her old voice cracking.
"Each day is sacred to a god."

"And today?" San Germanno asked quickly. "Whose day is this?" He
needed to know why she had chosen this day.

"Viracocha's," said Jasy promptly. "He rules—"

"Earthquakes and gorges," San Germanno finished for him. He
looked directly at Acanna Tupac's servant. "How was Viracocha honored, before the Spanish came."

"With sacrifice, of course, in honor of his power," said Jasy, and went
on as he saw San Germanno gesture his impatience. "On the holy days,
offerings were dropped from bridges. The High Priest would offici-

ate, and the Inca as well. There would be singing and—"

"What kind of offerings?" San Germanno demanded, anticipating the answer.

Jasy shrugged and looked down the corridor as if expecting the ancient procession to appear there. "In good times, flowers and pottery, occasionally feather garments, sometimes llamas and alpacas. In bad times . . . " His voice became a whisper. "In bad times, captives and slaves were offered."

"Slaves and captives," said San Germanno softly. "No others?"

Jasy would not look at him. "Not for a long time, not since the beginning of our power." He coughed. "There is a tale about Titu Inca, from centuries ago, that he preserved Sacsahuaman fortress by giving Viracocha two of his lesser wives, and the High Priest, as an offering. But that is only legend." He added the last swiftly, looking around at the other servants as if he expected them to argue with him.

"A legend every child of ten knows?" San Germanno suggested. "And where did this sacrifice take place?" Even as he asked, he knew where it must be. He would not be able to stop her now, though he could probably overtake her. He had neither the position nor the authority to thwart her; he would have to use every indication of his own position and authority to go after her without interference from the Spanish or the Incas.

"The bridge to Choqquerquirau," said Jasy quietly, doing his best to ignore the sharp looks of condemnation given him by the other servants. "The sacrifice was made when the bridge first fell into shadow," he muttered.

"Symbolic sundown," San Germanno said, and felt himself go cold at the very word. When the sun was gone, his full strength returned; he did not need to depend entirely on his native earth lining the soles of his boots to sustain him. Her farewell was intended not just for her own people, but to him as well, to his nature. Futile it might be, he admonished himself inwardly, but he could not stand by while Acanna Tupac made such an ultimate, desperate gesture. He signaled Rogerio. "My grey—the nine-year-old. Saddled and ready. At once."

"I will attend to it, my master. And I will charge your pistols, if you wish." His unruffled calm made this recommendation less outrageous than it might have been.

"Yes. Good; and one of you, Leilla or Gemica, look through the Yupanqui's chamber, to see if she has taken anything else with her. It does not matter how small a thing it may be," said San Germanno, striding out of the kitchen toward the stairs that led up to his private quarters on the floor above. He did not let himself think of what he was about to do, for that would serve only to discourage him. Instead he put his attention to providing the appearance of high station, formidable enough to keep all but the most foolhardy from stopping him. He chose his garments with care—not his usual Hungarian dolman and mente now, but a Roman ensemble of black sculptured velvet with a square, point-lace collar edged in silver with slashed sleeves lined in deep-red satin. Venetian breeches of the same sculptured velvet were secured below the knees with ruby studs, and his black silken leggings were all but concealed by high boots that were lined in the soles and heels with his native earth. At last he took the wide red-and-silver sash of the Order of Saint Stephen of Hungary and fixed it in place with the diamond brooch in the shape of his eclipse device, instead of the diamond starburst of the Order. He drew on black Florentine gloves before he strapped on his sword and reached for the wide-brimmed black hat ornamented with a silver band and a small red plume. Had he possessed a mirror—or had that mirror been of any use to him—he would have seen that he was by far the most elegantly dressed man in Cuzco, a man most soldiers would hesitate to impede. As it was, he paid no heed, but hurried out of the room, went down the back stairs, and along the corridor toward the rear of the house.

"Conde," said Jasy, very startled at San Germanno's appearance. Any doubts he might have had about San Germanno's rank disappeared at the sight of him now. Bearing more than clothing made his station in life undeniable.

"Is there a road Acanna Tupac is more likely to take than another?" asked San Germanno, apparently unaware of the stir he was making among the servants, four of whom had come into the kitchen. One of them stared openly, the others were less obvious in their examination.

"The old road, the ones our people built," he said, waving in the direction of the Sacsahuaman ruins. "If she is fulfilling the ancient ritual, she will have to take that road."

"And is she fulfilling the ritual, do you think?" San Germanno inquired, inwardly convinced that she was.

"Gemica says one of the feather cloaks is missing," Jasy reported uneasily. "That and a plain traveling cloak, I think to protect the feather cloak from the dust of the road."

"And to be less visible," he confirmed. "The road: is it still safe?" asked San Germanno, recalling the damage done to it by Spanish wagons and earthquakes. In the last two years, parts of it had fallen away, under-cut by water and neglect.

"It is, for someone on foot who knows the way and who is able to cross the two slides," Jasy told him, looking over his shoulder as if afraid of what might be overheard. Satisfied that no one was paying them much attention, he said, "You will not find her on that road."

"Why not?" asked San Germanno sharply.

"She knows the places to hide, and there are many of them." He hes-itated, looked down at the legs San Germanno had made for him, and sighed. "It would be wisest to go directly to the bridge. It will be eas-ier on your horse, as well. If she will be stopped, you may stop her there, not on the road."

He studied Jasy's face intently for a long moment, then, satisfied with what he saw there, he said, "I thank you."

At this Jasy looked embarrassed. "I . . . there is no need, Señor."

"You will have to forgive me if I think otherwise," said San Germanno quietly. He nodded to Jasy and was about to depart when Jasy made a sign indicating he had something more to add; San Germanno waited.

"The road is easy by day and difficult by night," Jasy told him hur-riedly. "You will need more time returning than you need to reach the bridge."

San Germanno recalled the way he and Acanna Tupac had returned from the burial of the High Priest; the path had been treacherous in places, and was undoubtedly worse now. "I will be careful, for the Yu-panqui's sake." With that, he made his way to the stables, the heels of his boots giving a sharp report with every step.

Rogerio was waiting, the grey Andalusian saddled, bridled, long mane and tail gleaming. "I have let him run his fidgets out; he will not misbehave on the road. You will need to keep him collected." He looked at San Germanno appraisingly as he handed him a charged pis-tol. "You anticipate opposition?"

"Perforce," said San Germanno tersely as he took the reins and swung up into the saddle. "I should return before midnight. If I am not back by morning, go to Don Ezequias."

"And tell him what?" Rogerio asked.

"Tell him I have gone in search of Acanna Tupac, who is missing." San Germanno was about to give the grey his head.

"You went to look for her kitted out for a Papal audience?" Rogerio inquired, hoping San Germanno would provide a reason for his finery that Don Ezequias could accept.

"She has taken ceremonial clothes with her, she could be in immediate danger because of it, and she is of royal blood," San Germanno replied with deliberate vagueness. "All of which is true."

"I hope you find her," said Rogerio, gesturing his acquiescence.

San Germanno touched the brim of his hat in agreement, nudged his grey with his leg and set the horse to a slow, extended trot toward the road. He could feel the well-trained, agile nine-year-old resist the urge to run, keeping instead to his magnificent passage as they threaded their way to the main plaza. As he passed Los Sacramentos, a number of monks appeared, intent on marking his progress, a few critical of his fine clothing and glittering jewels, most openly staring. San Germanno doffed his hat to show respect to the Catedral, then replaced it as he reached the Residencia and the road out of Cuzco leading to the bridge to Choqquerquirau.

There were few other travelers on the road at this time of day, and so San Germanno held the grey to a collected canter until the horse showed signs of flagging as the slope grew steeper. He told himself that his horse walking moved faster than Acanna Tupac on foot, but he could not wholly convince himself that he would arrive ahead of her. Reluctantly San Germanno pulled his mount to a walk as he scrutinized the area around him, looking for anyone who might tell him where Acanna Tupac was, hoping he could persuade her to abandon her intentions, although the blood-bond he had with her was eloquent, and he knew it was no longer possible to turn her from the path she had chosen for herself.

Finally, as the sun dropped lower in the sky and the first towering shadows angled across the steep slopes, San Germanno caught sight of the bridge, about half a league ahead of him. There were two men on burros crossing it, one of the burros carrying a double load of wood, the other bearing a huddled figure on its back. As San Germanno watched, the men paused in the middle of the span while the rider slipped off the burro. As the men moved on with their animals, the cloaked figure remained at the center of the bridge.

"Acanna Tupac," San Germanno said softly, and clapped his heels to the grey's sides, swaying a little as the Andalusian obediently bounded forward, drawing on the stamina for which the breed was famous.

She must have sensed his nearness, for she turned her head in his direction, then visibly shook off his hold as she shed her muffling cloak, letting it fall away into the gorge like a huge bird with a broken wing. Now the slanting sunlight struck her feather cloak; it blazed with color.

She lifted the headdress into place. Then she raised her arms and the colors rippled.

At the far end of the bridge, the men with burros stopped to watch. San Germanno noticed that other men had come down to the roadway, many of them standing with heads uncovered, their faces reverent, the last of the faithful: they knew what was coming and understood its meaning, just as Acanna Tupac had intended they should. The only sound around them was the moan of the wind.

San Germanno at last reached the bridge. He vaulted off his horse, letting the grey find a place to stand while he rushed onto the swaying bridge, only to stop still as she held up her hand to him. "Acanna Tupac!" he called to her, and heard his voice echo in counterpoint to the distant rush of the Apurimac. "Do not do this. For your people if not for yourself. The Spanish win if you do."

"The Spanish win if I do not," she said with serenity. "A Pyrrhic victory."

The first long shadow touched the bridge as San Germanno strove to call her back to him. "Then let me help you stand against them."

"It is too late for that," she said, adding in a clear, carrying voice. "Go away, San Germanno. This does not concern you."

"If it concerns you, it concerns me," he corrected her. It was disconcerting to hear her voice coming from that fantastic head-dress, and unnerving to try to find her eyes in the face of the bird mask. She was more than three dozen paces away, too far for him to reach her in a sprint, even with his preternatural speed. He remained where he was, saying to her, "You are blood of my blood now. There is no separation for us but the True Death."

"Then I release you from your bond and tell you good-bye, San Germanno," she said tranquilly as she drew a small metal case from under her magnificent cloak. "I loved you," she said as she struck.

San Germanno recognized the flint-and-steel at once, and realized what she intended. *"NO!"* he shouted, the protest wrung from the limits of his soul. He reached out, lunging toward her, already too late, already feeling the bridge swing with her movements, as the flames eagerly added their brightness to the feathers and Acanna Tupac arched over the rail of the bridge, to fall, burning, in the iridescent cloak of feathers and fire, to the torrent far below.

Text of a report prepared by Obispo Hernan Guarda and presented to Presidencia Don Ezequias Pannefrio y Modestez.

To the most respected and wise Presidencia de Cuzco, Don Ezequias Pannefrio y Modestez, the greetings and blessings of Obispo Hernan Guarda, with the hope that the information provided here will aid in the magisterial duties of your office.

As you are aware, the gracious lady Acanna Tupac's death of two weeks since has caused much disruption among the native people here, made the worse because only portions of her body have been found and she cannot be laid to Christian rest, or given those permissible pagan rites without the whole of her recovered. It is most troubling that only a portion of her corpse has been found. That is a matter for Don Alejandro's men to deal with, certainly, but it is hoped that you, Presidencia, are aware of the rumors concerning the body: that her bones have been taken for pagan rites, or, more terribly, for sorcerous ones.

So much of her ruined house has been ransacked since she left it that we cannot determine for certain what of hers she took with her and what has been plundered. Now the walls are crumbling. I am convinced that for the barbarian who has taken her goods we need look no farther than the man who offered his supposed hospitality. Her few servants have not been able to present us with a list of all the items missing. In my opinion, it was Ragoczy's intention to have all her belongings one way or another, and what she would not offer him willingly he determined to take. His accusations of Dom Enrique and his partner van Zwolle are nothing more than attempts to divert our attention to persons other than himself. Men at the barracks, including Diego Herrero, Matteo Maldonado, Lazaro Escaso, and Martin Vigaracimos have assured us that such charges against Dom Enrique are ridiculous and without any foundation whatsoever.

Little though you may wish to consider the matter, Presidencia, it is clear to us that your foreign friend, Francisco Ragoczy styling himself Conde de San Germanno, is certainly indirectly if not directly implicated in her losses and her death. You are aware of their illicit dealings together. You have turned your eyes from these truths out of regard for a friendship that does not deserve the honor you do it. This man has taken advantage of your sensibility and tolerant ways.

We have an account from one Gerard Toulon, a resident of the village of Agua Pura, a Frenchman by birth, who attests to the fact that when San Germanno came to the village to help after severe mud-slides had damaged the town, causing injuries and death, that this Ragoczy was able to return many of the residents to health. This would be a laudable thing were it not that too many of them recovered. It is the opinion of this Toulon that the recoveries are the result of witchcraft or something far worse than witchcraft. He has sworn that he has seen Ragoczy bring dead men back from the grave. Surely any man with such pride as the desire to emulate the miracles of Our Lord must be regarded as dangerous, for it is only through an alliance with Heaven or Hell that such things come to pass. It is apparent to all but the most naïve that Ragoczy is not one of Heaven's servants. A notarized copy of Toulon's statement is appended to this, for your perusal.

The neighbors of this so-called San Germanno, Don Gregorio Calderon y Mazez, attests to the fact that he, too, has witnessed cures provided by Ragoczy that were well beyond the capacity of human physicians. There are other, equally disturbing, matters that have come to his attention. He claims that he has seen Ragoczy abroad at hours of the night when no worthy man would step outside his gate, and has noted that he has never seen this man take a meal, which he believes is an indication that Ragoczy's sustenance comes from Satan's table, for he is not a man of Christian habits. His account is also appended to this.

For those who witnessed the death of Acanna Tupac, some are saying now that Ragoczy lit her cloak afire with a bolt of lightning from his hand, and cast her into the river himself, to strengthen his powers. They are saying that he compelled her to wear the ritual robes of her people to show how much stronger his magic is than theirs, and that he deliberately waited until she was on the bridge to confront her. We know he was determined to do this, to make a contest of their wills. He pursued her onto the bridge, which no other man dared to do, and it is known that he set off after her when she left his house. He made no secret of the fact—he all but paraded himself through the streets, in garments that held the eye of all who saw him pass. Those soldiers who saw him did not think it would be wise to approach him, for it would appear he wore the sash of a military Order, and his clothing was that of a man of princely rank. To lay hands on such a man would bring dishonor to the soldier who did it. Roman clothes and Hungarian honors! How he came by such things we may only guess. The rest who saw him that day have only related they have never seen anyone so grand other than Obispo Puente y Sello celebrating High Mass, which is a blasphemous notion in itself. It is known that he was displeased at her departure. Whatever his participation in the events on that bridge, he cannot be thought blameless in the death of Acanna Tupac, or the subsequent looting what was left of her house.

In my own instance, I have seen this man attempt to cure an injured monk lying on the sacred floor of the Catedral. Summoned here, and coming most reluctantly, Ragoczy claimed to be unable to help the man, and permitted him to die. It is my supposition that the great powers Ragoczy draws upon cannot be invoked or employed within the walls of Christian sanctuaries. If he had saved the monk, I would not have been so willing to question the source of his abilities, and for that laxness I will have to answer to God. But his incapacity to provide a cure within Los Sacramentos indicates to me that he must be considered a dangerous and profane man.

For the honor of your House and of España, think, Don Ezequias, of what this foreigner has done. Think of the excesses he has committed. Think of all he has done, and his reasons for doing it. Wealth may shield a man from justice in this world, but God cannot be bought off with gold and favors; it is not your place to put worldly power ahead of the obligations we have to God. It is known that this Ragoczy has much wealth, and for that reason alone he is forgiven much that would have condemned a lesser man. Detain him and permit those of us in the Church to question him about how he comes by the skills he possesses, and find out what he has done with the body of Acanna Tupac. It is not my place to order you to do this, but I pray you will set aside the sophistry of pleasing conduct and perform the duty you should have fulfilled months ago by arresting Ragoczy and confining him securely.

In the name of Our Savior and Holy Church, I earnestly implore you to remove this ungodly man from the society of Cuzco so that he can no longer advance his heretical cause through the good graces of your sponsorship. You besmirch your high office and the Viceroyalty of Peru by your continued indulgence of this miscreant. I eagerly await word of your decision regarding this man.

> *With my prayers and*
> *In the Name of Father, Son, and Holy Spirit,*
> *Hernan Sigismundo Bernal Guarda*
> *Obispo, Los Sacramentos*
> *By the hand of Frey Rafael, on the Feast of San Procopios,*
> *in the Year of Grace, 1644, at Cuzco*

13

Don Ezequias had the grace to look embarrassed as San Germanno came into the reception room. He bowed formally. "I regret that I must call upon you in this manner," he said, pausing to clear his throat. He had risen from his siesta less than an hour ago and had set himself this unpleasant task to resume his working day.

"And what manner is that?" San Germanno asked him, his manner as cordial as it was oddly distant; he returned the bow in the French style.

The Presidencia sighed. "Unfortunately, I am here officially." He took a long breath. "There is a warrant issued for your—"

"Arrest," San Germanno finished for him. "Yes, I thought so." Today he wore unrelieved black but for a small red rosette of mourning on the high Russian collar of his mente. He indicated one of the heavy oaken chairs. "Sit down, my friend. I will have my manservant bring you some refreshments."

Don Ezequias stared at him. "I am here to arrest you, to notify you that charges have been made against you," he said more firmly, as if he feared San Germanno had misunderstood him. "You will have to be guarded and prepare to surrender yourself."

"Yes," said San Germanno affably. "But it need not be this instant, need it? Permit me to do you the honor you deserve." He bowed in the direction of the chair again.

"I . . . that would not be prudent," said Don Ezequias, nonplussed at this casual response; he had expected protestations or angry denials, but this outward self-possession baffled him. He looked at San Germanno with a measure of curiosity mixed with wariness. "How did you know about the warrant?"

"I did not, until you spoke. It was a reasonable guess, given what is being whispered, and the events of the last month." He stared across the room to a branch of candles, and there was something haunted in the back of his enigmatic eyes.

Don Ezequias had never felt more ill-at-ease in his life. Flinging off his wool cloak, he paced over to the chair, walked around it as if expecting it to burst into flame, then turned toward San Germanno. Although he was a head taller than his foreign friend, he could not shake off the impression that San Germanno dominated the room; perhaps it was the smaller man's disquieting air of authority that caused it. He spread his hands to show his helplessness, his expression one of chagrin. "They are permitting me to do this, to keep from causing trouble for all of us. They do not want to have to send soldiers. Don Alejandro has said he does not want to arrest a member of the Order of Saint Stephen of Hungary. He says only heros are of that Order."

"That is gracious of Don Alejandro, and it would cause less of a stir to have me seen with you than being escorted by soldiers. The guard posted will cause enough comment," said San Germanno with an ironic note in his beautifully modulated voice. Again he indicated the chair. "Do, please, sit, my friend."

"It is not appropriate," said Don Ezequias, dropping into the chair as he spoke.

"Nevertheless, you will do me that honor, since it may well be some time before I am in a position to offer you hospitality again." San Germanno smiled slightly. "Wouldn't you agree?"

"If you insist," said Don Ezequias, his eyes moving restlessly, not lighting on any single object for any length of time and avoiding San Germanno altogether. He did not like the position he had been thrust into; San Germanno was adding to his ambivalence.

"Tell me," San Germanno said, making no effort to calm his visitor, "what is it that the Obispo wishes from me? Do not look so surprised. It must be the Obispo who commands you to arrest me. You come on his authority or the Corregidor's, for anyone of lesser rank could not compel you to this course, and I doubt Don Vicente would be overly concerned about me." The light, ironic tone was underlaid with purpose. He clapped his hands and in a moment Rogerio came into the reception room. "Wine and pastry for my guest."

Rogerio bowed and withdrew.

"It will be hard to explain why I accepted—" Don Ezequias said, feeling the bands of his collar suddenly tight.

"Then say nothing," San Germanno recommended. He went to face the hearth where a few logs smoldered. "The Obispo has been listening to the things they are saying in the market, I suppose. And is willing to believe them, to suit his own ends."

"I . . . I fear he may be, yes," said Don Ezequias miserably. "The report I have been given is . . . is credulous, or so it seems to me." He tried to shift in the chair to a more comfortable position but it eluded him. "I have draughted a reply, hoping to answer his charges in a satisfactory way, but—" He cocked his head.

"As you say: but." San Germanno continued to look down at the embers. "The Obispo is determined, and he will not allow any disputing the matter. He has been persuaded to take my presence as a personal affront, and will not permit the situation to continue, although it is wholly of his making." There had been so many times he had made preparations, as he was doing now, to leave a place hurriedly: Nineveh, Hydros, Trebizond, Rome, Poetovio, Crete, Baghdad, Tunis, Toledo . . . The list ran in his thoughts, filling him with melancholy. Lyons, Milano, Lo-Yang, Fiorenza, Moskovy . . . He had never been able to convince himself beyond doubt that leaving was a wise course to follow, even when he had no alternative than discovery and death, the True Death.

"The Obispo has been influenced by many," said Don Ezequias. "Not all of them as noble in their motives as they purport to be. They support Obispo Guarda's purpose, and so he does not question their accounts too closely." He rose abruptly and took a turn about the room. "Dom Enrique has claimed that you were the one who . . . " His words trailed off.

"He claims I have done what he did, that I looted the belongings of Acanna Tupac," San Germanno said without bitterness but without sympathy, at last turning to face Don Ezequias. "It is a workable ploy if no one challenges it too closely. And we know that no one is apt to challenge it."

"Truly," said Don Ezequias bitterly. He rubbed his chin, regarding San Germanno closely. "You have none of her things here?"

San Germanno's smile lacked warmth and his dark eyes glittered. "On the contrary, I have a great many of her things. She brought them here to preserve them from men like Dom Enrique." He resisted the urge to touch his mente where he had concealed the map she had entrusted to him. "My manservant gave you an account of what Dom Enrique and van Zwolle did at Acanna Tupac's house while I was away," he reminded him carefully.

"Yes," said Don Ezequias, his hand resting on the hilt of his sword. "And I believe his account. But I may be the only man in Cuzco—other than you—who does. Dom Enrique has been spending time at the barracks, filling the ears of the men there with tales. They believe him because they want to believe him."

San Germanno shrugged to conceal the alarm he felt. "And Don Alejandro? does he listen to these accounts?"

"He tells me he does not," Don Ezequias answered circumspectly. "But many of the others do, and he listens to them."

"Naturally enough," said San Germanno, his face showing only a slight frown, his mouth a stern line. He rubbed his eyes with his thumb and middle finger. "I suppose I would be foolish to expect otherwise."

"I fear so," said Don Ezequias, looking around as Rogerio returned to the reception room bearing a tray. "I assure you again, this is not necessary, San Germanno. You have ample reason to treat me as your foe."

"Possibly; but if I fail to be a proper host, there will be whispers in the marketplace within the hour that neither of us would want," he said, his manner smoothly polished and sardonic. Knowing how troubled Don Ezequias was, he relented, adding, "And it provides me a short while to enjoy your company without having to consider every word I speak, or assume that there is someone making note of all meetings. After tomorrow that will no longer be the case, will it."

At this last, Don Ezequias looked appalled. "They would not subject you to such examinations," he protested.

"Possibly not," San Germanno responded in polite disbelief. "But I must consider the alternatives." He watched as Rogerio set out the wine carafe, a goblet, and three pastries on the table facing the fireplace. "I hope my cook is up to his usual standard."

"You have always received me nobly," said Don Ezequias, trying to rise to the occasion and making a botch of it. He went to the table as Rogerio bowed and withdrew. His face was somber as he looked at the food left for him.

"If you would prefer chocolate?" San Germanno suggested, noticing Don Ezequias' hesitation.

He shook his head abruptly at once. "No. This is more than satisfactory, as you must know." He lowered his eyes. "I feel I am taking advantage of you—imposing."

"On a condemned man?" San Germanno ventured easily, his composure fully restored. "Even if I were such, you would not be imposing, my friend." He bowed slightly, enough to be cordial, not so much as to be ingratiating. "Come. While the opportunity remains."

"Was losing her very hard?" Don Ezequias asked suddenly, then reached to pour wine in order to mask any dismay his question might have caused.

San Germanno again looked at the dying fire. "Yes," he answered simply.

"I feared so," said Don Ezequias quietly. He broke one of the pastries in half and took a small bite. There was no savor to it for him, but he smiled his approval. "Obispo Guarda has required me to report the details of this . . . interview to him."

"Has he." San Germanno was not surprised. "I suppose you will have to, then."

Don Ezequias looked shocked. "I have no desire to do it. I am ashamed to have to do it, but—" He waited, as if asking San Germanno to provide him a reason to defy Obispo Guarda.

"I cannot blame you for that," San Germanno said wryly. "Dealing with Obispo Guarda is not pleasant." He regarded Don Ezequias with a speculative air. "I think it might be wisest, however, to do as he asks. It would not be prudent, given what you have endured in the past, to encourage him to question your devotion."

"No," Don Ezequias agreed heavily. "He is looking for an excuse to discredit me, and he would not be beyond using our . . . friendship as an opportunity to—" He stopped, chagrined at what he heard himself say. "I apologize."

"Why?" San Germanno asked, his demeanor still cordial. "You are not the one who is bringing this trouble about. If anything, you have offered me more protection than was in your best interests. You do not want me detained. You have done everything in your power to prevent this happening. That the Obispo and others have made it impossible for you to continue to extend your consideration to me does not compromise your trust, not in my eyes."

Don Ezequias listened eagerly to these words, grateful for them even while his conscience stung. "I might have found a way."

"And the Obispo might have started a Process against you, and me, for that matter," said San Germanno, as if a Church investigation were nothing more than a mild inconvenience, though he knew from experience that it was a grueling risk to run.

"They still might, if Frey Jeromo has his way," Don Ezequias admitted, putting the remainder of the pastry back on the plate. He reached for the wine, pouring half the carafe into the goblet.

"I would hope not," said San Germanno, and behind his light words there was grim purpose. He moved away from the hearth, letting Don Ezequias avail himself of its warmth; the heels of his high boots rapped out crisply on the tiled floor.

"Don Alejandro tells me that he does not want to put you under guard, out of respect to your Order." It was little enough consolation to offer, thought Don Ezequias as he sipped judiciously at the wine.

"That is very good of Don Alejandro," said San Germanno, speaking quietly; he wanted his guest to tell him more.

"Yes, it seems so," said Don Ezequias. He took another long drink. "But the Obispo could send monks to do the work of soldiers." This warning was given quickly, as if speed would lessen its impact.

"And do you think he will?" San Germanno asked. He had gone to one of the two tall, narrow windows and looked out on the patio of his house. The afternoon was clear, the air imbued with the fine, white light of winter; it was a pleasant place, one he would miss when he was gone from here. A series of images went through his mind: the gardens at Villa Ragoczy in Roma, the gardens in Toledo, the gardens in Lo-Yang; he had been fond of them, too, and they were gone.

"I think it could come to that, yes," Don Ezequias confessed after another mouthful of wine. "I told the Obispo I would allow you tonight to gather your things and make arrangements to close your house before taking you to the Residencia. He did not like the idea, but since he would allow more than twice that time if you were Spanish—" He stopped and went to refill his goblet. "Given that you have an encomienda and property, he could not require you to leave all in disorder. But there will be men posted around your house this evening."

"How many, do you think?" San Germanno asked.

"Four. To send more would be an insult," Don Ezequias said bluntly.

"Ah." It was not as desperate as San Germanno had assumed it might be. He studied Don Ezequias for a long, silent moment. "And they will be dispatched . . . ?"

"As soon as I leave this house," admitted the Presidencia. "They will stand guard all through the night."

"Changing at midnight, no doubt," said San Germanno, his tone dry.

"Yes." Don Ezequias hated to say the word. He was disgusted with himself for treating his friend so shabbily, for putting his own peace ahead of San Germanno's, but he could think of no course other than the one he was taking now, not with his wife and children in the balance.

"Since I am arrested, what must I forfeit?" San Germanno inquired smoothly. "Doubtless my encomienda is rescinded, and my servants taken from me. Will I lose the title to this house as well?"

It was difficult for Don Ezequias to answer. "Yes. All is claimed by the Church and the Crown, through the Audiencia de Lima." He coughed once, and swallowed more wine. "I have exempted your personal belongings from the confiscation. Obispo Guarda did not approve, but he could not give a sufficiently persuasive reason to seize your goods as well as your house and lands."

"And my horses and mules? What of them?" This next answer was crucial to his plans, but he did not reveal that in so much as a single inflection or flick of his fine brows.

"They will remain here for the time being," said Don Ezequias.

"But after tomorrow I will not," San Germanno finished for him. "There is some sense in that." He looked out at the patio once more.

"I was asked to take you into custody now," Don Ezequias admitted abruptly, unable to look at San Germanno.

San Germanno's full, enigmatic gaze fell directly on Don Ezequias. "But you will not."

"I refused. I said you need the time we would accord any gentleman to put his household in order. They could not deny that." He knotted his hands, his pacing more restless now.

"Very good," San Germanno said, continuing somberly. "For, my friend, I would not like to have to fight you. Or to kill you." There was no bravado in his words, only certainties. For a long moment he held Don Ezequias' eyes with his own. Then he made a single gesture and looked away, and broke the tension, remarking, "Will there be grooms to look after my horses?"

Startled and a bit shaken by the purpose he had seen in San Germanno an instant before, he said, "I will be sure to arrange it."

"Be sure the stalls are cleaned twice daily and new bedding put down," San Germanno told him. "The farrier will need to trim their hooves and reshoe them in a week; the shoes are stored with the pack-saddles, in a small chest, to keep out the rust. The horses are given a dollop of oil in their evening feed. The mules get oil every other day. You will find a keg of it with the tack." His expression remained unaltered, but a sadness came into his tone. "I would not like my animals to suffer because I am in disfavor."

"With horses like yours, that isn't going to happen," Don Ezequias said, and then realized he had said more than he intended.

"Oh?" San Germanno regarded him closely. "Who has a claim on my stock?"

At this question, Don Ezequias' face darkened. "Dom Enrique has . . . " He fumbled for a way to explain. "This is . . . His cousin is the wife of Don Vicente, the Corregidor." The last was hardly more than a mumble and ended with another gulp of wine.

"I see," said San Germanno, inwardly revising the plans he had started four days ago.

"Your Andalusians are magnificent horses. Everyone in Cuzco knows it," Don Ezequias said in a rush. "To have one of them would impart an advancement to the rider. To have more than one . . ." He stopped. "Don Vicente is supposed to get three of them, tribute to the Audiencia. That was the arrangement."

"Indeed," San Germanno said, coming away from the window.

Don Ezequias stared down into the wine. "I told them it was not an honorable thing to do. No one listened."

San Germanno heard this out without protest. Finally he said, "Dom Enrique is an ambitious man, one with cause to resent me. He will not be satisfied with getting a horse or two from my stables."

Don Ezequias nodded miserably. "He claims you have Incan treasures you stole from Acanna Tupac, gold and silver, and articles of great worth. He has sworn he has seen these things. He says that you seduced the soul of Acanna Tupac. She surrendered all to you. After you bewitched her." He hated the sound of those words and the taste of them in his mouth. "I have written to say this is not the case, but I do not know if Don Vicente will pay any heed to my accounts."

"It will depend on how well he knows his kinsman, and how great his ambitions are," said San Germanno, willing to reveal a little of the rancor that stung him.

Again Don Ezequias nodded. He wanted their meeting to be over, to be gone from this house so that he need not feel so much the traitor as he did now. "They will not take the horses for a few days yet."

"Why delay?" San Germanno asked, genuinely curious; the niceties of law intrigued him and never more than when they hid rapacity.

"The probanza has not been delivered yet; until it does, the horses remain here." He lowered his voice. "The courier will bring it from Lima shortly."

"Issued by the Corregidor, Don Vicente?" San Germanno inquired, certain of the answer. "To the favor of his wife's cousin?"

"Precisely," said Don Ezequias, and flung the goblet across the room, watching it crack and leak the last of the wine. He stood, shocked by what he had done. "Conde," he whispered. "I cannot . . . you must forgive my . . ."

"There is nothing to forgive, my friend," San Germanno assured him.

"I will have Rogerio bring another." He was about to clap to summon his manservant when Don Ezequias made a gesture of refusal.

"No. No." He was feeling clumsy and outsized, like a bear turned loose in a nursery. He did not trust himself to behave properly any longer. "The soldiers will be here directly." He paced down the room, and turned back abruptly to face his foreign friend. "There was nothing I could do, San Germanno. Nothing."

San Germanno nodded once. "I know," he said as Don Ezequias turned on his heel and left him alone.

A short while later, Rogerio presented himself to his master, saying, "Are there any changes in plans, my master?"

"I am afraid so, old friend," San Germanno replied, no sign of his emotions coloring his pleasant voice. "It seems we are being put under guard for the night. Tomorrow night I am expected at the Residencia, to answer accusations made against me." He waved in the direction of the cracked goblet. "This is not of Don Ezequias' doing."

"Certainly not," agreed Rogerio. His faded-blue eyes took in the other signs of difficulties: San Germanno's tremendous reserve, the uneaten pastries.

"There is a probanza coming, to lay claim to the horses. We will have to use the mules." San Germanno spoke as if they were in the middle of a conversation. "If we use the horses, the soldiers will be sent after us." He touched the mourning rosette on his collar. "They may pursue us in any case."

"It may be just as well to take the mules, if the road is as hazardous as the map would indicate," Rogerio said carefully.

"We must assume that it is," San Germanno said. "So, six mules and two llamas should be sufficient to our needs." He raised his hands in mock surrender. "You were right."

Rogerio held his peace, knowing his master was preparing himself to leave this place. He busied himself by picking up the fallen goblet and placing it on the tray with the empty carafe; he was willing to wait for his orders.

"How long will it take to be ready?" San Germanno asked suddenly.

"We can leave three hours before dawn," answered Rogerio, relieved at the question. "Jasy has promised his assistance, so that no one will notice what we do."

At the mention of Jasy's name, San Germanno looked troubled, aware that all his staff were at risk because of him. "Is it necessary? I do not want him to endure more hardship on my account. How will he fare, when we are gone?" He answered his own question. "If it is learned he helped us, it will go badly for him."

"And if they do not learn of it?" Rogerio prompted, knowing how his master thought about such things. "Why should they suppose he would help you? Let him plead ignorance."

"Then he might be left to his own devices." He smiled faintly, just a minute turn up at the corners of his mouth. "He is an Incan peasant, a simple man. They will not expect much of him, now that Acanna Tupac"—his voice dropped—"is dead."

"He came here with her. He does not have to admit anything more than that," said Rogerio.

"If they are willing to believe him," San Germanno added, his face somber. "If they are not, I will have done him a bad turn for his help."

"I will speak to him, my master; he will know what to tell them," said Rogerio.

"You had best include the rest of the staff, including Sor Maria. Obispo Guarda is likely to question them all." He shook his head once, chiding himself.

"If he receives the same answer, he will not harm them," said Rogerio, hoping it might be so.

"Do you think so," San Germanno asked, the ironic light back in his dark eyes.

"I think if we do not instruct them they are more apt to be harmed than if we do; and so do you," Rogerio answered with some asperity, and left San Germanno alone in the reception room where the fire was dying. He had much to do in the next several hours—the whole household did.

San Germanno went to his study a short while later, and set about the task of crating books and paraphernalia. He worked quickly, with the efficiency born of long practice. There was nothing in his demeanor to reveal the anguish he felt, or his growing apprehension that he would not elude danger as readily as he hoped he might. Occasionally he paused in his labors to listen to the rising wind.

By midnight most of the trunks were ready to be set on pack-saddles; San Germanno's red lacquer chest had been wrapped in two blankets to protect it on the road, and the rest were strapped with wide leather belts to hold them securely in their place.

"Have the guards been changed?" San Germanno had just come down from his private apartments for the last time, and now stood at the entrance to the kitchen as he pulled on the heavy leather gloves.

He was dressed in Hungarian hunting gear of tooled leather lined in fur, all black but for red piping at the collar, belted twice for wallet and sword. His dark, wavy hair was covered by a Russian cap of dense, black Persian lamb, and over his arm he carried his cloak of black alpaca wool.

"Just a few minutes ago," said Rogerio, who was standing with Jasy, Leilla, and Gemica near the open hearth where meat was cooked. "They came with Don Alejandro."

"They're being very official," San Germanno said quietly. "They want to be certain that there is not question about how they have conducted themselves." He took a pouch from his belt and held it out to Jasy. "There are forty-five pieces of gold in here. Divide it among yourselves, with my thanks." It was a lavish sum for a lifetime of service, but he went on as if there were nothing remarkable in the amount. "I trust Rogerio has advised you on how to deal with Obispo Guarda?"

Jasy was staring at the pouch, his hand on his cane so tense the knuckles were white edged in red. "He has. And I will do as he has told me, though it troubles me to let them think the worst of you."

"I am grateful; to all of you." He gave them all a fleeting smile. "Then accept my appreciation for all you have done. Sor Maria's convent has been given a donation as well, in the Yupanqui's name, for the relief of the suffering of her people, and the maintenance of the community." He pinched out one of the oil lamps that hung in the corridor. "You may all retire now, if you wish."

"Isn't there something more we can do?" asked Jasy, still staring at the pouch as San Germanno handed it to him. "This is generous beyond . . . " He shrugged, unable to express his thoughts.

"It is what Acanna Tupac would have done; take it in her name." There was a fleeting amusement in his eyes that displaced the sorrow. "If the Obispo should ask, tell him it comes from her. He will prefer that answer to any other."

Jasy looked shocked, and protested, "But she never had so much to give away."

"Obispo Guarda does not know that. Being a greedy man, he suspects all Incas have fabulous wealth hidden away in the mountains. He knows that the Spanish cannot have taken it all, for if they have, his work is in vain." There had been other conquerors over the centuries who had assumed the same thing about those they conquered, he reminded himself. They had been satisfied with explanations of this sort; Obispo Guarda was cut from the same cloth. And Don Ezequias, who knew better, would not question the story.

Jasy was able to laugh once. "He does, and so do many of the others. We are often asked by the priests to tell us where our damned pagan gold is," he agreed, and his hold on the pouch tightened. "Are we to share this with the rest?" He thought about the five servants remaining in San Germanno's household, and resigned himself to giving them equal parts of the gold.

"My servants have already received their parting gifts from me," San Germanno went on. "The same amounts as you have."

This revelation brought quiet to the room as the implications of San Germanno's wealth were assessed by the servants. Finally Leilla said, "I am grateful, Señor Conde, for your generosity." She curtsied, as did Gemica.

San Germanno bowed deeply to them all. "Go with the knowledge you have served Acanna Tupac well. And me."

"We can help you—" Jasy persisted.

"By going to your quarters and sleeping, so that there will be little disruption in the habits of this household," San Germanno finished for him. "I do not want to alarm the guards. If the house remains active, they may become suspicious." It was only part of his reasons, but it was sufficient to convince the three.

Jasy looked over his shoulder as if suddenly concerned that there might be someone listening. "Do you think they watch for such things?"

"They would be fools if they did not," said San Germanno. He was more relieved than he could say that Don Alejandro had refused to post guards inside San Germanno's house out of respect for the Order of Saint Stephen of Hungary; he knew it would be reckless to assume he was not under surveillance.

"When will you leave?" Leilla asked.

"It is best that you not know," San Germanno answered gently.

"We muffled the mules' hooves with rags," Jasy said suddenly. "So no one will hear you and note your passing."

"Excellent," San Germanno approved; he was aware that they did not want him to leave, for once he was gone, their last link to Acanna Tupac would be broken. He knew from the many times he had faced this situation in the past that there was nothing to gain but hurt in prolonging their leave-taking. As kindly as he could, he said, "I wish you a pleasant sleep."

The three servants muttered a few farewells and went away down the corridor toward the servants' quarters, leaving San Germanno and Rogerio to pinch out the lamps before going along to the stable.

"The mules are ready," said Rogerio just above a whisper as they entered the long row of stalls. "And the llamas."

"We will lead them out of the city and mount when we are beyond the ruins of Sacsahuaman fortress." San Germanno sounded remote now, as if all this were happening to someone else.

"Why should we go by that road?" Rogerio asked in mild surprise. "Wouldn't it be faster to take the Lima road?"

"Not necessarily, as we are not going to Lima, where they will look for us; there and Potosi, where they think there are more caches of Incan silver," San Germanno said. He pressed his hand to the wallet depending from his belt. "We will follow the road on the map Acanna Tupac entrusted to me. It will take us to Quito, and then we will go north to Nueva Granada, and Nombre de Dios." He stood very still, listening to the wind. "We will have a hard time tonight."

Rogerio nodded as he went toward the llamas. "They will need rest by mid-morning."

"As will I," San Germanno said with a trace of amusement. "I haven't enough of my native earth left to squander it with long daylight travel. And there will be fewer persons abroad in the night."

"And fewer questions to answer," Rogerio added. He spoke in his usual level way, but his demeanor indicated his satisfaction with this decision.

Suddenly San Germanno looked weary. "I will have to find sustenance along the way." He spoke of it as if confessing to an unacceptable weakness. "It will be necessary."

"There will be villages along the way," Rogerio reminded him. "You may give dreams and—"

San Germanno gave a sudden, quick sigh. "Doubtless." There had been long years in the past when he had resigned himself to taking what he needed from dreaming women, to a satisfaction that was safe but limited; it had been sufficient to his basic needs and of minimal risk for himself and the dreamers. His time with Acanna Tupac had renewed his longing for human contact, to be known without repugnance, accepted without disgust at his nature. After Antwerp, more than thirty years ago, he had withheld himself from anything other than the fulfillment achieved in dreams, fearing what might come with the bond of blood.

It was a short while before Rogerio said, "I have prepared chocolate for the guards." He looked directly at San Germanno. "In half an hour I will take it to them. The drug is not so strong that it will make their drowsiness seem unnatural, given the hour and the cold. They will not be astonished if they doze."

San Germanno nodded twice. "I'll get the nosebags ready."

Rogerio turned and went back to the kitchen. While he warmed the chocolate he pulled a thick woollen nightshift over his sensible traveling garments, and wrapped a houserobe around the lot. Then he mussed his sandy-colored hair so that he appeared to have just wakened from sleep. As the chocolate began to simmer, he reached for earthenware cups and a tray, and poured the aromatic liquid into the cups. He then took the tray and went out of the house through the servants' entrance, hunching his shoulder against the cold wind and the first onslaught of the sleety rain.

The most awkward part of his venture came next: he approached the soldier standing at the corner of the house, coughing a little to put the man on alert. "I hope you will have a cup of this," Rogerio raised his voice enough to be heard but not enough to wake those sleeping inside. "It's a servant's mistake: I made too much of it, forgetting only I was up."

The soldier cast a bleary eye in Rogerio's direction, then bowed his head slightly. "I won't say it isn't welcome on a night like this. We were given hot wine when we came on duty but it isn't enough to keep out the cold."

"I should think not," said Rogerio, extending the tray to the fellow. "Best not let it get cold."

The soldier chose one of the cups, wrapping his hands around the vessel to take full advantage of the warmth. He muttered a word or two of thanks before taking his first long sip.

Rogerio found the second guard half asleep and exchanged only a few words with him before passing on to the third.

"What're you up to?" the third guard growled. Everything about him was surly, from the angle of his jaw to the way he leaned on the side of the wall.

"I made more chocolate than I need. I knew you were awake and the night is very cold." Rogerio did his best to sound self-effacing; this soldier annoyed him. He concealed this with a display of propriety. "It isn't proper to provide for the household and neglect you guards."

"Um," said the soldier, and accepted the cup with obvious suspicion.

He tasted it warily, his tongue working over his lips.

Certain that the guard would drink the chocolate, Rogerio went to the fourth guard, who took the cup almost at once and drank deeply before uttering a modicum of thanks.

By the time Rogerio returned to the kitchen, two of the guards were beginning to feel heavy-eyed. He removed his houserobe and shift, putting them into a stack of rags marked for donation to charity, put out all the oil lamps but one, then went back to the stable where he saw San Germanno waiting, his hands holding the leads for two of the mules, with lines connecting the rest of the animals to their fellows and these leads.

"Are they—?" San Germanno asked as he took a long carter's whip from near the stable door. His alpaca cloak was wrapped around him, secured at the shoulder with a square silver pin. In the gloom of the stable, he appeared to be a bodiless head. He glanced in the direction of the rear door.

"Yes," Rogerio said, pulling on a Roman giustacorpo of heavy canvas lined with shearling. "They have had their chocolate."

"Is there any other reason to wait?" San Germanno asked, adding softly, "I can think of none."

Rogerio went to open the rear door, taking care to hold it against the wind as San Germanno tugged the mules forward. Two of the animals balked as they encountered the first swipe of the storm, but a smart slap on the rump got them moving forward; the llamas at the end of the train adjusted their pace to the mules'.

The walls of Sacsahuaman fortress loomed ahead of them as San Germanno led them along the backstreets of Cuzco toward the ancient Incan road marked on Acanna Tupac's map. Wind and freezing rain slowed their progress but concealed their passage. By the time the clouds turned pewter with the coming dawn, Cuzco lay almost two leagues behind them, as remote to San Germanno now as the fabled walls of Babylon, half a world and more than two millennia away.

Text of a letter from Gennaro Colonna to Dom Enrique; sent from Santa Marta in Nueva Granada.

To the respected Portuguese nobleman, the distinguished Dom Enrique Vilhao, currently residing in Cuzco, Audiencia de Lima, in the Viceroyalty of Peru, my most sincere and hopeful greetings.

It has come to my attention through the good offices of certain men known to us both that you have recently discovered a number of most remarkable Incan treasures that you have indicated you might be willing to sell if the price is acceptable to you. I will not make a direct offer here because I do not wish to insult you: as I do not know the full worth of your property, I am unable to indicate the limits to which I might go to acquire what you have. It may be useful to you to dispose of these things outside of the Audiencia de Lima, to avoid the tariffs required there. As soon as I have an indication of your interest and more information on the nature of your possessions, I will negotiate with you in regard to money. Be assured that I am not without means, and that I have a considerable amount at my disposal, and more may be obtained if your objects warrant such distinction.

Let me explain myself, so that you may be certain that this offer is without guile. As you may expect from my name, I am not without influential relatives and rich associates who have evinced some curiosity about the New World and all it contains. This curiosity extends beyond the desires of the Church, so you need not fear the consequences of our dealings. Due to certain misunderstandings, I have been sent here at the request of my family with the specific purpose to make my way in the world without their direct endorsement, although they are prepared to avail themselves of any advantages I may be in a position to procure for them. I intend to make the most of my opportunity to obtain for them such objects of interest or of value that might increase my fortune for the time when I return to Europe. It is in my immediate interests to make such alliances as the one I am proposing to you; I will not put you at a disadvantage for as long as our association is mutually beneficial.

To that end, I am requesting that you inform me specifically what you have to offer, and in what manner you will deliver it, and when you would expect the money involved to change hands. It would suit my purpose to meet you at any port convenient to us both in order to assess what you have that might serve my purposes. I earnestly entreat you to prepare an inventory and to dispatch it to me at Los Barcaderos in Santa Marta. I will be here for another four months at least, and no doubt during that time we may engage in transactions of mutual benefit.

Do not question my sincerity, for I cannot tell you emphatically enough how great my intent is, and how closely it marches with your own.

By my own hand, on this 19th day of August, in God's Year 1644,
                                                    Gennaro Colonna
                                                    Italian nobleman

14

At night the cold was bitter, sere, leaching heat from the very marrow of bones; in the day the sun glared down with relentless splendor that did little to alleviate the cold. The air was always thin, adding shortness of breath to the other difficulties they faced. Along the ancient Incan road few villages remained, and few of the old Incan guard stations high in the mountains were occupied, so San Germanno and Rogerio with their mules and llamas passing in the night disturbed almost no one, not even the magnificent condors in their distant nests, for they hunted by day.

Nine nights and sixty-five leagues from Cuzco, they crested the ridge between the gorge of the Apurimac and the Mantaro. The peaks rising formidably above them made the little pass all but unnoticeable until the road turned sharply and the declivity became apparent. From the state of the road, no one had come this way in a long time, and those who had had come on foot.

"Careful," San Germanno warned as he felt a portion of the road shift under his feet. It was late, and the gibbous moon was declined far in the west, providing what little light they had; San Germanno was not much troubled by this, but Rogerio had found the night hours on this ancient, narrow road harrowing.

"I will be," Rogerio assured him, holding onto the three mules' leads, and the llamas', more tightly than before, telling himself it was because of the cold and had nothing to do with fear.

The path swung to the west, revealing a stone wall with a large gate of rotted wood straddling the way; most of the gate had crumbled, revealing a wide, stone-paved street beyond, and a gathering of broken walls. Behind these were a number of large buildings, most showing signs of ruin: roofs collapsed, shutterless windows, fallen chimneys, plants forcing their way through the paving. A temple ornamented with weather-worn sun faces leaned precariously against the rising flank of the mountain above them. No sign of light or fire or guards could be seen; the city was deserted.

San Germanno halted his mules and stared, his dark eyes taking in as much as they could. Finally he moved forward again, listening to the echoes of the mules hooves as they ventured into the place, making their way down the middle of the wide central street. At last he turned back to Rogerio. "There must be a place we can pass the day. Not all the buildings are so dilapidated that they would be unsuitable." He pointed down a side-street. "The houses there appear to be intact. We could safely lodge in one."

"Except for the roofs," said Rogerio, squinting into the night.

"We can find shelter enough," San Germanno told him. "The mules and llamas need rest and feed. And both of us need sleep." His dark eyes were bruised with exhaustion, his skin looking like parchment on which a few creases had been set; though his appearance was of a man in his mid-forties, the quality of his skin now revealed something of his true age. His movements were strong, but his vigor had been sapped by hunger and high altitude.

Rogerio sighed once. "The food is getting low. We have some grain left, but not much; not enough to keep all the mules fed. In two days we will have to find a new supply or the animals will go hungry, and we will not be able to cover seven leagues a day, as we have done, not at this altitude, on these steep trails." His warning was not new, but now San Germanno gave him full attention.

Making a quick decision, he said, "In the next hour we will find a place for the mules and llamas to graze during the day. There must be some vegetation inside these walls they can feed on, enough for our purposes." He waved his hand expansively. "Let them take what they want. We will remain here tomorrow night as well, so they may rest." He, too, would be grateful for the respite, for without any sustenance the past few days had proven more enervating than he liked to admit. Only the rigors of their travel kept him from taking blood from one of their animals, for they were as vitiated as he and had nothing to spare him.

"Well enough," said Rogerio, welcoming the chance to recruit his strength as well. He glanced around as they made their way toward the buildings that seemed to be the most intact. He finally pointed to one that looked to be in less disarray than the others.

San Germanno signaled his agreement. "Excellent. I was thinking the same thing myself." He tugged at the lead, ignoring the grunt of protest from the lead mule. He approached the door of the place cautiously, examining the entry for signs of weakness. Satisfied that the stones were secure, he stepped inside and peered around the dim interior while

Rogerio waited patiently just outside, ready to act quickly if anything untoward should happen. As he surveyed the dark room, he heard a rustling sound in one of the corners; swinging around sharply, he was barely able to make out the shape of a small, raccoon-like coati huddled in the corner on a pile of what years ago had probably been bedding.

"Is anything the matter?" Rogerio called softly from outside.

"Not for me. There is a coati here who would disagree," San Germanno replied in the language of Imperial Rome. He moved aside, calming his skittish mules as the coati ran out, its long ringed tail held low, its long snout working. "The poor creature has only just returned from hunting. No wonder he dislikes being routed in this way." As he watched the coati disappear into another nearby doorway, San Germanno reminded himself they would have to be careful about the other wild things that had undoubtedly taken up residence in this city deserted by humans; not all of them would be as willing as the coati to defer to them.

"Do you think the water will be safe?" Rogerio asked, coming up to the door.

"Why not?" San Germanno asked, a faintly sardonic note in his voice now, and a trace of amusement in his eyes. "Who would have poisoned the wells?"

"If no one is here . . . " He shrugged to show he would accept any reasonable explanation for the vanished population.

"There is no sign of war—no cannon breached these walls, and no musquets have fired on them; we would have seen the impact had that happened. The faces of Illapa and Inti remain on the temple walls, so the priests and monks did not come here, either. No cross marks Christian worship. The people . . . left. It may have been to protect this place; its people did not want their city to be conquered. They probably fled the Spanish," San Germanno said, remembering the tales he had heard from the Spanish as well as the Incas of lost cities in the fastness of the mountains—cities the Spanish believed to be bursting with treasure of all sorts. "Or they died." The latter suggestion filled him with sudden dismay.

"Of Spanish diseases," Rogerio finished for him.

"Yes. Of Spanish diseases," San Germanno echoed. He was beginning to feel the full burden of his fatigue. They had made good time, he could not deny it, along the long-forgotten road indicated on Acanna Tupac's map, but they were still a vast distance from their goal. He began to doubt he could cover the distance without nourishment to restore him.

Rogerio's question cut into his reflections. "How many lived here, do you think?"

San Germanno frowned. "Two to three thousand, by the looks of it, maybe half again as many outside the walls." His tone changed. "Not much of a city by European standards." His father's ruling city, more than three thousand six hundred years ago, had not been much larger, he thought: perhaps four thousand subjects, with an additional seven thousand slaves, who were not numbered as people.

"But important enough to be guarded," Rogerio said. "There are breastworks on the peaks above us."

"I saw them," San Germanno told him. "And the signal-tower half a league from here."

"Is this place on the map?" Rogerio asked, curious about what Acanna Tupac knew of the empty city.

"I will look, later." Redirecting his thoughts to more immediate concerns, San Germanno said, "For now, I will find the well. Light a few of our candles and do what you can to make this room useable."

With a sense of great relief, Rogerio said, "At once, my master," and extended his hand for the leads San Germanno held.

Leaving Rogerio to his work, San Germanno made his way back toward the temple, convinced that the marketplace, and hence the municipal well, could not be far from it. As he walked, he listened to the report of his heels on the neglected paving, and heard the movement of animals in response. Glancing upward, he studied the sky, sensing the approach of dawn. He would have to hurry if he was going to locate the well and a grazing place for the mules and llamas before the sun drove him into the annealing shadows for the day.

The well was on the north end of the marketplace, its stones green with moss and damp where the enormous stone basin had been overflowing steadily for decades, fed by springs deep underground. Beyond it the remnants of livestock market stalls leaned at tipsy angles, thick grass growing in the rich earth left behind. Four stone pillars similar to those in Cuzco marked the limits of the livestock market; they had once been linked by wooden fences, but those had long since fallen. The area was well-defined. It would be easy to tether the llamas and hobble the mules and leave them to feed in the wide plot of ground. Returning to the house where three candles now burned, he began to remove the pack-saddles from the animals, remarking to Rogerio as he did that there was enough food for all eight beasts.

"And the water is sweet?" Rogerio asked anxiously.

"There are no bones around the well, and the moss is healthy, so I must suppose it is," answered San Germanno. "I saw nothing that made me think otherwise." He accepted a brush from Rogerio and went to work on the lead mule, starting from his head down his neck and front legs, across its back and flanks to his rear legs. When the worst of the dust and mud was removed, San Germanno began on the second mule, plying the brush steadily, methodically. And all the while the sky was growing lighter, the street outside the door more distinct. He would shortly have to rest, for without the revivification of blood his enormous endurance gave away to fatigue; even his native earth could offer only minor restoration. By the time he and Rogerio led the animals to the deserted livestock market, the rim of the sun was showing above the peaks and birdcalls welcomed its arrival.

"My master," Rogerio ventured as he put the last pair of hobbles on a mule, "is there no way you might . . . "

"I doubt it," San Germanno said when Rogerio did not elaborate his meaning.

"Then you had best get back into the house. Save the strength you have. You will want to make a bed on one of your chests of earth, to restore yourself, since you will not use the mules." Rogerio assumed his most pragmatic manner; long experience had taught him that when San Germanno became remote and polite, little could be done to reach him. "I will follow shortly."

"Ah, yes," San Germanno said, pausing and half-turning. "A bird or two will hold you, will it not?"

Stung by this sardonic observation, Rogerio snapped, "An advantage enjoyed by ghouls, I think."

"Truly," San Germanno agreed in the same maddening, courteous tone. He inclined his head and strode off in the direction of the house, his clean stride covering the distance quickly without appearing hasty. It was nearly an hour later when Rogerio found him there, lying atop one of the chests containing his native earth. "Pardon me, old friend," he said as Rogerio stepped inside.

"Pardon you for what, my master?" Rogerio asked with concern, hearing contrition in San Germanno's words. "You are tired. Everyone gets testy when he is tired."

"True enough," San Germanno allowed. "But you are tired, too, and you were not churlish."

"I had less to trouble me." He had caught two birds roughly the size of pigeons, fletched them and eaten them raw, using his knife to joint the birds; now he was pleasantly full, ready to rest for a few hours before tending to the mules and llamas.

"That may be so, but it does not excuse me." He had wrapped himself in his alpaca cloak and made a pillow of his Persian lamb cap, and a certain drowsiness fuzzed his speech. He made himself be more alert. "I had a look at the map while you were breaking your fast."

"And what does it say?" Rogerio asked, coming a step closer and looking down at his master, trying not to appear too concerned.

"Auquicanipu is the name on the map," San Germanno said, adding, "It has something to do with a prince—auqui—and a military honor—canipu. Whether the city was a military honor for a prince or the place where a prince was given a military honor, I cannot tell. It could also mean a badge, that is, a military honor bestowed by a prince, so this might have been a special garrison for the prince's use." He placed his hand over his wallet where the map was kept. "At sundown we will decide where we will go next."

Recognizing San Germanno's exhaustion, Rogerio bowed slightly and moved to the pack-saddles, gathering together a heap of saddlepads and dropping atop them for a short, intense slumber. He was awakened at midday by the cry of a raptor—hawk or eagle, he could not tell. As he rose, he noticed that San Germanno, contrary to his usual habit, was still profoundly asleep. This brought a resurgence of worry, for if San Germanno did not find sustenance soon, he could slip into a dangerous lethargy. It had happened before, twelve hundred years earlier, beyond Constantinople, when the attack of the Huns had cut them off with Niklos Aulirios in that miserable fortress, and again, in the Polish marshes, nine centuries ago. Both times Rogerio had been filled with despair, unable to persuade or coerce San Germanno from his listless melancholy. What came after was a hunger so overwhelming that its ravages lingered within him long after the need drove San Germanno to batten on the living. The last time San Germanno had suffered the consequences of long deprivation was thirteen centuries since, and the horror of his actions continued to scar his soul: to face such agony again was almost unendurable to Rogerio—the prospect infinitely worse to San Germanno.

By mid-afternoon Auquicanipu had fallen into shadow, the massive shoulder of the Andes shutting out the sun. Only then did San Germanno stir sluggishly on his chest of earth. As he sat up, he rubbed his face as if to restore feeling to frozen skin. "How long?"

"Most of the day, my master," said Rogerio without inflection.

"Ah." San Germanno stretched slowly with the thoroughness of a cat. Satisfied that he was not stiff, he stood up. "Better, I think."

" 'Sleep is a meal,' " Rogerio quoted, remembering the first time he had heard that aphorism, in Crete, shortly before the first attempt on San Germanno's life.

"So it is, even for vampires," San Germanno concurred. He cocked his head toward the door. "Our mules and llamas?"

"I checked them earlier. They look rested. They are active, fretting at restraint. They are eating well." It was a relief to make such a report. "By tomorrow night they will be eager to go on."

"By tomorrow night, I will have to go on," San Germanno murmured, his fine brows flicking into a frown. He reached for his wallet and drew out the map. "Let us consider our route." He sat down and smoothed the Incan parchment out on his thigh. "This is the place we are now." He put his finger down on the indication of the pass. "The road goes along this side of the slope, to Andamarca. At Andamarca the road divides. Look here. One follows the Tulumayo down into the jungles, the other goes around the north flank of the peak toward Huancayo and follows the Cordillera Occidental to Huantar and along the Maranon until the river turns east."

"It is a hard journey, my master, no matter which road we take. The mountains are hazardous, and the jungles as well . . . and there are few villages where it would be safe for you," Rogerio said, tapping the map.

"All the more reason to use the mountain trail, to the north, instead of the river trail to the east. The authorities will not be likely to follow us." He achieved a wry smile. "And who can blame them."

"The sun is growing stronger," Rogerio reminded him.

"Yes. We are nearing the equator; I am aware of it. It is like a bludgeon. You need not remind me of its power: I feel it even in my sleep." His finger moved. "It is roughly here, to the north of Quito."

"Your native earth will need replenishing before the year is out," Rogerio warned him. "If Bondama Olivia has sent more, you will have to reach where it is being kept before you can use it."

"Olivia has sent more, without doubt. There will be chests at Guayaquil in New Granada, Cartegna, and Cartagena as well as in Nombre de Dios. If only half of them arrived I will have more than enough for a decade. During that time more can be obtained, I trust. And before you speak, old friend, yes, we are a long way from all of them, and they will be of little use to me if I cannot reach them." He sighed once, and then his voice dropped. "But we cannot return to Cuzco or Lima. For the next two or three months, I will have to manage with what I have."

"Then you will need—" Rogerio began.

"—blood. I am aware of that, as well. Believe this." His tone was light but his eyes remained somber, inward-looking. San Germanno rubbed his face again, this time as if to wipe it clean. "I cannot afford to raise the alarm anywhere, not with the authorities of Church and Crown eager to find me. I will have to proceed circumspectly." He straightened his back. "So. We will continue to travel by night. If we come upon those we can employ in good faith, we may be able to obtain one or two chests of earth from"—he hitched his shoulders—"a merchant going from the mountains to the coast and back again: one who will be eager for gold and will not be inclined to tell his Confessor too much."

This was the first indication Rogerio had that San Germanno had a specific destination in mind. This realization shocked him, as much because he had not been aware of it than where it might be. He met San Germanno's gaze with his own. "Tell me where, my master?"

San Germanno pointed to a place not marked on the map. "Here. You see this valley? Not far from Popayan there is a Carmelite community, one dedicated to the service of the native people; it is outside the Audiencia de Lima, which makes it less hazardous for us. As for the Carmelites, occasionally they are in dispute with their superiors within the Order, for not all the Obispos in Peru approve of giving the native people Christian burial. So the Carmelites do so, according to their mandate, and treat the sick. They will not question a tertiary too closely."

"A tertiary Carmelite," Rogerio repeated as if he had misunderstood what San Germanno said. "You will put yourself in the hands of the Church?"

"Indirectly. The Carmelites are not God's Hounds, after all, and their community is remote. And in so isolated a location they will not be apt to hear rumors that could prove . . . awkward." San Germanno refolded the map, adding, "And the Church, if she goes in search of me, I trust will not think to look among the Carmelites in the mountains near Popayan."

Rogerio was not convinced but he held his peace; after his long association with San Germanno, he knew it would avail him nothing to question his decision now. Perhaps later, he told himself, when we are nearer Popayan. That was a considerable distance—not that they had not covered the same and more many times in the past—but it was far enough that any number of things might change their plans.

As if reading Rogerio's thoughts, San Germanno remarked, "Better to be with the Carmelites than have the people of the region talking about a foreigner: don't you think?"

Rogerio nodded at once, his expression one of comprehension. "Yes, my master, if those are the alternatives." He indicated their refuge. "Were there no other choices?"

"You mean taking one of da Gois' ships to Nagasaki?" San Germanno suggested. "A long ocean voyage on a Catholic ship. Now, that *would* be a bold move, one that would startle everyone. Once in Japan I would be beyond my chests of native earth, with the destination a port where there are priests waiting and a ruler who is suspicious of all foreigners. I might arrange to travel to China, of course, but how long that would take, given the dealings in the past between the Chinese and the Japanese, who can tell. Then it would be necessary to return to my native land across two thousand desolate leagues. You recall Karakorum, surely. We were there—what? four hundred years ago?—I doubt it has changed much in the intervening decades. And I would return to my homeland to witness yet another conqueror plundering it." He held up his hand. "Oh, you need not remind me that the Turks have been there for two centuries. I am aware of it, as I have been aware of every conquest since the Scythian allies of the Hittites conquered my family. I knew when my people left the region, and I knew when they arrived in Italy, and when the Romans finally vanquished them." He shivered at a sudden memory.

"What is it, my master?" Rogerio asked, not wanting to interrupt but struck by the change in San Germanno's visage.

He did not answer at first, then said, "One day, outside Fiorenza: I was with Laurenzo. There were others along as well—Ficino and Pico della Miradola, but not Poliziano, all the forgotten gods be thanked, for he would never have allowed the occasion to be dismissed. We came upon an ancient temple, just a ruin, of my people. Laurenzo insisted on exploring it, though the other two were not as curious about the place. An old man found us there, doubtless mad, who . . . who sought to . . . honor me." For an instant, he saw the temple-keeper before him on his knees, attempting to cut his own throat in offering. It had troubled him then and it sickened him now. "He called me Rasna," he added, remembering this last suddenly.

"That was the name of your people in Italy, wasn't it? Or something very like it?" Rogerio asked, and saw San Germanno nod in answer. Then San Germanno had been il Conte Francesco Ragoczy da San Germano, whom Laurenzo de' Medici had called *mio caro stragnero,* and Rogerio had been known as Ruggiero; he appended a speculative observation, "I do not recall your mentioning it at the time."

San Germanno looked slightly embarrassed. "I thought it would be unwise to speak of it. I hoped everyone would forget about the incident. Lauro referred to it only once again, Ficino never."

"They were being prudent, perhaps?" Rogerio ventured.

"Perhaps," San Germanno said at his most neutral. Then he shook off his memories. "This place must have reminded me of the temple."

Privately Rogerio thought the matter was more complex, but let it pass. He busied himself with flint-and-steel, lighting their candles again as dusk closed in. "I saw no villages down the slope."

"That does not surprise me," said San Germanno, grateful for the shift in subject. He paced the length of the room, testing his strength. "In such a place villages would only serve to alert the Spanish to the existence of this city."

"Or all their people died as well," Rogerio commented.

"Yes," San Germanno said quietly. "In two generations this will be a legend, a fabulous tale of a great citadel."

"You are certain of that?" Rogerio inquired as he opened the chest where the last of the food for their animals was stored. "I will give each a handful of grain. That will lend them strength in this depleted air."

"A sensible precaution," San Germanno approved. "I am going to explore this place. If a coati has lived here, there might be other creatures, more suited to my purpose." Disgust turned the corners of his mouth down for an instant, and then his expression became remote. "I will be here before sunrise; have no fear, old friend." He made no gesture of farewell; one moment he was in the house, the next he was gone into the night.

An hour before dawn, San Germanno returned, renewed energy in his step, an expression of grudging relief on his attractive, irregular features. His dark eyes met Rogerio's enigmatically and briefly. Then he reached out for one of the cleaning cloths Rogerio had been using to wipe the saddles. He neatened his clothes, then ran a brush through the wave of his hair. As he put the brush away, he said, "After three and a half millennia you would think I would have grown used to it by now. But I haven't."

Rogerio knew San Germanno well enough to say nothing in response.

With the dawn came clouds; first nothing but streamers at the top of the sky, but then heavier ranks arrived, reducing the sun to a silvery glare and making the mountains look like badly painted murals. By afternoon the wind had risen enough to prompt Rogerio to bring the animals into the house for saddling and loading. The cold took over the little house, promising worse to come at sunset.

"We will have to carry lanthorns," San Germanno conceded as he looked out at the building storm. "I can manage without, but you cannot, and I would not be astonished to discover the mules would need a little more illumination." He had swung his cloak around him, and with his Persian lamb cap drawn down, he moved about the room like a restless shadow, testing the tack as Rogerio finished the last of their preparations.

"A little light on this road would be useful," Rogerio said quietly.

"You are thinking of our long climb up the mountains from China to the Land of Snows; I share your recollection of that journey," San Germanno said, certain of it. "These mountains are as forbidding, in their way as those were, after Tzoa Lem . . . forsook us. And we cannot hope to find as kindly a reception as we were given at the Byagrub Me-long ye-shys lamasery here in Peru, or in Nueva Granada, or Nueva España, if we go so far."

Rogerio nodded his agreement and continued to saddle and pack their animals. Finally he said, "It might be best to leave while there is still dusk."

"To permit eyes to adjust," San Germanno said, understanding Rogerio's intent. "Yes, it would probably be sensible." He had taken their lanthorns from the chest in which they were carried and was in the process of trimming the wicks and filling the reservoirs with oil. "Four will be sufficient, won't they." Finished with those tasks, he swung around and affixed one lanthorn to the chest that had just been loaded onto the pack-saddle. "Which is to bring up the rear?"

"This one," said Rogerio, patting the rump of the mule with the speckled coat. "He is a good walker, and does not need to be prodded along, the way the dun does."

"Four will be enough for tonight," San Germanno said again as he put the second one in place and handed one to Rogerio, keeping one for himself. "It would be foolish to light our way so well that we guide others to us."

Aware of the limited state of their supplies, Rogerio said "Yes," although he would have preferred six, in case they had to put their mules and llamas on longer leads, which could become necessary if the storm turned violent.

"You and I will carry one each, and the middle and last mules as well." San Germanno's decision was quickly made. "How many waterskins did you fill?"

"Nine," Rogerio said. "Enough."

"I need not have asked," San Germanno told him with a fleeting smile before he stepped out into the bitter wind, drawing three of the mules and one of the llamas after him.

Rogerio waited until the string had passed him before leading his animals out of the abandoned stone house. He huddled against the wind, turning his shoulder to take the brunt of it, and thinking that when the clouds opened at last, sleet and snow would ride on a gale.

But the night brought nothing worse than the maniacal wind. Along the way trees swayed, some of them falling. An hour was lost while San Germanno struggled to tug a long trunk off the track they followed. When at last the tree rolled away down the slope toward the river below, the night was more than half over, and they were without protection from the day.

"We will press on," San Germanno announced in a shout that was barely audible in the bluster of the wind.

"It might be better to build a shelter," Rogerio yelled back.

"We press on," San Germanno reiterated, and started his mules and llama following him along the narrow path.

By morning the wind and clouds had harried their way to the northwest and San Germanno and Rogerio had come upon an outcropping of boulders that offered relief from the sun. The animals were unsaddled but kept close with leads and halters so that they could not inadvertently wander into danger. Just before the sun reached their place on the mountain, San Germanno said, "I think we are being watched."

Rogerio peered out of their hiding place. "Where?"

"The other side," San Germanno told him, indicating the opposite slope. "About two-thirds of the way up."

"You mean that dip?" Rogerio asked, his faded-blue eyes narrowing in concentration.

"That is the place," San Germanno acknowledged. "Two men, I think."

"Should I charge a pistol?" The question was asked carefully, without emphasis for any specific decision.

"I hope it will not be necessary," San Germanno said, settling back on one of his chests of earth. "Will you reline my soles for me, old friend? while I rest."

"And keep watch. That I will," Rogerio said firmly.

"Of course," said San Germanno, letting his eyes drift closed.

It was late in the afternoon when a middle-aged man in full Incan regalia—mascapaicha head-dress, feather cape, and champi in hand—approached, the head of the champi lowered to show peaceful intent. He stopped a respectful distance away and said in very poor Spanish, "You are welcome in our village."

San Germanno was not fully awake, but he rose gracefully and bowed. "What village is that, Apu?" The use of this Incan title caught the man's attention, and San Germanno went on, "The map we carry has no village on it."

"Spanish maps!" the newcomer scoffed.

"The map is not Spanish," San Germanno said, and paused to make the kiss-like mocha toward the setting sun, as he had seen many of the people of Cuzco do in the marketplace as the day came to an end. "Acanna Tupac entrusted it to me."

At the mention of her name, the Incan visitor gripped his champi more tightly; its massive head rose slightly. "How do you know that name?"

"She and her servants honored my house as guests when her own burned," San Germanno told the man. "She permitted me to have many of her belongings in my house."

"And you took it from her in payment," the man said with hard conviction.

"No. I would not so dishonor myself," San Germanno replied in such a calm voice that the man gave him a chance to explain this.

He folded his arms inside the radiant cloak of feathers. "This map: how do you come to have it?"

"Acanna Tupac herself gave it to me," he answered in the same quiet manner. "Without it, my servant and I would not have known of this road." He bowed again, this time with a sweep of his arm that included Rogerio in the display of respect.

"Acanna Tupac is dead," the man said flatly.

"Yes. And all who honored her alive mourn her now," San Germanno responded, waiting to see what would happen next.

"Soldiers follow you." It was an accusation.

"Only to do us harm," San Germanno told him, and said in the Latin of Imperial Rome, "No pistols, Rogerio. He has others with him."

Rogerio carefully slipped his charged pistol back into the capacious pocket of his Venetian breeches; he made sure all the leads to their mules and llamas were secure in his hands.

"If what you have said is true and you are a foreigner who has been the host of Acanna Tupac, we must be permitted to show the gratitude of her people. It is fitting that you feast with us tonight," the man continued, watching San Germanno with acute attention.

San Germanno bowed a third time. "A most gracious offer, worthy of the Yupanqui. Alas, I have sworn to fast in memory of Acanna Tupac. But we would be honored to visit your village, if it is what you wish."

"It may be a trap, my master," Rogerio warned in the same Roman dialect.

"So may this be; we do not know how many men are watching," San Germanno said quietly, then addressed their visitor. "I was told by Acanna Tupac that when a man wears the mascapaicha he does not fight. I will accept your offer of hospitality, and so will my manservant." He signaled to Rogerio. "Keep a tight hold on the animals. They are more likely to be the targets of these people than we are."

"Why would that be?" Rogerio asked, as much to keep direct contact with San Germanno as to acquire information.

"They have chests on their pack-saddles and they are edible," said San Germanno bluntly. He touched his sword belt, assuring himself he could reach the weapon quickly.

"We will show you the way to our village," said the man in Incan finery. "You will follow."

"Certainly," San Germanno declared, signaling Rogerio to keep near. "Find out how many are watching, if you can. We will have to get free before we reach the village." He spoke in Byzantine Greek, his voice low.

"What are you saying?" the man demanded.

"I am telling my servant to make sure our animals do not lag behind us." San Germanno bowed again.

"Why do you think we are in danger? These are poor people, trying to maintain their own ways." He had already fixed the lanthorns to the packs, and was preparing to light them when he saw San Germanno signal him not to.

"We have been accepted much too quickly," San Germanno said in Greek, adding in Spanish for the benefit of their escort. "I agree; we will have to fill the waterskins in the morning."

"But if he, or they, were planning to attack . . . " Rogerio protested, still in Greek.

"They want what we carry, and not the map alone." He returned to Spanish. "Let these generous people lead the llamas. To show our mutual trust." In Greek again, he said hurriedly, "Consider what the Spaniards have done to these people. Why are they not reluctant to deal with us? We have been accepted much too quickly."

"All right. That is a matter for concern," Rogerio agreed, holding out the llamas' leads to their visitor.

"That, and he did not tell me his name," San Germanno reminded Rogerio. "If he was truly intending to receive us as guests he would have done so at once." He tugged on the leads Rogerio had given him, adding, "As soon as it is possible, one of these animals is going to stumble. Be ready." He could sense the urgency of the man who they were to follow, and he was aware that he would not have long to get away.

"I will," Rogerio promised, and added in rough Spanish. "Remember the speckled mule has been limping."

"Yes. I remember," San Germanno answered as he scanned the slopes for movement. In all he spotted nine men, each with three spears, prepared for hunting. He weighed their chances, trying to recall everything on the map about this region. At least, he thought, the soles of his boots were newly lined with his native earth. He glanced at the western ridge and calculated the amount of light remaining.

Their guide noticed this, and said, "Yes. It will soon be dark. You may wonder at my offer, this hour in the day. Since the Spanish came, we have had to perform our ceremonies at night, so that they will not be seen and reported. The Spanish have left us alone for now, but we do not want to tempt them."

"So Acanna Tupac explained to me," San Germanno said, thinking that this man was making the mistake of all deceivers: the man was telling too much. He noticed a dip in the road ahead and thought it would be the one chance he and Rogerio would have to escape with their mules and their lives. He coughed twice, alerting Rogerio.

The track narrowed as it dipped, and the mules became restive, one of them braying in protest. This distraction was enough to distract the men escorting San Germanno and Rogerio.

With a loud cry, Rogerio seemed to loose control of the mules he led, and in the next instant, one of the animals stepped off the steep path and began to slide down the rough slope toward the river. Rocks bounced and rattled around him as Rogerio plunged after him, appearing to drag the rest after him inadvertently. One of the mules San Germanno was leading reared, answering a covert jab given by San Germanno, and the remaining two mules bolted after their fellows, all but rolling down the precarious terrain in pursuit of the others. The mule that had reared now balked, then jumped off the trail, pulling San Germanno after him.

There was consternation among those men escorting the strangers. Two of them rushed to the edge of the trail, their spears up, already trying to aim in the gathering shadows.

Their leader held up his champi. "Do not waste your weapons," he ordered them in their own language. "We will find them in the morning. By then they will need our help or be dead. Either way, we are at the advantage."

One of his men offered a complaint, but the rest were reluctant to hunt the foreigners in the dark. After a while, they drifted away to their homes, the llamas accepted as temporary loot; all of them looked forward to the next morning when they would be able to claim their prizes at last.

Near the bottom of the canyon, San Germanno found Rogerio bent over one of the mules. "What's wrong?" he whispered, knowing their voices would carry in this stone declivity.

"A broken canon-bone, off-side," said Rogerio, his hand on the animal's sweating neck.

"What of the others?" San Germanno inquired, and went on, "The three I led are tethered a short way downstream."

"The other two are well," said Rogerio. "This one will have to die."

"What does he carry?" San Germanno asked as he recognized one of his chests of native earth. "Well." There were many concerns in that single word. "It will not do to lose that."

Rogerio looked up at San Germanno. "The mule will have to be killed, for kindness if not for our protection," he said. "Before that, he has blood . . . not as you would want it, but enough to—"

"—to give me the strength to carry that chest," San Germanno finished for him. "Yes. Doubtless you are correct. But I dislike the means."

He frowned at the sky. "Twilight. Good enough." And he steeled himself against his own need as he knelt down next to the mule while Rogerio began to unfasten the chest from the pack-saddle.

An hour later, the dead mule left behind them, San Germanno steadied himself to carry the chest now strapped to his back. He hoped that the added benefit of his native earth would provide sufficient stamina to allow him to continue to bear this burden on his journey north.

Rogerio gathered up the leads of the mules and fell in behind San Germanno, carefully putting the whole of his attention on the narrow road so that his apprehensions would not overwhelm him through the long night.

Text of a letter from Obispo Hernan Sigismundo Bernal Guarda to Corregidor Don Vicente in Lima, Audiencia de Lima, Viceroyalty of Peru.

> *To the most excellent Corregidor of the Audiencia de Lima, Viceroyalty of Peru, Don Vicente Angel Luis Jorge Yniguez y Nieviereos, Hidalgo, in Lima, the greetings and blessings of Obispo Hernan Sigismundo Bernal Guarda, at Los Sacramentos in Cuzco;*
>
> *Most worthy Corregidor, it is not my intention to admonish you in regard to the administration of the Audiencia de Lima, but I cannot suppose you have been apprized of the unfortunate turn of events which has taken place here recently and which casts serious doubts on the abilities of your Presidencia in Cuzco, Don Ezequias Pannefrio y Modestez, who has been so lax in the discharging of his duties that he has permitted the notorious foreigner Francisco Ragoczy, styled el Conde de San Germanno, to escape from his jurisdiction in spite of being informed he was under detention.*
>
> *It has come to my attention that this Ragoczy was informed, by Don Ezequias himself, that he was to surrender to the Residencia. The Presidencia allowed the perfidious Ragoczy to have the night in which to make ready. The foreigner used the time to engineer an escape of such cunning that the four guards posted at his house could not stop his departure. The guards have given it as their opinion that a spell was put on them, although it is the opinion of Don Ezequias that the chocolate they were given was drugged. In either case, it must be noted that this Ragoczy has gone far beyond acceptable conduct of one under the demands of authority.*
>
> *I am of the opinion that the reason for this lapse in judgment comes from Don Ezequias himself. Who is to say he did not warn Ragoczy to*

depart, and offer him his support in the process. The staff at said Ragoczy's house all claim ignorance of the events. They are simple people, incapable of deception of the sort evinced here, and I do not hold them in any way answerable for the departure of Ragoczy, although it is my belief that he drugged them as well so that the sounds of Ragoczy's departure would not alert them to what was taking place. Had Don Ezequias sent over servants from the Residencia, this would not have taken place as it did, I am confident of it.

It pains me to make complaint against Don Ezequias, for few things are so disruptive to a city like Cuzco as dissention among its leaders. I know he has done his best, as he judges his best to be, to fulfill the high office you have entrusted to him. But I must tell you that I am not so satisfied with his decisions that I can applaud his other actions and deplore this one alone. If he had made but one such error, I would have to, in charity, accept it as proof of the fallibility of man. Yet I am aware of many other times Don Ezequias has failed to support the decisions made by you, and by other officers of the Crown in positions superior to his own. This so-called independence of spirit has shown itself to be nothing more that simple, unacceptable rebelliousness and defiance.

Therefore I must ask you, Don Vicente, to consider removing Don Ezequias from his position as Presidencia in Cuzco and replacing him with an honorable hidalgo more capable of forwarding the aims of the Crown and Holy Church. Your failure to make full inquiries into this matter will compel me to direct my concerns to those in a position to relieve you of the necessity.

Prayerfully, and in the sure and certain hope of your compliance and wisdom, I assure you of I will remember you in all things, and bring your acts to God's attention,

Hernan Sigismundo Bernal Guarda
Obispo, Los Sacramentos
Cuzco, Audiencia de Lima
Viceroyalty of Peru
By the hand of Frey Jeromo,
on the 24th day of October, in the Year of Our Lord, 1644

PART II

Francisco Ragoczy, el Conde de San Germanno

Text of a letter from Jules Mazarin to his second cousin Gennaro Colonna in the New World, written in French.

To my errant kinsman now in the New World, your cousin in France sends greetings, and the hopes that his prayers will aid with those of others to bring you once again to honor and Grace, for the reputation of our family and the triumph of our religion.

You have informed me in your most recent letter that you have encountered nothing but the most heathen of savages, all of them decked out in gold and jewels and flaunting their false gods in the face of the Christian monks and priests who have come to teach them the ways of Christ. I have read the reports that show some of the same observations, but without the consequences of your own impressions. Your sense of frustration at the lack of faith on the part of these heathen, and their lack of Grace, is understandable enough, and if that were all your message, I would rejoice and inform our relatives that at last you have set your feet on the true path and have started the journey that must ultimately lead to the salvation of your soul and the restoration of your position within the family. But, sadly, you do not stop there. You are not content to observe those who are obdurate in their resistance to the teachings of Christ, and the tranquility of soul that comes with acquiescence in the Will of God, which is the reward on earth given to true Christians. You give it as your opinion that since these heathen are not won to the cause of Christ and are not willing to bow down to the Cross, that they are therefore unworthy of anything but the most unforgiving treatment, and any sort of degradation that you and your companions,

*as soldiers of the True Faith, can mete out to them for their obstinate re-
fusal to accept Christ.*

*For the sake of the Saints, why should they, those poor, ignorant sav-
ages, accept the promise of salvation and paradise when you, who carry
His banner, treat them as you would hesitate to treat animals. Your letter describes—with hideous pride—the way in which you violated the
women of a chieftain's family, and then killed them by pulling out their
intestines and nailing them to the floor. This is not the act of a good
Christian soldier, and certainly not the act of one who professes to
accept the laws of Christ as binding on his own fate. This is an overwhelming denial of the very nature of the Word of Christ, which is pos-
tulated on peace and love in His Name. To cause such terrible carnage
shows a complete lack of respect for the oath you have taken as a soldier fighting in the name of the Christian King of Spain and the Church.
You say that this was not the only incident, but the most recent, and
therefore the one you have the most knowledge of. You say that without
such acts the heathen will not be subdued to the Christian faith. You
claim that the fact that these are heathen excuses everything you do, but
I cannot and I do not agree with you. You have taken the teachings of
Christ and perverted them to your own nefarious purposes, making
them worse than the most intolerable behavior of Nero and other debauched Emperors before the salvation of Christ found its heart in Rome.*

*I will offer you this homily in the fervent hope that it will create within
you some understanding of the enormity of your trespasses against the
Holy Spirit, and will stand you in good stead in future when you are
tempted to indulge again in the excesses you have described and have
not repented of, neither in the act itself, nor in the sins that drove you
to such atrocious errors.*

*There was a man who had lived all his life in disfavor with his fam-
ily and with his God. He was not a bad man, if badness is measured by
the ferocity of his sins, but he was one who viewed the world and those
around him with contempt; he respected no one and nothing in this
world, and feared nothing in the next. He was thought to be a man without conscience by those who had cause to work with him, and as a hard-
ened sinner by those who heard of him from others. He cared nothing
for their thoughts of him, and when questioned on the matter, he said
he was well-content to live alone and thus be freed from the company
of rogues and fools. He was so unwilling to enter into the society of his
city and his family that he chose to live away from them, and to regard
them as nothing more than travelers, with no obligation or claim shared*

with them greater than their human necessities, which for him did not include love, honor, or religion. It was his contention that to have friends was to have liabilities, and to have family was to have constant unjustified demands made on him. When he learned that his father had disowned him and taken away his inheritance, the man was amused for it justified his vexation with the world. He declared that he had had nothing from his father while the man lived and it was nothing to him that he was disowned.

Think of that unfortunate being, my cousin, and apply his lamentable actions to your own life. Before I continue with the tale, I wish you will take the time to review your own statements, and letters, which are not unlike the contentions of this most unhappy mortal. You may think that there is nothing to see, but I assure you that there is, and I am convinced that you have fallen into the same terrible trap as this fellow did. If you are able to discern the similarities, then hear the end of this unhappy story, and profit by it. You have said that you do not wish to be read lessons and that you have seen enough of the world to know what is what, but I, as your affectionate cousin, cannot agree with you.

Let me continue with this narrative, with renewed implorations that you read what is here as being for your benefit, a timely warning—albeit an unwelcome and unsolicited one—given to one of my own blood who appears to be willing to damn himself forever as a gesture of pique.

This man, the fellow I have mentioned who cared so little for his fellow man, was rumored to have wealth hidden in his house. Because he kept few servants and did not pay them well or treat them with respect, two of them were willing to speak of their master with strangers who accosted them at a local inn. They revealed, for the price of a small meal and two tankards of wine, that they had never seen the treasure their master was supposed to possess but had never been given any information by him that it did not. They were venal enough to accept a small bribe to inform these strangers of the best way into the man's house, and then, being full of food and wine, wended their way back to their master's house smug in the knowledge that they had at last some profit for their dealings with the man.

The strangers were, of course, thieves, and desperate men, who two nights later broke into the house and began to search for the treasure they wished to find. The man had only three servants who slept in the house itself, the others being required to stay in the farmers' houses on his estate, and these three were quickly overwhelmed by the robbers. Had their master shown them more regard and thereby sealed their loyalty, it might have gone otherwise, for it was apparent that his servants were not much moved to protect him. So it was that the robbers plundered through the house, searching for the treasure said to be hidden there. When none was found, the robbers determined to extract the location from the man who owned the estate, and they took up the task with skill and determination. First they bound him and hit his ankles with metal rods, demanding that the man tell them where he had hidden his gold. It was useless for the man to protest that he had none, that his father had left him none, and that he was of a solitary nature and not merely a miser. The robbers, as is often the case with such violent men, did not believe him, and so worked greater harm on his flesh, culminating with blinding him. Then they set fire to the house, so great was their disappointment and anger at not discovering the gold they were sure was hidden there.

So the man was now without any property, he was crippled from the blows to his ankles, and he was blind. In vain he called for his servants, who had fled upon the arrival of the robbers. No aid had been summoned on his behalf, no one had come to help him when he had cried out. He might have died in the fire that consumed the house but that the robbers had left one door open and the man was able to drag himself out of it. Once beyond the door, he collapsed, and it was there he woke in the morning, quite alone. None of his servants returned to aid or succor him. When he hauled his maimed body to the nearest church, he was turned away from there because of his apostasy, and the monks at the monastery had no place for him when he at last reached their portals. They promised to pray for him, as they had always done in the past, but they could offer him no shelter and no food, for he had disavowed the company of those in the true faith of God.

So this maimed and ruined man was left to be a beggar on the road, without shelter or aid. His relatives, after a few attempts to find him, abandoned the search and brought the man's nephew to work his land and rebuild his house. They revered his memory as one dead to them already and they strove not to speak ill of him; in consequence they spoke very little of him at all. The man knew suffering without end and distress beyond imagining because he turned from those who would have been his staunch support in his ordeal, and he mocked the very soul of charity, so that it was no longer available to him. When he died he was left to rot in a ditch and wild dogs fed on the flesh of his carcass while his soul descended to Hell, to the ministrations of devils more cruel and cunning than the robbers had ever been. His prayers were useless then, for he had not repented and God no longer had jurisdiction over his soul.

I pray that you will come to your senses in time to keep from treading the same road this unfortunate man trod. I beg you to think of your soul and the souls of those yet unconverted, for they are as much in your hands as are the souls of innocent children who entrust you to bring them protection from evil. You will find no profit in what you do, and you will not thrive if you continue in this way. I urge you to seek the advice of the priests who accompany you and to act upon their recommendations, for that way is the road to salvation and the preservation of your life.

This letter will be carried to you by Frey Andreas on the Sagrada Familia *which departs for the New World on the 22nd day of July, the Feast of Marie Madelaine; it would do well for you to remember her in your thoughts and your devotions, for she was guilty of far more serious sins than you have committed—or so I trust—and was absolved of all of them when she undertook to live a virtuous life. Consider how grievous her trespasses were, and how exalted she is now. You are not incorrigible unless you will make no effort to improve yourself. God will lend you His strength if you will but ask for it. That is the promise which His Son won for all of us with His precious Blood. Do not spurn it, cousin, and never despise it, as you have professed once to do. That Blood was shed for you, and your soul is as much a treasure in Heaven as that of the holiest monks and nuns. Repent your past sins and resolve to sin no more; God will welcome you with the blessed if you truly put your errors behind you. Mère Marie will intercede for you if you will ask it in her Son's Name. How can I tell you what joy it would bring to me to learn that you had put your past behind you? It is always in my thoughts.*

With all my prayers and all my hope that you will turn from your disastrous course and establish yourself with the righteous and the blessed, I send you my blessing.

> *Your cousin,*
> *Jules Mazarin*
> *Cardinal and First Minister of France*
> *On the 8th day of July, 1645*

1

A single small bell gave the six chimes of midnight; in the chapel the Hour was greeted with soft chanting that reached all the way to the infirmary where San Germanno bent over a man far gone in fever. The two monks serving the dying paused to cross themselves and were no longer astonished that San Germanno waited until he was finished with caring for the man to do so.

Frey Angelito shook his head as San Germanno came toward him, the sleeves of his black camisa rolled up to his elbows, his black ropilla left negligently over a hook by the door, although the infirmary was almost cold this early spring night. The monk peered down the row of simple beds toward the man San Germanno had just finished tending. "He will not live past sunrise."

"Probably not," San Germanno agreed quietly, wishing Frey Angelito would lower his voice. "But he can have what little comfort we can give before then."

In the year and a half San Germanno had been a tertiary in the Carmelite community, Frey Angelito had not been able to trust the foreigner, and it bothered him to realize it: the man was too calm, too willing to treat the dying, too competent for the monk to believe the tale that San Germanno was a minor noble and an instructor from the Universidad de Salamanca who was seeking to expiate the errors of his studies through humble service rather than face the questions of the Inquisition. From the time he had arrived at the community, leading three mules and accompanied by his taciturn manservant, he had become an object of intense curiosity. His background was believable, of course; many men with radical notions had braved the perils of the New World to escape the limits of the Old. But to Frey Angelito, this was not explanation enough. There had to be something more to him, something he had not revealed, something that would account for his fearlessness in the face of the most hideous diseases, and for his preference for tending to the dying at night. That last was particularly troublesome to Frey Angelito, who thought that those who preferred the night did so for nefarious reasons. He filled the silence between them by signaling to Frey Joaquin, who was preparing a five-year-old child for burial. "How many more?"

"I do not know—six, perhaps seven." Old Frey Joaquin never indicated any distress in his work, another thing that bothered Frey Angelito, who could not summon the stoicism he knew was expected of him.

"And tomorrow?" Frey Angelito pursued, hoping to force a response from the old monk. "How many tomorrow?"

"Another five or six," said Frey Joaquin. "The fever has not yet run its course through the villages. We will see more before it is over. This is a hard year for these people."

"A hard year, yes," declared Frey Angelito. He made no effort to keep the sarcasm out of his voice. "This place does not give easy years, does it? They have been dying in droves for a century here. No one living in these mountains can claim an easy life."

Frey Joaquin shrugged as he continued to bathe the child's body, preparatory to wrapping it in a shroud. "Down in the jungles, along the rivers to the east, there are sights that would make the worst of what you have seen here appear mild. While I was at the Siete Santos mission, we were driven out by a vast army of ants that devoured all in their path—nothing lived where they had been: no tree, no creature, no man. But there were other hardships in that place, and doubtless these evils continue. It was a sign from God when our Order founded this community. We should have been content with what we had, but we went into that terrible green hell, and thought the Devil could not touch us. There are men in that place with a kind of leprosy that rots bones instead of flesh. There are insects whose bites are so venomous that their victims swell beyond the limits of their bodies to contain it; their skin splits open like ripe fruit. This place is nothing compared to Siete Santos."

Frey Angelito laughed. "Tales for children and old maids!"

"You were not there," said Frey Joaquin, and crossed himself as he moved to the next child's corpse.

"And you, San Germanno: do you believe any of this?" Frey Angelito challenged, wanting to dismiss all the old monk had told him.

He did not raise his head from his tending to a woman with a large suppurating growth on her thigh. "I do not disbelieve," said San Germanno quietly.

It was not the answer Frey Angelito sought. He made an impatient gesture and then informed them, "I am not an infant, to be gulled by such accounts."

"It would be unwise to discount all you hear," San Germanno said quietly, "and only because you dislike it, or it is not in accordance with your opinions."

Frey Angelito was stung to a hasty reaction. "And I am no simpleton, no matter what you think."

"No one has said you are," San Germanno reminded him, his manner unfailingly courteous. "You are the one persisting in asking questions; it is strange that you should so dislike the answers."

"Well, someone must ask," said Frey Angelito, feeling ill-used. "If no one questions you, we may come to learn that you have committed terrible crimes before and will do so here, when we have grown lax in our attention."

San Germanno paused in his work to regard Frey Angelito with a steady, enigmatic gaze. "Do you truly think so."

Those dark eyes seemed to contain secrets that Frey Angelito dreaded; he looked away and coughed once. "I am only concerned for the welfare of the community. I did not mean anything uncharitable."

"Certainly not," said San Germanno cordially. He went back to cleaning the growth and coating it with a substance the color of berries. "A shame this was allowed to become so large before she asked our help: it cannot be removed now without causing her to bleed to death in the process. Had she come when it was small, there might have been a way to stop its growth without harming her with our treatment." He looked about for the ewer of wine, and poured some of it into a cup, then added a little of a honey-like substance from a large stoneware jar. "This will lessen her pain."

"What is it?" asked Frey Angelito.

"Syrup of poppies," said San Germanno, recalling that his supply would not last him much more than another year, given his current rate of use. He would have to send word to Olivia to provide more when she sent her next shipment of his native earth.

"But it may kill her," protested the young Carmelite monk, recalling all the dire warnings he had heard about this evil substance. "Doubtless she will fall under its influence. Surely that is wrong."

"Why?" San Germanno's attractive, irregular features were hard to read in the low light, but a world-weariness came over him that made him appear suddenly older and less amiable. "The canker will kill her, no matter what we do; that is certain and beyond our power to remedy. Her death is inevitable. If she has the syrup of poppies at least she will not die in unspeakable pain." He looked directly at Frey Angelito. "Your Superior does not prohibit my using this: why should you?"

This last goaded Frey Angelito into a hasty reply. "You have cozened Frey Ardo. We all know you have. You cannot hide it from us." He slapped his hands together as if to rid them of dust. "Since you came, Frey Ardo has permitted you such liberties as no tertiary Brother is entitled to have. Look at you, with your silken clothes, serving with monks in homespun. You are allowed to keep your manservant. You wear that signet ring, for pride. You do not take Communion, you—"

"But I do not wear my device as a pendant, nor my diamond Order of Saint Stephan; surely that counts for something." His eyes were ironic as they met Frey Angelito's. "If Frey Ardo is not displeased, why are you? Do you not accept his guidance in all things?" San Germanno inquired gently. He had finished tipping the poppy-laced wine down the woman's throat.

"Some of us do not deceive ourselves in your regard. We do not accept your pretense at humility," Frey Angelito went on, his voice lowered in response to a disapproving frown from Frey Joaquin. "Some of us are aware that you have taken advantage of our Superior's goodness. It brings no honor to our Order to have our Superior taken in by one who may be a fugitive. We are not pleased that you have done this."

"Why do you say so?" It was not San Germanno's question, but Frey Joaquin's. "How do you claim to speak for more of us than yourself?"

Knowing that he was treading on uncertain footing now, Frey Angelito softened his words. "We notice things, some of the others and I. We . . . have expressed our worries and found them shared."

Frey Joaquin made an abrupt motion, indicating that Frey Angelito had overstepped his bounds. "Gossip is forbidden. You need not be reminded that we are enjoined not to gossip, for it leads to great errors and much shame. You will have to Confess what you have done."

"Confess?" repeated Frey Angelito indignantly. "If this . . . this foreigner had not brought gold with him, do you think Frey Ardo would tolerate his ways?"

"As a tertiary, I cannot see what cause we have to complain of him; if he were a novice, it would be different, but he has taken no vows but his promise of assistance to us, and life in accordance with our Rule," Frey Joaquin said quietly. "And I will not continue to speak of this with you, for that will lead me into the sin of gossip myself, which I do not want on my soul." With that, he went back to washing the body of a dead child, this one a girl of about four, who was wasted by fever and thirst. "Have the graves been completed?"

Frey Angelito accepted this indirect rebuke as well as he could. "I believe so. Frey Anselmo has gone to bed. He would still be working if the graves were not ready."

"Very well," said Frey Joaquin. "These four are ready. Frey Roberto will sing the Office with you." He watched as Frey Angelito placed the shrouded children on the two-wheeled handcart. "The others will be prepared by the time you have completed the rites for these."

San Germanno went on with his tasks, and only when Frey Angelito had left the infirmary did he say, "Thank you," to Frey Joaquin.

"Frey Ardo will have to speak to him, I fear, about obedience," he said, and apologized, "It is not fitting that I make the same error for which I rebuked him; I should not speak of these things to you. It is not seemly, or humble in him or in me. Forgive me this imposition."

"You have not offended me," San Germanno said steadily. "Not even Frey Angelito has offended me, try as he may." Wry amusement twisted the corners of his mouth and faded at once. He rose from the woman's side and moved to the next bed, his face carefully composed so as not to distress the young man who lay there; he had shown himself to be very perceptive in reading the expressions of those caring for him and his acuity increased as his disease grew worse and his world narrowed down to the cot and those around it. "So there, Sipu, how are you tonight?"

"Frey Silvandros is saying the Requiem for me now," Sipu answered in a voice roughened and hushed by infected lungs.

"Did he tell you?" San Germanno asked lightly, inwardly cursing Frey Silvandros for a consciousless fool; if Sipu doubted the mortality of his disease, Frey Silvandros had removed any chance of hope. He could tell by the odor clinging to the young man that the end was not far away.

Sipu coughed, and fresh blood spots appeared on the sheet that covered him. "He did not have to." He looked at San Germanno, his eyes shining with fever. "He is right to pray for me."

San Germanno could not find it in his heart to offer Sipu false cheer, so he said, "Do you want his prayers?"

Sipu was startled, and took a short while to consider his answer. "So long as they are not the only prayers."

"That will be arranged," San Germanno promised him. "I will see to it myself."

"I am grateful," said Sipu, knowing San Germanno could be trusted.

"It isn't necessary to be grateful," he said, feeling a rush of chagrin for all the times he had heard these mortal words, and how little he had been able to do. Arranging for prayers was a small matter; watching Sipu die was far more difficult.

"The monks will not do it," said Sipu, and coughed up more blood. "I will speak of you to the old gods, when I am in their company."

"Shh," San Germanno admonished him, wiping his face with a damp cloth. "You need not talk. Save your strength." Ever since he had served as a slave at the Temple of Imhotep he had witnessed the final hours of those beyond recovery, and he had long ago learned he could not grant his particular semi-immortality to them: vampire-life was not sought by most, and those few who had come to his undead state had done so with reservations, a few learning they could not endure it. This realization San Germanno was always discovering afresh, and never more poignantly than now, when he felt Sipu's life slipping the moorings of its fragile human bark.

"Not long," Sipu whispered, perceiving some hint of San Germanno's thoughts on his countenance.

"Probably not," San Germanno said, knowing it was cruel to lie.

"Good." Sipu stopped struggling to speak; he lay back, his chest rising and falling with effort, a low fluttering accompanying each breath.

San Germanno moved away from Sipu and gave his attention to an old man whose greyish skin and irregular pulse indicated his death was near. "There is nothing more we can do for him," he said softly to Frey Joaquin. "He will pass from this sleep by midday."

"His brother has asked that we send word when that happens," said Frey Joaquin. "I will do it though Frey Ardo does not encourage such things."

San Germanno had heard the Superior's animadversions on the subject many times, and said, "He will have to pardon the people of this region if they are not as willing to surrender all to God as the Carmelites are."

Frey Joaquin achieved a slight smile. "I suppose so," he agreed; he regarded San Germanno in silence for a short while, then said, "Are you never afraid?"

"Afraid?" San Germanno repeated, his demeanor unaltered but his full attention now on Frey Joaquin. "Afraid of what?"

"The fever, for one. The flux, for another; all the things we treat." He folded his hands briefly to show his respect for these terrible things.

"*You* do not seem to be frightened of them," San Germanno pointed out, aware that he was not answering the question.

"I am old and called of God," said Frey Joaquin.

"Does that make a difference?" San Germanno asked. "No one seeks to die like this, yet everyone dies, in time."

"In time, I reckon they do," said Frey Joaquin, and continued to prepare winding sheets for the bodies awaiting burial.

The rest of the night was uneventful, marked by silent routine among the cots of the dying. San Germanno went about his duties with an efficiency Frey Joaquin might have envied had he not suspected that the capacity the man displayed was hard-won. The two men spoke rarely, and when they did, their voices were low so as not to disturb those Indians they cared for. Shortly before dawn, Frey Roberto came to collect the last of the bodies to be buried before the first Mass of the morning. He kept his face in the shadow of his hood in order to conceal the large, mulberry-colored birthmark that covered most of the right cheek and jaw.

"The fever is taking a high toll. Frey Angelito has complained of it tonight," he said to Frey Joaquin as the two of them loaded the shrouded bodies onto his two-wheeled handcart. "If it lasts much longer we will have to enlarge the cemetery."

"That will have to be done eventually, in any case," said Frey Joaquin, pausing to cross himself. Then he lifted the body of a child onto the cart and stood back. "That is the last for now."

"*Deo gratias,*" said Frey Roberto with feeling. He glanced in San Germanno's direction. "Still helping, is he?"

"More than any other," said Frey Joaquin.

"His manservant has assisted with digging graves," Frey Roberto admitted grudgingly.

"Then perhaps the Superior was wise to let the man remain with his master," said Frey Joaquin. He saw that his suggestion fell on deaf ears. "At a time like this, a pair of willing hands is useful."

"That it is," said Frey Roberto. He prepared to depart, then added to Frey Joaquin in an undervoice, "There are some who are saying the fever is here because of him." He hitched his shoulder in San Germanno's direction. "They say the reason he treats it so well is that he brought it with him."

"And do you believe that?" asked Frey Joaquin with enough scorn to make it apparent which answer he sought.

"Certainly not," Frey Roberto blustered, continuing in a hurried whisper, "But Frey Angelito has alarmed some of the Brothers, telling them that he has seen San Germanno do things that no Christian could permit, things that only the ungodly would consider doing. He claims the only reason he did not stop the foreigner was that he did not want to disobey the Superior."

"It is true he does not bleed most patients," said Frey Joaquin in a reasonable manner. "He believes it causes more harm than it does good. Nothing any of us have told him has changed his mind."

"Frey Angelito says—" Frey Roberto began, only to be cut off by Frey Joaquin.

"Frey Angelito would do well to keep a still tongue in his head." The warning was clear; Frey Joaquin wanted no more gossip.

Frey Roberto took Frey Joaquin's meaning and shrugged. "I had better get these unfortunates into the ground before Mass." With practiced ease, he grasped the handles of the cart and steered it out of the infirmary.

When he was gone, San Germanno spoke from his place beside a middle-aged woman who was dying of childbed fever. "He will not be silent long."

"No, I do not think he will," said Frey Joaquin with a sigh. "If you were not a foreigner . . . " He faltered, steadied himself, and began again. "If you were Spanish or Portuguese or even Italian, they might not be so suspicious; if you were willing to join the Order, fewer doubts would be felt. But you have skills exceeding their own and you are from Hungary, and that to them is as remote as the shores of China."

"And, as you say, I am only a tertiary," San Germanno added for him. "If I would become a novice, they would not mind as much." He laughed softly. "A novice. At my age. With my history."

"God would not mind," Frey Joaquin assured him.

"The Brothers would," San Germanno countered with certainty. "Little as you and I may want to think ill of them, they are like most men: they do not trust what they do not understand."

"Does that include God?" Frey Joaquin challenged him.

"Of course it does," San Germanno replied, an expression of reluctant amusement lightening his face. "Who among us, being mortal, is certain of the nature of God? Do you not think that when most men declare their trust in God, they are expressing a hope and not a conviction?"

"No wonder you left the Universidad de Salamanca," said Frey Joaquin. "Such opinions cannot have won you many allies. And no wonder the Holy Office of the Faith wanted to have words with you, through the Secular Arm." Even this passing reference to the Inquisition sobered the old monk. "Better to remain in the Viceroyalty of Peru among the most heathen of people than to risk the Office's displeasure."

"I agree," San Germanno said quietly. He came across the room to Frey Joaquin. "I do not mean to burden you with my opinions, dangerous as they might be. Pay no attention."

"As you wish," said Frey Joaquin. He stood aside to permit San Germanno to make his way to the door. "I will see you after Vespers?"

"Yes. After Vespers." With a gesture that was almost a flourish, he draped his ropilla over his shoulders. "God keep you, Frey Joaquin."

"And you, San Germanno," came the response.

Striding out of the infirmary he went across the compound of the Carmelite community toward the simple two-room house Frey Ardo had granted him and Rogerio. It was the last in a line of two- and four-room plank buildings that housed all the members of the community. Overhead the sky was silvery with the coming dawn. Today, thought San Germanno as he squinted upward, today I will prepare a letter to be carried to Olivia. When I waken, I will write. Or better—I will write before I sleep. Remembering Olivia gave him an intense pang of loneliness. How was she faring in Paris now? if she was still in Paris; had her fascination with that young Gascon Guard deepened into passion as she had hoped it would? He longed for one of her letters, filled with her affection and exasperation. As he stepped into the spartan interior of his lodgings, he felt his isolation keenly.

Rogerio was pulling out San Germanno's long camisa for him to sleep in, shaking out the long black folds with the efficiency of long practice. He did not turn as San Germanno approached. "They are saying that a party of monks traveling with an armed company is coming this way."

"Who says this?" San Germanno asked, knowing how quickly such rumors spread through communities like this one.

"The women in the market," Rogerio replied quietly. "The women you visit in dreams."

San Germanno gave Rogerio a thoughtful stare. "Are you suggesting I risk being discovered to find out about the rumor?"

"No," Rogerio answered.

"But you think that we should be prepared to move on: you are right," San Germanno said with an abrupt, hard sigh. "It may be past time to leave."

This time Rogerio's response was oblique. "They say the fever is getting worse."

"And it will continue as long as their well remains compromised," San Germanno said. "That is the cause. There is contagion in the water. As it was when we stood with Niklos Aulirios when the Huns came. Had the wells been pure, we would have held them off much longer."

"You are certain it is the water?" Rogerio asked, turning to hand the camisa to San Germanno.

"As certain as I can be without tasting the victims' blood." San Germanno went to the single table in the room and drew out the straight-backed wooden chair. "Is there vellum left?"

"A dozen sheets," said Rogerio. "The ink is—" He opened the lid of an inlaid box to reveal the ink-pad, seals, wax, and untrimmed quills.

"Very good, my friend." He was about to pare a nib on one of the quills when he thought of another thing. "When does the next courier leave for Quito?"

"In two days," Rogerio told him. "He will arrive tonight unless there is some mishap."

"Is there any reason to think there will be trouble?" San Germanno asked with a slight lift of his fine brows.

"No," Rogerio answered. "But the fever is spreading, and many of the people in the villages around this place have fled in the hope of saving themselves. You are aware of this."

"And their flight will spread the fever," San Germanno said with a slow nod. "Of course. It will be more virulent and last longer because more people have left the region." He continued to work on fashioning the nib he would need. "Two sheets of vellum should be sufficient," he told Rogerio, adding his thanks when Rogerio laid them on the table in front of him.

"You may want to ask her to send more vellum when she arranges to ship your native earth," Rogerio recommended as he went into the other room where San Germanno's narrow, austere bed lay atop one of his few remaining chests of his native earth.

"So I might," San Germanno agreed. He moistened the ink-cake and rubbed it with a smooth jade stone, then dipped his nib into it. His handwriting was small and precise, without flourish or elaborations that were the current fashion in Europe; the lines were straight and the language he used—the Latin of Imperial Rome—was eloquent without formality or artifice. He wrote quickly, making no corrections or changes as he went. Once an errant drop of ink spattered on the page and he blotted it with a corner of the cloth reserved for that purpose. All the while, as he wrote, he thought of Olivia herself, of the fifteen hundred years they had shared since she came to his life through his blood; he was missing her with such immediacy that it shocked him. He did what he could to put the emotion into words, and knew she would sense this, as those who shared blood did, far more clearly than he could describe the emotion.

When the letter was completed, he had covered one of the vellum sheets with words. The other he folded around the first, wrote her name and the name of her small estate near Paris on it, then sealed it with ribbon and wax kept in the same box as the ink-cake, fixing the seal in place with his signet ring. He held the letter in his hand for a short while as the room lightened with the rising sun. Then he set it down and rose, stretching.

"How much longer, my master?" Rogerio inquired as he saw San Germanno get up from writing.

"Not much longer, old friend. It wouldn't be wise; I am aware of it. Perhaps there will be a party we may travel with, away from Lima and Cuzco." San Germanno looked about him. "It has been a respite, staying here, but it will not be much longer."

"Do you know where we will go next?" There was nothing in the way he asked to imply that he had any preferences at all.

"Not back to Europe yet, I think," San Germanno replied. "Not if the news we hear is accurate. But there are more places in the Americas we might consider. Places where the Viceroyalty of Peru is not the final authority, and where the Church has not yet taken hold of the minds of the people." He paused. "I am relieved that we saw this place before all the people and their way of life died."

Rogerio studied San Germanno's face, then said, "Because your own people are gone?"

"In part," San Germanno agreed, a twinge of impossible homesickness for that distant place in the bow of the Carpathians making him blink away distant memories. He glanced toward the window. "And it is time I slept; so near the equator the sun exacts a price."

"I will prepare the bathing tub for you at sunset, my master,"

Rogerio said as San Germanno went into his chamber.

"Thank you," San Germanno said. "And if something can be done to wash these camisas? The monks may call it vanity to keep them clean, but—" He stopped, his face showing slight distaste.

"Certainly," said Rogerio smoothly. "It will be attended to."

"And Rogerio," San Germanno added quietly, "I will be going beyond the walls tonight, before I report to the infirmary."

"I will make sure there are no questions asked." He had told the monks that his master met with Indian teachers who would only speak to him under cover of darkness, a tale that had the advantage of being partly true.

"Very good," San Germanno said, and began to remove his clothing, handling the garments with pragmatic care. "If you must awaken me—"

"I will," Rogerio assured him, and went about his duties as San Germanno lay down to sleep the sun away.

Text of a letter from Francisco Ragoczy in Peru to Atta Olivia Clemens in France, written in Latin.

To the Bondama Atta Olivia Clemens, Roman widow, residing at Eblouir near Chatillon in France, the enduring affection and greetings from the Viceroyalty of Peru, the Audiencia de Quito, which may as well be the moon.

This is to tell you that I will shortly be leaving this Carmelite community, bound to the north, so I hope, or west. When I have established myself elsewhere, I will send you word of it, and arrange to receive the chests and anything else stored in Santa Marta, for I cannot bring myself to undergo the agony of another Atlantic crossing quite yet, and this is not a voyage I intend to make twice. When I have learned more, then it will be time to seal myself in a chest of my native earth and endure miseries of the Atlantic Ocean. In the meantime, I ask you to send me a dozen crates of my native earth to the care of Eduardo Medallo, builder, in the port of Santa Marta, and three stoneware jars of syrup of poppies: I have never seen any place but a battlefield so in need of medicaments as this one.

They say that when the Spanish came these mountains were thickly populated. That is no longer the case. And it was not war that struck them down, but oppression and disease—simple things, not cholera or Plague or typhus. Measles would seem to be the worst, although many

*others have taken their toll as well, including smallpox, which has rav-
aged the Spanish along with the Indians. The records of Bartolme de las
Casas chronicle this all too clearly, that whole villages died out in two
generations, and the people are dying still. There are fevers here that
have struck back but not with the virulence of those brought from Europe. I have been studying the ways in which the people of this land treat
their diseases and have learned a great deal of which the monks do not
approve, in large part because they work.*

*Cherished Olivia, I cannot tell you how much I miss the Old World,
and not simply because my native earth is there: I miss having many
books, and hearing madrigals as well as chants and hymns. I miss the
splendid statues and frescos of Firenze, and the turmoil of Rome. I miss
having the viol and virginals to play. I miss the theatre, and booksellers,
and well-sprung carriages. I miss my homes, even those no longer as elegant as fashion demands. I miss the nearness of you. However, I do
not miss the wars being waged from Sweden to Egypt in the name of
religion, or the relentless persecution of those who disagree with the
powerful. I do not miss the pettiness and arbitrariness of officials who
pretend to mete out justice. I do not miss the continuing cruelty of need-
less poverty and the indifference to those in despair. Yes, it is likely I can
find no place in the world where such things do not happen. For the sake
of those who dare to think, I would wish it otherwise.*

*To answer your question, no, I have taken no one but in dreams since
the death of Acanna Tupac. Even you would agree it would be dangerous to attempt such a thing surrounded by monks as I am. It is true
that no disease can touch me, but those in my care deserve other treatment at my hands than diminishing my needs, so I do not presume upon
any who come here. And to be candid, I am not prepared to lose another lover: not yet. Let me have some time to mourn before you upbraid
me for maintaining my isolation. The pleasure found in giving dreams
may be ephemeral, but it will suffice for now.*

*In this regard, I trust you continue to enjoy that Guardsman with the
eyebrows. You tell me he is not easily discouraged, and that you no
longer want to discourage him. Were it in me to be jealous, I would be
jealous of him. As it is, I am at once joyful and not sad but perhaps wistful for your alliance with the man. To have someone know you for our
nature and to love you, not in spite of it, but because of it is a thing I
have sought for millennia and have never found. What luxury, to be
accepted without reservation. Savor it, treasure it, and honor him who
gives himself to you; as I know you do.*

*This carries my continuing love as well as my longing for the day
when I see you face to face once again,*

*Ragoczy Sanct' Germain Franciscus
with the Carmelites
(his sigil, the eclipse)
By my own hand, 17th day of October, 1645*

2

Don Vicente's mourning medallion was properly worn above his heart, the portrait of his wife enclosed in silver cypress boughs. Aside from the medallion, nothing in his dress or demeanor suggested bereavement: his garments were official, his posture was upright, his brow was lowered in a glower, and his mouth was set in hard lines. He studied his hands as they lay bunched on the table, and when he spoke, he did not look up at Dom Enrique, who waited before him. "I would not impose on your siesta, but the matter we must discuss cannot wait: I have been informed that you have exceeded your encomienda."

"Exceeded?" Dom Enrique exclaimed, posturing indignantly as he tried to think who might be seeking to slander him. Of all things he had expected in the summons to the Corregidor, this was not one of them. He had supposed his cousin had left him a legacy of some sort, perhaps a jewel or two as a remembrance. At most he had expected to have to pay a higher bribe to Don Vicente for his continued tacit assistance. "How? In what way? Who makes such a claim?" He felt two threads of sweat run down his neck to be lost in his lace-edged collar; he decided it was caused by the heat of the summer day and not the tone the Corregidor took with him.

"Be quiet," said Don Vicente reasonably, startling Dom Enrique into silence. "I have said you have exceeded your encomienda, which permitted you to explore, not to pillage. I do not make such an accusation lightly. I have here a number of complaints from Cuzco—"

"Don Ezequias!" Dom Enrique scoffed.

"Not only he, and not that it is important that he notified me as he did, given the information I have been provided from other sources."

He patted one of the papers under his hand. "I have it on the authority of Don Alejandro Morena y Osma that you and your associates have gone so far as to commandeer servants from households and farmers from the fields. You had no mine needing workers, and no land to put under the plow. Taking the men was an abuse of the encomienda." He looked up at Dom Enrique for the first time. "There have been arrests. I have received word that certain of your . . . fellow-miscreants have been incarcerated."

Now Dom Enrique was alarmed. "Who has been arrested? And jailed? You say that we have done wrong, but why do you say so? How have we offended, that anyone might accuse us? Of what crime? What purpose does it fulfill? And why? Why would you so abuse a kinsman?" He was blustering, and it bothered him to realize it; he felt his cheeks darken as he spoke.

"Three of the men said they were acting on your authority, the authority of your encomienda," said Don Vicente as if he had not heard the barrage of questions. "Lazaro Escaso. Martin Vigaracimos. Diego Herrero. There are others, but these claimed to have had permission from you for all they did."

Uncertain as to how to proceed, Dom Enrique folded his hands and looked at the huge crucifix on the wall above the Corregidor's head. What damage would it do if it fell? he wondered. It would be divine intervention, without doubt. It was tempting to laugh at the notion, but it would not benefit him now. He composed his thoughts for an answer. "These men have helped me, it is true. And help is needed if we are to find maps to show us where the hidden cities are, with their treasures. We had to investigate many places, to try to discover what the Indians have hidden from us for so long. Van Zwolle and I could not accomplish all together. We sought deputies. They were eager to be part of the work I am about. I did not issue them many instructions, thinking we were in accord. But I did not tell them to do . . . whatever they have done." He caught himself in time. "If they have gone beyond the law, it is their own doing. I never told them to do anything contrary to the law. I swear it on the grave of my mother."

"That remains to be seen, although the first reports do not support your claim," said Don Vicente, rising abruptly and going to the partially shuttered window. "It is like you to place the blame on others, and to give a lying vow. You are not above compelling others to your will. You do not always uphold the limits of the law." He swung around. "Or do you wish to deny what you said to me in the whorehouse?"

The protestation he was going to make died on Dom Enrique's lips; he strove to recover his self-possession, protesting, "That was because Don Ezequias did not want to grant me—"

Don Vicente held up his hand to silence Dom Enrique, saying in a world-weary tone, "Spare me your denunciation of Don Ezequias, and your protestations of innocence. I am not so gullible as you think me, nor so trusting. It would not serve the purposes of the Crown if I were. I have long experience of Don Ezequias, and men of your cut, as well." He looked out into the street again, squinting a little against the brilliant light piercing the shadows of his office through the shutters. "You did not suppose I would accept your account of the matter on face value, did you? Or that I would not inquire what you had done with the authority granted to you? I may be venal, my erstwhile cousin, but I am not wholly corrupt."

It took Dom Enrique a moment to find his voice. "I would never . . . You cannot suppose I would accuse you?"

"You did threaten to accuse me," Don Vicente reminded him. "And while my wife lived, I had no choice but to accommodate you in this matter, for I would not bring disgrace upon her. I owed her that much respect. You had her favor, although la Virgen alone knows why, and she would hear nothing to your discredit. She required of me that I protect you, and I obliged her. But," he went on with a sigh, "she is dead now, and I am not constrained to honor her family as I was."

"May God welcome her in Paradise," said Dom Enrique, crossing himself.

"No doubt, no doubt," said Don Vicente. "And I must be grateful to her for choosing such an opportune time to depart this sinful world, making it possible for me to find the whole of your crimes before you fled with your gains." He strolled away from the window, going past Dom Enrique. "I am pleased to be released from my duty to you. I am no longer prepared to indulge you, Dom Enrique, as you wish to be indulged. And I no longer have to." He rounded on the young Portuguese nobleman. "Your encomienda is revoked as of this morning. You have no licenses of any kind from this Residencia, and it will avail you nothing to seek new ones, not in the Viceroyalty of Peru."

"What do you mean?" Dom Enrique had gone pale about the mouth.

"My couriers left at dawn for the Audiencias of the Viceroyalty with my notification to the Presidencias of what you have done, and warning them that they will be held accountable for your acts should they disregard my orders. You will not be permitted to abuse my position again." His smile was satisfied, and he walked the length of the room more quickly. "You overstepped, Dom Enrique. You have gone much too far, too greedily and too obviously."

"I . . . I have done nothing wrong," Dom Enrique began and heard himself whine.

"You stole from Acanna Tupac's house, and not an old map, as you may claim. If you found such a map, you had no need of it. You took masks and cloaks and urns. You sold what you took. You raided the house of the foreigner Ragoczy with the supposed authority of the probanza, which only entitled you to his horses. Do not"—he raised his hand in warning—"attempt to deny it. I have statements from several men of honor. Don Gregorio Calderon y Mazez was good enough to inform me of what you did at Ragoczy's house, for he felt he owed his neighbor some assistance; there was no one to guard the man's belongings, and so you ransacked the place, which disturbed Calderon y Mazez. Ragoczy had been of help to him in the past, and he did not like to see an honorable gentleman treated like a desperado."

"Ragoczy *is* a desperado," Dom Enrique insisted, clinging to the hope that he could persuade the Corregidor to change his mind. "Ask anyone who has met him. He is a charlatan, at the least."

"I doubt that," said Don Vicente dryly. "All reports but yours favor the man, giving him credit for many worthy acts."

"The better to suborn the unsuspecting," said Dom Enrique, trying his best to appear righteous. "He is taking advantage of those around him, putting them in his debt and using their good will to his own ends. He is without scruples of any kind."

"He may seem to be to you, but he wears the Order of Saint Stephen of Hungary." In response to the look of astonishment in Dom Enrique's eyes, he said, "You have a very poor opinion of me, Dom Enrique. You think I know nothing of the people living in the Viceroyalty. A fine Corregidor I would be if a foreign nobleman came here and I was unaware of it."

It was worse than Dom Enrique had thought. He cleared his throat. "You do not call him Conde de San Germanno," he pointed out weakly.

"No. I call him by his highest title: Infante Don Francisco Ragoczy; he is the heir to his father's lands, and his father was a king. Conde de San Germanno is the only title he uses while his country is in the hands of the Turks, for the county remains his." He paused to allow Dom Enrique to consider this. "And before you question this authority, I have it from the personal secretary of His Holiness, Urban VIII. And again, before you claim he influenced the late Pope, I have assurances from the secretary of Innocent X, stating that all information regarding Ragoczy is correct."

"But if his lands are controlled by the Turks, isn't he without anything, and might he not be eager to make a new place for himself here?" Dom Enrique thought the question was feeble, but he could not stop himself from asking it: anything to make it appear he was within his rights to seize the property San Germanno abandoned.

"Not according to all reports I have," said Don Vicente. He went back to his place behind his writing table and stood beside his chair. "After you approached me the last time, I made a few more inquiries, including ones carried to España and to Rome. I thought it would be useful to know as much as possible. I received the first of my answers a year ago, and I have had confirmation from many sources since. There is no reason whatsoever to think that this Ragoczy wishes to establish himself here, in any capacity at all; I have made the necessary inquiries and I am convinced he has no such purposes in the New World. The bulk of his fortune—and it is formidable—remains in Europe, and he has five houses he keeps in readiness against his return. So," the Corregidor went on with false affability, "I hope you will admit you have taken on more than you can handle."

Dom Enrique folded his arms. "How was I to know these things? You had to send messages to Europe to learn of them. You will not tell me I was wrong to be suspicious."

"No; I will not tell you that," Don Vicente allowed. "But had my wife not been your cousin, I would have asked more pointed questions than I have. And I would have asked them sooner, no matter what you know of my tastes in amusements." He sat down, separated two sheets of vellum from the others in front of him and handed them to Dom Enrique. "You are under warrant to surrender all goods currently in your possession that you have seized on the authority of your encomienda. You are to present all of them to Don Ezequias for restoration to those entitled to have them. This includes the work and services of the men and women you have demanded." He looked Dom Enrique directly in the face. "If you fail to do this within two days of your return to Cuzco, or if you leave Lima for any other city in Peru, you will be subject to arrest."

"But . . . how can you . . . what justification do you have?" He stood a bit straighter. "We are the conquerors here."

"And as such we do not have to disoblige our fellows or misuse the people we have conquered." He sighed, shaking his head in mild disbelief. "Dom Enrique: how short-sighted of you. You did not suppose that Don Ezequias was the only man in Peru who was sent here for unacceptable ideas, did you? Or that he was alone in his convictions about the people of these mountains? I must inform you that he has allies in his thought. Some of us believe we cannot look upon the Indians as less than human. Some of us are willing to put our beliefs to the test." He smiled slightly, mirthlessly. "I was sent here for much the same reason as Don Ezequias was, and I have not changed my opinions any more than he has."

Now Dom Enrique was thoroughly confused. "You do not support the claims of the Incans, do you? How can you do it? We are the people sent by God to . . . to bring their souls to . . . "

"Not that you are concerned for anyone's soul, including your own," said Don Vicente with a gesture of resignation. "You made a crucial error, Dom Enrique: you assumed that because I take my pleasures in ways you regard as immoral that I have no regard for those around me."

Dom Enrique gave an irate stare at the pages still held out to him. "You said yourself you are venal."

"And I am. But I am also sworn to uphold the honor of my office and España, and I will do that to the limits of my skills, though I like to sleep with two whores at a time, and pay to watch others in the act." He reached for a small bell on the side of his writing table. "Padre Bocan will see you out," he said as if abruptly disinterested.

"How can you do this!" Dom Enrique burst out as Padre Bocan came into the room.

"Oh, I could do much worse," said Don Vicente blandly. "I could imprison you at once. But for the sake of my late wife, I will permit you the chance to make restitution before you answer for your depredations." He pointedly took another sheet of vellum from the loose stack, giving it his whole attention.

This was more than Dom Vicente could endure. He flung down the sheets he had been handed. "I will not! You will not compel me!"

"Of course I can," said Don Vicente. "I am Corregidor. And you are a Portuguese hidalgo whose only link to my authority has been buried for five weeks."

"In España—" Dom Enrique began only to be cut off.

"But we are not in España, we are in Peru," said Don Vicente so reasonably that Dom Enrique wanted to bellow in outrage. "In Peru, you answer to me."

Padre Bocan picked up the two vellum sheets.

"You will have your wife's curse upon you," Dom Vicente declared. "You have disgraced her family."

Don Vicente signaled to Padre Bocan to be still; he cocked his head. "Strange," he mused. "I thought you had done that."

"Not half so much as you," blustered Dom Enrique. What was he going to do? he wondered furiously. He would not give Don Vicente or Don Ezequias the satisfaction of shaming him before all Cuzco. He had to make up his mind what to do now, and quickly. Returning there was out of the question. But that would mean he would have to flee at once. Something occurred to him: Duca Roldo Vila Nova de Gois had a ship getting ready to set sail for Mexico, and de Gois was Portuguese. He would be willing to take him on, and van Zwolle as well. He regarded his dead cousin's husband with contempt. "So you will honor dirty Indians before you defend your relatives."

"In this case, yes: they are more worthy of defense," said Don Vicente. "I have other matters to attend to."

The hint was broad enough, and Dom Enrique decided to take it. "It would be fitting to wish you prosperity and the favor of God and Crown. Yet I cannot find it in me to show such hypocrisy."

"I had not expected it," said Don Vicente, and gestured to Padre Bocan. "My late wife's cousin is leaving."

"Come with me, if you will, Dom Enrique," said Padre Bocan, his face set in the same severe expression he always wore. "You will not want to impose on the Corregidor any longer."

"Certainly not; he may have Indians who need his attention," sneered Dom Enrique as he allowed himself to be led away. He forced himself to think, though his mind was sluggish as if he had been at siesta like the rest of Lima, and he had dreamed the whole. It was not possible for Don Vicente to be as determined as he claimed. Men who passed their afternoons as Don Vicente passed his had no strength of purpose within them. It was the loss of his wife speaking, not his good judgment. Her death had set him against her relatives, out of his missing her: he had seen it before. But it would take a year before the Corregidor could recognize what had happened to him, and for that year, Dom Enrique would have to put some distance between himself and Peru.

"Your partner is waiting," said Padre Bocan as he opened the courtyard door. "May God guide you."

"And you, Padre, and my cousin's husband," said Dom Enrique in what he hoped was a pious voice.

Van Zwolle was waiting in the courtyard of the Residencia, his hat drawn low over his brow to protect him from the stark sunlight. He must have read something of their predicament in Dom Enrique's movements or expression, for he came quickly, saying, "What's gone wrong?"

"Don Vicente," said Dom Enrique, his scowl as deep as it was abrupt. "We have plans to make. Come. There must be somewhere we can get a tankard of wine at this hour, siesta or not."

"Is it bad?" van Zwolle persisted.

"I will tell you when I have had something to drink," Dom Enrique announced with force. "Do you know of such a place? An inn, perhaps, or a tavern?"

"The tavern by the Callao gate? behind the customs shed?" suggested van Zwolle, remembering the many times he had been able to get food and drink there in the past. "They do not close the taproom at siesta."

"Then let us go there at once," said Dom Enrique with a single look over his shoulder at the closed doors of the Residencia. He wanted to be shut of the place, away from Don Vicente, his ridiculous demands and his smug confidence.

The streets were all but deserted, the heat of the day oppressive although it was not yet November, the sun overhead as brilliant as polished brass. A few natives and mestizos were still about, most of them struggling in the midday heat. At the next plaza, a dying mule was being unharnessed from an overladen cart, and a man was readying a pistol to end the animal's suffering.

"What happened?" Van Zwolle kept his distance from the mule, and jumped at the report of the pistol.

"There has been someone working against us. I suspect it is Don Ezequias, for the Corregidor"—he said the title with unflattering flourish—"has revoked the encomienda." He clapped his hand on van Zwolle's shoulder. "I will explain it all once we have tankards of wine in our hands."

"Very good," said van Zwolle, knowing that they might attract undue attention even at this quiet hour. He indicated the alley next to the customs shed, remarking, "Watch out for beggars. They often wait here."

"Let anyone dare to approach me, and he will taste my boot for his pains." Dom Enrique rested his hand on the quillons of his sword, the fingers straddling the hilt. "I will not waste steel on such dregs."

Thinking that his companion was truly in a foul mood, van Zwolle kept his peace, and pointed out the rest of the way until they reached a building with bottles and tankards on the sign over the door. "This is the place," he said.

Dom Enrique shoved through the door ahead of van Zwolle and found himself in a dark taproom, long plank tables set about with benches beside them. He noticed a middle-aged slattern of a woman standing behind the bar, a ragged apron tied around her ample middle. "We want wine."

"We sell wine," she answered, unimpressed by his manner. "It is three silver crowns the bottle at the least to a gold real for the best." She recited this in a singsong as if the words had long since lost their meaning.

Dom Enrique tossed her a gold real, watching with some amusement as she snagged it out of the air. "Two tankards. And something to eat."

"We have stewed goat," she informed him.

"Stewed goat," repeated Dom Enrique. "Well, why not? Two bowls of it, and flat bread, if you have any."

"We have. It is four silver crowns. Apiece." The last was added on impulse, in the hope of earning more money for the tavern.

At another time Dom Enrique would have argued about it, but today, with all that he had endured, he simply nodded and produced the desired coins. "Be quick. We are thirsty men. Who knows but that we will have another bottle of your best before the day is over."

"Who knows?" she repeated owlishly, and left them to themselves.

"Now then," said Dom Enrique, looking about the room as if he expected to find spies lurking in the corners, "I will tell you what Don Vicente has done. We are without the encomienda, and cannot continue our work here. He rescinded it."

"You said it was because of Don Ezequias?" ventured van Zwolle. He said nothing about their work; it had been apparent to him from the first that they would not be permitted to continue their raids indefinitely.

"Someone has done this, and Don Ezequias has never been my friend. He has sought to bring me bad cess from the first. He has allowed some of our men to be arrested. He refused to grant me the encomienda I required, which is why it was necessary to obtain it from Don Vicente," Dom Enrique reminded him. "And now it seems that Don Vicente has been busy making inquiries. They are not to our advantage." He glowered toward the narrow windows. "I see it is all of a piece. We have been made the villains, while the Indians are the suffering innocents in this. As if any of them knew the worth of what they have. According to Don Vicente, if we have taken anything from them, it was not ours by right, but theirs by tradition, and we have overstepped the line." His voice had risen to a near shout.

"Why have there been arrests? Who has been arrested?" van Zwolle asked, hoping to stem the tide of Dom Enrique's anger.

Van Zwolle laid his hand on Dom Enrique's arm and angled his chin at the interior door. "She's coming back."

As he said this, the door swung open and the woman came back into the room carrying a tray with a bottle and two tankards on it. "The goat will be ready in a moment," she said, putting the tray down and setting out its contents. "The wine is five years old, Curaca," she said to Dom Enrique, using the Incan word for a high official.

He rounded on her, his face thunderous. "I am Portuguese, not Indian. I am Dom, not Curaca."

She quailed, glared, then shrugged. "Curaca, Dom, it is all one to peasants," she said as she departed.

"We'll have to wait for the food," van Zwolle said, his complaint heart-felt; he had not eaten since the night before and he was seriously hungry. "Why did you have to impose upon her?"

"The wine will take care of us," Dom Enrique said, pouring almost half the bottle into van Zwolle's tankard and ignoring his question before giving himself a like amount. "It will ease the sting of Don Vicente's rebuke." With that, he lifted the tankard and downed half its contents.

Van Zwolle copied him, but more cautiously. He traced the warmth of the wine all the way down to his stomach; the warmth gathered there, then spread. A little of his apprehension began to dissipate. "How bad is it?"

"For a local vintage, not too bad," said Dom Enrique.

"I meant how bad are Don Vicente's restrictions?" He watched Dom Enrique closely.

"Bad enough, if we comply with them," said Dom Enrique with a show of bravado that fooled no one, not even himself.

"You were not thinking of defying him?" Van Zwolle all but choked on his wine as he asked.

"We must do something. We cannot permit Don Vicente to disgrace us, not in front of these natives. They will see it as permission for them to demand more of all Europeans. They will suppose they can gain support from the authorities, and will take advantage, the way the black slaves have done in the Caribbean." He made a quick movement compounded of disgust and scorn. "To think that Don Vicente should be fool enough to champion such creatures as the Indians of this place, and at the expense of his wife's kinsman."

Van Zwolle shook his head slowly. "Still, running away would—"

"It would give us an opportunity to make a place for ourselves in this continent. We may establish ourselves well if we do not lose our heads. We can do nothing for Vigaracimos or Escaso or Herrero." He stared down into his tankard. "It may be they will turn on us."

"You cannot think so," van Zwolle protested. "They have too much to lose if they do." Even as he spoke, he felt the same uncertainty that possessed Dom Enrique. He squared his shoulders as if to bolster his argument from within.

"And Don Alejandro will make sure they have something to gain, such as their freedom, or a similar favor if they will but swear that you and I are responsible for what they have done." Dom Enrique drank again. "They will do it. They will tell Don Alejandro and Don Ezequias all they want to know, and will add anything that will make our crimes seem the greater to claim their errors are less than they are."

"They would not," said van Zwolle without conviction. "They would not betray us after all we have done for them. They have money, thanks to their ventures with us. They would be without it had we not given them the chances we did."

"True," mused Dom Enrique. "And they enjoyed the work. If they do not succumb to the threats and lures, you may be right and they will not give away what we have done." He waited for van Zwolle to say something more; when he did not, Dom Enrique went on, "I think it may be San Germanno who began all this trouble for us. Before he fled, he may have sent word to Don Ezequias of what he suspected we had done. Don Ezequias would give his complaints credence."

"It is possible," said van Zwolle, sharing Dom Enrique's desire to blame someone for their ill fortune. "The two of them often talked, and it may be that San Germanno gained influence with the Presidencia that he turned to his advantage and against us." He paused to look at Dom Enrique, hoping to assess his state of mind in order to avoid being the target of his temper. "It is possible that a man of San Germanno's skills was able to blind Don Ezequias to his intentions."

"That is so," said Dom Enrique, relishing his sense of abuse now. "And with Don Ezequias his defender, San Germanno might say anything with impunity. What man could withstand his intentions?"

"Alchemists have many potions and charms to work their will," said van Zwolle, satisfied that Dom Enrique would direct his anger at the missing foreigner. "It is unfortunate he took his cache of jewels with him."

"We were entitled to it," said Dom Enrique, adding the last of the wine in the bottle to his tankard. "Where's our stew?"

"You offended the woman," van Zwolle reminded him. "She will not bring it quickly now."

"But you are hungry. And we need another bottle." He rose to his feet and started toward the inner door, shouting, "Bring our meal! We have paid for it and we will have it! And bring more wine! The best you have!"

There was a bustling sound from the other side of the door and two half-grown children rushed into the taproom, each carrying a large earthenware bowl with steaming goat stew in it. Giggling, they put the bowls down, and one of them attempted a bow to Dom Enrique before running out of the room again in the wake of his smaller companion. As soon as they were gone the woman reappeared with another bottle of wine and a basket with several flat breads set out in it. She also carried two large spoons which she offered to Dom Enrique. "The wine. Pay for the wine."

Dom Enrique fumbled in his wallet on his belt, handed her the coins and took the spoons. "Very good. Now leave us. And do not listen."

Few things, thought van Zwolle, would excite the woman's interest more than being told not to listen to their conversation. He sighed once as he drew one of the bowls across the table and bent over it, inhaling the rich aroma of meat and onions that wafted up from it. "If you do not object?" he said to Dom Enrique as he grabbed a spoon and helped himself to a large mouthful.

Dom Enrique looked at him in disgust. "How can you be such a barbarian? At least use the bread to soak up the gravy," he admonished van Zwolle as he poured out a little more wine. "It is unseemly to wolf your food that way."

"I'm hungry," said van Zwolle, the words muffled by the stew. He chewed vigorously, taking pleasure in the toughness of the meat that demanded he use all the strength in his jaw to pulverize it. It was good to overcome opposition, though it was only a piece of stewed goat.

"Is it decent?" asked Dom Enrique as he took a long draught of the wine. He regarded the stew in his bowl with suspicion.

"It is savory," said van Zwolle, still chewing with determination. "Try it. The gravy is very tasty."

Reluctantly Dom Enrique dipped his spoon into the gravy and then tasted it as if it were possibly poisoned. He waited, swallowed, then shook his head. "Well, if we must travel, I will have to accustom myself to such slop." With a shrug he began to eat, pausing often to wash the stew and then the bread down with wine. Only when his bowl was empty did he say, rather groggily, "We will have to leave tonight if we are to find a ship to carry us tomorrow."

"It is several leagues to Callao," said van Zwolle, thinking that he disliked dealing with Dom Enrique when he was drunk. "We will not be able to cover the distance tonight, I think."

"But we will," said Dom Enrique with the mulishness of growing intoxication. "There are horses to be had."

"But no horse will cover that distance tonight," protested van Zwolle. He was beginning to miss his siesta now that he was pleasantly full and his wits fuzzy with drink.

"Four leagues!" Dom Enrique jeered. "We could walk it if the moon was bright enough."

Privately van Zwolle doubted that Dom Enrique could walk to the Plaza della Nuestra Señora, let alone to Callao, but he kept his opinion to himself. "Four leagues where soldiers might be looking for us."

"All right. We would have to use some caution. All the more reason to go at night," Dom Enrique stated with inebriated confidence. "Four leagues. It's nothing."

"Esta buen," said van Zwolle, his face set into a rictus of compliance. "Four leagues. On horseback. At night."

"Yes. No one will think we're doing it. They will expect us tomorrow morning, and by then we will be talking to captains, to find out which ships will take us." He paused and frowned. "It might be best to go north, to Panamá."

"In case you decide to return to Portugal," guessed van Zwolle.

"Or go on to Japan," said Dom Enrique grandly. "And you will come with me, wherever it is we go." He drank the last of the wine in his tankard and poured in the last from the bottle. "There is a man in the north who has bought from me before. He might be useful."

"The Italian?" said van Zwolle uncertainly. "You said you thought he was too greedy."

"And I do," said Dom Enrique as if there were no contradictions in any of this. "But he has relatives who could be useful to us. Relatives who might want the things we can supply and would be willing to retain us to do their searches for them." His smile was supposed to be roguish, but seemed only fatuous as he finished up the wine. He folded his arms on the table, his bowl and tankard pushed aside. "Tonight we leave. Remember." With that he dropped his head on his arms and fell asleep almost at once.

Van Zwolle looked up at the low-beamed ceiling and considered his position. It would be easy to get up and leave Dom Enrique here alone, drunk. It was certain that the tavernkeeper would rob him of his money and perhaps take his clothes as well. He had done much the same thing himself with Dom Enrique many times, and had thought nothing of the eventual fate of those they robbed. But perhaps it was the knowledge of this inevitability that kept him at Dom Enrique's side, dozing from time to time, and wondering how they were to acquire horses without being reported to Don Vicente. He did not relish dealing with Dom Enrique when he awoke, when the fumes of the wine he had imbibed would have settled in his head, making him surly and groggy. He took out his pipe and smoked a while, his thoughts turning to all the stories he had heard of Aztec treasure in Mexico. As he dazzled himself with visions of gold and silver, the day faded toward evening and their hour of departure.

Text of a letter from Gennaro Colonna to his second cousin Jules Mazarin, written in Italian.

To my esteemed relative, the First Minister of France, Jules, Cardinal Mazarin, my greetings and much-belated thanks for the interest you have taken in my welfare. I have only now come to appreciate your efforts on my behalf, and I wish to inform you of my gratitude for all you have done.

Let me tell you how this comes about: the company of fighting men in which I was enrolled was ordered into the coastal mountains on the west side of the southern Americas, to the place where the Incas live. During our journey there—partly by sea, partly over-land—I took a fever. It was severe and it did not improve. The physician of the company feared for my life and my companions were ready to dig my grave by the time we reached our destination. I remember little of the travel, for the illness had me in its grip and I was often not wholly in my right mind. Oftentimes I was taken with chills that left me palsied and weak as a sick puppy; other times I burned with fever and raged. It is not remarkable that my comrades despaired of my life and were more willing to send for a priest than another physician.

Yet to my everlasting thankfulness, a physician came. He was with another party of soldiers and priests, and he had been in these mountains for almost ten years. He was identified as a tertiary Brother of the Carmelite Order, serving religious and soldiers with equal deliberation. Being a tertiary, he was not bound by monkish vows, but lives with the Carmelites and follows their Rule as far as he is able, as he was not born a Catholic. He travels with the monks and treats those whose wounds or illness require his skills. He recognized my malady and at once set about to procure chinchona bark. He told me Pedro Barba had used this bark to cure la Condessa de Chinchon, and as it returned her to health so it would return me. It mattered little to me, for I was certain that I would die and that God had numbered me with the goats bound for Hell. I tried to resign myself to death and damnation, but took the elixir given me by this tertiary Brother. Either from his skill as a physician or the Grace of God, or both, I began to recover.

It is now two months since I made my first improvement. I am not yet strong enough to fight with the company, but I am able to aid my physician in his treating others, and I have found solace in this. San Germanno—for that is the name of the physician who has cured me—tells me I have some ability as a physician and has suggested that I take up the study. I have given him my word to consider this. Before I was taken with fever, I might have dismissed the notion—to be candid, it would have seemed ridiculous to me—but now, having come so near to death, I find I cannot ignore what I have survived, or the suffering it gave me. In six months I have sworn to give San Germanno my answer, and while I am weighing my decision, I have promised to continue to assist him, to learn from him, although I know I will never attain his degree of ability. Daily I am amazed at the capabilities of this man, whose genius exceeds all physicians I have known of before now. I have asked him where he came by these extraordinary skills and he said that he learned them in Egypt.

I mention this man not only because he has saved my life and shown me another way to live, but because he claims to know one of your embassy, the Roman widow Bondama Clemens. He has informed me he knew her when he was much younger and that he has maintained an occasional correspondence with her over the years. From what he tells me, they are relatives of one sort or another, for he said that he and she share the bond of blood. I ask that you commend me to Bondama Clemens and convey my admiration for her relative to her. Surely one such as San Germanno is a credit to any family, and she must know that she is blessed to be of the same blood as he.

That brings me to my last observation of this letter: in the past I have regarded your instruction as unwelcome and ludicrous, and I have been inclined to dismiss everything you were kind enough to impart to me. Now I am aware that I have been worse than lax in my behavior and my thinking. You have not been a bothersome intruder, but a pardoning sage, willing to try to pull me back from the brink I was so determined to cast myself over. I wish you to know that I truly value all you have striven to do for me, and in future you will find me an attentive and grateful student, eager for instruction.

This letter will be carried by Frey Estanislao on the ship Los Sacramentos, bound for Spain in ten days. I pray passage will be swift and the seas quiet, so that you may receive this before the start of Lent next spring.

It is presently my intention, should I be able to progress as a physician, to take my mentor as my example and become a tertiary Brother of the Carmelites. I will not be beyond the reach of my family that way, and will have no monkish vows to uphold, if the family makes other plans for me. In time, that may change, but for now, I believe that I was saved for more reason than a whim, and I know I have turned away from all that was worthy in my life and endangered my body and the salvation of my soul. No more need you or any others of our family fear for me. I have seen the danger at last, and I have drawn back from it as I would from the fires of Hell itself. Your prayers have been heard, cousin, and I hope with all my heart that my previous abuse had not made me odious to you so that my awakening has come too late for friendship between us.

Every night and every morning I number your name in my prayers. I beg you not to shut me out of your heart, but to accept me, penitent, as one who seeks your guidance. If you continue to pray for me, then petition Madre Maria and San Lucca to aid my learning so that I may, in time, be a capable physician.

Your cousin, in contrition,
Gennaro Colonna
On the first day of November, 1646

3

Buenaventura huddled, sweating, under a midsummer squall, the wooden buildings seeming to pull together for protection from the onslaught of wind and rain. Known for heat and fevers, it was a place most Europeans ignored when they could and cursed when they could not. Out in the Baia de Buenaventura the ocean frothed as if rabid.

"It is not a busy place, this port," remarked Capitan Rodrigo Vinay, his eyes on the foreigner traveler in elegant black satin of French fashion and cut, and his middle-aged manservant in good Spanish homespun. "It is odd you should come here, particularly a man so well-dressed." He studied the two speculatively, trying to assess their worth. "Unless fine clothes are all you have."

"Our escort has gone on; they departed four days ago," said San Germanno smoothly. "Ask at the taverns; they will tell you about them: a company of monks and soldiers. They were bound into the mountains to the south, and I am looking to get passage to the west coast of Nueva España. I would prefer Mexico, not simply the Audiencia, the region."

"What port?" asked Capitan Vinay as if the answer were of no interest to him.

"Whichever you are sailing for—the northernmost of your ports-of-call." San Germanno touched the silver collar holding a small version of his eclipse device, hoping what the innkeeper had told him was accurate. "I would prefer not to have to stop in Guatemala."

"Ha!" He slapped the table with his hand. "What would be the use to you?"

"In Guatemala?" San Germanno asked as if puzzled. "Little use, except it would bring me closer to my goal."

"Tell me where you are bound: I go no farther than Acapulco, which is Mexican territory," said Capitan Vinay, looking sharply at the window of the inn where a loose shutter banged.

"For the silk on the ships from Manila, and to trade mercury and copper for it," said San Germanno smoothly, not allowing the apparent indifference of Capitan Vinay to put him at a disadvantage. "As any sensible coasting merchant would do."

Capitan Vinay raised his head, interested for the first time. "You, too, have interests in silk?"

San Germanno answered honestly, if not fully. "I own four ships plying the ocean between Manila and Acapulco. Some carry silver, some carry silk. In the Viceroyalty of Peru silver is not in short supply but silk is. It would make no sense to trade in silver, but silk is another matter." He nodded once to Capitan Vinay. "If it would help me to secure passage, I would provide you with bona fides for any ship of mine in port, so that you would get the most favorable rates from the brokers."

Chuckling unpleasantly, Capitan Vinay shook his head. "Oh, no. You will say the ships were lost at sea, and I would have nothing for your passage and no advantage in trade. Lies of this sort may convince less canny men, but I have been about the world. Thank you, Señor, but I am not so—"

"I fear you are under a misapprehension. I do not lie, Capitan Vinay. I plan to pay in gold for the passage," San Germanno interrupted him as politely as he could. He bowed slightly. "It would please me to pay you well for the trouble our presence might cause."

"Um," said Capitan Vinay, to indicate he was listening.

This was not very encouraging, but San Germanno was as aware as Capitan Vinay that no other ship in port was bound as far north as *La Noche Blanca,* which gave the square-jawed, squint-eyed offspring of a Spanish sailor and his Philippine mistress an advantage he intended to use to the fullest. "It will not be possible to leave for at least another day," San Germanno said calmly, knowing now how he would have to deal with this man. "So tonight you have to keep your men paid if they are to sail with you. Given that this storm was not expected, it is unreasonable to have to pay for your crew in port; I will set aside nine gold reales to offset your costs. And I will pay the same amount for every day we are at sea, with a bonus of thirty gold reales if you reach Acapulco in less than twelve days." To punctuate his offer, San Germanno put a pouch of coins on the table. The thongs holding it closed were sealed with an impression of his eclipse device. "You may count them, if you wish."

Capitan Vinay seized the pouch, pried the wax off, and unfastened the thongs. His eyes widened at the glittering cascade that poured from it. "Very well. You have more than enough to meet your promises." He set the pouch aside and rested one hand on top of the coins. "This is for you and your manservant?"

"And some chests and crates, a dozen of them. If necessary, I will pay for taking up space in the hold. You see, I have certain belongings I wish to transport as well." San Germanno did not appear desperate or devious, which served only to rouse Capitan Vinay's suspicions.

"And what might these chests and crates contain?" he demanded, his brow clouding as fiercely as the sky outside the inn. "There are high penalties for smuggling."

"Clothes. Supplies. Books. Earth." He spoke reasonably enough, and waited for the inevitable questions.

They came sharply, as San Germanno had expected. "What supplies? And why earth?"

San Germanno was prepared with his answer; he fixed his dark eyes on Capitan Vinay's. "I am something of a physician, and I have medicaments in my supplies which I prepare from certain plants with medicinal properties. Many of them must be grown in their own earth, or they will not retain the virtue for which I grow them. I have the earth for this purpose, so that my . . . work may flourish." His voice was low and penetrating, and there was something in his manner that held Capitan Vinay's absolute attention. "I must take them all with me, or I cannot do my work. It is not unreasonable to make such a request, is it."

"No," said Capitan Vinay in a dazed voice. "It is not." He touched his brow as if he was not certain he was awake. He blinked and looked down at the coins again. "It is a generous sum," he said at last. "Who are you, Señor, that you carry a pouch with so much gold?"

"I am el Conde de San Germanno," he answered. "My manservant is Rogerio. He is from Cadiz," he added, trusting that Rogerio's origins would help to preserve them both from any more probing questions.

"You are willing to pay a great deal, Conde de San Germanno," Capitan Vinay said, his acquisitiveness warring with his curiosity. His tongue slicked his lips and his eyes strayed to the pouch of golden coins now inside his camisa. "There are those who would be made wary by such a sum."

"Considering what is being asked, I do not think so," San Germanno said. "There are a few other matters to settle now." He paused while Capitan Vinay gave him a speculative glance. "There are some requirements of which I must inform you: I will have to remain in my cabin for the entire voyage. My manservant will take care of me; there will be no demands made of your crew." He coughed once. "I am prone to seasickness."

At that Capitan Vinay laughed aloud. "Then why not go overland? Spare yourself the money and the suffering?"

"And get there months after my ships have landed and started back across the Pacific? What is the use in that, pray?" he replied, as if the answer was obvious. "Two are supposed to arrive by the end of January, and I would like, for once, to inspect the cargo before the brokers rob me of it." His answer had enough truth in it to keep Capitan Vinay's attention.

"They are dogs," he growled in agreement. "Thieves and rascals, the lot of them."

"Too often in the past, the charges they have made for selling the cargo have been excessive. I want to be there when the next ship arrives." He recognized the greed in Capitan Vinay that would accept such an answer readily. "I want also to instruct the Capitan in regard to future cargos."

"A good precaution in these times." Capitan Vinay toyed with the coins, then nodded decisively. "Be completely aboard by midnight tonight, Conde. This storm is dying now. We will go with the turn of the tide, and that will come shortly after midnight." He began to return the gold to the pouch, taking pleasure in the clink of the coins. "I will hold this against your passage." With that he surged to his feet and started toward the door. "My ship is moored in the mouth of the Rio Dagua, away from the fishing boats. The longboat will bring you out. Be at the dock no later than ten, with all your chests and crates. You will be ferried out to—"

"*La Noche Blanca,*" San Germanno confirmed. "I saw you arrive in port day before yesterday, before the storm came up."

Capitan Vinay did his best to conceal his surprise. "Yes. We came in shortly before noon." He sighed once, adding, "A pity the climate here is so bad; this port has not changed much in the hundred years since it was founded. The Isla Cascajal is easily defended, and were it not for the heat and the fevers it harbors as well as ships, it would be one of the strongest ports in all of the Viceroyalty of Peru. No smugglers would dare venture here." He did something with his face that might have been a wink, then went out into the warm, pelting rain.

"What do you think?" San Germanno asked Rogerio as he closed the door against the storm. He remained silently with his back to the door and held his hand up for silence; he wanted to be certain Capitan Vinay had actually left them and was not listening to them from outside.

"He is a dangerous man," said Rogerio without any inflection.

"That he is," San Germanno seconded, indicating that Capitan Vinay had departed. He came back across the room, his small feet making little or no sound. "And you will have to be on guard for the whole of our voyage, in case he or his men attempt to claim more than we are paying them." His smile was apologetic. "I do not mean to make such demands on you, old friend, but on water . . . "

"On water," Rogerio said in the Frankish of Charlemagne when San Germanno did not go on, "ghouls fare better than vampires."

"Precisely," San Germanno said in the same tongue, then resumed Spanish. "It means we had best prepare to leave. We would not want to give him an excuse to leave without any part of us but that pouch of gold." This last sardonic observation was punctuated with a single raised eyebrow.

"You will have to be careful, my master. I doubt the Capitan would hesitate to make the gold his own without encumbering it with our presence." Rogerio paused. "He may have done such things before."

"Very likely," said San Germanno. "But this is not Tunis, and Capitan Vinay is not apt to press his advantage with a man with a title, not in these waters, not with Don Ezequias and Don Gofredo in the Audiencia de Panamá keeping track of all travelers. I do not doubt Mazarin's nephew could ask questions, and ask them in high places, that would be hard to answer if any such misadventure befell us. Much as the good Capitan may hanker for gold, he does not want his position compromised." He sighed once. "He is not Shuisky, either, all the forgotten gods be thanked: his treachery is obvious."

Rogerio favored San Germanno with a direct stare. "You would not say this if you feared some betrayal."

San Germanno nodded once. "And I do, but not from Capitan Vinay."

Catching a note in San Germanno's voice that alarmed him, Rogerio demanded, "What are you saying? What do you fear?"

"There are those who might still hold me responsible for the death of Acanna Tupac." Although the event happened almost two years ago, the memory of it remained fresh with San Germanno.

"Other than you yourself?" Rogerio challenged, concern in his faded-blue eyes. "Who would do so, after all this time?"

"Obispo Guarda, for one," San Germanno answered, the reserve back in his manner. "Possibly the Corregidor, Don Vicente, depending upon what he has been told, and by whom."

"But why would anyone continue to blame you?" Rogerio had seen this in his master before, this anguish of responsibility. San Germanno had been all but overcome by it after the death of Ranegonda, seven centuries ago; as he had after the slaughter of Ten Chih-Yu, more than four hundred years ago; not quite two hundred years ago the suicides of Estasia and Demetrice had weighed heavily upon him, each in her own way a burden he bore still; when Xenia had died defending him less than a century ago it had been three years before San Germanno was anything more than a remote, polite stranger to everyone; even Olivia's affectionate upbraidings could not break the formidable isolation he imposed upon himself.

"Because she deserves better than to be forgotten," San Germanno said softly. He went toward the window and stood for a while, looking out through the slanting rain to the bay beyond the island. "I loathe sailing."

By that night the squall had passed, as Capitan Vinay had said it would. The long waves coming in off the Pacific for once lived up to the name, curling along the shore like gathered lace. The sky overhead was uncommonly clear as if the stars were set in deep, flawless glass. Out toward the ocean the water was dark under the black sky. Only the wind, coming lazily from the east, carried with it the pervasive green stench of the equatorial forests.

Amid their crates and chests, San Germanno and Rogerio waited at the dock. They had arrived almost an hour before the appointed time, wanting to provide Capitan Vinay no excuse to leave them behind. Both were wrapped in long, hooded cloaks; neither looked tired.

As the longboat drew up to the dock, a man in the bow holding a lanthorn stood up, calling out "You there, Conde?"

San Germanno answered at once. "Yes. We are here. Our things are ready."

"Very good," the man called back in a disappointed tone. He shouted a few terse orders to the men at the oars, and in the next moment, he was climbing the ladder to the dock. He was angular, and so weathered his face looked like leather but for the wide, white scar running from his forehead, along his nose to the top of his lip. Catching sight of San Germanno and Rogerio, he bowed clumsily. "I am Cornelio Dis. I am Capitan Vinay's first mate." He peered at the chests and crates. "It will take two trips to carry it all to the ship."

"So I thought," said San Germanno. "And when the first load is ready, Rogerio will go with you, to help you stow it properly." It would also, he thought, keep the men from making off with his things. "I will come with the second load."

Dis' smile turned sour. "Muy bien," he said.

"Truly," said San Germanno at his cordial best, gratified that the first mate would not be able to take him and not his belongings and sail off.

Rogerio recognized this unfailing politeness for the disguise it was; San Germanno was prepared for trouble. He went up to Dis, bowed slightly, and said, "I am Rogerio. Tell me what I may do to assist you."

"How many crates and chests?" Dis asked, attempting to count them for himself.

"Seven crates, five chests," said Rogerio. "If you will permit, I will help you select which to take across first."

It would be improper to refuse him, Dis knew it. He jerked his head up and down in assent. "We'd best be about it now." He snapped his fingers and two men from the longboat below answered sharply. "Secure the boat and hustle. This must be loaded within the hour," he snapped as the first of the two appeared, making his way up the ladder.

"Is there a loading crane we may use?" asked the sailor in German-accented Spanish. He was no older than twenty-five and already the sea had set deep creases in his face.

"There is," said San Germanno before Dis could issue orders to procure one. "I took the liberty of having one brought. The tide may be high, but not high enough to load without one."

"True, very true," said Dis, scowling. "Very well, lads. You heard him. There's a crane ready. Listen to what this fellow has to say"—he clapped Rogerio on the shoulder—"and get ready to take this all out to the ship."

The two sailors gave Rogerio a suspicious stare, but resigned themselves to following his orders. The one with the German accent pointed out the largest of the chests. "How heavy is it?"

"They are all heavy," said San Germanno. He walked to the edge of the dock planks and looked down, experiencing the same vertigo he always felt over so much water. Only at slack tide did the ocean lose its potency for a short while; the rest of the time it was the most powerfully running water on earth, and not even the mightiest river was as enervating to San Germanno as the ocean. He swallowed hard, conquering his fear of being lost at sea. Being un-dead he would not drown, but would lie on the floor of the ocean, conscious, until something mercifully ate enough of him to destroy his nervous system and bring the True Death. No torture he had endured could equal that, he told himself, and strove to master his anxiety.

Dis watched him. "Can't swim, can you?"

"Not very well," San Germanno replied; he swam well enough in pools lined with his native earth, but not in the ocean. He looked away from the water. "How long will this take?"

"The loading?" Dis asked. "About an hour to load and ferry for each; we will be ready by the turn of the tide." His smile was not at all convincing. "Then we're off, on to the north and bound for Mexico. If the wind were stronger we would make very good progress by morning, but as it is . . . " He shrugged and waved one rough hand in the air; he went on in the same quiet way. "Capitan Vinay tells me you're giving a bonus if we reach Acapulco in twelve days."

"I am. Do you think you will earn it?" San Germanno watched the sailors secure the first of his chests of earth with the crane sling and prepared to lower it to the longboat below.

"We've done it in less. We aren't so heavy laden that we will lose time for it." He saw the crane swing out over the dock and lower the chest. "How did you get those here?"

"With mules and an oxcart," said San Germanno. "The Carmelites had three wagons; the oxcart hardly made a difference. The mules were mine." He had bought them near Quito not long before he had left the Carmelite community; he had given them to the monks and the soldiers when they parted company a week ago.

"The Capitan says you have business in Acapulco," Dis continued with a speculative glint in his eyes.

"Yes," was San Germanno's terse answer.

Aware that he had overstepped the bounds, Dis put his hand to his chest in a gesture of apology. "Didn't mean to pry, Conde."

San Germanno looked directly at him. "Didn't you."

Dis tried to appear indignant. "Of course not. Just wondering why a fine gentleman like yourself should be sailing from a place like Buenaventura, not Guayaquil?"

With a sigh, San Germanno answered as if speaking to a child. "By the time I reached Guayaquil, I would not be certain of getting to Acapulco before my ships were gone again. And my escort was not going north to Panamá, where I might have found passage. So I came here. This seemed the most prudent choice." He regarded Dis thoughtfully. "There are cargos awaiting my inspection in Acapulco." Four more chests of his native earth had been shipped there three months ago by Eduardo Medallo, on his orders.

"And your ships are coming from Manila to Acapulco," said Dis, understanding that San Germanno had just told him his arrival was expected and his disappearance would be investigated.

"As your Capitan already knows," said San Germanno, his attention held by the men with the loading crane; another chest was being lowered into the longboat. Rogerio was pointing out the next to go.

"Your servant is experienced in this," Dis approved, hoping to gain some of San Germanno's goodwill.

"That he is. I would be lost without him." The few times in their long association that they had been separated, San Germanno had felt as if he had sacrificed half his sight and hand. Rogerio, and before him Aumtehoutep, was not only San Germanno's invaluable servant, but his treasured friend.

Dis thought that most of the hidalgos he met were lost without their servants, although few were willing to admit it; San Germanno's statement gained Dis' grudging respect as well as a justification for the contempt he felt. He spat once into the ocean. "How long's he served you?"

San Germanno answered honestly. "Not quite half my life." He did not add that when they met, Vespasianus was Caesar.

Again Dis spat in the ocean while he watched Rogerio continue with his work. "Have you anything to do, Conde?" he asked suddenly.

"Not just at present," said San Germanno, wondering what was on Dis' mind now. "Aside from watching you ferry my belongings to your ship."

"No last farewells? No bed to rumple? We have an hour yet." He laughed at his own wit, and was a little surprised at San Germanno's ironic chuckle.

To his mild surprise, San Germanno felt offended. "I have not been here long enough for such . . . entertainment." On the ocean he would feel the lack of blood keenly, but he would not take it from one who was unwilling, and he had not had the opportunity to find which women he could visit in sleep, bringing sweet, fulfilling dreams in order to sustain himself.

Dis saw something in San Germanno's face he was unable to understand; he put his hand to his chest once more. "I meant no disrespect," he said seriously. "It is just that so many hidalgos are—"

"I know what they are," said San Germanno, remembering what Gennaro Colonna had told him of his past. In Cuzco there had been men like Dom Enrique Vilhao, who had been the model for Dis' complaint.

Rogerio shouted a warning; the two sailors on the dock reached out for the crane as it began to swing over the longboat. They caught the arm in time and secured the crate more thoroughly.

"Clothes," murmured San Germanno. An awkward loss, but not an impossible one. If he had to leave something behind, clothes would be better than his native earth. He gave a single, satisfied nod as the crate, now fully protected, was lowered down.

"A full crate for clothes? Just clothes?" inquired Dis, who had overheard San Germanno.

"Certainly," said San Germanno in a tone that did not invite further comment.

It was nearly midnight when San Germanno descended slowly into the longboat, chiding himself at every step for the queasiness filling him like an illness. He leaned against one of the chests of his native earth and fixed his dark-seeing eyes on *La Noche Blanca* waiting at its moorings, sailors scrambling in the rigging in preparation for standing out to sea. As they rowed out to *La Noche Blanca,* he concentrated on maintaining his composure, and when he climbed aboard the ship, he kept his jaw clamped shut.

Capitan Vinay greeted him with a nod and an impatient flick of his hand. "The tide will turn shortly. Then we'll haul canvas and be underway." He did not smile, but he showed his teeth. "Your manservant has a cabin ready for you. Unless you'd like to stay on deck."

San Germanno recognized the mischief in the Capitan's eyes, and answered dryly, "I would think *you* would prefer I did not."

Making the inference—an incorrect one—San Germanno had intended, Capitan Vinay abandoned his game. "Christ of the Fishes! Let your manservant deal with the mess." He indicated the entrance to the companionway adding, "The first door on the . . . left is your cabin."

"A thousand thanks," San Germanno said, and went in the direction indicated, his bones feeling weak inside him as the water did its baleful work upon him. He felt under his ropilla for the short sword hanging there, grateful for its presence because he was certain that before the voyage was over he would need it, or one of the other, more formidable, weapons he carried.

Rogerio was waiting in the cabin door; he bowed slightly. "Your bed is ready," he said, pointing out one of the large chests that had been brought aboard in the first load; it was set up at the end of the cabin where a small wardrobe had been moved out of place to accommodate it; there was a thin mattress atop it, and a single blanket above that.

"Excellent," San Germanno approved. "How did you explain needing this in the cabin?"

"I said you had medicaments in it that would lessen your seasickness," he replied. "It is not entirely a lie."

"No, it's not," San Germanno said, removing his ropilla and handing it to Rogerio. He hesitated before going on. "I think we may rest easy tonight and tomorrow, but after tomorrow night, we will need to be on guard."

"I would think it best," Rogerio seconded. "Otherwise, who knows what mischief these fellows may get up to?"

"They are greedy enough to make an attempt if we are foolish; if we stop them once, I doubt we will have to stop them a second time." San Germanno rubbed his face as if trying to keep awake; he was fighting off the pervasive sense of vertigo that had been increasing steadily since he set out on the water. "Where is my—"

Rogerio gave him his long silken camisa in which he slept. "And there is a dressing gown, if you want it."

"This should suffice," San Germanno answered as he finished undressing, as always turning his back when he was naked so that Rogerio would not have to see the wide swath of scars across his torso and abdomen. When he had drawn the black silk camisa over his head, he sat down on his make-shift bed. "My sword?"

Rogerio touched the place where the hilt could be found. "Under the mattress. It is the Japanese one—Masashige's."

"You are expecting trouble," San Germanno said, recalling the Japanese warrior he had fought in China, more than four hundred years ago. Masashige had given him this katana when San Germanno had recovered from his wounds and it had been with him ever since.

"As you have said, not tonight, but it is best to be prepared," Rogerio said. He began preparing to put San Germanno's clothes into the press next to the wardrobe.

"You might as well sleep tonight, then," San Germanno said. "I will stay awake."

"And by day, you can sleep," Rogerio offered, aware that San Germanno was not always eager for such concessions.

For once, San Germanno chuckled. "I suppose you're right. Native earth in the soles of my boots would not be proof against so much water and sun as well."

"No, it would not," Rogerio said with a slight sigh of relief.

San Germanno pulled the blanket aside and lay back. "I do not mean to be such a trial to you, old friend. You would think that after so long a life I would become accustomed to the restrictions vampirism imposes upon me. But as we both know, that is not always the case." He drew the blanket up. "It will probably be wisest if you refill the soles of my boots every day we are on the water."

"As you wish," Rogerio said, pleased that San Germanno was being sensible about his predicament. He went about his duties in silence while San Germanno took strength from his native earth in the chest; although his breathing was slow and regular, Rogerio knew his master was not asleep.

By the time Rogerio had completed his tasks, *La Noche Blanca* was leaning into the freshening wind, headed north by west for Nueva España, Audiencia de Mexico, and the port of Acapulco.

> *"Oltras arenas, oltras mujeres:*
> *Cuando los sueños me llevo*
> *A donde las olas me ahogo*
> *Entonces te m'amas, Mercedes,*
> *Entonces te m'amas."*

The song of the man on watch heralded the middle of the second night at sea. For the next hour, he enumerated the other sands and other women who had captivated him, and the perfidy or treachery of each of the women. *La Noche Blanca* was steady on course, judging by the stars overhead, making good speed toward Mexico. A bell announced the hour as San Germanno sat on his chest of earth and listened; since midnight he had been waiting, all his senses alert, all his attention on the soft sounds around him, from the groan of the hull and the hiss of the waves to the luff of the sails and snap of the wind. He felt a growing stealth gathering, and he strove to concentrate on all he heard in order to be prepared for the attack he knew was coming.

At first there was a soft scuffle of stockinged feet in the narrow confines beyond the door, and a number of whispered admonitions. San Germanno reached out and shook Rogerio's ankle with one hand while he drew the katana from under his mattress with the other.

Rogerio came awake quickly and silently, a poignard in his hand. He nodded once to indicate he was prepared, and then he directed all his scrutiny on the door, anticipating its opening.

That came abruptly. One moment there was a muttered order, and in the next instant the door slammed inward as four men tumbled into the cabin. All were armed, and each man had his weapon at the ready. San Germanno rose from his bed, his katana held negligently in his left hand. "Is there something you wanted?" he asked politely. He had accustomed himself as much as he could to the upsetting influence of the water beneath him, and the rest on his native earth had helped him to regain some of his strength.

The sound of his voice startled the men, whose forward rush stopped in confusion as they realized they were discovered. One of the men— a squat lout with a mashed nose and disfigured ear—swore loudly only to be silenced by a sharp word from the others.

"So Capitan Vinay did not send you," San Germanno surmised from the continued secretiveness of the men. "Very well." He took one step toward the men so that he would have more room to swing his blade, then he smiled at the men. "If you seek a fight, I am at your service."

The cabin was still for two heartbeats, then the tallest of the men moved swiftly: he raised a cutlass and shoved through his companions to cleave it down at San Germanno's head. His blue eyes were alight with the glory of fighting.

A flick of the katana and the cutlass was turned aside at the same moment the man's right hand was severed halfway to the elbow.

The sailor let out a terrible bellow of pain and outrage as he grabbed his arm with his one remaining hand to stop the blood pumping out of him.

Another of the attackers—the one with the mashed nose and battered ear—fled, cursing as he went as the injured man dropped to his knees, now keening in terror.

"Is that all?" San Germanno asked coolly.

For an answer, another man, one of those who had helped load the crates and chests onto the longboat, did his best to take a slice at San Germanno from the side.

Once again the katana moved, this time only to block the knife. "I would rather not hurt you, too," San Germanno told him. He gave the sailors a little time, then said, "Your friend here will have to have help or he will bleed to death."

In response to this, the sailor with the severed hand shrieked.

Finally the sailor with the other cutlass uttered an obscene oath and threw down his weapon. He glared at San Germanno. "Who warned you?"

"You did," San Germanno answered quietly. "It was certain from the time Dis came to the dock that some of you would attempt some . . . mischief." He looked at the remaining three sailors. "I trust this is the last of it?"

The apparent leader shrugged. "Probably has to be. With these—" He kicked his cutlass out of the room. When he returned his stare to San Germanno, he became servile. "What will you tell the Capitan? He will keel-haul us for this."

San Germanno glanced away; he had seen what keel-hauling did to the wretches punished with it; the memory was sickening. It was a hideous way to die. "It must be reported. If it has not been already. Your Capitan will wonder at this noise."

"Yes," said the other man. "Hespiro's arm will have to be treated, and the Capitan will have to know why." He made a gesture of futility. "We haven't a surgeon aboard."

"I will do it," San Germanno offered, hearing himself with surprise, and trying to ignore the stifled oath from Rogerio.

"You?" the man said in blunt amazement.

"Yes." Now San Germanno looked down at the sailor he had maimed. The scent of his blood was disturbing, reminding him of how long it had been since he had received blood knowingly. Long ago he might have used the bleeding sailor for sustenance, but not anymore, not since his first days in Egypt. There was, he distantly recalled, a perverse thrill in terror and pain, for the emotions were powerful, but such feeding brought no contact, no end of isolation, no matter how brief, and blood without touching might as well come from goats, or donkeys, or rats. And he was hungry. He returned his attention to the man who led the attack. "Well? He will faint soon."

The sailor gave a hiss of frustration, then said, "All right. The cook would probably poison him." He glared at San Germanno. "See that you do not." With that for farewell, he turned and was out the door.

San Germanno nodded once, as much in dismissal as agreement. "Rogerio," he ordered as he dropped to his knee beside the man. "Bring my red lacquer chest. It is stowed under your bunk, I believe."

Rogerio put his poignard into its sheath on his belt before rising and tugging the chest from its place. He said nothing, but there was disapproval in every line of his body. As he set the chest upright, he made himself say, "What will you need?"

"Bandages, the leather strap for a tourniquet, the salve in the red jar, for cauterizing the wound." He was relieved that the cut had been so clean. Certain that they were no longer in danger, he held out the katana to Rogerio. "You know what to do with this."

"I do," said Rogerio, taking the Japanese sword and setting it carefully aside on the edge of his bed while he selected the items San Germanno needed; later San Germanno would clean the blade as its former owner had instructed him to do.

By the time San Germanno had treated the man's arm, Capitan Vinay had arrived, his face reddened with wind and wrath. He glared down at the wounded sailor and then glowered at San Germanno. "Did they attack you? Mary's Tits! Damn every whoreson one of them!"

San Germanno did not answer at once. He made a last check of his patient, satisfying himself that the man would sleep for many hours. Then he regarded Capitan Vinay. "They tried."

"Who was it?" the Capitan demanded.

"A few men. I do not know their names." He gestured to the unconscious man. "As you see, they were not successful." He signaled to Rogerio, his face blank with distaste. "The Capitan will want the hand."

"Of course," Rogerio said, and held out a wide linen strip on which the severed hand lay.

Capitan Vinay saw how clean the cut was. "Even the bone is sliced; there is no splintering," he whispered as he studied the grisly trophy.

"I have an exceptional sword," San Germanno said, and knew that word of his katana would be all over the ship by midday.

"So you must," allowed Capitan Vinay. He cocked his head toward Hespiro. "You are strongly built, but no taller than most men. A big man like that, he would expect to have the advantage against—"

"A smaller man. Yes, he might," San Germanno interrupted. "But it was over very quickly. He had no time to use his height."

"It must have been quick, if only Hespiro drew his weapon," Capitan Vinay said, regarding San Germanno with new respect.

"I did not notice any others," San Germanno said, not quite accurately. He indicated the blood drying on the floor; the odor was making him dizzy. "If you will arrange for this to be cleaned, I would be most grateful. And if your men would carry Hespiro to his bunk?"

Capitan Vinay nodded once, a show of capitulation. "I will send one of the men. One or two, no more."

"Thank you," San Germanno said quietly; the Capitan turned away.

As he got to the door of the cabin, Capitan Vinay turned back. "Tell me, Conde: had you wanted to, could you have killed them all?"

San Germanno disliked the truth, but he gave it. "Oh yes," he said quietly, bowing slightly as Capitan Vinay closed the door.

Text of a letter sent in multiple copies from Obispo Hernan Sigismundo Bernal Guarda to other Bishops in the Viceroyalty of Peru and the Viceroyalty of Nueva España.

To my dearest Brothers in Christ, my prayerful greetings and my pious hope that this New Year finds each one of you thriving in God's favor and the faith of your flock, and that the remembrance and celebration of the glorious Nativity of Our Lord has filled your hearts and souls with renewed purpose and strength to persevere in the face of opposition and heresy.

Lamentably, this notice is not one to inform you of the progress of our faith, or to praise la Virgen for her many mercies to us in these difficult times, but to alert all of you to a danger that might well have come upon you already. I regret the necessity of making this notification, but it is sadly true that the Corregidor has seen fit to ignore the threat of the danger I mentioned, and so I must, in the service of God and the Church, perform the warning Don Vicente is unwilling to do in the name of the Crown.

Somewhat more than two years ago there fled from Cuzco a foreigner, an admitted alchemist, Francisco Ragoczy, styling himself Conde de San Germanno. The man is said to be Hungarian by birth, and noble of blood, although no proof of either assertion has been offered. There is no report of his return to Europe; he is believed to be still in the Americas, and so I am fulfilling my duty as I am convinced I must, to put all of you on alert in regard to this man. He was thought to have influenced many persons here by black magic, for he was acknowledged a skilled alchemist, and a powerful healer of many deadly ills. Whether or not these distinctions are merited, no one can tell without the proper examination of him, which only those priests skilled in the detection of witchcraft and devils' work can know.

The reason for this warning is to alert you and your priests to the danger this foreigner represents. He is wealthy enough to be able to ensure the favor of Presidencias and Corregidores wherever he goes. It remains to you, guardians of our faith, to see he is not permitted to bring his damnation to any of your flocks. He is a subtle and well-spoken villain, and you must not let yourselves be persuaded that he means no harm to anyone but seeks only to do good. No alchemist can make this claim if he is truly an alchemist. His claims of healings are, of course, exaggerated, and are not to be taken as credible, for only the spirit of God heals the ills of man. You will do yourselves and your people a disservice if you permit this so-called San Germanno to be welcomed among you. He has been implicated in the death of a distinguished woman—perhaps he drove her to suicide, perhaps he killed her himself. This has not yet been satisfactorily determined. If he is brought to answer the Crown, he may well find a way to excuse himself. But the Church is not so easily suborned; it is our task to determine his degree of responsibility in her demise, and to mete out a fitting punishment for his errors.

I pray you will inform me if you have any report of this man. It is most necessary that he be apprehended, no matter where he is. We would like to have the opportunity to learn the extent of his predations, and it would spare all of us unwonted suffering to rid the world of him and his like. It is entirely fitting for you to give him up to us, for we will engage the Secular Arm to learn all that we are able to learn from him before dispatching him, as he deserves to be dispatched, in the flames of Hell to which he is bound.

For your diligence and your devotion, I bless you all and thank you for the dedication you bring to your work in this benighted land. Surely God will triumph here or we will be the worse for it, and will answer for it on Judgment Day. In prayerful anticipation of your revelations, I commend myself to all of you and to the Mercy of God, here and in the life to come.

Hernan Sigismundo Bernal Guarda
Obispo, Los Sacramentos
At Cuzco in la Audiencia de Lima, Viceroyalty of Peru, the 6th Day
of January, 1647

4

During siesta, San Germanno retired to his laboratory in the room behind his library and worked on making new compounds from the herbs he had acquired on his travels in the Viceroyalty of Peru. It was the safest time for the work: while Acapulco dozed in the heat of the day,

San Germanno was certain he would not be interrupted. In the six months since his arrival on *La Noche Blanca* he had established himself among the rich merchants who kept houses here in order to oversee their Pacific trading. Spanish and Portuguese predominated, but there were also a handful of French and English merchants as well. Here in the far-flung Viceroyalty of Nueva España he had found a temporary refuge; he had gained a modicum of acceptance from the other Europeans in the city, but it was tempered with competitive suspicions. He was content to leave matters as they stood, so that he would not be subject to the social demands others faced. Reflection and work distracted him so that he did not notice footsteps approaching the laboratory door.

Rogerio knocked twice, then let himself into the laboratory, securing the lock again as he closed the door. He was neat as always, his manner flawless; his faded-blue eyes were filled with concern. "I think I have found a translator for you." He made this announcement quietly, without fuss, as if he had not spent three months on the task. He held out a square of vellum to San Germanno. "I have spoken to her this morning. She knows the tongues of ten of the peoples to the north, according to Padre Epeso, who has employed her with good results. He said she has done much good for him and his preachers. This is where she may be found."

"Her? She?" San Germanno asked with mild surprise, then looked at the name on the vellum: Oaxetli. "How do you pronounce this?"

"Wah-zhet-li," said Rogerio, accenting the last syllable slightly. "It's close enough, though the t and l are more . . . stuck together." He hesitated. "She's blind."

San Germanno regarded his manservant with slight surprise: for an instant he was back again in the temple of Imhotep, holding a hideously burned, sun-blinded girl in his arms while she died. "And still you believe she might be willing to go north with us, and serve as translator?"

"If she is satisfied as to your purposes, yes," Rogerio answered. "I told her you would visit her this evening."

"Very well," said San Germanno, his questions answered. "I will go to see her after sundown."

"She will be expecting you." Rogerio knew that San Germanno wanted more information. "She is at the most thirty, very likely younger. Because of her blindness, she is not likely to find a husband, and she has no religious vocation. Her own people sent her off to the Freyes when she was seven or eight; they were not able to care for her any longer. It is rumored her grandfather was Spanish; she does not look entirely Indian." He hesitated. "She made herself useful to the monks—Passionists and Franciscans—by learning languages and translating for them. Most of the Indians trust her, and so do the Freyes."

"Thank you, Rogerio, for all your . . . wisdom," said San Germanno, a touch of sardonic amusement in his words. "It seems you have found the very person for our travels."

The continued reserve San Germanno displayed was at once troubling and exasperating: Rogerio sought to find a way to pierce San Germanno's formidable isolation. "She might suit your purposes, as well, in ways useful to her as well as you. No doubt she would welcome dreams if nothing else." He had intended to shock San Germanno. He did not succeed.

"Perhaps," was all the Conde was willing to say.

Glaring in spite of all his good intentions, Rogerio bowed slightly. "If there is nothing else, I will leave you alone, my master."

Almost reluctantly, San Germanno smiled with one side of his mouth. "I do not mean to be such a trial to you, old friend. It is not my intention to make matters so difficult for you."

"And I do not mean to be churlish," Rogerio responded, mollified.

"If you are, it is only due to my provocation," San Germanno told him without any sign of irony. "I appreciate your intentions. Believe this." Then the edge of humor came back into his demeanor. "How much of a task was it, I wonder, to find the translator I need, and a woman as well."

At this Rogerio stood very still. "She was given the highest recommendation of any translator I have learned of, for she knows more of the Indians' tongues than any other. She is said to be more capable than most of the men who serve in that capacity." He stared down at the floor. "I would not engage anyone who was not suitable for the work. I know it would do no good."

"And now I am the churl," San Germanno said with a glint of genuine amusement at the back of his dark eyes. "Very well. After sunset, I will go speak with this Oaxetli. When I return I will tell you my impression of her capabilities."

Rogerio bowed, his mind relieved. "I will set out your Italian clothes."

"To impress a blind woman?" San Germanno inquired with a lift of his fine brows.

"No, to impress those around her, for surely she will be told about your appearance, and the Italian ensemble is the most remarkable of all your garments." Rogerio waited for San Germanno to decide.

"A very good choice; it is certain no one else in Acapulco has clothes like those," said San Germanno, trying to forget that the last time he had worn them he had watched Acanna Tupac fall, flaming, to her death. "It would be folly to go in this." He gestured to the black linen kalasiris he wore; the garment had been popular when Akhenaten ruled in Egypt. San Germanno had chosen the kalasiris for his laboratory clothing since he had served at the Temple of Imhotep.

"There would be questions asked," Rogerio agreed, and started for the door.

"And Rogerio," San Germanno called after him, "I thank you, whatever your intentions might be."

Rogerio made a gesture of dismissal and was gone.

San Germanno went back to his work with a pulverized compound of three different barks which had proven to reduce certain fevers. He had recently made an athanor, and had to admit he would miss it when he went north. But he knew it would be necessary in a short while. He had remained here longer than he had intended, and had become the target of speculation, which in turn created danger for him. As he measured out a little of the distillate he made from mouldy bread, he found himself reluctant to make plans, no matter how wise it would be to leave. He weighed his alternatives in his mind as he had done every day for the last two months: he could remain in Acapulco and risk being investigated by the Corregidor or Presidencia, or the Obispo; he could cross the Pacific Ocean in the hold of one of his trading ships—but the suffering would be hideous; he could cross to the east coast and take ship for España—more suffering, but the voyage was not as long; he could return to Peru and the possibility of legal action against him; he could plunge into the jungles of the south, where few Europeans had gone, to take his chances with the people of the trackless forest; or he could go north, into the lands which were largely unexplored, and learn from the peoples living there, which is what he had come to the New World to do.

A quickening of sounds outside his house and a glance at the narrow beams of sunlight from the tall windows made San Germanno aware that siesta was at an end. He scolded himself inwardly for wasting his precious laboratory time in useless self-debate. He looked at his notebook, the page open and blank. The time had slipped away from him as he attempted to unravel his options; he had intended to put the hours to better use than he had. There were other opportuni-

ties for assessing his situation, when he did not have so much to do.
Perhaps, he thought, this Oaxetli would help him to make up his mind.
With that notion to assure him, he resumed his measuring.

By sundown the streets of Acapulco were filled with people; hidalgos rode their high-bred horses to show off their wealth and mastery
of their animals, their garments and tack as gaudy as their mounts; ven-
dors of all sorts of food and trinkets stationed themselves at intersec-
tions and plazas, all of them calling out what they offered; many of the
residents were out to stroll, to find entertainment, to look at the ocean;
monks in their various habits went about on errands, many of them
with rosaries in their fingers; poor children pestered anyone they could
for coins; youths in rough clothing competed with one another in dis-
plays of strength and bravery; sailors from the ships at anchor made
the most of their evening ashore, searching for the houses where
women waved from open, second-story windows. Few of any of them
paid much attention to the splendidly clad foreigner on the grey Andalusian, except for one or two who marveled at the diamond starburst
of the Order of Saint Stephen of Hungary.

In the Calle della Ribera, not far from the Misericordia Convent, San
Germanno found the house he was seeking: it was small but in excellent repair, with a neat garden just inside the gate where a number of
fragrant blossoms lent their odors to the twilight. Leaving his horse tied
to the hitching-post, he went to the door and knocked twice. "I am
looking for the woman called Oaxetli."

"And who are you?" a voice answered from within, in Spanish that
had less of an accent than San Germanno's.

"My servant, Rogerio, spoke to you earlier today. I am Francisco
Ragoczy, Conde de San Germanno." He had a sense that his title would
not impress her but his foreign name would.

There was the sound of footsteps, and then the door-latch was lifted
and the woman said, "Yes. I am expecting you. The nuns know you
are here." The door was opened halfway, as was proper for a meeting
like this one. "If you will come in, Conde?" She stood aside, revealing
a neat room with no lamps or candles lit. For other guests this could
be a disadvantage—for San Germanno it was not; he saw her face, and
her eyes, focused on some place far away.

"Thank you." San Germanno had a moment to peruse her, face and
body. Rogerio had been right: she was no older than twenty-five
or -six, half a head shorter than he. He realized why there was the assumption of Spanish blood, for her jaw was narrower than many of

the Indians of the region, and her dark hair had the suggestion of brown in its color, and a slight tendency to curl. She stood very straight, her simple ropa of polished rose-colored cotton modeled on the Spanish styles of two decades ago, the petticoat beneath it unadorned. There was little outward sign of her blindness other than a tendency to hold her head so she could listen more carefully. Her manner was pleasant without being subservient. She was not a beauty, but there was something engaging about her, a quality of vitality that was more captivating than prettiness. "There are chairs, if you would like to sit. And a bench," she added, pointing in its general direction. "The Freyes usually prefer the bench."

Once again he was reminded of the woman in Egypt, so long ago. "A chair would suit me quite well," he said, and went to the one with a straight back and a leather-upholstered seat. He remained standing until she had gone to her chair—distinguished by two cushions and a shawl, as well as a guitar leaning against it—and sat down. "I trust I am not interrupting."

She laughed once, her face half-turned in his direction. "No, you are not. I was only picking out a song I heard one of the sailors singing today." Her hand strayed to the neck of the guitar, but she did not pick up the instrument. "It isn't a very good guitar. The pegs will not hold the strings in tune."

San Germanno felt an intense pang at the loss of music. It had been so many years since he had touched a fiddle or a lute or virginals. The guitar was mute testimony to all he had left behind and he longed to play a melody, or a few chords, even on so unpromising an instrument. The silence that descended between him and Oaxetli should have been awkward, but was not; the soft sound of women's voices chanting echoed from the convent, punctuating his grief for so many lost things. Finally San Germanno said, "How much did my manservant tell you?"

"He said you would need a translator, one who speaks the languages of the people," she replied. "He had been given my name by more than one religious. You may rely upon me, in spite of this." Her voice was aggravated; her hand went to her eyes. "I need only hear to translate."

"And did he tell you what I intend to do?" San Germanno watched her carefully, measuring her response with a mixture of concern and curiosity.

She answered at once, her manner direct. "He said you wanted to go north, into the regions where the Indians and not the Spanish still rule." She cocked her head, listening closely. "Few Europeans are willing to undertake such journeys. Why do you want to do this?"

He considered his answer carefully. "There are many things I would like to learn from these people, before the Spanish urge them to forget, and the ways are changed beyond recall." He saw her nod, and went on, "So much has been lost already, and it will not be long before what is now truth becomes legend, a tale for children instead of the wisdom of the people."

"A noble intention." She was unconvinced. "Might this search have anything to do with the Seven Golden Cities of Cibola?"

"No," he said calmly. "Even if those cities do exist—which I doubt—they would be of interest to me only because of their people."

"You have no desire for treasure." The statement challenged him.

"If by treasure you mean gold and silver, no, I do not; I have considerable wealth already." He realized as he said it that she had excellent reason not to believe him. "If you mean knowledge, then I must admit I am eager to find it, and it is what I am seeking; the knowledge of the people while they still understand it."

"Knowledge." She swung around toward the sound of his voice. "And why does it matter to you?"

To his surprise, he answered candidly. "Because my people are forgotten." The admission left him feeling strangely exposed; he watched her carefully for any sign of fear or dismay.

He saw neither: curiosity lit her face; she leaned toward him impetuously. "What people are they?"

"They are gone. No one remembers them." He paused as the singing of the nuns swelled, then faded. He regained some perspective on what he was saying. "It troubles me that so many others suffer the same fate."

She rose abruptly and came toward him, walking with the confidence born of being in familiar surroundings. "You have not asked for lamps."

"No," he agreed.

Stopping less than an armslength from him, she said, "I would like to touch your face."

He stood. "Please. If that would assure you of anything in my regard." The last was intended to assuage any apprehensions she might feel about him.

Her hands reached his shoulders first. "Not as tall as I thought," she said to herself, and then began the exploration of his face. "What is it about your skin?" she asked a little later. "It is fine, but like smoothed parchment. How old are you?"

"Older than I look," he replied.

Her fingers continued to memorize his features. "Your eyes are—?"

"Dark. Blue to the point of blackness." He had not seen this for himself since his death; others had described them to him óver the centuries.

"That is unusual." Oaxetli resumed her discoveries, her nearness causing him some disquiet; reluctantly he thought Rogerio might be right after all, and shut the idea away in the next instant. "What troubles you?" she asked.

"Nothing that need concern you," he replied, hoping it was so. He studied her pensively, hoping he was not attracted to her for purely esurient reasons, that what had cracked the armor of his reserve had been more than appetency.

Her lower arm brushed against the Order of Saint Stephen, and she uttered a little cry. "What is that?"

"An honor. It is a starburst of diamonds. Those of us who have fought against those invading . . . our homeland, have been awarded it by the leader of our allies." It was accurate enough as far as it went; the Order of Saint Stephen was fifty years old—San Germanno had fought invaders for more than three thousand six hundred years.

"What did you do to deserve it?" she asked, one hand tracing out the Order. "It is a fine ornament."

"Many things I would rather not remember," he said to her.

The finality of his tone impressed her; she brought both hands to his head again. Finally she took two steps back from him. "You have a good face." She hesitated. "Not so handsome as some, but a good face."

"Thank you." His acknowledgement was awkward, and he sought to put both of them at ease once again. "How did you learn this skill?"

"I have done it all my life," she said simply. "Touch and sound are sight for me."

"Does it bother you?" As soon as he asked, he wondered if he had gone too far, and was trying to find a way to modify the question when she answered.

"Certainly it does." Oaxetli held up her hand to keep him from speaking as she gathered her thoughts. "But it is a gift as well, in its way. It does not leave me wholly bereft." She went back to her chair. "I have never seen flowers, but I know them by their scents more keenly than a perfumer. I have petted cats, but I do not know what their fur looks like, no one is more able to enjoy their purring. I know the voice of every child in this neighborhood, but I have never seen them run, though I hear their footfalls, and know each of them from their steps. And I know the thousand sounds most people never hear." She directed her blank gaze at the far wall. "It is also the reason I learned so many languages. What else was there for me to do?"

"It took great courage," San Germanno said, his voice low.

"Courage?" She chuckled angrily, pacing away from him in the confines of her room. "What courage? Courage had nothing to do with it. Necessity demanded I have some ability that would make my blindness less of a burden. It was fortunate that I was willing to dedicate myself to learning. Had I not studied, I would be a beggar now, or a whore, or a wanderer starving to death, or a slave to the Freyes, eking out a living by scrubbing their floors and washing their clothes. My own family was required to send me away." She rounded on him. "What else was I to do?"

"You might have resigned yourself to it; that is not uncommon," San Germanno suggested, recalling the many times he had seen others do just that; he had known that temptation more than once himself.

"For what reason would I do that?" she protested with heat. "What would I gain but servitude and grief?"

He went to her side and touched her arm gently; when he spoke it was in a deep, still voice. "I did not say I thought you ought to do it, Oaxetli, I only marvel that you did not."

She shrugged his hand away but could not keep from smiling a little. "You are flattering me."

"No, Oaxetli, I am not." He said it bluntly. "I am telling you what I have observed, and crediting you with a strength which, believe me, is rare. Were you only an honorable translator, I would respect what you do. That you have overcome much adds to my regard."

"Does that mean you are going to employ me?" she asked, mischief lightening her voice. "Or were you going to say lovely things about my character to soften the blow, that you would find a blind woman a liability on your travels? If it is the latter, I would prefer you do not waste time in flattery."

He answered at once. "I need someone with your skills in tongues. My servant and I both have excellent vision, but we do not understand the languages of the peoples to the north. I suspect that many of them do not want to converse in Spanish, even if they know the language." He paused a moment, choosing his words carefully. "I do not know what dangers we may confront, or what hardships. It may be that you would prefer to remain in this place, where you know your surroundings."

Oaxetli tossed her head; concealed in her defiance was an intense longing. "I am bored with familiarity. I am weary of caution. I am tired of being looked after. I do not want to translate the Gospels into Indian languages for the Freyes, so that they can go to the people and cast out the old gods in favor of their God and Son. I would like to have an adventure, once in my life; I would like to use my skills for something other than the work of the Freyes." She reached out for his hand, holding it in straining fingers. "If you mean what you say, that you want to preserve the knowledge of the people, then I will go with you into the maws of volcanos to do it."

"I hope to avoid volcanos," San Germanno said wryly. "It will be hard-going, or so I have been told."

"It is not wise to say that in this place, even now." She made an impatient gesture to show it meant nothing to her. "I have a cousin who will keep this house for me while we are gone. He has done it before, when the Freyes have sent me to distant villages. If I send word, he can be here in two days."

So it was settled; San Germanno was relieved to have the decision made. "I am prepared to pay you three gold reales for each month we are gone, and a silver angel for each page of translation you provide, with an additional ten gold reales on our return." He knew the sums were high, but given what they might face, he thought it was reasonable. "If you can ride"—he saw her nod—"you will use my horses and tack. I will supply you with any clothes you may need, and all gear for traveling. You have a better notion than I of what you will need in the way of clothing. Tell me what you require and I will put the seamstresses of Avenida de Coches to work at once."

"Does that mean you will take me with you?" she asked, as if she had not understood what he had just said.

"Since you say you want to go, and I need your services . . . " He took her hand, bent and kissed it.

"Truly?" she pleaded.

"Truly," he vowed.

Her excitement made her seem younger than she was. "My cousin will be here in two days. You can wait that long, can't you?"

San Germanno sighed. "It will take a week to prepare. You have seven days to change your mind."

"Seven days!" She turned toward the sound of his voice. "So long."

"They will pass quickly," he promised her. "With so much to do, they will be gone in an instant." He was already thinking of all he would have to do in the coming week: the horses would have to be reshod, and the pack-mules; chests of earth would have to be readied for the journey; there was food to purchase, for Oaxetli and the animals; he would have to decide if they were going to hire a guide here in Acapulco or wait until they were farther inland; clothes and boots would have to be—

"Conde," she cut into his rumination. "I am so grateful to you."

He shook his head. "No; say that at the end of the journey, if you still wish to." Spanish formality demanded that he leave her now, their business completed; to remain any longer might harm her reputation. He stepped back. "My manservant will come in the morning, to arrange about your clothing and boots."

She reached out to touch him again. "You will not change your mind?"

"No. But you may change yours; I will not fault you if you do," he reminded her, making his way toward the door. It was full night now but he went effortlessly, his vision unobscured. "And the Freyes might forbid it, since you are an unmarried woman."

"Never. I will not change my mind, Conde." She said it softly and comprehensively, with such feeling that he was struck again with the strength of her.

He hesitated at the door, wondering if he ought to reassure her again. "I do not want to put you at any . . . disadvantage. I will offer a pledge to the Freyes, if that will make your employment less questionable."

"If you think it is necessary," she said, unwilling to involve the Church any more than prudence required.

"I think it wise." At last he turned and bowed to her, although she could not see him, and said, "Many thanks, Oaxetli, for hearing me out and for consenting to help me on my search."

She had risen and now bounced on her toes, like an anxious child. "May I ask one thing of you?"

He gave her his full attention, aware that this request was one that mattered greatly to her. "Of course you may ask: what is it?"

"Will you bring books and read them to me? Not Scripture, but . . . oh, anything." She stared downward, confused and suddenly awkward as she had not been before. "That is the hardest thing about blindness—that I cannot read, and I so want to. I know the Freyes would not want to teach me, but if I had sight, there would be a chance I could learn from someone, but . . . "

"Certainly," San Germanno said with dawning sympathy for her. "I often carry books with me. It would please me to read to you."

She clapped her hands once, grinning with delight. She pressed her advantage. "I know Latin. If you have works in Latin, I would like them as well as Spanish ones."

"All right," he said, captivated by her enthusiasm. "Latin and Spanish." His dark eyes were quizzical as he stood half inside and half outside her house. "Is there anything else you would like?"

She hesitated, then said, "If you know other languages, will you teach me?" Before he could answer she went on, "You have an accent I have never heard before. What is your native tongue?"

He did not answer at once. "I come from mountains called the Carpathians. There is a war there now, a continuing one. You would not have much occasion to use my native language, Oaxetli." This was true enough, for he was the last native speaker of the language of his people for three millennia. In the intervening centuries he had learned more than a hundred languages, many of which were now forgotten.

"What is it?" she asked sharply; she had heard something in his voice that troubled her.

"It is not always . . . easy to remember," he said, taking care to offer her the truth.

She realized she had overstepped the bounds. "No, I suppose not. I did not mean to pry, Conde." She prepared to close the door, curtsying a bit to show her respect. "It will be wonderful."

"I trust you will continue to think so." He waited until the door was closed and the latch in place before he turned and left the little walled garden, taking care to make certain the gate was latched. As he swung onto his horse, he realized that two nuns were standing in the side door of the convent, watching Oaxetli's house. He considered acknowledging their presence, but changed his mind as he realized they were concealed; ordinarily they would be virtually invisible; his vampire eyes pierced the dark as mortal eyes could not. He touched his horse with his heel and set off through the streets once again, preoccupied with assessing his impressions of the woman he had just engaged as his translator.

By now, the streets of Acapulco, so busy an hour ago, were all but deserted. Most of those who had promenaded, strolled, and roistered were gone indoors to their various evening pursuits. From behind many gates came the sounds of voices, some convivial, some lascivious, some angry. Between this hour and dawn, the streets belonged to dangerous men. San Germanno put his hand to the hilt of his sword, and concentrated on the alleyways and other places where such men might hide and nudged his grey into an extended *passage*.

San Germanno reached his own house without incident, and discovered Rogerio waiting for him in the stables. He led his horse toward his stall, and busied himself with unsaddling the grey. "What is it you want to say?" he inquired in Imperial Latin as he lifted the saddle off the horse and set it on the stand immediately outside the stall. "Well?"

"Pedro will do that," Rogerio reminded him.

"He is with his family for the night; there is no good reason to summon him." San Germanno put the saddle-pad atop the saddle. "I hope I am not too proud to groom my horse."

Rogerio handed his master a brush and took the bridle from him, answering in the same language. "Is her blindness too much of a hazard, do you think?"

"It is a disadvantage, I grant you, but nowhere near as great a hazard as going into the regions of the north without a translator, one that is not in Orders. Since she is willing, it would be absurd to refuse her company." He worked the brush over the horse's shining coat, beginning at the top of the neck and going down, then from the shoulder back. "She has the skills we will need; you said that yourself. We would accomplish little going to these people if we are unable to speak with them. But you are having second thoughts: why is that."

After a brief silence, Rogerio said, "I would not like to bring her into danger."

"It is not what I intend to do, either, although it may come to that." He bent to brush the horse's belly, smoothing out the hair where the girth had been. "She does not seem to mind the prospect."

"She has no notion of what risks are," Rogerio scoffed unhappily. "That is what concerns me. She may long for adventure, but I doubt she realizes what it could mean."

San Germanno changed the subject. "We will take five horses, two for reserve, and two pack-mules. The tack will have to be inspected and repaired if necessary, and we will have to have tents and bedrolls."

"We haven't settled the matter of Oaxetli. It is not like you, my master, to take anyone into danger without giving them warning. You know we may face many hazards. Yet you do not seem to have given any hint of what she might face to this woman." Rogerio frowned as he spoke, aware as he heard himself just how uncharacteristic of San Germanno this was.

"I will not deny that," San Germanno said, righting himself again and going to the other side of the horse. "But she, I suspect, is not so fragile as either of us are inclined to think. She has wanted this, or something like this, for a while. She does not want to do all her work for the Church."

"Aren't you worried?" Rogerio asked.

San Germanno paused in the grooming of the grey and looked directly at Rogerio. "Of course I am worried. I haven't taken complete leave of my senses."

Had Rogerio not known San Germanno for so long, he might have missed the odd note in the Conde's voice. He folded his arms. "So."

As if he had not heard Rogerio, San Germanno continued. "We will have to make extra provision for her, of course, and she will not be able to guide us as I hoped she might. But she wants to go, and her Spanish is excellent." He had reached the grey's rump. "That is no minor consideration. Many another speaks the languages of the people, but does not have a good command of Spanish."

"Of course," said Rogerio with such deference that San Germanno stopped his work again and gave his manservant his full attention.

"All right; since you insist. Yes, she is an interesting woman. I am . . . intrigued by her." He picked up his brush again. "It was what you intended, isn't it?"

"Yes," Rogerio admitted. He held out the large, bone comb to San Germanno and took the brush from him. "But I am unconvinced I was right. I am not so certain that an alliance would be as beneficial as I first thought."

"Are your doubts about me, or about her?" San Germanno asked as he set to combing the Andalusian's luxurious mane.

"Perhaps both," Rogerio said. "If she does not provide all that you seek, would you not fare better—"

San Germanno cut him off. "It is not my intention to make her my lover."

Rogerio stared at him, appalled at what he heard. "If you do not—"

Again San Germanno interrupted him. "She has dreams, Rogerio, as all those living do. The ones I give her will be sweet, and will do her no harm. And I will manage well enough."

"Are you sure she will find that sufficient? Might she not want something more? Might not you be persuaded?" Rogerio asked as if flinging a gauntlet at San Germanno.

For a long moment San Germanno said nothing. "Ah." He finished the mane and went to comb the tail, his dark eyes contemplative. "Let us hope you're not right."

"That is what troubles me," Rogerio said as San Germanno reached for a hoof-pick.

"I must confess, that had not occurred to me," San Germanno said as he lifted the grey's off-side front foot and bent over to clean it.

Text of a letter from Frey Ardo, prior of the Carmelite community near Popayan, to Obispo Hernan Sigismundo Bernal Guarda, in Cuzco.

To Su Excelencia, Obispo Hernan Guarda, Los Sacramentos, Cuzco, Audiencia de Lima, Viceroyalty of Peru, the most humble, respectful greetings from Frey Ardo, with prayers for the Obispo's long life and Godly favor.

Your letter has reached our community and has caused me much trepidation and consternation. In all duty, I am bound to answer you, for the man you seek served with us in this community as a tertiary Frey for seventeen months, yet I must inform you that he never once displayed any of the sins you have indicated he embraces. It may be that he had no opportunity to do so, but nothing he said or did caused me to suspect him. While he served with us, he did prepare a number of medicinal compounds, some most certainly alchemical in nature, but they permitted us to treat many whom we would only have buried before San Germanno arrived. I cannot credit this man with the vile motives you assign him, but I cannot doubt your assertions, either.

Without contradicting any imputation Su Excelencia may have for this man, I must give an account for how he has been behaved while he remained with us, so that you may more fully understand my confusion. There is a marked difference from what you described to what I have witnessed. It may be that after he had been in Cuzco, remorse seized him and he determined to expiate his errors through dedication to this community and the people we serve. There is no other way I can account for the pronounced discrepancy between the man you describe and the man who worked with us with such selfless devotion. He was always keeping the night hours in the infirmary, and there was no disease so terrible that he declined to treat it. Often he has gone to those suffering from the most ravaging fevers and given them constant care. When he has been confronted with injuries that many men would despair of treating, he has ministered to the injured unceasingly.

Certainly we do not offer society of the grand sort you enjoy in Cuzco, and it may be that San Germanno—for so we have called him—is one who becomes ensnared in the ambitions of the great ones. As a foreigner, he would not always recognize the snares laid out for the unwary by those in power, for those of his blood are not engaged in Spanish affairs, or our efforts in the New World. If that is the case, he has shown that away from such influences he is honorable and without guile. We must thank God that he was able to rid himself of those venal influences that threatened to corrupt his soul, as his work here has revealed he has done.

I am puzzled that you assert he conspired in the death of an Incan noblewoman. While he was with us, San Germanno has held the people of the region in high regard, taking care to respect them in all that they do. Nothing he has said here would suggest to me that he was dissembling. He has consulted with their healers and has recorded many of their tales. It may not be wholly appropriate to do this, but I am convinced that he undertook the task in the belief that it was a service to the people we are dedicated to help. It is also fitting that I tell you he made no mention of contempt for any of the people of Cuzco, not Indian and not Spanish. He has conducted himself here with exemplary courtesy to all; his humility has been constant. I am satisfied that he had no nefarious purpose in coming to this community, and I will not denounce a man who has given of himself without ambition or regard for his personal safety. He has provided an example I pray more of mankind will learn to emulate than we see in the world in this age.

May this account serve to mitigate the apprehension you have in regard to San Germanno, and may God give both of us the vision to know the truth. May your steps be always in the path of righteousness, so that at the Last Judgment we may see God in His Face. I pray it may come to pass in the Name of Our Lord and la Virgen. With all respect and Christian obedience, by my own hand.

Frey Ardo
Carmelite and Prior
Communidad della Sagrada Familia
near Popayan, Audiencia de Quito
Viceroyalty of Peru
The 11th day of August, in the Year of Grace, 1647

5

Forests of ferns and high-topped trees had given way to grasslands, wooded hills and small, fertile valleys, and occasional stretches of dry scrublands. San Germanno with Rogerio and Oaxetli followed narrow roads and indistinct trails from one village to the next, occasionally pausing for a few days while San Germanno sought out the local healers and through Oaxetli asked questions about herbs, earths, and water. They avoided the cities of Guanajuanto on the east and Guadalajara on the west, choosing instead to remain on the roads of the Indians, past high mountain lakes and remote communities. Occasionally they met travelers bound for one Spanish enclave or another, but most of those on the road were bound for neighboring markets, or visiting relatives. Occasionally bandits pursued them, but without any success to their intentions: San Germanno was deadly with a sword, and Rogerio used bow and arrow with a skill few could match.

In some places the three of them lingered for more than a week; in most they were gone in two or three days. Once the local Passionists asked San Germanno and his company to move on, and twice the people they found forced them away with spears and arrows. One village they found was totally deserted for no apparent reason, and another was in the final throes of a deadly outbreak of measles. By the end of the first month, they had gone more than fifty leagues from Acapulco, into the Audiencia of Nueva Galicia. They found fewer Spaniards as they continued north and west, and most of them were monks, the bulk of the Spanish and mercenary soldiers being posted far to the southeast of them, at Mexico and Veracruz. Gradually the frequency of Christian buildings and missionaries lessened, becoming rare by the time they had covered a hundred leagues.

When camp was made each night, San Germanno would do as he had promised and read to Oaxetli while Rogerio tended to the meal; that this was done without any light but the glow from the fire was unimportant. It was a companionable way to pass the long evening hours, and San Germanno was able to breathe life into the works he selected. He began with Tirso de Molina's *El Burlador de Sevilla y covi-*

dado de piedra, then moved on to Lope de Vega's *Fuenteovejuna.* Four times in the first seven weeks of their traveling, San Germanno had visited Oaxetli, always in her sleep, and always leaving her with the delicious rapture of her dreams which were revealed in smiles when she woke. Reluctantly he had to admit that Rogerio had been right; it was becoming more difficult for him to be satisfied with the ephemeral gratification he received from these encounters; he was coming to know her too well to be content with so little genuine intimacy. He could not discover how Oaxetli felt about the dreams he gave her. Little as he wanted to have his needs intrude on his working with Oaxetli—for he feared her detestation as he feared few things—he realized that it had already begun, and that the farther they went, the greater his desire for her acceptance of him grew.

It was a tenuously warm, clear afternoon in late November when they picked up what appeared to be an animal trail, crossed a ridge and saw below them a swath of dry grasses in a tree-fringed high valley; a number of baked-brick houses were clustered in an elbow of the valley, so carefully located that from any other vantage point they would be invisible: anyone passing on any path but this would not see the village at all and would assume the valley to be empty. San Germanno, Rogerio, and Oaxetli were now at least one hundred fifty leagues north-by-northwest from Acapulco, and near the edge of the desert of central Nueva Galicia, in territory generally undelineated on the single map they had obtained before leaving Acapulco.

"What do you think?" San Germanno asked the other two; he shaded his eyes as he studied the houses; his gelding pawed restively at this unexpected halt.

"It looks to be a peaceful place," said Rogerio, making *looks* the strongest word. "No sign of walls or fortifications. But still protected."

"Describe it to me," said Oaxetli, her sightless eyes turned toward San Germanno's voice.

San Germanno complied. "It is a high valley, shaped like a long arrowhead with a bend in it near the tip. The valley is grassy, one end sewn for harvest, the rest untouched. From here it is possible to see down the bend to the village, which is in the far end. There are perhaps thirty or forty houses arranged in threes and fours around a central fire-pit."

"Is there a church?" Oaxetli asked.

"Not that I can see," San Germanno answered her carefully. "If there is, it is very small." He shaded his eyes, thinking as he did that he needed a new lining of his native earth in the soles and heels of his boots; the sun was beginning to bother him and his head ached from the brightness.

"Is there a wide platform, or shelf on the side of the hill? To the west?" Oaxetli shifted in her saddle, and pointed in the direction she meant; it was westerly, toward the angle of the sun.

"Yes," said San Germanno, and turned to look at her, surprised at the accuracy of her description. "Do you know this place?"

"I know *of* it," she replied, her features brightening with curiosity. "There are many stories about it. I thought it might be a legend."

San Germanno felt his interest ignite as well, taking inspiration from her. "Why is that? What place is this?"

Oaxetli smiled as she told him. "This is the valley of la Dona Azul, or it may be. I never thought it was real."

"The Blue Lady?" Rogerio repeated. "It has a Spanish name?"

"*She* has a Spanish name," Oaxetli corrected him.

"Why did you think it was not real, Oaxetli?" San Germanno asked her, and gave her a little time to respond, for he had come to know she would reveal more if she was not pressed.

"I thought it wasn't real," she said after a brief moment of frowning cogitation, "because the story about it seemed so . . . convenient. I thought it was a story made up by the Freyes."

San Germanno knew she was making a game of the tale; he indulged her. "What is convenient about it?"

She sighed gently, a certain indication she was getting ready to reveal the whole. "It was said of the place—perhaps this place, perhaps another—that the first Conquistadores came here, and brought the religion of Christ to the people, and then vanished, their tasks completed, leaving only their faith behind. No one knows who these noble Conquistadores were. It is said that here they conquered with the Word, not the sword, and that the people have continued to worship as they were taught." She paused. "Most of the Freyes seek to do this, and it is the sort of story that they want to believe. So I have thought it was only a tale made up to keep the Freyes happy, but if this is truly a high valley shaped like an arrowhead with a bend in it and a platform on the side of the hill, it may be the valley of la Dona Azul."

"But why la Dona Azul?" Rogerio asked when San Germanno did not. "Why that name and why in Spanish, if it is not a legend of the Freyes?"

Oaxetli shrugged, her indifference feigned. Finally she said, "It is the one part of the story the Freyes don't like: they say that the one who converted these people was not a monk or priest but a woman."

San Germanno chuckled. "No priest or monk would like that." He paused, musing. "La Virgen traditionally wears a blue dress. So did camp followers, a hundred years ago, blue or red." He frowned against the light. "Married women wore black."

"Blue, black. Why would that matter here?" Oaxetli inquired, leaning forward in her saddle to hear the answer.

"I did not think Cortez came this far," San Germanno said remotely, aware that he had not answered her question as he thought back on all the accounts he had heard during his stay in Acapulco. Of all the stories of the Conquistadores, none of them had mentioned leaving women behind with native people, although it might be more from disapproval than knowledge that the tale was not often told.

Oaxetli studied the sound of his voice. "You sense something."

"Nothing so certain as that," said San Germanno apologetically. He could not keep from being direct with her.

"Do we investigate this place?" Rogerio was aware of resistance in his master, and could not help but share it; he continued to speak Spanish out of respect for Oaxetli. "It may be nothing more that a myth, that story, and this place chosen for the setting because it is so remote."

"Yes, I am aware of that. And this cannot be the only high valley in Nueva Galicia with a bend in it," San Germanno said with a touch of asperity. "I will curse myself if I pass by such an opportunity. And I may curse myself for being reckless enough to go to the place." He looked at Rogerio. "Well?"

"If we do not go there now," said Rogerio philosophically as he tugged on the leads for their pack mules to bring the two closer, "you will only want to return in a day or a week."

San Germanno gave a rare, open smile. "You know me too well, old friend."

"Does that mean we are going into the valley?" Oaxetli asked.

Rogerio answered her question. "Yes. It does." With that he set his horse in motion behind San Germanno's, tugging on the lead lines of the two spare horses as well as the lead lines of the mules.

The track descended into the valley at a steady angle, cutting a straight path between the occasional trees; the horses and mules were kept to a strict walk, not only because it was unknown territory, but because the incline was sharp enough and the track so narrow as to be hazardous at a faster pace. The two horses being led frisked on the ends of their leads, one of them trying to push ahead of the rest, tossing her head to show her rebellion.

San Germanno swung around in the saddle to pull the spotted mare back into line with the rest, his attention on the animal and not the trail ahead. So he was startled when he finished with the mare to find two men holding spears, the tips pointed upward, standing on the track fifty paces in front of him. He swore once in his native language as he shifted his seat. He held up his hand to signal the others to halt as he pulled his grey Andalusian mare to a stand-still.

"What is it?" asked Oaxetli, knowing something had happened. "I hear something, but I . . . What is happening?"

"I'll need you to translate, I hope," San Germanno said to her. "Come up beside me." He kept his eyes on the two men, noticing they were wearing woven garments, which reassured him; had the men worn leather, it was probable they spoke a language unknown to Oaxetli, as it was, it was still a possibility.

"What is it?" she repeated as she reached his side.

"Two men. With spears." He saw her flinch, and hastened to reassure her. "They are not threatening us, but they are blocking the path. If they mean to hurt us, that is not apparent in how they are standing now."

"Describe them," she said, listening as if the intensity of her attention would allow her to know more.

"Dressed similarly to the people of Zacatecas, but with sashes of blue and a cross painted on their upper arms." He held out his hands to show they were empty, then turned to Oaxetli. "There are crosses on their headbands as well. The headbands are white."

She nodded to show she understood, and called out a few words to the men, adding softly to San Germanno, "I said we are travelers bound for the north and we mean them no harm."

"Excellent," he approved, watching the two men closely; they were whispering together, the larger of the two making an emphatic gesture with his fist. He decided to try again. "Tell them," San Germanno suggested, "that we have come a long way and are tired."

She spoke again, this time more quickly. When a terse few words were given for an answer, she said, "We are to wait here."

"You do understand them?" San Germanno asked in spite of his conviction that she did. He was puzzled by the clothes these people wore; the patterns on the cloth and the cloth itself were unlike any others he had come across in his travels in the New World. He began to hope he might have found people untouched by the Spaniards.

"Yes," she replied, unperturbed by the question. "It is something like the language of the people of Nazayote; they are similar enough for my purposes. I will manage, if they will not try to confuse me."

"Why should they do that?" San Germanno wondered aloud, and answered the question for himself. These people might have excellent reasons to confound strangers, to mislead and deceive those they did not know.

"What is he saying to you?" demanded the larger of the two men.

Oaxetli answered him promptly. "He wanted to be certain that I know your tongue."

"You speak it strangely," the man remarked, and repeated, "We must wait."

"Why?" Oaxetli inquired politely after she had translated the last exchange for San Germanno.

"Because la Dona Azul must see you here," the larger man told her curtly. He put his hand on the smooth tunic he wore and patted the design; San Germanno could not determine if the pattern was woven or painted, for the cloth was flat and oddly shiny, like dull satin.

"Dona Azul makes decisions here," the other man stated.

"What is it about la Dona Azul?" San Germanno asked sharply, having heard the words.

Oaxetli looked puzzled. "He said she must see us here," she answered, and shook her head once to show she knew nothing more.

"She must see us? Here?" he echoed, hoping to persuade the two men to explain more. "What does that mean? And how does she come to have a Spanish name?" He glanced at the men again, not wanting to appear anxious about them. There had been many times in the past when he had had to be approved by a village leader in order to enter it, and a few times when he had had to make an offering to a village deity; surely this was one or the other. He wished he knew which.

Oaxetli spoke to the men again, received an answer, and told San Germanno. "He says she will come. Until then we must wait."

"All right," San Germanno said, prepared to have the village elder inspect them as a condition of being received there. He made a sign to Rogerio. "Let the horses graze. Not the mules: we'll never get them moving again."

"It is done." Rogerio dismounted, took the leads of the spare horses and his own mount, tugging them out of line and holding them as they lowered their heads into the dry grasses, searching out greenery.

The smaller man said something to the larger, then clapped his hand to his chest. His fellow scowled at him, and grumbled, his tone argumentative; he pointed at the mules and spat out a few terse words. The smaller man thrust a finger in San Germanno's direction, his mouth square with anger.

"What—?" San Germanno began, only to have Oaxetli interrupt him in an undervoice.

"It is the horses they wonder at. One says it is a sign. The . . . I think it is sky men ride horses. They have burros, it seems, but horses are as wonderful as flying serpents." She leaned forward and listened. "The other says that it is not a sign."

"A sign of what?" San Germanno thought aloud. He had been told that until the Spanish came there were no horses in the Americas. He was willing to believe it, if only because there were no llamas in Europe, or giraffes.

Oaxetli shook her head in annoyance. "I can't hear everything. They're speaking very softly. Something about the sky men."

"Are you sure that is the word—sky?" San Germanno had difficulty accepting the word. For a moment he recalled his first encounter more than a thousand years ago with Shamda on the Irrawaddy, who thought all Europeans were ghosts because of their pale skins, and sought to exorcise them for the protection of his people. If this sky men was more of the same, he would have to be very careful, not just for his own safety, but for Rogerio and Oaxetli as well.

"What is bothering you about the word?" she asked acutely. "What do you think it will mean?"

"I wish I knew," he answered with great sincerity just as he became aware of a commotion a short distance away. Crude bells, more like gongs than bells, were being clamorously hammered, and a number of voices were singing something about la Dona Azul; the two guards fell to their knees and pressed their hands together as if in prayer.

"My master . . . " Rogerio called out, tugging the horses closer to him. "There are others coming."

"Yes, I can see them, but I cannot count them yet. Keep the animals quiet; they seem to disturb these people, and the animals are restive already," San Germanno told him. "This noise might upset them." He reached out and seized the reins of Oaxetli's gelding, saying, "He's getting nervous." The horses were not the only ones, San Germanno observed to himself; he had to fight his own mounting apprehension as he strove to quiet the horses.

"I am aware," she said, letting him take charge of the gelding without protest. She did her best to listen for phrases in the cacophony coming toward them. "I'm sorry. I can't hear enough."

"It would be astonishing if you could," San Germanno said, raising his voice, for the gong-like bells were drowning out all other sounds around them. He had his hands full holding his remount mare and Oaxetli's gelding; both horses were pulling at the reins, bouncing on their front feet. Behind them a mule brayed.

A procession appeared on the narrow trail, three men with mallets and t-shaped trees of long, metallic chimes which they struck with single-minded determination. After them came six men with a litter on their shoulders on which sat a woman in a chair; she was wearing a strange blue dress, unlike any worn by those accompanying her. Behind her trooped a dozen men, all carrying spears, all in the same puzzling cloth, all wearing the same blue sashes and white cross headbands as the two kneeling.

"Tell me," Oaxetli said to San Germanno. "What do you see?"

San Germanno kept his voice level. "This looks very official. A number of men are escorting a woman of about twenty-five or thirty, in blue, who is being carried on a litter." He did not know what more to tell her, so he added, "The bells are leading them. Three men play them." Her dress, San Germanno noticed, shone as much as the tunic-like clothes of her guards.

"Three men and all this noise? How do they achieve it?" Oaxetli remarked to show she was not frightened.

"Amazing, isn't it," he agreed, watching the procession narrowly.

The bell-ringers were suddenly silent, the absence of their clanging making ears ring. They knelt and held their bell-trees upright. Then the litter-bearers set their burden down with great care before they, too, knelt facing the woman in blue, who now rose slowly and came forward.

"Ought I to kneel?" Rogerio asked San Germanno in English.

"Not yet," San Germanno said without looking at him; his whole attention was on the woman in the blue; the shining dress had begun as a wide-skirted shift, but a wide silver belt had been clasped around her waist, in imitation of European styles of the last century. Several ornaments hung from the belt, though San Germanno was not near enough to make out what they were. The woman looked to be roughly the same age as Oaxetli, tall for her people, with a sinuous walk that reminded San Germanno of Estasia. As she drew nearer, he spoke in Spanish. "Greetings to you. We are travelers who come to you asking

for a place to rest among you. We are weary, and so are our animals."
Then he listened while Oaxetli translated this for him.

The woman in the blue dress rapped out a single question; Oaxetli
said, "She wants to know who you are. At once."

"Tell her I am Francisco Ra—" He got no further than that. The
woman in blue cried out, raising her hands over her head and repeated
the same words over and over again. "What the devil—?"

"She is thanking the sky-god for the return of . . . I do not know what
she means, but she says the bringer-of-the-god." Oaxetli turned toward
San Germanno. "Francisco is the name of the bringer-of-the-god."

San Germanno felt cold grip him; he could not shake off the impression that his name had triggered this woman's outburst. He sat very
still on his mare, waiting for what would happen next, wishing he had
brought his musquet as well as three swords, two poignards and his
francisca tucked inside his belt, lying concealed along his back. Until
now, this had seemed more than sufficient in combination with Rogerio's hunting bows. He was no longer as sanguine as he had been about
this. "Are you certain about the meaning?"

Oaxetli did not answer at once. "Yes; I suppose I am," she said after
reflection. "The words are not so very different that they can mean anything else."

The woman in blue continued to exclaim her thanks, and the people kneeling around her took up the chant. The three bell-ringers
began to hammer once more. The sound welled, growing louder and
stronger with each repetition. It was hypnotic, this repetition, and
many of those kneeling wore the dazed look to prove it.

Rogerio had his hands full when the spotted mare suddenly tried to
bolt, the clamor having frightened her enough to make her want to
flee. He jerked hard on the lead, and brought the mare to a trembling
stop, sides working and ears half-back.

"What are we supposed to do?" San Germanno asked Oaxetli, tension mounting within him; he would have covered his ears with his
hands if he did not have the reins of two horses to hold.

"I don't know," she said testily, raising her voice to be heard. "Why
should I know?"

Once more the sound stopped with ear-numbing suddenness. The
people watched the woman in blue, their hands clasped reverently. A
few of the people swayed on their feet, caught in the rhythm of the
chant, though it had ended.

The woman in blue fixed her eyes on San Germanno and, with an expression of determined purpose, started toward him. When she was four paces away from his horse, she stopped, raised her hands joined together over her head and addressed him directly.

Oaxetli translated for her. "She welcomes you once again to this valley that is dedicated to the sky-god, and makes the sacrifices according to the law that was laid down for them when Francisco brought la Dona Azul to them. She tells you that they have been faithful to your commands and praise you for bringing la Dona Azul to them when you came before; they beg you to accept their devotion." She did her best to keep any color from her words, but she was not entirely successful, for she was unable to hide her apprehension from San Germanno.

"What Francisco?" San Germanno wondered aloud. "When did this happen?"

Oaxetli asked the question for him, and when the woman in blue had spoken, she said, "She accepts your test, thanking the sky-god again that it is she and not one of the others honored by your return. You came here with many men five Donas Azules ago, bringing the first of us in your company. You left the first Dona Azul to teach us and bring us to the laws of the sky-god. You said you would return to claim la Dona Azul and carry her back with you to the rising sun. I am the fifth, and the sky-god has shown me favor above all others."

"But I am going north," San Germanno said, hoping that so simple an assertion would serve to end the adulation he was beginning to view with alarm. The woman in blue was expecting something from him, something she was convinced he understood and sought.

"Francisco came here going north when he came before with the first Dona Azul," she said to the kneeling people, reminding them of their history.

"It is the test," Oaxetli said for Dona Azul when she had relayed San Germanno's words to the woman in blue and received her answer. "You are Francisco."

"Yes," said San Germanno with a patience he did not feel. "That is my name, as it is the name of many other men who are in the New World." He let Oaxetli translate this for him before he went on. "I am Conde de San Germanno, not a Conquistador. I am here only to learn, not to—"

There was another outburst from the woman in blue, her tone insistent. She pointed to Oaxetli and added something San Germanno needed no translation to know was an insult.

Oaxetli's cheeks darkened, and she recoiled as if slapped. "She . . . she does not want me with you," she told San Germanno.

"That much was obvious. What was the rest of it?" He brought her horse a little closer to his own, as much to show he regarded Oaxetli as important to him as to protect her from the woman addressing them. "Tell her that you have already passed the tests I have given you. She has not yet done so."

She was shivering as she did as he instructed her. When she was done there was another outburst from the woman in blue. Oaxetli heard her out. "I think she is willing to prove herself to you, so that you will take her east to the sky-god, in recognition of the worship they have given since . . . since you were here before. That is what she said." This addition was sullen, so she would appear less frightened. "She is prepared to do all you require to show her worthiness."

San Germanno knew he was being challenged and he disliked the feeling; he had no well-defined idea of what it was that this woman expected of him, but he was uncomfortably aware that she believed otherwise, and believed it with the full fervor of her religion. He looked at Oaxetli and said, "Tell her I do not understand what she is saying. This land is unknown to me. Say that whatever Francisco came here before, it was not I." He could not keep from the ironic reflection that he had been alive when the Francisco to whom she referred was here, and few men, if any aside from the few who were of his blood, shared his position.

Oaxetli did as she was told, her speech meticulous as if to add weight to what she said. Then she waited while the woman in blue spoke out heatedly. "She is saying that she does not know why you are behaving in this way, but she will not lose heart, for the son of the sky-god was denied by his followers, so she supposes she must be by you."

San Germanno swore under his breath in the language of his people, then brought himself to order. "This is going to be difficult," he said softly in Spanish. "I do not want to make her angry, but . . . Tell her that I have no test to make of her; that I am not who she thinks I am; that I am a foreigner looking to learn about the peoples of the New World."

This time the woman in blue exclaimed enthusiastically, seemingly not the least put off by what San Germanno had said. She turned and addressed her followers in a firm, satisfied tone.

"She is saying that is what you said before, that you were not the God of Obsidian, who is sometimes called the Dark Mirror, as the old legends told, but the voice of the sky-god, who is the God of the Foreigners, and who is the master of sacrifice." Oaxetli was worried, and she put her hand over San Germanno's on her horse's reins. "I do not know why she troubles me so much."

"Are you afraid they are still cutting the living hearts out of their captives?" San Germanno asked, hoping to make this notion sound absurd.

"No, not that," she replied seriously, unamused.

"Then what?" he persisted, giving some attention to the woman in blue, who had returned to her litter and was searching for something underneath the chair where she rode.

"They speak as if they had a new god, one that took the place of the old when the first Dona Azul came here in the company of Francisco. She says that the first Dona Azul came from far away, from the place where the sun rises." Oaxetli directed her sightless eyes toward the sound of the Dona Azul's voice. "She is certain that you are the Francisco they have waited for to return. She knows you will have to test her, because the sky-god always tests His people, to be certain they are worthy of His favor."

"I wish I knew who this Francisco was," San Germanno said quietly. "Then I might be able to speak with her sensibly." He scowled, thinking aloud, "Francisco is Spanish. Perhaps one of Cortez's men came this way."

"Or a missionary," suggested Oaxetli.

"With a woman in blue?" San Germanno mused. "I doubt it." He listened to the woman in blue again, disliking his own inability to understand her. "What is she saying now, Oaxetli?"

"She is saying that the sky-god will deliver them from all misfortune when they have purged themselves of their errors through worthy deeds and sacrifice. She says they will be saved by the sacrifice of those who have done great crimes." At the last word, Oaxetli shuddered. "She used the word for a blood sacrifice, Conde."

Suddenly the woman in blue turned around and faced San Germanno. She spoke directly to him, paying no heed to Rogerio or Oaxetli. When she was finished, she pointed to the kneeling men nearest to them.

"What is going on?" San Germanno asked.

"She has said that she will bring you back to their village. You are to be the guests of these people until you reveal yourself." Oaxetli had no emotion in her voice, but her hands were shaking.

"In other words, they are taking us prisoner," San Germanno said dryly. "And only they know what they expect us to provide them." He raised his voice, and spoke in English. "We'll go with them, Rogerio. We're in no position to try to fight our way out."

"No, my master," Rogerio responded, pulling the horses and mules as the men with spears approached him.

"Keep your eyes open. We will talk later." With that, he started his grey moving, pulling Oaxetli's mount after him. As they were surrounded by the escort ordered by the woman in blue, San Germanno said in Spanish, "Have courage, Oaxetli. We will come through this."

"I trust you are right," she said.

As San Germanno drew abreast of the woman in blue, she made a motion that brought her men to a halt; San Germanno pulled in his grey, wondering what the woman wanted now.

Dona Azul had a long string of beads not unlike a rosary depending from her wide belt. At the end of it there was an oval object which she raised, extending it toward San Germanno, exclaiming dramatically. She indicated her dress and spoke to Oaxetli.

"She says that the Dona Azul taught them to weave this cloth as part of her mystery. Only women weave, and only Dona Azul can have the knowledge of patterned cloth. And you have patterned clothes of patterned cloth." Oaxetli would have said more, but she was abruptly shoved aside as Dona Azul thrust the object in her hand near San Germanno's face.

Too late, San Germanno realized that the oval object was an obsidian mirror, and that he cast no reflection in it. He swung around to ask Oaxetli, "What is she saying?" as well as to escape the black obsidian surface.

"She says that the Dark Mirror cannot contain you, and that your clothes are of figured cloth, that your name is Francisco," Oaxetli answered, puzzled by the words. "She says that is because you are from the sky-god. San Germanno, what does she mean?"

"I wish I knew," San Germanno replied with genuine feeling, even as he began to fear that he had put all three of them in mortal danger.

Text of a letter from Jaime Ramos of Durango, Audiencia de Nueva Galicia, Viceroyalty of Nueva España to Dom Enrique Vilhao at Guatemala, Audiencia de Guatemala, Viceroyalty of Nueva España.

To the Portuguese hidalgo Dom Enrique Vilhao, the most sincere greetings of Jaime Ramos, formerly of the garrison of Saltillo, Nueva Gali-

cia, now engaged in enterprise of a different nature in which Dom Enrique may be interested.

It has come to my attention from mutual acquaintances that you may be in the position to acquire certain rarities of this and other regions that are not as easily come by as one might wish. During my time with the garrison, I had occasion to explore many places in the northern part of Nueva Galicia, and struck bargains with various authorities in the Audiencia from which all of us have benefitted in the past, and hope to continue so in the future. In that regard, let me assure you that I am capable of procuring many things that you might otherwise despair of obtaining.

My participation in such arrangements would be a percentage of what you are paid for the material I supply. It is not unreasonable to ask for forty percent of the price you eventually realize. You may at first believe that this figure is unreasonable, but I assure you it is not unjustifiable. Consider all I have done to gain access to these items, and the costs of what I do. Rather than charge you a price that might put you at a disadvantage, I think it is more to our shared desires to work on a percentage basis. Upon reflection, I am confident you will agree with me and will avail yourself of my help. Otherwise you will have to travel to these remote regions yourself and do your best to bargain with those willing to speak with you, which will not be easily accomplished. The people of this region are not often willing to enter into contracts with foreigners, and, I fear, with good reason.

You will find that there are many advantages in dealing with me, and in dealing with me first. I will not pass off shoddy goods that have little value as being worth more than they are. I will not promise what I cannot deliver. I will not hold up delivery for any reason than failure on your part to pay me the percentage you owe me. I am willing to extend you all the time you require to collect payment for any items you have sold, but once the funds are in your hands, my share must be dispatched to me immediately, with a bona fides record of the amounts in question. If at any time I discover you have withheld monies due me, I will at once cease all transactions with you and I will report you to the Presidencia at Zacatecas.

Let me know what you decide to do with all dispatch. I will be in Durango through February, but then I will be gone until August. If you wish me to procure items for you during my travels, your answer will have to reach me speedily. Direct your answer to the tavern at the head of Calle San Gelasias; it will find me without delay. As soon as I have

*received word from you, I will put myself at your disposal, assuming
the conditions I have outlined are acceptable to you. There is much to
be accomplished, and between us, we should both have reason to be
pleased with our partnership within a year. To that end, I give you my
word that I will do nothing to endanger our partnership, either by word
or deed.*

*In this season of holy joy, may your fortunes flourish and God show
you favor in all things.*

*Jaime Ramos
By my own hand, the 21st day of December, 1647*

6

"I am so scared," Oaxetli whispered as she sat beside San Germanno
in the open courtyard in front of the two small houses Dona Azul had
assigned to them three days ago. It was early evening and the air was
redolent with odors from many cooking fires which lent the air a false
warmth that would fade with the embers. "I'm afraid of what these people intend to do."

"We do not know what that is, yet," San Germanno told her gently,
wanting to ease her fretfulness. His ropilla was open and his camisa,
white silk edged with lace, was startlingly bright in the fading day. His
black boots were scuffed, but he had brushed most of the dust from
them an hour ago, giving some of the leather a trace of shine.

"That is what frightens me the most, not knowing," Oaxetli admitted, taking his hand and hanging onto it with the determination of a
lost child. "Aren't you afraid, Conde?"

"Not precisely," San Germanno said. "But I am not entirely . . . com-
placent, either."

From his place at their cooking fire, Rogerio said, "It is troubling that
they are keeping us so isolated." He inspected the half of a fowl he
was roasting on a spit for Oaxetli; he had already eaten the other half
raw before he had returned to the village to light the kindling in the
pit. He had rubbed the bird with sage and wild onion and the savor
of it made the fire smell sweet.

"They said there was a reason for it," Oaxetli reminded them, her brow drawn down.

"But not what the reason is," San Germanno appended, and felt her fingers tighten on his. "I believe it is that which is so troublesome." He did his best to make light of their situation, but he was unable to conceal his apprehension completely.

"It worries you," said Oaxetli with a degree of satisfaction, as if his concerns made her fears more acceptable. "Why should they want to keep us here if they have no desire to speak with us?"

"That is part of the reason for my misgivings," San Germanno said, gazing off toward the rest of the houses, a hundred paces from their allotted place. What he saw ought to have quieted his foreboding— women cooked over the fire-pits, men, returning from the fields and hills, busied themselves with evening chores while the children interspersed their assigned tasks with playing, romping, and battles—but instead made him more alarmed than outright hostility would have done, for he perceived in these ordinary things an acceptance of what was to come. "Man is never so ferocious than when he is certain it is in the cause of good," he said aloud, and was startled to hear himself speak.

Oaxetli turned toward his voice. "Why do you say that?"

San Germanno realized she was upset by his inadvertent observation. "My darkest assumptions, Oaxetli. Nothing of substance." He looked toward the village. "You went to bathe with the women today. Did you learn anything?"

"Their bathhouses are very hot," said Oaxetli. "They use rough cloth sheets to cleanse the skin, at least they say that's what it does. Dona Azul, the first one, used to rub her skin with rough cloth to rid herself of sin." She smiled slightly. "The cloth is not unpleasant used lightly."

"And is it like their other cloth?" San Germanno asked; he was still intrigued by the unfamiliar textiles of these people.

"They say all cloth starts rough, which is the virtue of it. Dona Azul taught them how to weave certain fibers, and then to pound the rough cloth until it is smooth." She knew he was pleased with her answer. "I said I had never touched anything like it, and because I am blind, they told me how it was done."

"I'd like to see the rough cloth," San Germanno said.

"I will try to get a piece for you, but it may not be possible. Only women use it, to purify themselves. The cloths remain in the bathhouse.

It is wrong for men to see them." She shrugged. "The men bathe in the river, and may not have bath sheets as the women do."

"That's strange," San Germanno said as much to himself as to Oaxetli. "In most places it is the men who have bathhouses, isn't it?"

Oaxetli shrugged. "So it has seemed to me. I am to bathe after my blood comes. All the women do." She paused, her head cocked. "I do not know what is expected of men, but—"

"Your supper is almost ready," Rogerio announced to Oaxetli as he took a rag to protect his hand as he reached for the spit. "It will be hot."

"Thank you," she said, still frowning in San Germanno's direction, not yet satisfied with his explanation. "I am feeling cold." As she rose she released San Germanno's hand. "Where is the plate?"

Rogerio put her half of the roasted bird on a plate for her and held it out, placing it in her hands. "And here is a knife."

She took the plate and the knife, then went to sit down opposite where San Germanno remained. Expertly she cut off a section of meat and speared it with the knife. As she ate, her expression grew thoughtful, and when she had almost finished her meal, she said, "How is it you do not eat when I do?"

The question was addressed to San Germanno, but it was Rogerio who answered. "It would not be fitting for a servant to eat with his master." While there was a degree of truth in this, particularly among Spaniards, he did not add that he consumed his food raw, a habit that most found upsetting if they learned of it.

Oaxetli would not be put off. "Conde? Why is it?"

San Germanno was prepared to answer; he explained in his most matter-of-fact tone, "Among those of my blood, taking nourishment is a very private matter."

"Do you never eat with others?" she pursued, her face intent.

It was difficult to answer her; his words came out clumsily. "Under certain rare circumstances: for specific reasons." It was painful to remember his few nights with Acanna Tupac, and to feel his need for the intimacy beyond dreams rekindle as he stared at Oaxetli.

From the look of her, she had more questions, but she nodded and held her peace as she finished her supper. "This is very good. Rogerio, you cook well. Do you never cook for San Germanno?" Her face was turned toward the Conde, an expression of doubt mixed with curiosity clearly evident; she set her plate and knife aside, she asked, "Will you read to me this evening?"

The two previous evenings Oaxetli had retired to the house she had chosen to occupy and spent the hours before sleep in thought, so this request startled San Germanno. "If you wish it."

"Oh, yes, please," she said, animation returning to her demeanor. "That one you started last week."

"La Duquesa de Amalfi?" he asked; he had enjoyed turning John Webster's thundering English into elegant Spanish, but the murky story would do little to dispel the malaise that had taken hold of them. "If that is what you want."

"I want to know if those brothers of hers are punished for their crimes," said Oaxetli; she lowered her voice and went on. "They are an evil pair, Ferdinand and the Cardinal."

"That they are," San Germanno agreed, glad to have this to discuss instead of any continued mulling about their current circumstances. "Do you like the play?"

"It answers many questions," she said without elaborating on what those questions might be. "I will fetch the book if you like. I know its size."

"I'll get it," San Germanno told her, and rose. In the two-room house he shared with Rogerio he found his books arranged on a rough plank. There were sixteen of them, and at the moment the number seemed pitifully small. He took the Webster play, made certain the page they had reached was marked with a silken ribbon, then returned to the fire-pit.

Rogerio was standing by the fire; he was very still, his eyes turned toward the wide path that led to the rest of the village. Oaxetli had not moved, but her head was cocked as she listened. Beyond the area between the two houses a group of men in blue headdresses had gathered, each holding a spear. Their demeanor was respectful and their stance was full of intent.

San Germanno took all this in at the flicker of his eye. He approached the nearest of the men, saying to him, "Finally we have a chance to welcome you to our fire: a most courteous gesture."

Oaxetli knew that something had happened; she brought her head up sharply at the unfamiliar voice, and regained her composure rapidly. She translated his words at once as if she had expected to do this all day.

"It is our fire, stranger, and we will tell you when you may welcome us," said the man leading the group.

"Not very cordial, after all," San Germanno remarked when Oaxetli had repeated the words in Spanish. "Tell them that I would like to know what they want." He waited while Oaxetli spoke for him.

"They have been told to watch you eat," she answered, visibly flustered by the answer.

San Germanno concealed the shock that went through him. "I regret that is not possible," he said politely, determined to keep these men from imposing upon him. He listened to them as they spoke once more, no longer emphatic; they were all but pleading with him.

"They say the Dona Azul demands it," Oaxetli informed him, growing more distressed. "It was wrong of me to speak of it, Conde. I should have said nothing about your eating. It was a very great mistake. I apologize for my error. I have caused this to happen."

"No, Oaxetli. It has nothing to do with you or your question; these men have reasons of their own to want to know the thing they ask," San Germanno said, wanting to keep her from becoming upset. "Ask these men what the Dona Azul wants to know about my eating, and why."

It was an effort for Oaxetli to relay San Germanno's request, and when she did, she added to him, "I will say nothing, Conde, nothing. They cannot make me speak. I will not tell them anything that—"

"Oaxetli, *querida*, let them answer. We will decide later what we will tell them." His voice was gentle but stern. "I need you to listen closely to everything they say."

She nodded, stunned at the endearment he had used, and strove to concentrate on what the men were saying, all the while hearing *querida* ring in her mind. It was an effort of will not to ask him what he had meant by saying it. When the men were done speaking, she was pale. "It is not just the eating, or what you eat. There are other signs Dona Azul wishes to know of. They have been told to discover how many of the signs you possess."

"What signs?" San Germanno asked, none of his increasing dismay coloring his words. With the sun gone, the valley was chilly, and the wind, mild in the afternoon, was getting sharper and colder.

The question was relayed to the men, and brought a long recitation in answer to it, the men standing proudly but uncomfortably as they did their best to fulfill their mission.

"They say there are signs that will make it clear you are the one promised to the Dona Azul, the bringer-of-the-sky-god. She will know them, for all the Donas Azules have had this secret since the first one came to these chosen people." She was more frightened, but the fear had caused her to take more control of herself. "I will tell them that you eat alone."

"Thank you," San Germanno said, hoping this would end the matter and equally certain that it would not. He listened courteously as Oaxetli spoke to the men and had them answer her.

"They will have to tell Dona Azul something. If they do not, they will be punished for displeasing the sky-god." She folded her arms so she would not tremble.

He gave a short, hard sigh. "Then tell them that I suffer from a . . . a malady, one that brings limitation of diet with it which makes it necessary that I eat . . . privately."

"Is that true?" she asked him, her question sharp.

"Near enough," he replied, unwilling to say anything more. "Ask Rogerio if you doubt me." He made a show of opening the book he held as if the page were more interesting than the men.

"I? No, Conde," she hastened to tell him.

"Then translate what he says for the men." He bowed slightly in their direction. "I have no wish to cause them disappointment."

She did as he said, doing her best not to be nervous. "Yes; I think they want to hear what Rogerio has to say."

"Ask him, by all means," San Germanno said, aware that under other, less hazardous circumstances he would find this exchange boring.

Oaxetli turned to Rogerio. "Will you tell them that San Germanno does not eat with others?" she asked, her voice strained.

Rogerio looked directly at the men as he answered them. "I have served my master many, many years, and I have not known him to . . . dine with company, not as you mean it. There have been certain times of . . . celebration when he will dine with one other person, never more than one."

As she translated this, Oaxetli scowled, and while she listened to the men, she turned the ambiguity of Rogerio's remark over in her mind, worrying it like a bone. Finally she said to San Germanno and Rogerio, "They will tell this to Dona Azul. There will be other questions tomorrow."

"How fortunate," said San Germanno sardonically as he turned the page. "No doubt there is a ritual to this, if only we knew what it was."

The men said a few words in unison, held up their hands, palms outward, then turned and went away, trooping back toward the main part of the village in double file.

"They hold you in reverence, they say, because of the sky-god." She listened closely to anything he might offer by way of response.

"The sky-god," San Germanno repeated, thinking how ironic it was that he, of all men, should be seen as a messenger of the sky when he was so much a creature of the earth. "I would like to know more about this sky-god."

"And of the Dona Azul? Would you like to know more of her?" asked Oaxetli sharply, not knowing until she heard her own voice that she was jealous.

San Germanno recognized the emotion. "Yes: in order to deal with her. I do not want to increase our danger here through my own ignorance." He went to her side and laid one small hand on her arm. "She does not interest me in any other way." There had been other women, he remembered—Pentacoste, Djahliele, Estasia—who had sought things from him it was not in him, or anyone, to provide; Dona Azul was of the same nature. He had sensed it from the first sight of her, and he had no reason to think he had assessed her inaccurately.

"She wants you; she wants to possess you," said Oaxetli softly. "I can feel it in the air. It is like a smell coming from her house, like hot iron."

Although he had some of the same perception himself, San Germanno said, "It is her obsession with the name Francisco. She wants the name, not me. She has no idea of who or what I am beyond that name." It would not be pleasant if Dona Azul discovered he was more of a stranger than she assumed. His situation was already precarious; he wished he knew more of the legends of the Francisco who had become a hero in this place. He gave Oaxetli a little time to reflect on what he had told her, and himself a chance to regain his composure, then said, "I have the play, if you still want to hear more of it?"

She did not answer at once. "I want to go inside," she declared. "If you will come with me and read to me?"

"If that is what you want," he said, and glanced at Rogerio. "Call me if you have need of me."

"That I will, my master—be certain of it," Rogerio said, setting more wood on the fire to keep it from going out.

The house Oaxetli had been allocated was the mirror image of the one San Germanno and Rogerio occupied: a workroom and a bedroom. The workroom was empty, with not so much as a stool to sit upon. The bedroom had a low frame with a rough mattress on top of netted ropes, and it was here Oaxetli went, moving with care. She sat down on the bed and turned her face in San Germanno's direction. "It is strange to have you here," she said as she fussed with her skirt, pleating the fabric with her fingers; she shook her head as if to deny his presence.

"If you would rather I left . . . " he offered, seeing ambivalence in every line of her body.

"I . . . no. I . . . I want to hear this tale you are reading me. It is very . . . informative." She folded her hands in her lap and composed herself. "La Duquesa and Antonio have declared they are married, and they have had a child." Her mouth felt suddenly very dry. "Her brothers do not know that, only that she has a lover."

"Yes," San Germanno said as he opened the book and looked down at the page. In the dim light he had to concentrate to read, although it was not an impossible task for him as it would have been for most others. "We are at Act Two, scene five." He began to translate, only to have Oaxetli stop him.

"Let me hear it as it was written," she said, the eagerness she expressed tempered by an urge to secrecy, as if, with the Duchess, she had to conceal her interest.

"But it is in English," he reminded her.

"I do not understand the language," she agreed, "but I would like to know how it sounds. I will learn much from that. You may translate it for me later, when it is appropriate." As she said this, she held out her hand to him, waiting for him to take it. "You hear the tongues I translate for you, and from what you hear, I can tell you garner much."

"True enough." He took her hand, holding it lightly in his own, his small fingers curled over hers. "I will do as you wish."

She pulled on his hand. "Then sit beside me." Her words were rapid and a little breathless; having him so near to her would be as disquieting as it was reassuring. "You will not have to speak so loudly if you do. And I will be less alone."

He complied, keeping more than a handsbreadth's distance between them. "Are you comfortable?"

"Certainly," she said mendaciously. "I am just tired. That makes me nervous." She coughed once, experimentally, and gave him her attention. "I am ready."

San Germanno began with Ferdinand's impassioned denunciation of his sister, letting the drama shape his reading, his mellifluous voice giving color and presence to the speeches, and when he had finished the whole of the scene, he went back to the beginning of it and translated it into Spanish, remarking as he did that there were a few constructions in English that did not readily adapt to Spanish forms. "I am sorry I cannot give you the whole of it at its full meaning."

"Every language has such problems. I have it often enough, changing the words of these people, and others we have met, to Spanish for you. It is always the same. We have a word for the moving of lava down a mountain. Spanish does not, so I must describe it, not translate it, since the word does not exist in Spanish." She seemed slightly more relaxed now; her head was held at a less rigid angle and her eyes did not move restlessly as if movement would provide sight.

"It is ever thus," San Germanno said, trying to remember the first time he had heard such sentiments expressed. Finally he decided it must have been in Nineveh, when he was still considered a demon; then the phrase had justified confining him in constant darkness. He resumed his reading, speech by speech, first in English, then in Spanish.

Some time later, Oaxetli moved closer to him, her head resting on his shoulder. She had been silent through his reading of the whole of Act Three and into the second scene of Act Four, and the strangling of the Duchess. Then she said, "Do Europeans truly commit such acts as these? Or is this only a tale?"

"Yes, sometimes they do," San Germanno answered dryly. "And most of them not half so eloquently."

"Is it necessary for them to do this? Is it a tribute to their leaders? Do their gods require it?" The apprehension was back in her voice, and she grasped at his shoulder with one hand while trying to close his book with the other.

"Many of those who commit such acts claim it is for their King, or their God," he answered.

"It is a dreadful thing." She was almost inaudible. "To kill that way."

"Would you rather not hear any more, Oaxetli?" he asked softly as he prepared to set the book aside.

She nodded abruptly. "The story is . . . difficult."

"That it is," San Germanno agreed, making no move either toward her or away from her as she clung to him.

"It is so sad, what they do to her. And to her Antonio." She put her other hand on his shoulder, joining them behind his neck.

"Yes," San Germanno said, aware that she was vulnerable to him now as she had never been before, and wary about pressing his advantage with her, for he did not want her to seek him out of fear. He could not persuade himself to leave her, though he knew it was the prudent thing to do; he told himself she would be vexed if she were left alone with their situation as uncertain as it was. At the same time he chided himself inwardly for sophistry.

"San Germanno, I am frightened," she confessed hurriedly, doing her best to get closer to him. "These people and their Dona Azul frighten me."

San Germanno put his arm around her; he felt her longing for comfort as intensely as he felt her pulse. "They are frightening people," he said quietly, knowing it was useless and demeaning to make light of her fears, or to pretend they were groundless. "If you were not afraid, I would be more troubled than I am."

"They do not intend to let us leave," she whispered, her hold on him tightening. "They have some purpose for us."

"That much is obvious," he agreed, keeping his need at bay as he strove to give her the solace she sought. "You are wise to be troubled, Oaxetli. We are in danger, and it is greater because we do not know what the danger is, or why we have been put in it. But I give you my Word that I will do all that I can to protect you, if you require it. I hope it will not come to that."

She was shaking now, determined not to weep. "This is a bad place." She pushed her forehead against his shoulder. "This is like the old ways, when the blood flowed to please the gods."

He stroked her hair as he wrapped her in both arms. "Oaxetli," he whispered, "I apologize for bringing you into danger. If I had thought we might encounter such trouble as we have in this place, I would not have come here."

Her trembling became silent sobs; she tried to pull away from him to hide her shame. "It is my fault. I should have known. I heard the stories before we reached this place. You did not know them, but I did."

"And you were curious," San Germanno said, unwilling to release her to her misery. "So was I. If there is a fault, we share it. A place like this one, hidden from the world, is more often than not a legend, an imperfect memory from the past, or a tale to amuse travelers. To discover people who have been forgotten is . . . rewarding. You did not think that this place was real. Had I been in your place, I would have made the same assumptions."

She refused to accept his exoneration. "I was foolish. I never thought it would not be safe. You would have known the dangers here, if you knew the story. You . . . you understand many things I have never encountered."

He had nothing to say to that. He held her more securely, rocking her gently to provide consolation as well as his nearness.

With a swift twist she broke free of him, but only to reach for one of his hands. "You want to touch me, don't you?"

The question startled him, but he answered candidly, knowing any other response would alienate her. "I would like to, if you want me to," he replied carefully, her sudden change perplexing him even as his esurience flared.

Her laughter was short-lived and reckless. "I have never been touched that way by any man, not in the ways I have heard of in tales and songs. Until I met you, I thought such meetings were as much tales as the adventures recalled of the old gods. If I am going to die here, I would like to have you touch me, and more than touch me, before that happens." She pressed his hand against her abdomen.

"Why do you think you may die here?" San Germanno asked her, troubled by what she had told him; the rough cotton of her skirt was bunched beneath his fingers. "Have you heard something?"

"It gathers," she answered obliquely, and reached out to him.

It was a turbulent kiss, prolonged and searching, her mouth softening and opening to his only after she had tugged his ropilla fully open, and, when that was done, his camisa, and slid her hand over the flesh beneath, as if finding certainty in her fingers she could not achieve any other way. She sighed as she pushed back from him, a look of resignation about her. "My mother told me that men are ready quickly. If you are ready, I will lie down. You will do as you must."

San Germanno put his finger to her lips to keep her from speaking. "It may be true of many men: it is not true of me." He waited a moment, gaining understanding of her. "My readiness comes from yours." He saw she was puzzled, and he tried to explain. "You have not been roused, have you, Oaxetli? You do not know what I am talking about, and so you doubt it is possible, just as you doubt what the songs promised. You have not found your gratification."

She squared her shoulders. "I am not a virgin."

As he gathered her into his arms again, he could not help but wonder how that had come about. Perhaps, he thought, in time she would tell him. "What is between us has nothing to do with your virginity, or lack of it; virginity is nothing to one of my nature," he told her in a deep, musical undervoice.

"It is worse than that: I am not chaste," she said, in self-condemnation, her hands fixed on his shoulders tenaciously as claws. "I have not confessed the whole of my sins. The nuns have told me that I have no chance for Paradise unless I repent and name the man who took me. They used to ask me every time I went to Mass. Last year they finally stopped insisting; now they only pray I will tell them." She turned away from San Germanno. "They do not believe I do not know who it was."

San Germanno enfolded her more closely, her confusion and hurt causing him an inward pang. "Chastity is in the mind, not the body," he said softly. "You have nothing to repent." He kissed her brow. "No one can think you have erred."

"The nuns do," she countered sharply. "They have said that once a woman is no longer virgin, she is lost forever if she will not name her lover."

"And was he a lover?" San Germanno asked, mildly surprised. "I would have thought you would have known him, if he were your lover, even if you wanted to protect him." He held her close, one hand on her hair, the other across her back. "If he seduced you, you would be able to identify him. So I must suppose he attacked you, taking advantage of your blindness." It was impossible to conceal his detestation of whomever her attacker had been.

Oaxetli heard him out in growing dismay. "He would not have come had I not lured him." She had courage enough to sound angry.

"Is that what the nuns told you?" San Germanno looked down into her face. "They lied."

She was rigid with shock. "How can you say that? They are promised to God, and keep their purity. How can such women lie?" she demanded, her whole body stiffening in his embrace.

He was not discomfited by her outburst. "I can say it because it is true," he told her kindly. "You tell me you do not know who took your virginity, and that you were not roused by what he did. I must suppose that you were set upon, and if you were, the nuns had no right to blame you for what was done to you, whatever that was." He strove to contain his indignation, for his anger was long-standing and without any purpose but to remind him that he and religion disagreed on more than matters of blood.

She swung back toward him, her hands again seeking the affirmation of his skin under her fingers. "You want to take pleasure of me."

His single chuckle was deep and quiet. "No; not as you imply. For those of my blood, that isn't possible." He stroked her hair. "What I would like is to give you pleasure, and find my own through yours."

"In your sons?" she asked, more perplexed than ever.

He dismissed the notion with a shake of his head. "What I seek of you has nothing to do with offspring, Oaxetli. Those of my blood increase in other ways. If you are willing to have me, I would be honored to—"

"I did not quicken," she said hurriedly, as if admitting a wrong.

His response was soothing, his voice low. "Nor will you from me. If you want me to . . . to love you." The enormity of his offer filled the air between them.

This time her shivering came from a different sort of fear. She sat very still. "How can you?"

"Love you?" he asked gently. "I can love you because you are Oaxetli, and because it is what you want of me."

She put her hand on his chest again as if to convince herself he was actually with her. "If I tell you not to, will you go?"

He could not keep the regret from his voice, or a trace of exasperation from his manner. "Of course. It would benefit neither of us to force you to accommodate me. I do not want to bring you anything but pleasure."

"But you could, if you decided to. You could force me. You are a powerful man," she said with growing apprehension. "You are not tall, but I have never encountered anyone stronger."

He was still for a moment, wondering what he had done that had alerted her to his strength. "You have no reason to be afraid of me," he said kindly, knowing she was not convinced. He wished he could find the phrases to reassure her. "I would never do you harm, Oaxetli."

She laughed once. "Do you think so?"

"I know it would never be my purpose." He wanted to promise her that she would never suffer because of him, but realized that already such an assertion was false. He felt a great despair come over him, and he almost released her. "At least I will not compromise you, Oaxetli." It was hard to leave her, he thought, now that his need was so keenly awakened.

"To hear what the nuns say, I was compromised long ago. My own people did not think I was fit to live." Abruptly she began to weep, and as quickly made herself stop, shame making her push back from him. "I did not mean to do that."

"Who would blame you?" San Germanno asked with great sincerity. He had lost his tears with his life; since then he had come to envy those who were capable of crying. As he drew her back toward him, he said to her, "Let me give you what comfort I can, Oaxetli. For my own sake as well as yours."

She turned toward his voice. "I wish I could see you."

"You may touch my face, if you wish," he offered in compensation. "I would be glad of your touch."

Her hands were light as the wings of butterflies as she explored his features, her concentration intense as she continued her investigation of his hair, his neck, then down onto his shoulders, struggling with the restrictions of his ropilla and camisa, for though she had opened them a little, it was not sufficient to permit her the explorations she sought. "Let me touch your skin, San Germanno. I want to know your skin." Her words were hushed and urgent, as if she had suddenly reached a decision and wanted to act upon it before she changed her mind again.

"Will you let me touch yours?" he asked; he began to remove his clothes, tossing his ropilla aside as he pulled his camisa out of his belt.

Her hands continued their investigation, faltering only when she reached the base of his ribs. "What—?"

"Scars," he said in an undervoice. "Those are scars, Oaxetli."

"But . . . so much." Her astonishment was conveyed through her hands. "The wound must have been very bad."

"Yes." He had died of it, three thousand six hundred years earlier.

"But you did not die," she marveled.

"Apparently not," he said quietly, and caught her hands in his. "They need not trouble you; it happened long ago."

"And if you had died, I would not have met you." This overwhelmed her and she wrapped both her arms around him, holding on tightly, her head pressed against his chest. Although she trembled, she did not cry.

Very slowly he embraced her, saying, "And I would not have met you." His small hands stroked her back and her shoulders. Nothing was hurried, nothing was rushed, but there was a sense of sparks where they touched. Finally, when she had been soothed out of her distress, he said, his voice very low, "You have taken off half my clothes."

"Yes." She tensed again, but for a different reason. "Shall I take off mine?"

"If you want to take them off, then do. But I would enjoy doing it, as well." He was taking a great chance to admit so much. He waited for her answer with more doubts than he dared express.

She found his hands and guided them to the base of her neck. "I did it for you; you may do it for me."

Until she gave him her permission, he had not realized how much he had dreaded her refusal. With a humbled nod, he removed the long, tunic-like woven chepa she wore; her flesh beneath was flawless and warm. As he put the chepa aside he said, "You are a very lovely woman, Oaxetli."

Her scoff failed as her breath caught in her throat. She tried to look indifferent to this compliment but did not succeed. "I want to believe you," she told him.

"I will show you." His hands were as reverent as they were expert in seeking out the ways to gratify her. Although his movements were never hurried, they were more passionate for lack of haste. From the moment he laid his hand on her shoulders, to the time he took caressing her breasts, to the slow removal of her skirt, to the interminable seconds he sought the hidden treasure between her thighs, he drew her toward a fulfillment she had thought could only be found in devotion to God. Where his hands began, his lips went with kisses more evocative and varied than any song had promised. Oaxetli clung to him, as if without him she would fall into some great chasm. As San Germanno's kisses deepened, she at last let herself release her dreams for the far better reality he offered. Her body shook as if the ground were quaking, and the spasms that came with her fulfillment dizzied him as his lips opened to her and to an intimacy so comprehensive that the secrets between them were banished.

She lay beside him silently for some time afterward, content to be cradled in his arms as she tried to recall all the wonderful things that had just happened to her; he had been right: nothing that she had known before had prepared her for all she had experienced with him, or for the turmoil he had given her with her joyous gratification. Most of that was welcome, but she was increasingly aware of what she had encountered in him, and gradually the realization lessened her euphoria.

"What?" he murmured to her hair, though he was more cognizant of what was happening to her than she was.

She had not been aware she had spoken. "I . . . " The words eluded her. "It is very wonderful, what you do."

"It is what *you* do, not I," he whispered, the first chill of despair beginning to move over him. "I can do nothing you have not in you."

She sighed. "But it is all you do, isn't it?"

"For me and those like me, it is all we have: the quality of the passion we can impart to others is what sustains us," he said sadly, for he knew these questions of old, and what they led to.

"It is the blood, isn't it?" she said, moving an infinitesimal distance from him that might as well have been leagues. "It is what you seek."

"I seek you," he said, aware of nightbirds calling. "The blood is the very core of you. Without you, and all you are, the blood is nothing more than chaff. If blood was all I needed, I might live as well on goats, and at less risk." There had been times he had been forced to do just that: the memories were not pleasant.

She thought about this while he remained silent. "You died when you got those scars, didn't you?"

"For a short time," he confessed.

"And now?" It was more of a challenge than she had intended.

"Now I am . . . what I am." Why was it so difficult to speak of this with her, especially now? How was it that her distress caused him such anguish? What made him ache with every syllable?

She crossed herself furtively, averting her face as if he could not then see her do it. "It is . . . I do not mean . . . to cause you . . . I do not want to repay such kindness . . . but I must . . . I cannot . . . " She made herself speak more clearly. "You took my blood; you did not take . . . my body. I thank you for that—"

"There is no need to thank me for my nature. I could not use you as living men do: I thought you understood." He had long since accustomed himself to explaining his impotence, but Oaxetli's confusion troubled him.

"Yes, but I did not know you could . . . there were such ways as . . . your pleasures." She took a long breath, doing her best to keep from trembling. "What you are is . . . " She laid her hand on his arm. "I am truly more grateful than I have words to tell you, and that will never change. But—"

"But?" he prompted when she did not go on; he knew what she was trying to say.

At last she steeled herself. "I love what you have let me feel, San Germanno, I respect you, and I appreciate all you have done for me; I admire your learning: but I abhor what you are."

"I know," he said tenderly, regretfully, moving off her bed. "It is in your blood."

Text of a letter from Eduardo Medallo in Santa Marta, Audiencia de Panamá, Viceroyalty of Peru, to Atta Olivia Clemens at the embassy of Jules, Cardinal Mazarin, First Minister of France, in Paris.

To the most excellent Bondama Clemens, through the good offices of the First Minister of France, Jules, Cardinal Mazarin, the greetings of Eduardo Medallo of Santa Marta. May God show you His favor in all things, and bring you to bliss, and may your sins be taken away through Grace and Salvation.

It will please you to know that the nine trunks of earth you have sent me for the use of the Conde de San Germanno have arrived in excellent condition. Two have already been sent on to Acapulco, as you instructed. Another two will be shipped in a week's time to Panamá, and Nombre de Dios. I will be sure they are delivered to the addresses specified, and will hire agents, as you have instructed, to guard the shipment until el Conde de San Germanno is able to come and claim them for himself.

As to the other requests, I regret to tell you that I have had no direct contact with el Conde for some months. He sent word to me that he was bound to the north of Acapulco, and since his departure I have heard nothing from him or of him. I have been told by the officers of the Presidencia of Nueva Galicia that there is no report of his death—they do not yet consider him missing. The last account of him came from a small village two days' ride from Durango. At that time he said he was bound to the northwest with his manservant and blind Indian woman said to be an excellent translator. Nothing more has been heard of him since.

Be of good cheer, Bondama Clemens, for I have been informed that a party of Passionists are set to go in that direction before Lent and are expected to cross the territory San Germanno has been exploring, which until now has been unknown land. The Passionists will seek him out if he has not presented himself to one of the garrisons before the monks find him. The Indians of the region, I am told, are respectful of foreigners and are not likely to do him any harm. There is no reason to fear for his safety, or for his soul: I am informed that many of the Indians have become Christians in the last two decades, preferring the Glory of God and the Salvation of Our Lord to the bloody rites of their old gods, who demanded the sacrifice of many lives in order to sate their hungers.

As soon as I have any word, I will have a letter to you on the next ship leaving Santa Marta. If the pernicious pirates do not seize the ship carrying it, or this, you will have news within five weeks of when I receive it. Godspeed the messengers between el Conde, me, and you.

With my thanks for the opportunity to be of service to you and San

Germanno, I pray God will bless you in all things, and bring all our ships to safe harbor,

Eduardo Medallo
By my own hand in Santa Marta, Audiencia de Panamá, Viceroyalty of Peru, on the 16th day of January, 1648

7

"It is the most sacred time of the year," Dona Azul announced to the villagers assembled around the platform carved out of the side of the hill. The wind cutting through the valley was cold enough to make most of her flock uncomfortable, but none of them complained as the traditional recounting went on. Dona Azul addressed San Germanno, Rogerio, and Oaxetli where they stood at the rear of the platform. "From now until the days and nights are the same length, we must devote ourselves to the glorification of the sky-god, so that our summer will be fruitful and our people will know the favor of the sacrifice given to him in exchange for his son. Our people are most fortunate. We were chosen to have the greatest gift of all the people of this world by Dona Azul, when she was left to minister to us. When the first Dona Azul came here with Francisco and his men, she remained with us to tell us of the sky-god who sent his celestial son to bring salvation to us, and to end our errors in sacrifice and redemption. He came at the dark of the year, which has just passed and was honored by great chiefs who came to do him reverence. He was an infant, and he was known as the son of the sky-god whose mother knew no semen to make the child." She took a stance and launched into what was obviously a ritual recounting of the coming of the Dona Azul. "Before Dona Azul came, we were steeped in blood. Death was all around us. Death was the greatest force in the whole of the world, mightier than anything else. In those days, we were like all the others, benighted and in the thrall of earth, following the ways of the Black Mirror, the god in the glass of volcanos, and like all the others, we made offering to him, taking the hearts from living men as the Black Mirror took the heart from the earth in lava. Countless hearts were given, still beating, in honor of the Black Mirror who came from the heart of the earth, opening the breast of the earth with great explosions and vast rivers of lava, the blood of the earth which we revered with the blood of men. We thought that in emulation of the Black Mirror we would enrich the earth and our souls, as the lava enriches the earth with the blood of the earth."

"It is a true thing," the people of the village responded in unison, clanging bells accompanying their words.

Oaxetli struggled to keep up with the recitation, her voice low and hurried. Once in a while she faltered, trying to translate the phrases as accurately as possible.

"Then the first Dona Azul arrived, and taught us many things. We have learned from her and we venerate her words." Again she changed her stance, lifting up her hands to heaven as if she held something precious in them. "She taught us that all people are created in error to bring glory to the sky-god through their redemption. She taught us that we, those of us in this valley, were the children not of the earth but of the sky-god, whose realm is the sky and the sun. She explained that the sky-god accepted sacrifice for his glory on behalf of his son. She showed us that we had been wrong to worship the Black Mirror and the blood of earth, for that brought us nothing but death. We were told to stop revering death, for that brought more sin. To be rid of her sins, she brought her salvation to all of us, that we might achieve it with her. She taught us that we were favored by the sky-god for our sins were great, and the greater our sins, the greater our redemption. We heard her and we opened our hearts to the ways of the sky-god and his son. We gave up the Black Mirror and the offering of hearts to him in favor of the sky-god, and his promise of salvation."

"It is a true thing," said the people again, with a greater clamor of bells.

San Germanno had heard of the Black Mirror god, who was sometimes called the Smoke Mirror, and he recalled the polished stone Dona Azul had attempted to use to find his reflection, without success. He gave her recitation and Oaxetli's translation his full concentration, certain that the answer to their predicament lay in the tale Dona Azul was recounting. He dared not speak to his two companions, or do much to bring them notice for fear that any disruption of this ceremony might have immediate and unwelcome consequences, but he made an encouraging gesture to Rogerio and briefly put his hand on Oaxetli's arm.

"How is it that we were chosen above all others?" Dona Azul demanded of her people.

"The sky-god sought us out through the Dona Azul," they answered. "She was the messenger of his mercy. She brought us salvation, for she came to us filled with sin. For that we thank the sky-god."

"It was Francisco who left her here among us. And she brought with her the true god, the one greater than the Black Mirror who came as the bounty of the volcanos when the hot blood of the earth spews out. The giving of hearts to the Black Mirror brought no glory to the Black Mirror or to the sky-god, for the living hearts were not what the sky-god sought. The Dona Azul showed us that the sky-god was more loving, for our errors would bring us to the realms of the sky-god, for our sins were many and the glory of our redemption all the greater. We learned the ways to sacrifice to the sky-god in a manner that would bring us greater favor, by repeating the sacrifice of the son of the sky-god." She began slowly to circle the platform area, her stately dance accompanied by the steady unmoving march of her people's feet. "Behold the sky-god above us, from one edge of the earth to the next. The sky-god is vast, and constant. The veins of the earth are opened rarely, but the sun crosses the sky every day, and the sky-god gives us more than the Black Mirror ever could, from the sun to the winds, to the rain."

"It is a true thing," said the villagers in heavy rhythm.

Oaxetli reached out for San Germanno's hand, wrapping her fingers around his. She strained to listen to everything she heard.

"We who are chosen by the sky-god are chosen because, we, like Dona Azul, are filled with sins, and by our redemption the glory of the sky-god is fulfilled, and the Black Mirror is sent back into the bowels of the earth where he dwells in torment. We have seen the truth of this, and we humble ourselves to the sky-god, who sees all, night and day. Storm clouds cannot prevail against him, and the wind brings his voice to us." She turned slowly, her arms extended more forcefully upward. "To the sky-god we give all our errors and from the sky-god we receive forgiveness, attained through the trading of his son for our errors. The Black Mirror gave us only pain and blood, the sky-god brings us the joy of going into the sky to him when we are dead, to be one with the stars at night." Abruptly she stopped, standing still as if petrified. "The sky-god will take our sins and make us like him, without any fault or flaw."

"This is a true thing," her people declared.

"It is fitting that we should be grateful to the sky-god for sending Dona Azul to bring our salvation, and it is fitting that she sinned greatly, so that Francisco was not willing to have her among his men again. It is fitting that we show our gratitude by doing those things she taught us to honor the power of the sky-god. It is fitting that it has taken more than one Dona Azul to end the sin the first of us carried so that the presence of the promise of the sky-god could not be forgotten by us. She was left here to cleanse herself so that she would be worthy of him when he returned to claim her. We have lived in accordance to what she taught us, always seeking to be worthy of Francisco's return." The ecstatic cry she sent up to the heavens was loud enough to make the horses neigh in alarm. "And he is come! *He is come again!*"

This time her people did not reply in unison and a few of them looked dismayed; this was a departure from their ritual. Oaxetli hesitated as she sensed the disruption of the ceremony.

"In coming again, Francisco has shown that Dona Azul is worthy to accompany him again to the distant lands where the sky-god holds sway. Her sacrifice is sufficient to restore her to Francisco and his great King over the waters, in the lands of the east where the sun rises always." She approached San Germanno and held out her hand to him. "I will serve you as the first Dona Azul served you. I will show you my worth in her name, which is mine as well."

At this, Oaxetli made a cry of protest and crossed herself for protection. Her face was pale and there was a white line around her lips. "San Germanno," she whispered, "this woman will not be persuaded that you are not the man she wants you to be."

He agreed with her, but he said, "She will come to accept it."

"I do not think so," Oaxetli said in a tone of utter despair. "She will punish you if you deny her."

San Germanno could think of nothing to say to assuage her distress. He looked at the people gathered at the foot of the platform and for an instant recalled the faces of good, pious Christians standing around the pyres of heretics, waiting eagerly for the moment when the wood would be set ablaze. These people had the same intensity of devotion about them; it was a frightening realization. He tried to comfort Oaxetli, but his words rang false even to him. "Nothing is going to happen to us, querida."

"We will claim our place with the people of the sky-god and with Francisco in the place where the sun rises," Dona Azul declaimed. "It is our right and our heritage through the sins of Dona Azul which have now been expiated."

At last San Germanno had an idea. He rose, interrupting the woman's chanting, and said, "Dona Azul, we do not wish to profane your ceremonies, or to insult your sky-god in any way. We do not come as emissaries of the sky-god, nor will we return to the lands of the east to where the sky-god rules. If you persist in your assumption, you will offend the sky-god, which may bring his disfavor. It would be a poor repayment for your hospitality and kindness to us." As Oaxetli translated phrase by phrase he saw the ire flare in Dona Azul's eyes.

"You continue to deny what you are. You test our faith with your obstinacy." She stood squarely in front of him. "Well, I will not be put off by your refusal to own your purpose here. Dona Azul said that Francisco would come again for her, and here you are."

"Many men are named Francisco," he pointed out. "Many men from España have it, to honor many saints with the name."

"Dona Azul said that Francisco was a sinner who would bring glory to the sky-god through his redemption. When her child died, she took it as a sign that Francisco was forgiven for leaving her with us, that her child was accepted by the sky-god as the payment of his father's sin." Dona Azul indicated a small cross at the far end of the earthen platform. "The child was buried here, to join the others in sacrifice to the sky-god. The child is buried here as an offering, so that it will not truly die. She said that when Francisco returned, he would be without sin and he would once again give her a child, one that would live."

"Dona Azul, listen to me, and Oaxetli, translate this faithfully: a Spaniard named Francisco came this way a century or so ago; he was exploring in the hope of finding treasure, for they all were doing that. He left a camp-follower in this valley because she was pregnant and could not keep up with him and his company, and told her he would return for her when he came back this way. She was the same religion as the Black Robes who have come to other villages, and she taught you to worship as she did. Your people took her in. Without other teachers to instruct you, you made her teaching your own, and practiced it as you practiced your old faith." He said it bluntly, piecing together what he thought was a reasonably accurate account for the events that had brought this odd version of Christianity—for surely it had begun as the Christianity of the Spaniards—to the people of this valley. "Whoever that Francisco was, he has died long ago, either in the New World or the Old." Privately, San Germanno thought it likely that Francisco and his company had been killed by Indians, which was why there was no record of him or his travels. "His woman had her child and it died. That is unfortunate, but it was not a sacrifice to the sky-god."

"You are testing me," said Dona Azul angrily, when Oaxetli fell silent, frowning with apprehension at what she had said. "What more must I do to show we are faithful to the teaching we were given? We have sacrificed as we were taught to do. We know our favor came through our sin, as does all favor."

"I am not testing you. I have no reason to test you." San Germanno did not like having to urge Oaxetli to repeat what he told her, but he could not keep the brusqueness from his voice. "I am telling you how I believe all this began."

"You are Francisco," Dona Azul accused him, angered at the bewildered stares of her people.

"That is one of my names, certainly," San Germanno said at once. "It is as much mine as Ferenc, or Franz, or many another." He waited while Oaxetli reluctantly repeated what he had said in the language of Dona Azul. "But the Francisco who came here was not I, nor am I his descendant or deputy. We share the same . . . Christian name. He was Spanish, I am not. He had men accompanying him, I do not. He came to conquer, I do not." Again he waited while this was translated.

"It was promised you would return," Dona Azul stated, looking from San Germanno to Oaxetli. "It was promised you would put no other in her place until then."

"No doubt that Francisco made such promises," San Germanno said once Oaxetli had done her work. "And when he gave them, he was sincere."

"He was the angel of the sky-god, sent to bring Dona Azul to us," Dona Azul declared, and for once her people responded with a ringing of their tuneless bells.

"This is a true thing," they said with relief at this more familiar homage.

"But I am no angel," San Germanno told them. He knew that his true nature would appall these people; he strove to find a way to convince Dona Azul she was mistaken. "If I am what you want to believe me, let the sky-god give you a sign of it."

Visibly shaken, Oaxetli repeated his challenge, her voice shaking as much as her knotted hands.

"Yes, we will have a sign," said Dona Azul with intense satisfaction. She held her hands up to the sun again, and shouted, "If this is Francisco come again, let us know it now."

The people drowned out Oaxetli's translation with a frenzy of bells and cries. When she tried to repeat it more loudly, San Germanno waved her into silence.

"I have the jist of it," he said sardonically.

For the greater part of an hour the noise continued; Dona Azul stood very still in a posture of anticipation while San Germanno returned to the place on the platform assigned to him, where Rogerio waited, apparently unperturbed.

"If there is no sign?" he asked in Russian after a short while.

"I wish I knew," San Germanno replied in the same language.

"They may kill us," Rogerio warned him.

"They may try," said San Germanno, then gave his attention to Oaxetli. "Do not worry, my little friend. Nothing evil will touch us."

She swung around and fixed her blind eyes on him. "How can you say that? You, of all creatures?"

He accepted her anger as part of her fear, and did not seek to assuage either. "It is because of what I am that I can say this," he told her, reaching for her hands. "I will not permit you or Rogerio to suffer on my account."

"That may not be possible," she said, trying to pull her hands away. "Dona Azul does not like you to touch me. I may not be able to see it, but I sense it." She lifted her head in pride and defiance.

He released her. "I will do all that I can to guard you, Oaxetli."

She nodded once to acknowledge she had heard him. "I can't hear anything in all this—" Her fingers moved to indicate the jangling bells and the shouting.

"Then we will wait until it is over," San Germanno said, certain Oaxetli heard him. "As soon as they tire of this, we will try again."

When at last Dona Azul lowered her hands, she pointed at San Germanno with the whole length of her arm. "If you are a deceiver, you have brought sin back to us, and you will be made to answer for it. You—"

"I have not deceived you," San Germanno reminded her when Oaxetli had translated the denouncement. "From the first, I said I was not the Francisco you had been promised would return. I have never claimed to have come here for the Dona Azul, or as the emissary of the King in the east."

"Your name is Francisco," Dona Azul persisted.

"And I come from far away. There are hundreds of men in this part of the world of whom you could say the same." He let Oaxetli translate this for him, adding to her, "Do not worry so, *querida*." The winter sun was beginning to wear on him; he would need more earth in the soles and heels of his boots soon. He had the contents of two chests left and in three months would be critically low on his supply as the days lengthened and the sun made its way north in the sky.

"But none of them have come here." Dona Azul pounced on this argument as if he could not dispute her claim.

"True enough," he replied with Oaxetli's help. "That will change in time." He gave Dona Azul a long, speculative look. "You would not want to overlook the man coming to you on behalf of the Dona Azul simply because I stumbled upon this valley before he does. She must have told you that there could be Franciscos who came here to mislead you, to discover if you have held to the teachings of Dona Azul." This was a risk and he knew it, but he had to challenge her. "When Dona Azul brought you the secret of making cloth, she must have said that many would wear clothes with patterns woven into them, and that most would be deceptions."

"No one stumbles upon this place. Those who come here are sent by the sky-god, as the Dona Azul taught us." Her cheeks were flushed with emotion and she glared at San Germanno. "Unless you have been sent to keep us from our mission."

The people gathered around the platform murmured with dismay, and a few of them put their palms together to gain protection.

"I came here of my own accord," San Germanno said steadily. "I was hoping to learn from the people of the New World before the Spanish had control of it all." He waited while Oaxetli conveyed this to Dona Azul. "As I have said from the first, I have no purposes but my own, and no mission beyond what I have set for myself."

"You have deceived us," Dona Azul screamed. "And there is no sign!"

"I have not deceived you. I have never claimed to be the man you wait for. Because I am not that man—" San Germanno began only to be cut short.

"You will be held in your houses, you and your whore! And your henchman!" Dona Azul spat at Oaxetli. "We will wait until we have a sign, and then we will deal with you as the sky-god wishes."

Oaxetli translated this in a flat voice as if the words meant nothing to her. When she finished, she added to San Germanno, "She will take vengeance for this, Conde. She will not permit you to embarrass her."

"I share your worry," said San Germanno, his emotions at war within him. "I would like to think she will listen to reason"—Oaxetli snorted in derision—"but that is too much to hope for. Tell her that we will do what we can to comply with her orders." He saw Oaxetli hesitated, and repeated his order.

"You will not gain my favor through compliance," Dona Azul vowed. "You have disgraced our faith and I will not tolerate such contempt."

Again Oaxetli translated without inflection. "There is no reason to doubt her."

"I am aware of that," San Germanno told her, and added, "If we resist now we accomplish little but to put them on their guard. If we show we are willing to cooperate, they may not be too careful with us."

Oaxetli shrugged and said to Dona Azul, "We will do as you require."

Dona Azul was not quite finished. "Tell that man that I will not be content until he has abased himself before me and done penance for his lies."

When San Germanno heard this translation, he said, "It would be useless, I suppose, to point out that I have told no lies."

"Yes, it would be," Oaxetli said sharply. "For you have not told all the truth, either, have you?"

"No," he allowed. "I have not."

Rogerio approached San Germanno, no expression of worry marring his regular features. He spoke in the language of the Chinese Imperial Court. "Do you think we will be able to get out of this place?"

"Not tonight, or tomorrow, but in a few days, perhaps, if we do not resist them. They will grow lax and we will be able to leave in the long hours before dawn." San Germanno glanced at Oaxetli. "One hour will be like any other for her."

"Do you think they will come after us?" Rogerio asked, keeping urgency out of his demeanor.

"I think they may, but once we are beyond this valley, I reckon we will be safe enough. They do not want to draw attention to themselves, and they must know that they could be discovered if they ventured too far beyond their village." San Germanno gave a wide gesture with his hand that appeared to take in the sky, but Rogerio knew he meant to indicate the people standing around the platform.

"Not in these times, certainly," he agreed. "They must know that there have been changes in Nueva Galicia."

"Or they do not want to know of them," San Germanno said, and said to Oaxetli, "Tell her we are discussing arrangements we have made that may suffer because of our delay here. Tell them that we are expected in other places."

Oaxetli kept up her indifferent manner but also contrived to do as

San Germanno requested. "They will escort us back to the houses they have provided for us; they will see we are fed and kept clothed," she said when Dona Azul had responded. "We will be kept under guard."

"I thought we might be," San Germanno said with a trace of sardonic humor. Why, he asked himself, if these people feared what he might do to them did they contrive to keep him captive? Why not take him and Rogerio and Oaxetli a long distance from the valley and abandon them? If they were going to be killed, why delay the hour? Was there a ceremony to prepare? What was the use in holding them here? He had never been able to answer that last question, no matter how many times he encountered the behavior. These people did not want ransom, they did not have anything to gain by his presence, and yet they were determined to hold him and his companions. He shook his head in bafflement.

"What is it, my master?" Rogerio asked, this time in Spanish.

"Nothing that need concern you," San Germanno answered in the same tongue. "An old question."

Six of the village men had stepped forward, all of them carrying spears and a throwing sling with a stone in place.

"We are to go with these men. They are our guards until sunset. Others will come then." Oaxetli listened intently to the voices around them, and added, "They are afraid you are a wizard, or something worse. If you escape, they are afraid misfortune will come upon them all."

San Germanno's brow rose. "Do they not have faith that the sky-god will protect them?"

"What did he say?" Dona Azul demanded.

Oaxetli translated, softening San Germanno's sharp remark as much as she could. The answer was a long one, and Oaxetli had trouble keeping up with the pace of Dona Azul's tirade.

"The sky-god is forever our protector. That was promised us by Dona Azul. But we can fail him by entertaining his enemies and showing them reverence to which they are not entitled. If we should fail the sky-god in this way, we will be punished for our blindness and our error. It is taught to us that we must seek our redemption through sin. A sacrifice will be made in expiation of our sins, and to keep the sky-god from turning away from us, bringing us endless famine and drought. We will find the one who has sinned the most and his sins, being great, will bring redemption on us all, as the sky-god's son was traded for our sins long ago. We know the lessons we were taught, and we will keep the laws the sky-god set for us through Dona Azul. We will remain faithful to the sky-god so that he will not put us beyond his favor. Our devotion will be demonstrated through a sacrifice that will please him, according to the rites we were given by Dona Azul."

A few unmelodious bells rang unenthusiastically as she finished.

"This way," said the senior member of their escort. He pointed toward their houses with his spear. "Try nothing foolish."

"Guard them as you would guard yourselves from perdition," Dona Azul charged them. "And fear what will befall you should they escape."

Oaxetli translated these warnings with seeming indifference as she fell in beside San Germanno and laid her hand reluctantly on his arm.

"There are four steps down," San Germanno said.

"I remember," she responded curtly, wanting as little of his help as possible.

Sensing this, San Germanno slightly increased the distance between them, a pang of loneliness going through him. "I will do nothing you do not want me to do, Oaxetli," he said as they made their way down the stairs.

"I want nothing from you, San Germanno. I have had more than—" She stopped abruptly, her footing uncertain.

Realizing that she would take nothing more from him, San Germanno called out, "Rogerio, if you will take Oaxetli's arm?"

"Of course," said Rogerio, coming to the blind woman's side and taking her hand. If he was aware of the distress Oaxetli experienced, he made no comment about it.

When they reached the two houses, Oaxetli went into hers and remained there, isolated herself from everyone around her. As the day lengthened, she made no effort to get food or water and gradually San Germanno became concerned.

"She must be hungry, and thirsty," he said to Rogerio. "It is time she had food and drink."

"I know enough of their language to ask for meat and water," Rogerio told him. "As do you."

"It would be better coming from you, and not too clearly; let them think you have only a rudimentary command of the tongue," San Germanno said to him. "Struggle with the words."

"Of course," said Rogerio. "There is nothing to be gained by letting them know how much we have learned."

"Precisely," San Germanno concurred, and turned away to go into their assigned house as Rogerio approached one of the guards.

Pointing to Oaxetli's house, he purposefully put the accent on the wrong syllables of the words he spoke. "She. Water. Meat." He paused and repeated the words again, a bit more loudly than the first time.

The guard nodded and muttered a response before signaling to one of his fellows and rapping out a series of instructions to the man, who went at once back toward the rest of the village.

Satisfied, Rogerio went to the door of Oaxetli's house. "They will bring you food and water shortly."

"Thank you," she called to him formally. "I am grateful to you."

"There is no need," he said, and waited in case she had something more to say. When the silence had dragged on long enough, he went into the house where he and San Germanno stayed. "It is coming."

"Good," said San Germanno. He was sitting on top of one of his remaining chests of earth, his dark eyes focused some distance beyond the wall. "She loathes me now."

Rogerio could think of nothing to say.

"She despises what I am," San Germanno said a short while later. "Given what she believes, who can blame her?" He expected no answer to his question and got none. After a while he rose and went to the single window. "Is there anything I can say, do you think?"

"To Oaxetli?" Rogerio answered. "I doubt it. As you know, it is what she believes."

San Germanno rubbed his face. "I will need a shave soon."

"I will attend to it," Rogerio assured him.

Again San Germanno was still. Then he shrugged, dismissing whatever reflections had taken hold of him. "Who was the Francisco who came here, I wonder? and when?"

"A Spaniard, as you told Dona Azul." Rogerio coughed diplomatically. "She did not want to hear what you told her."

"Small wonder." He frowned out at the dusk. "Those guards are being very careful."

"And will be for a while. Remember the guards in Chotin." Rogerio did not quite smile although he showed his teeth.

"Or the guard at Olivia's house. A pity we cannot drug the wine these men drink." He paused to study the village. "Someone is coming." He pointed out the window. "Look."

"Dona Azul?" Rogerio ventured as he peered through the window.

San Germanno nodded. "We will need Oaxetli's help." He indicated the door. "We will have to receive her by the fire-pit."

"The guards will see her," Rogerio said, knowing that was San Germanno's intention.

"And Oaxetli will not feel . . . pressed by my presence." The sadness in his dark eyes was concealed by the fading day.

Rogerio almost said something, but did not. His face was somber as he went across the space between their two houses to get Oaxetli. He found her sitting alone, the remnants of her supper littering the single bowl she had been provided; she was softly reciting passages from *Después del Ultimo Oracion,* and he waited until she came to the end of one of the verses before he said, "Your pardon, Señorita, but we need your services. Dona Azul is approaching."

Oaxetli tried not to wince at this information. Her hands shook as she got to her feet. "I will be with you directly."

"We will be at the fire-pit. We want the guards to observe all that passes between us." Rogerio saw Oaxetli relax. "I do not know how long this will take."

She came toward his voice. "Do not be angry with me, Señor Rogerio," she whispered as she reached his side.

"I? I am not angry." He paused, knowing she would not accept so facile a reply. "I am . . . disappointed perhaps. But I am not angry, nor is my master."

She flinched at his mention of San Germanno. "I know he is a good man, and if that were all he is, I would never . . . But he is not a man like other men, and I cannot forget that."

"I realize that. So does he." He started toward the door, then added, "It has happened before."

She lowered her voice to barely more than a breath. "What he did to me? Or—"

"You are not the first to feel as you do about his nature." Rogerio bowed slightly. "No one has been compelled to accept him for as long as I have known him, and that has been a very long time. You have nothing to fear from him."

"So he told me." She nudged him to resume their walk out into the evening. "Is Dona Azul here yet?"

"She has just arrived," said Rogerio, and escorted Oaxetli to the stone bench beside the fire-pit. "You won't get cold here."

"Very well," Oaxetli said, the terror gone out of her. Rogerio was right; the fire was warm enough for her to enjoy it, and the wind had died down in the last two hours.

"I would prefer we talk in private," Dona Azul said to San Germanno as soon as Oaxetli reached them.

"That is impractical," San Germanno replied cordially. "You will have to speak through Oaxetli, as will I."

Dona Azul stared at San Germanno with ferocious hunger. "When Dona Azul has Francisco's child and it lives, then we will all be united with the sky-god."

Oaxetli translated this and added, "Tell her what you are and she will leave you alone."

"If she believed me, and if she did not decide to rid the world of me," San Germanno appended. "Tell her that I am not the Francisco she seeks and that I cannot give her a child. Say I was . . . spoiled in youth."

Oaxetli translated for Dona Azul, saying to her, "He is not Spanish, Dona Azul. He is not the one you seek."

"Spoiled in youth!" Dona Azul scoffed. "Do not tell me he is one who only lies with men. Dona Azul taught us to consign such monsters to the flames."

Color mounted in Oaxetli's face. "He is not one of those."

"Ah!" Dona Azul pointed directly at Oaxetli. "Then he has done the act with you."

"What is she saying?" San Germanno asked.

"She has asked me if you have ever . . . taken me." She was flustered.

San Germanno watched Dona Azul as he spoke to Oaxetli. "I have, after the manner of those of my blood. I have been in your bed to that purpose. Tell her we have lain together."

Oaxetli spoke to Dona Azul, her voice dropping to a whisper. "She will think me a harlot," she accused San Germanno.

"She does already," San Germanno reminded her, not without kindness. "Tell her that you have touched my scars. Do not diminish their severity or extent. Let her know how extensive they are."

Again Oaxetli relayed San Germanno's remarks to Dona Azul, and described the wide swath of scarring that began just beneath his breastbone and stopped at the base of his abdomen. "He is intact," she said to Dona Azul, "but he does not . . . he cannot . . . he has no stiffness."

"Liar!" Dona Azul approached Oaxetli, her mouth square with rage, veins standing out in her face and neck. "You lie!"

San Germanno stepped between the two women, facing Dona Azul. "She is saying a true thing," he said clumsily in Dona Azul's language.

Dona Azul directed her wrath at him. "You cannot escape your vow.

You will do as you gave your oath you would, Francisco, or you will die. And your man will die. And your whore will die."

Oaxetli repeated this in Spanish, feeling more shame than fear at the threats.

"Dona Azul," said San Germanno calmly, "how often must I tell you I am not the Francisco who came here. I cannot do what you want of Francisco because it is not my oath to honor."

When Oaxetli had finished translating this, Dona Azul glowered at San Germanno. "You will regret this." She turned on her heel and strode away.

As he watched her go, San Germanno said quietly, "I regret this already."

Text of a letter from Presidencia Don Ezequias Pannefrio y Modestez to Obispo Hernan Guarda at Los Sacramentos both in Cuzco, Audiencia de Lima, Viceroyalty of Peru.

To Su Excelencia, Obispo Guarda of Los Sacramentos, the respectful greetings of Cuzco Presidencia Don Ezequias Pannefrio y Modestez, with his hope that we may be able to avoid a misunderstanding.

Lamentably, I must officially protest the warrant you have extended to all clergy and the Secular Arm as well for the arrest and imprisonment of Francisco Ragoczy, el Conde de San Germanno. While I do not question your authority to do so, I must remind you that the Corregidor and the Crown have refused to issue a warrant for the arrest of this man, each stating that while some of San Germanno's activities may be suspect in regard to his purpose, there is no evidence or complaint to support the accusations contained in your warrant. You have chosen to accept the most inflammatory statements in regard to this man's activities and you have taken as valid the rumors that have made the rounds of the marketplace since the day Acanna Tupac took her own life.

I have no doubt that San Germanno played no part in her death, beyond a fruitless effort to save her. The assertion that she was killed by him is wholly unsubstantiated and only credulous natives who distrust all foreigners believe this to be true. I am also persuaded that San Germanno used no deviltry in his medicines which saved many lives here, in part because he was not able to save everyone he treated. Such is the way with all physicians, no matter how skillful. Those men who are men of the cloth who have devoted their lives to treating the sick do not save all their patients, and you have the word of Frey Ardo in the Audiencia de Quito that San Germanno's service in his community was above reproach.

This warrant, and the reward accompanying it, can lead to nothing but trouble and acrimony. Those who have in the past upheld San Germanno's reputation will now be afraid to do so, for fear of what may become of them at the hands of those hoping to claim the reward and advance themselves in your favor. You know as well as I that many scoundrels are in the New World to make their fortunes and will do it at any cost to others. Those Indians who have benefitted from San Germanno's aid will now have to return to their villages, for to remain in the cities would be inviting disaster: those same men who would trouble Spaniards would torment the Indians and that would lead to many complaints by distinguished men whose households would be disrupted.

I recognize your desire to test your authority against that of Obispo Puente y Sello, and in Cuzco you may be certain you have the higher position no matter how the Church may see the question. But you have extended the warrant throughout the Viceroyalty of Peru and the Viceroyalty of Nueva España, which surely is beyond the limits of your bishopric. I must request that you rescind the warrant and vacate all complaints held against San Germanno.

It is not merely the bonds of friendship that lead me to make this request of you, but the obligations of my office, which cannot be made subject to the Church in matters of administration. If this redounds to my discredit, so be it. I am not willing to place myself and all Presidencias in the New World beholden to the Church in issues of policy of the Crown. I would have to abjure my oath to the King if I permitted this warrant of yours to go unchallenged, and that would make me a traitor. The Church must not require administrators like myself to betray the King in order to accommodate the Church.

In opening the New World to our exploration and government, the Church has allowed the Crown to decide in what manner the Viceroyalties should maintain justice. The Crown has placed these matters in the hands of the Corregidores and Presidencias, and the Church has not challenged this decision. We who have been granted this authority answer to the Crown for our actions. If you are determined to allocate magisterial rights for yourself, let me register my protest at once, and beg you to submit the whole debate to the Pope himself to decide, for there is much at stake here that neither you, Excelencia, nor I, are in a position to decide.

*It is not only San Germanno who is affected by this, but all foreign-
ers coming to Spanish territory in the New World. You presume your decision will have impact on only one man, and for a single reason. But
each action is like a stone cast into a pond: there are always ripples. Little as we may like it, the Protestants have a toe-hold in many places, and
if you pursue San Germanno for apostasy, the Protestants may well rise
up against us all. You know what that argument has done to Europe.
Do you truly wish to see such conflict in the New World as well?*

*With my prayers that God will guide your meditation and answer our
prayers with peace and justice, I am*

Don Ezequias Pannefrio y Modestez
Presidencia of Cuzco
Audiencia de Lima
Viceroyalty of Peru
*By my own hand, and with a bona fides copy sent to Don Vicente,
Corregidor at Lima; witnessed by Capitan Don Alejandro Morena y
Osma this 26th day of February, 1648*

8

Ominously still weather hung over Acapulco; the sky was brassy and
flat, turning the bay to a sheet of quicksilver, with hardly a trace of
froth to break its metallic sheen. The Indians from the region muttered
and put small stone skulls above their doors while the sailors in port
alternately cursed and blessed their guardian angels for stranding them
here for the last four days.

At la Posada de las Joyas, Dom Enrique Vilhao took a long pull at
the bottle of French wine he had ordered as part of his midday meal.
He grinned as he set the bottle down and grabbed a large chunk of
savory goat from the platter set between him and van Zwolle. "We will
see the Harbor Master this evening. Don Oviedo is a reasonable man,
not given to questioning legal documents."

"Good," said van Zwolle brusquely. His long experience sailing had
taught him to distrust weather like this; he was growing uneasy.

"And with that deed of gift we were able to . . . obtain, we should have title for the *Queen of the Pacific* and *The Golden Empress* before another two Sundays pass. Don Oviedo will have to file the deed of gift with the Presidencia, but that will not take long." Dom Enrique chuckled. "It is fortunate that San Germanno seems to have disappeared. His advocate has nothing to keep us from making our claim." He took another long pull from the mouth of the wine bottle, sighing as the pleasantly muzzy sensation came over him.

"We will have to make it worth his while to keep silent," said van Zwolle gloomily. He pronged a collop of goat on his fork, but did not eat it, inviting though it was. Instead he looked past their balcony to the bay. "The longer the calm the harder the storm. I can feel it in my bones."

At this Dom Enrique laughed outright. "This isn't the Lowlands. The New World is a warmer place, and I have been told by the landlord that there have been no terrible storms for more than five years." He began to chew vigorously, a thin trail of gravy at the corner of his mouth.

"It will be the same here as any place in the world," van Zwolle predicted unhappily. "Storms are storms from China to Egypt to the top of the world." He bit into the goat, nodding approval at its taste.

"Then we must keep within doors when the weather turns. That should not be so difficult." Dom Enrique gave van Zwolle a smile of encouragement. "I have arranged an appointment for us this evening at the house of Dona Amelia. She is said to have the best whores in Acapulco. They have come from all over the world, from Prussia to Africa, from Peru to the Malay Islands. I was told one of them is Japanese." He rolled his eyes in exaggerated lasciviousness.

"We will see for ourselves tonight." Van Zwolle did not share Dom Enrique's anticipation. For him, a woman was a woman no matter where she came from, and he had but one use for her. He took another bite of goat and looked away from the bay. "If the weather holds through tonight, we should have a pleasant evening."

"You and your damned northern blood!" Dom Enrique burst out, still smiling but without a trace of humor. "Does nothing move you? Have you no passion?"

"I cannot afford passion," van Zwolle said. "You are well-born. That alone entitles you to the pleasures of life. For those like me, we take our enjoyment as we may and we thank our Guardian Angel for keeping us from harm." He pronged another collop of goat on the tines of his fork. "If you bring us to the good life at last, I may learn to indulge myself as you do, but—"

Dom Enrique interrupted him. "Oh, stop your carping, van Zwolle. No one has made your life hard but you." His mouth was sullen now, and when he drank he was more reckless than before. "You always anticipate the worst, and I think you are disappointed when you do not achieve it."

"One of us has to consider the risks, and you are not willing to," said van Zwolle.

"How can you say that?" Dom Enrique demanded. "Who was it who arranged to have a deed of gift forged in Panamá, before we got here, by a man who knew nothing of San Germanno? Who was it who asked Obispo Rueda y Bandejero at Santa Maria de la Luz about San Germanno, to determine if he could be reached? Who was it who filed a complaint against San Germanno with Don Ezequias before we left Cuzco? Who was it who made the contacts to dispose of the things we took from San Germanno's house in Cuzco? Did we get caught? Did anyone question us?"

"We have been lucky," said van Zwolle. "If I asked the things you have asked, we would long since have been detained."

"Are you certain it was only luck?" Dom Enrique challenged as he finished the last of the wine in his bottle. "When we call upon Don Oviedo, it will not be luck that will gain us title to San Germanno's ships, it will be the planning we have done, and the preparations we have made."

"You are assuming there will be no difficulties," said van Zwolle.

"There you go again," Dom Enrique chided him. "You will not have faith in what we have done." He grabbed more goat with his fingers and popped the meat into his mouth.

"Dom Enrique, these officials are not stupid. With San Germanno gone, they must realize many men will covet what he has and try to seize it for themselves. You are not prepared to deal with questions we may be asked. You expect the deed to be accepted without any reservations. For all you know, San Germanno left instructions regarding his ships and his other property that we have no knowledge of, and that lack would cause us to be held under suspicion, if nothing else." He regarded Dom Enrique with growing apprehension. "Don't drink any more until we see the Harbor Master. You will need clear wits."

"All right," Dom Enrique conceded genially. "If you will stop jumping like water on a hot griddle, I will not have any more wine until we reach Dona Amelia's tonight, when we will have reason to celebrate."

Van Zwolle coughed. "And you suppose we will have San Germanno's funds at our disposal to pay for our entertainment?"

"Of course. We have not been questioned thus far, have we? The deed of gift we carry is most convincing." Again he laughed, his fading, handsome features showing deep lines around his eyes and bracketing his mouth, the first sagging of dissipation transformed into a mask of good-fellowship.

"If anyone should discover that the deed is counterfeit . . ."

"They will not," said Dom Enrique confidently. "Who is to challenge it? San Germanno left this city months ago and there has been no word of him since October. He may well be dead. Whatever his fate, he has no need of his ships, nor of his house, nor his possessions." He licked the fingers of his right hand, relishing the gravy. "The women tonight will end your unhappiness."

"Possibly," said van Zwolle. "But the Harbor Master will be the one whose judgment will have the greatest impact upon us, not the favors of prostitutes."

"At least for the moment," said Dom Enrique, stifling a sudden yawn. "I am going to have my siesta."

Van Zwolle was relieved that Dom Enrique would have a chance to sleep away the wine fumes. He made a gesture of approval. "Both of us would do well to lie down for an hour or two. It will be a long night, if your plans come to fruition."

"If?" Dom Enrique echoed. "It is all arranged."

"There may still be disappointments for us," said van Zwolle, his delivery as crisp as Dom Enrique's was slurred. "You think everything has been done satisfactorily, but until we have the documents in our hands with the official seals on them, I will not be sanguine about the arrangements."

"I tell you, there is no reason to worry," Dom Enrique stated.

"And I tell you, we had best be prepared to answer many questions. It is possible that we are getting into trouble we know nothing of." He folded his arms and gave Dom Enrique a fixed stare.

"All right, all right. I will go over our deed of gift and see if any consideration has been left out. Will that satisfy you?"

"Not entirely, but I suppose it is the best I can hope for." He ate more of their meal in silence, not wanting to cajole Dom Enrique out of his fit of the sullens; he had done it often enough in the past and accomplished little by it. He broke off a section of flat bread and soaked up the gravy with it, relishing the flavor almost more than he relished the meat.

Finally Dom Enrique rose. "I am going in to lie down. You do whatever you Dutch do at midday."

"I will lie down as well, since we have so fine a night ahead of us." Van Zwolle noticed that Dom Enrique was not quite steady on his feet as he made his way indoors; he hoped that by late afternoon Dom Enrique would be sober again. The prospect of facing the Harbor Master with Dom Enrique half-drunk was troubling, and with that uneasy notion for company, he retired to his own room and paused only to take off his boots before sprawling on the bed, to spend the next two hours staring up at the ceiling.

By late afternoon there was a hint of a breeze out of the northwest, though the sky had not lost its ominous shine. There were a number of prominent men out on their high-bred horses as Dom Enrique and van Zwolle emerged from la Posada de las Joyas and set out for the Almirancion where the Harbor Master's office was. Dom Enrique had regained his good spirits and he carried their forged deed of gift as if it were a marshal's baton. Beside him, van Zwolle looked ill-favored and scruffy, but the pace he set kept Dom Enrique striding more quickly than he liked.

"Once we have presented this, we will not have to worry about money again," Dom Enrique announced as they approached the Almirancion. "We will own ships and the contents of the warehouses where San Germanno stores his goods. You will see. We will have what we are due at last." The courtyard was full of men from the Pacific merchant fleet; men with leathery faces and rolling gaits gathered here to present their records to customs and to obtain permission to set sail once again. Catching sight of one man in lavish silks, Dom Enrique snapped his fingers. "We can send our ships to Nagasaki. I am Portuguese, and we will be allowed to land there." His smile was smug. "There are many Spanish who will want to do business with us, since the Portuguese alone are permitted to trade from Nagasaki."

Although van Zwolle was well-aware of this, he said, "It could be profitable."

The main doors stood open; Dom Enrique entered the building with a flourish, bowing to the clerk who sat at the massive writing table. "I am Dom Enrique Vilhao here to see the Harbor Master regarding title to two merchant ships."

"Are these ships yours?" the clerk asked. He was a young man, properly attired for the son of a Spanish property owner. His hair was a trifle too long to be truly fashionable, but the lacings on his ropilla were more than enough to make up for this lack.

"They are now," said Dom Enrique, holding up the rolled deed of gift. "I want to arrange for the title transfer as soon as possible."

The clerk favored him with a look of mild distaste. "I will tend to it at once, Señor."

"Dom Enrique," he corrected, still smiling.

"Certainly. Dom Enrique." He consulted his ledger. "You are expected," he said with a trace of disappointment.

"Yes. I thought it wise to be prompt. The Harbor Master is a very busy man." He signaled van Zwolle to come closer. "My partner and I are at Don Oviedo's disposal."

Now the clerk sighed. "I will have him informed you have arrived." His face was a mask of propriety as he rang for a servant. "Take these two men to the Harbor Master. He knows they are coming."

"Gracias," said Dom Enrique as he and van Zwolle fell in behind the servant. They went up a flight of stairs and along a corridor to the end of the building nearest the harbor. Here the servant indicated a bench in the anteroom where they were to wait while they were announced.

Van Zwolle sat down at once, using the time to gather his thoughts. He watched Dom Enrique pace, his lavish ropilla swinging with every step he took.

"I trust we will not have to wait long," said Dom Enrique to the servant as he emerged from the Harbor Master's office.

"It should not be long," said the servant; he went away without offering any refreshments, which annoyed Dom Enrique.

"What sort of place is this, leaving us to wait upon Don Oviedo's pleasure with not so much as a sip of wine to sustain us?" He spoke loudly enough for the departing servant to overhear.

"If our wait is short, there is no time to bring us a tray," van Zwolle observed, secretly pleased that Dom Enrique would not have a chance to start drinking before they spoke with Don Oviedo. He did his best to make himself comfortable on the hard bench and resigned himself to their delay as best he could.

"Possibly, but he should have offered us something." The mulish cast to Dom Enrique's handsome features boded ill for their meeting. He scowled in van Zwolle's direction. "When we are with Don Oviedo, let me do the talking. He is said to be very aware of rank and position."

If you speak—" He hitched his shoulders to show he could not be responsible for what happened next.

"I will not speak," van Zwolle assured him. "Unless you ask me to, or there is information I might offer."

Dom Enrique had to be content with that. "Make sure you remember."

After a quarter of an hour, Dom Enrique stopped pacing and took a seat at the other end of the bench from van Zwolle. He tapped his fingers on the wood and looked prepared to spring up in an instant.

More than half an hour after their arrival they were admitted to the office of the Harbor Master. Don Oviedo Mauricio Sanson Durandarte Carterez y Atrevido was too old to be a dandy, but he attempted to deck himself out as well as he could; his hair was improbably black and the curl to his thinning locks was the product of curling irons rather than the bounty of nature. His ropilla was silk, a deep shade of gold with accents in black, as his position demanded. He rose from his chair behind his writing table and bowed deeply to Dom Enrique. "I am sorry to have kept you waiting," he said with patent insincerity.

Dom Enrique answered with equal mendacity, "It was nothing." He bowed and made a sign to van Zwolle to do the same. "We have been in Acapulco for six days. We were told by Padre Juanbatista at San Matteo that you were the official we must contact in regard to this deed of gift." He held out the rolled parchment. "I made this appointment four days ago."

"So my clerk informs me." He sat down once again but gave no indication that Dom Enrique or van Zwolle were to do the same. "Tell me about this document."

"El Conde de San Germanno has granted the two of us title and use of two of his ships. You will see them described in the fourth paragraph. We are to take control of his goods stored in this city as well, and we are licensed to trade as we see fit." He opened the roll and spread it before Don Oviedo.

The Harbor Master peered down at the page as if he had trouble reading. "This document was signed in Panamá," he said at last.

"Yes, it was," Dom Enrique allowed. "On the authority of San Germanno, as you can see." He pointed to the witnessed signature.

"Um. Indeed," said Don Oviedo, considering the signatures. "It entitles you to the sum of two hundred gold reales."

"To be paid to me upon delivery of this deed of gift," Dom Enrique pointed out. "To make it possible for me to begin to do business without putting my purse at risk."

"That is what is stated here," Don Oviedo said nodding. "It is not a small sum, but not so great that anyone would question it. Provisions for a Pacific crossing can cost twice that amount." He watched Dom Enrique to see what the man's response to this would be.

"So much," Dom Enrique mused. "I thought it was nearer to three hundred." He saw by the slight shift in his expression that Don Oviedo was satisfied with his figure.

"The largest ships require the greater sum," said Don Oviedo, dismissing the issue. "It says also that you are to be given the use of San Germanno's house and his staff until San Germanno himself returns."

"There are records at the house that will be useful to me, and being he is giving me this deed, it would place me at a disadvantage to be unable to use his house. He saw no purpose in letting it sit empty." The smile Dom Enrique offered was modest, the sort one might see in the Spanish court rather than in the New World. "It was a generous addition to the deed, the house."

"And the staff," said Don Oviedo, fingering his precise mustache, which was as improbably sable as his hair. Perhaps, thought Dom Enrique, both were wigs, made for a mature man. If they were, no doubt they were French and cost more than Don Oviedo's clerk made in a year.

"It would serve no useful purpose for me to have to hire new servants when there are servants at the house already." This was an answer he was prepared to give, and he added, "This way my associate van Zwolle and I may live under the same roof and occasions for misunderstandings will be lessened because of it."

A sudden yowl of wind took the attention of all three men, and the papers on Don Oviedo's writing desk danced as the shutters swung open. Don Oviedo clapped his arms down on the pages, trying to keep them from being blown about the room.

Van Zwolle went to close the shutters and looked out into the sunset, seeing that to the northwest dark clouds were boiling. At the quays men were rushing to secure their boats or to take their ships out into the bay to moor them away from danger. The movement was hectic in response to the sudden threat.

"At last," said Don Oviedo as he rang for a servant. "We will have the lamps alight in a moment." He continued to scrutinize the deed of gift. "I think it would be useful to let me and my advisors review this. In the morning I will send for you and we will settle the matter then. Where are you staying?"

"La Posada de las Joyas," said Dom Enrique in an off-handed way as if he were unaware it was one of Acapulco's most lavish inns. "We have the fourth suite, the one overlooking the courtyard and the bay."

Don Oviedo refused to be impressed. "One of my staff will find you there at midday, I trust."

"Certainly." After an evening at Dona Amelia's, he should be about ready to rise at midday.

"I will have to pass on my recommendation to the Presidencia before all can be transferred into your name. He may have to inquire of the Corregidor for approval." Don Oviedo managed to sound bored, as if these legal matters were an intrusion upon him.

"Certainly," Dom Enrique repeated, and bowed slightly as if to honor the new Presidencia of Acapulco, Don Augustin Murado y Bonsuerte who had taken the office just two months earlier; Dom Enrique was greatly relieved that the Presidencia had never met San Germanno, for they might have discussed San Germanno's property and its disposal in his absence. "A man in your position must use his best judgment. I have faith that your sense of justice will treat me fairly."

"Ya lo creo. And my recommendation can be only that—a recommendation. If the Presidencia should decide not to accept my recommendation, his decision will be final. You would have to go to the Viceroy to have it overturned, and that would be costly both in time and money."

"Well enough," said Dom Enrique, determined not to show any apprehension. "But I will remind you that *The Golden Empress* is expected in port in two to three weeks and the *Queen of the Pacific* is expected a month later. Without a final decision both ships will have to remain in port doing no one any good at all."

Don Oviedo tapped the parchment with one finger. "This would enable you to begin to arrange for cargo for the ships."

"Of course," said Dom Enrique, his impatience not quite concealed.

"And no doubt the Capitans and their crews will be eager to set out again for Manila. Barring need for repairs, the ships serve no purpose staying in port." Van Zwolle startled both men with his remark; he looked abashed at their astonishment.

"Yes," said Dom Enrique, striving to regain his mastery of this interview. "And someone will have to arrange transfer of the cargo going on to Europe to be carried to Veracruz to meet with San Germanno's Atlantic ships."

"This would give you the authority to tend to such things," said Don Oviedo, stating the obvious. "Well, that will have to be addressed sooner or later, and the Presidencia may have to review the whole of San Germanno's estate before summer is over, no matter what the final disposal of this deed of gift may be. When San Germanno has been absent for a year, it will be necessary to assign his authority if this does not stand."

It was an effort for Dom Enrique to control his temper. "Don Oviedo, if those two ships are not provisioned, the chance for them to begin their crossing during good weather will be lost. It is not advisable to force them to remain in port half a year if they have no need of repair. In half a year, San Germanno's other three ships will have reached Acapulco from Manila, and then he will lose a year of trading. How am I going to answer him, when and if he returns, to explain the reason for the lack of trade? He provided that deed of gift to enable his ships to continue their enterprise while he was away." He held up his hand. "I know he has an agent; I have spoken to Lazaro Cerritos in this regard. You know he is an old man: fifty-three. He will not be able to do his work much longer, and San Germanno would not want him to remain at his desk until his health is completely gone."

"Yes, yes," said Don Oviedo. "There is much in what you say." He rolled up the deed of gift and rose. "I will send you word tomorrow at midday. Thank you for presenting this to me. You have done the right thing." He offered a meager bow and indicated the door. "My servants will escort you out."

Dom Enrique wanted to protest, but knew it would be unwise. He bowed to Don Oviedo respectfully and was relieved as he saw van Zwolle do the same. "I appreciate the time you have given us." With a final flourish, Dom Enrique and van Zwolle left the Harbor Master alone. They were almost to the stairs when a servant found them to lead them out.

The courtyard was all but deserted; the wind rampaged through it, bludgeoning shutters and pounding on the walls. Both Dom Enrique and van Zwolle had to clutch their hats to their heads to keep them from being snatched away.

"There will be rain within the hour," van Zwolle shouted to make himself heard.

"Then we will have to hurry," Dom Enrique yelled back. "We would not want to arrive at Dona Amelia's drenched."

"Do you still insist on going there?" van Zwolle asked, prepared to argue with Dom Enrique.

"We must celebrate. Where better to wait out the storm?" He was half-running now, taking the wind head-on and laughing at it.

"And if we cannot return to the posada before Don Oviedo's men reach it tomorrow at noon?" He did not like to think how unfavorably that would be received by the Harbor Master.

"We will. I will leave word we are to be wakened before ten. No matter how bad the storm we should be able to get from Dona Amelia's to the posada in an hour; we will break our fast at Dona Amelia's and it will not matter if we delay our noon meal." He rocked on his heels as the wind buffeted him.

Van Zwolle sighed, and prepared to follow Dom Enrique to the whorehouse, though he thought it was too early to celebrate and too stormy to enjoy the night.

In his office Don Oviedo finished his first memorandum to Presidencia Don Augustin, and reached for another sheet of vellum: *To the respected agent Lazaro Cerritos,* he wrote. *I have just received a deed of gift requiring your review. If you would do me the kindness of coming here next Thursday at three in the afternoon, I will present this to you for your evaluation. I will require a report from you, made under oath to be received here no later than the fifteenth of March. I trust this will not inconvenience you.* His signature was an incomprehensible scrawl but the seal of the Almirancion was unmistakable. When he finished sanding the message, he rang for a servant. "This is to be taken to the house of Lazaro Cerritos. I do not know where it is, but someone will provide his direction. He is to have it in his hands tonight. You will have to see him personally. Do not entrust this to a servant." The memorandum to the Presidencia would be delivered more formally in the morning.

The servant bowed, thinking the evening was too ferocious to venture out into. He left the Harbor Master alone, and cursed his fate as he went to the clerk at the entrance to the building to find out where Lazaro Cerritos lived. "I hope it is not far, or in a steep street," he complained as the young man consulted a large, leather-bound record book.

"Not far at all." He scribbled an address on a slip of vellum. "Here. Turn to the right at the old church San Rafael el Arcangel. It is two streets further on, to the left, the fourth house on the right."

The servant sighed. "At least it is not on the far side of the city."

"Verdadamente," said the clerk as the servant went out into the gathering storm.

Just as the servant reached the little church of San Rafael el Arcangel, Dom Enrique was tugging on the bell-pull of Dona Amelia's house, calling out for someone to open the gate.

Two men opened it for him, both of them large, strong young men with hard faces and cold eyes.

"We are expected," said Dom Enrique, indicating van Zwolle with a sweep of his hand.

"The storm is going to be very bad," said the taller of the two.

"All the more reason to pass the time in pleasant amusements," said Dom Enrique, stepping through the gate. "Let us get indoors before the rain."

The two men stood aside, one of them saying something under his breath in the language of the natives, the other shrugging as they closed the wrought-iron door behind the new arrivals.

Dona Amelia herself greeted Dom Enrique as he came into the house. She was not as effusive as she usually was and her expression was not as accommodating.

"Do not worry, my girl," Dom Enrique assured her. "I have here fifteen gold reales to pay for the evening."

"A handsome sum," she said, trying to sound enthusiastic. "There will be a supper laid for you at midnight, if the storm is not too severe."

"Why should that matter?" Dom Enrique asked her, putting his arm around her waist and pulling her toward him, nuzzling her neck as she came near enough. "You smell so good."

"If the storm is severe, trees may fall, the roof may be damaged, and there could be shutters torn off by the wind," said Dona Amelia, unresponsive to his seductiveness.

"It will not be so bad," said Dom Enrique, impatient with her for delaying their enjoyment of one another.

She tugged free of him, her manner brisk. "That is nothing for you to say. This is not your house, and if it is damaged it is only inconvenient. But if something should go wrong—truly wrong—I will be without a business and that troubles me, Dom Enrique."

"You are not without friends," said Dom Enrique, determined to bring her back to him.

"I am also not without enemies. All women in this line of work are not favored by the authorities, not officially. What they do privately is another matter, but it is nothing I or any other woman like me can depend upon." She tossed her head. "Floria will tend to you, Dom Enrique, and your friend may choose among my girls who are not already spoken for tonight. There is a girl from the South Seas who is quite lovely and knows only a dozen words of Spanish."

Van Zwolle heard this with interest. He had heard many tales of women from the South Seas, all of them intriguing. Such a woman would not object to his curses or his roughness; it was known that all native women liked their men to be strong with them, not like European women, who cringed and complained if their men did more than strike them with an open hand. "Show me which she is."

Dom Enrique was dangerously near pouting, but he allowed himself to be led into the main reception room where a number of beautiful and exotic women waited for their evenings to be filled. The room itself was wonderfully and eclectically arrayed with silks from China and Japan, pillows from Morocco, brass tables from Turkey, and masks of silver taken from the peoples of the Audiencia de Mexico fifty years ago. The women were dressed with as much variety, many wearing jewelry on their ankles as well as on their fingers, wrists and necks. The earrings were lavish, many with jewels winking in them. One woman in gauzy silks had chains of coins draped around her waist and her eyes were outlined in dark paint.

"The tall one is the girl I mentioned," said Dona Amelia, standing aside so that van Zwolle could have his pick of them. "If she does not please you, there are others." She turned to Dom Enrique, keeping her distance from him. "Floria is in the second room at the top of the stairs, the one with the hawk on the door."

Dom Enrique did not like to be dismissed; at the same time, he did not want to linger while van Zwolle decided which of these women most delighted him. He compromised by saying, "If you want two of them, I will pay for it." It was doubly satisfying to realize that San Germanno's money was paying for the evening. The strongbox he had found in San Germanno's house, unbeknownst to van Zwolle, had held thirty gold reales and eighty silver angeles, enough to keep them in style until Don Oviedo released the ships to them.

Van Zwolle's face lit up. "Excellent." For the first time that evening he began to feel they would succeed. His hunger increased sharply as he gazed at the women. "The dark one," he said at last, pointing.

"I will leave you to your decision," said Dom Enrique with a deep bow. "I will want wine," he said to Dona Amelia.

"There is a bottle in the room with Floria," said Dona Amelia with an uneasy glance at the shutters as the first of the rain struck.

"I should not have spoken," Dom Enrique said as a kind of apology.

"Enjoy yourself," van Zwolle said over his shoulder.

"And you," was Dom Enrique's departing remark; it was almost lost in the clatter of the rain.

Text of a letter from Gennaro Colonna to his cousin, Jules, Cardinal Mazarin, First Minister of France, written in Italian.

To my most revered and esteemed cousin, Giulio Mazarini now calling himself Jules Mazarin, former Abbe and now First Minister of France, the greetings of his most grateful cousin, Gennaro Colonna, in Maracaibo, Audiencia of Santo Domingo, the Viceroyalty of Nueva España, on the eve of his entry into the Passionist Order.

I pray you will bless me in my endeavor, good cousin, for this is truly the most momentous occasion of my life. I am called of God. That has become clear to me in the last year, and I can no longer refuse the summons of that sweet inner voice, nor do I wish to. Now that I have studied to be a healer, I can think of nothing more fitting than I dedicate my life to God, Who makes all healing possible, and Who is the font of mercy for all suffering humanity. This is not the result of the sin of pride that I seek to give myself and my skills to God's cause in this New World. No man may truly call himself physician if he will not rely on God's help in all his work, and I am no exception to this rule.

My training will begin in two months, and I am already preparing myself for the disciplines that will be imposed on me. I realize I will have to temper my skills with the requirements of my Order, for Obedience is one of the Rules we follow, as do all those dedicating their lives to the service of God. In this capacity, I will not be permitted to correspond with you or anyone known to me before I enter the Order for a period of five years. I tell you this so that you need not fear on my behalf when you have no word from me. Rest assured that I am in the care of my Order and under the protection of God. I am willing to accept whatever God sends me to do, and if that includes the sacrifice of my life, I cannot give it for better purpose. I have given your name to the Superior of my community, in case any notification must be made. You are the only member of the family I have revealed, and it is fitting, because without your wise advice I would not have achieved this gift God has given me. I rely on you to inform all our family should any misadventure befall me. You will be the first I will contact once I am again permitted to correspond with those from my worldly life.

Should it happen that through Bondama Clemens you have occasion to exchange word with San Germanno, I pray you will extend to him my most profound thanks for all he has done for me, and tell him I will mention him each night when I commend myself to God. Had he not restored me to life when all was thought lost, I would never have known the joy of salvation. My gratitude to him is unending. As yours should be, sweet cousin, for he made me aware of how I had erred in a way you and all your preaching and admonitions could not do. I do not fault your for your efforts; everything you told me has proven to be correct and for that I am humbly in your debt. Had you not concerned yourself with the fate of my soul, I would face perdition now; I am aware of how much you tried to show me the magnitude of the sins I had committed and what awaited me if I died without repenting my wrongs. But it was San Germanno who dedicated himself to my recovery when all others were preparing my Requiem, and that selfless determination has become my model as a physician and will continue to inspire me, I hope, when I have become one of the Passionists.

Until I write to you again, I ask you to remember me in your prayers as I will remember you in mine.

He who in the world was your cousin
Gennaro Colonna
By my own hand, the 2nd day of March in God's Year 1648

9

Oaxetli drew her shawl more closely around her shoulders and did her best to smile at San Germanno. "I am sorry," she whispered, huddling on her bed, her two blankets in disarray at her feet. She had passed from fever to chills again with frightening suddenness. "I did not—"

"You have no reason to be sorry; you have done nothing wrong," he said as he wiped her vomit from his clothes. "It is not your fault you are ill."

"You could have been gone from here had I not . . . " Her words straggled off as she gagged again. "You could have left me here."

"No, I could not," he said sternly, helping her reclaim her blankets. "As I have told you before."

"But you have nothing to gain by remaining," she said, and retched. "God, what is happening to me?"

He held out a pail for her, but this time it was unnecessary; she had nothing more in her stomach. As she clutched the edge of the bed, he told her, "Your illness is not any infection I have ever seen, and I have seen many," he said when he was certain he had her attention. He said it as gently as he could. "I fear you have been poisoned, Oaxetli."

"So you intimated yesterday," she said a little later, her voice shaky. She was trying to keep herself under control but so far was not able to. "But who would poison me? And why?"

"I think we both have an answer to that," he said dryly.

"You cannot be right. Dona Azul is a religious. She may be glad I am ill, but it would not be fitting for her to do me harm." There was a stubborn light in her fever-glazed eyes.

"And no one ever hurt another person in the cause of religion?" he asked with such sadness that she was unable to answer at once.

"No. I didn't mean that," she whispered. "Certainly not. The priests of the old gods killed thousands upon thousands to honor the gods of the earth." She struggled to make herself comfortable.

"And not those priests alone," San Germanno added, recalling the slaughter he had seen over the centuries; it was at its worst when the cause was religious.

She shivered and clung to her blankets. "So many gods want blood on their altars."

Realizing she was too exhausted to deal with these questions, he said, "I will not tire you with these unhappy thoughts."

"I wish I could go to the bathhouse," she complained. "But I am ill, and they would not allow me inside."

"You would be warmer," San Germanno said, watching the tremors pass through her.

Oaxetli reached out for his arm. "I must continue to put my attention on things other than my body. If I do not, I will despair."

There had been many times at the Temple of Imhotep he had experienced this insistence by those gravely ill to seek refuge in distractions; often it was the only relief he could provide to those suffering.

He put the pail aside and sat down on the stool beside the bed. "Very well. What do you want to talk about?"

Her brief, difficult smile expressed her gratitude eloquently. "You said that we harm one another for faith. Surely that is not true of the Christians?" She looked more composed as she asked.

"Thousands of your people have died because the Spanish came here, and they are Christians," said San Germanno levelly. "Your people have died from disease and battle and the demands of the Spanish for laborers: that cannot be excused by conversion." He said nothing of the abattoir Europe had become as Protestants and Catholics battled to show their devotion to the Prince of Peace.

"But those who have died in the service of the Spanish have found salvation, and they have not had to fear the wrath of the gods who demanded living human hearts for their tribute," she said quietly, her breath coming in wheezes. "The priests of the old gods slaughtered thousands to appease the earth with the blood of innocents."

"Is that what you were taught by the nuns?" San Germanno asked, not expecting an answer.

"It is taught by the Padres and Freyes, the ones who took me in when my own family abandoned me. I cannot think badly of them, for they gave me charity when no one else would. They showed me compassion when my family would not. Their ways have been kind. I have believed their teaching; I have had no reason to doubt them." She closed her eyes, shaking with the pain of body cramps which had tortured her for the last four days. "I'm so thirsty."

"Let me get you something to drink," San Germanno offered. He had prepared a number of compounds that would lessen the impact of the poison, but so far, Oaxetli had refused to take any of them, preferring water to medicine.

"No. I will not keep it in me." She sighed heavily and lay back as he put her blankets back over her body. "You need not spend all your time with me, Conde. I do not expect it of you. As much as it pleases me to talk, I do not want to keep you from things you must do."

"Do I distress you?" he asked, knowing the answer already.

"Yes." The word was nothing more than a breath. She recovered enough to say, "You have better things to do."

"I cannot think what they would be; if you would be easier for you if I left, tell me," San Germanno said to her and saw her shake her head. "I have a wet cloth. Let me put it across your eyes." The cloth held soothing herbs that would help reduce her headache.

"Then tell me why you ask so many questions about the cloth these people make." She fidgeted, but gave a nod of agreement. "My hands are swollen," she complained as she tugged the blankets up to her throat.

"Yes, they are," he said, seeing the telltale redness around her nails and her cracked knuckles. There were similar patches on her arms and chest and back. Beyond question Oaxetli was being poisoned. Gently he put the cloth over her eyes and stepped back from the side of her bed so as not to trouble her with his nearness. The poison was relentless in its ravages, leaving him feeling helpless to combat it. He had not yet discovered how the poison was being administered: it was not in her food or her water, of that he was certain. His attempts to examine her clothing and bedding had been inconclusive, revealing nothing more than traces of a substance he did not recognize. Since the first symptoms appeared ten days earlier, he had tried to find out what was being used, but so far he had not succeeded. "I was curious about the cloth because I had not seen its like in the New World before, and only a few times in the Old. The fibers used here are not like those of the Old World, so it struck me that these people may have found it on their own."

"They say the Dona Azul, the first one, taught them," she replied. "They had used the fibers for making nets and baskets before, or so the women told me." The smile she attempted was heart-breaking. "And my face feels . . . tight." She was apologizing again, as much for her distrust of him as for her deteriorating health.

He did not want to tell her that her cheeks and forehead were covered with abrasions and skin eruptions; it would serve no purpose but to alarm her. He paused. "Do you want to be alone?"

"Not yet," she said with urgency. "You are . . . dreadful, but not so dreadful as lying here alone. You are good at nursing me, I know it." This confession ended in spasmodic coughing; she motioned to San Germanno to keep away from her. "Give me nothing. I want nothing of yours."

He realized the reason for her anguish: his own was almost as keen. "Oaxetli, I will not force my blood or my love on you. I ceased that folly more years ago than you could reckon. When I offered to share it with you, it was to save your life, for it is all I can do now. You refused." His words became softer. "I would not compel you to take what you . . . loathe."

She turned away from him. "It is not you I . . . I . . . "

"Abhor," he finished for her, the word emotionless.

"Yes," she admitted, her face turned toward the sound of his voice. "I do abhor the thing you are, but I esteem you, Conde. As we are told to hate the sin and love the sinner." Her face flushed as her fever returned; she wrestled her blankets from around her shoulders to just above her waist.

He glanced toward the window and the spring-brightened hillsides beyond. "In my case, it is somewhat more complex. I fear, querida, that who I am and what I am are the same thing."

"But you could give up—" she began impetuously.

"No, I could not—any more than you could give up eating, Oaxetli, or breath; there have been long periods when I could not take blood as I would prefer, but the need, the esurience, never left me." He returned his full attention to her, sympathy and regret in his face which she could not see. "If I had syrup of poppies, you would have less pain." If he only had a few of the supplies he had left in his laboratory at his house in Acapulco!

"So you've told me. The willow is helpful." She put her hand to the cloth over her eyes as if to block out an unwelcome sight. "Have many taken your blood? Have they been willing to have it?"

The answer was not an easy one, for he realized his candor would increase her repugnance. "Not many. A few."

"And they became like you for it?" Agitation made her breathing uneven. "Your blood changed them when they died?"

"Yes," he said.

"And those you came to as you came to me, they accepted you? They did not turn away from you because of what you are?" She was visibly upset by her own question.

He leaned forward, his voice deep and filled with kindness. "Do not fret, Oaxetli. I was in earnest when I told you I do not impose on those who do not want me. It provides nothing for either of us if I do." Except in dreams, he added inwardly, if they had not spurned him before; the pleasure of the dreams he provided had in the past sustained him for decades on end.

"Tell me what I want to know," she insisted with fragile determination.

"All right." He sat back. "Some did, some did not. Most would have preferred another lover to me, but took what I offered in place of their true desires." Two millennia ago such a recognition would have sunk him into despair; now he could speak of it with only a trace of melancholy.

"And you were not jealous?" she asked in surprise.

"Why should I be jealous?" he countered. "For those of my nature jealousy is . . . impractical." His single chuckle was without anger. "And your lives are so short, it is folly to waste precious time in jealousy." There had been a time, so long ago he barely remembered it, when he had been jealous of life itself, and those who had the capacity to engender life, but that had faded before he left Nineveh.

She considered his answer. "Were all of them women, these lovers?"

"Most of them," he replied. "There have been a few men; and one remarkable child came to me out of . . . worship."

"A child?" she repeated, aghast. "How could a child be willing to . . . do what you require?"

"He was a child in years only," said San Germanno, his recollection of Tibet acute to the point of hurt. "He knew me for what I am when we met, and he sought me out for healing." The healing, he did not add, was his, not SGyi Zhel-ri's. He saw that she was starting to doze, so he said nothing more.

A short time later she stirred. "And the men? Did they seek you out? Or did you pursue them?"

"One did: sought me out." Kozrozd had accepted his blood in order to live as he would have accepted anything from Sanct' Germain Franciscus; the gift proved fleeting enough, for Kozrozd had died the True Death not long after on the sands of the Roman Circus. "The others I approached."

"And did they receive you as you wanted? It is a sin to do it." She stifled more coughing. "Did they?"

"All but two did," he answered. "One tried to kill me because he was shamed by his desire. The other . . . " He did not go on: the memory of Yslan and his betrayal was too painful, even after a thousand years, to speak of.

Oaxetli shuddered. "Are women . . . better?"

"Not better, no." He frowned, his dark eyes focused inward. "Women who seek men know they will find someone unlike themselves, and so my . . . strangeness is not so alien that all of them reject it out of hand; they are willing to accept the pleasure I can give. Men who seek men expect to find the same as they are, which I cannot be. Men are more troubled by my impotence than women are."

"Is it so simple as that?" Oaxetli asked.

"No; but this is a part of it, I have come to think." He saw her begin to convulse and moved to hold her down. "Do not be afraid of me, Oaxetli. I will not require anything of you. I want only to help you."

She tried to speak and failed. She felt his strength and took solace from it. As she regained some control of her flailing body, she murmured, "Soon."

He knew what she meant; the nearness of her death was an all-but-palpable presence in the little house; as much as he wanted to, he could not save her if she would not take blood from him. As she fell into an abrupt, fitful sleep, he returned to the stool and occupied his time folding herbs into more cloths to put over her eyes.

By midafternoon she had sunk into a delirium, her occasional bursts of speech no longer coherent. She had ceased to respond to anything said to her, or to the care San Germanno gave her.

Rogerio brought another pail of water and took away the one San Germanno had supplied in the morning. "Not much longer," he said quietly, his face creased with sympathy.

"No," San Germanno agreed. "Not long. It will be over before sunrise." He regarded Rogerio with stricken eyes. "What is doing it? It looks something like arsenic, that rash, but how is she given it? Her skin has those abrasions, and the crust has poison in it, but how did it get there?" Without warning he seized one of the earthenware oil lamps and flung it across the room, staring as it shattered against the wall. "Why can't I find it?" he demanded of the air. "How is it being done?"

Although he said nothing, Rogerio's faded-blue eyes revealed his dismay.

"It is not in her food, or her water. I have tested both and found nothing harmful. It is not in the utensils she uses. I have looked through her garments in case a vial was hidden there, but I have found nothing. I even examined the blade of her knife, in case that had been tainted, but nothing! I do not recognize the residue I have found which I think is generated by the poison. I have been thwarted at every effort I have made." He glowered at the open door leading to the empty sitting room. "And there is nothing—*nothing*—I can do."

"You offered her blood," Rogerio pointed out.

"And she will not take it. She would rather die than become one of my blood." He lowered his head in defeat.

Rogerio shook his head. "It is hard enough for you to live as you must. For her, being blind, to be a vampire would be . . . unimaginable. Do not think the less of her for preferring death." He was about to leave, but hesitated, and added, "You hold yourself to blame. You think if she had not come she would not be dying."

"Of course I think that," San Germanno said, his formidable self-possession restored again. "Were she still in Acapulco, the nuns would be looking after her, and although some of her work might be tedious, she would be alive."

"Yes. But she wanted to come with you. You told her there would be risks in travel. She could have refused." He bowed slightly. "You did not poison her, my master."

"No. But I brought her to where she was poisoned," San Germanno said quietly. "Go on. If there is anything you can do, I will call you."

Oaxetli lingered through the last of the day and into the night, her breathing growing more uneven as the hours went by, her skin more cracked. By evening she was no longer able to swallow anything, not even water. She had two more convulsive fits, each one weaker than the last. Her skin went from hot to clammy to hot again. Finally the effort to hold on to life was too great and she ceased to try; her heart fluttered and stopped and her breathing sighed to nothing.

San Germanno had stood beside her bed for the last of her struggle, his hand laid on hers for whatever comfort it could bring her; her coming death was as bitter to him as any he had known. He spoke to her from time to time, his voice low and soothing, offering her the solace of poetry. When it was over he took the cloth from her face, put her arms at her sides, then drew one of her blankets up and over her face before wrapping it securely around her as if to keep out the cold. He had long since lost count of the deaths he had witnessed; none of them were alike, although all were the same. How much and how often he longed for the luxury of weeping! The loss of Oaxetli filled him and he found no anodyne in knowing she had been willing to die. She had told him that among her people it was considered ill-omened for the dead to lie indoors. Grief made him clumsy; he kicked over the stool as he went to carry her out of the house. She was so light in his arms, as if the poison had consumed her insides leaving nothing more than a husk behind.

Rogerio was waiting for him by the fire-pit. "One of the guards has gone for Dona Azul," he said as if it had no importance for either of them.

"At least we can arrange for her burial; Dona Azul will not begrudge her that," San Germanno said distantly, thinking that he should do something more for her though it was past the point where there was anything he could do.

"She has what she wants from Oaxetli," said Rogerio, somewhat obliquely. "What will she do to get what she wants from you?"

San Germanno frowned with disgust. "Not now."

"Better now than later," Rogerio said firmly. "Without a translator we are at her mercy, and Dona Azul has little of that. She will take full advantage of you."

"You think we should leave this body and flee, taking our chances in the hills." He nodded once, showing he comprehended the suggestion. "We do not know this country, not as the people of this valley do. We do not know what lies beyond the valley to any direction but the south, where they will expect us to go. How far would we get, do you suppose, before they caught us again? We would have to leave all our things behind, including my native earth. Once the sun rose, I would have to seek shelter for the day, and that would give them an advantage in hunting us. My strength would fade rapidly." He carried Oaxetli to the long bench near the fire-pit and set her down, taking care to keep the blanket securely around her.

"I think it is our only chance. If we remain we will be wholly in their hands, with no means to appeal to their compassion, if they possess any. We have escaped with less and prevailed," he reminded San Germanno.

"True enough," San Germanno said.

"You are not going to make the effort, are you?" Rogerio asked, knowing the answer.

"What would be the use?" San Germanno responded, his tone light and disinterested. "What would the advantage be?"

"You cannot speak in your defense," Rogerio persisted, "not without Oaxetli to translate for you."

"I have learned some of their tongue; I should comprehend most of what they say. I would rather know what we are supposed to have done than flee without discovering what they have decided has happened here." He regarded Rogerio steadily. "You need not remain, old friend, if you would rather not."

Rogerio made an impatient gesture. "You do not truly believe I would go when you are in danger, my master."

"Let us say I hoped you would not; I would not fault you for going," San Germanno said with a wry, fleeting smile. "If we have guards around us here, we must assume that there are others posted about the valley, charged with our capture if we leave. It would be foolish for us to try to get beyond this place without some information about the guards, or the country."

"And how are we to acquire that, pray?" Rogerio turned on his heel and walked a short distance away from San Germanno. "This is not Russia, or Tunis, or the Polish marshes. We are not wholly isolated. There are Spanish monks and soldiers twenty leagues from here."

"That is supposing we could reach them. Without our horses and mules, I doubt we would have that opportunity; they will not let us near our mounts. These people would anticipate our intentions; they are not stupid. And when they caught us again, they might well suppose we were guilty of more than a wish to be gone from here." He said it reasonably enough, but under his words was an agony that was too enormous for anything but howls.

"If you insist on putting yourself in danger to show you are mourning, there is little I can do about it." Rogerio folded his arms and shook his head. "But I will not stand by and see you take punishment for something you did not do."

"I might as well have killed her," San Germanno said quietly. "I could not keep her from dying."

There was a clamor of bells from the far end of the village, and in spite of the lateness, the people came rushing from their houses in answer to the summons.

"She could have lived," Rogerio said over the sound of the bells.

"Not as she would have had to live," San Germanno replied, his dark eyes enigmatic. "You are right: a vampire would suffer terribly if she were blind. And she thought vampires hideous."

Rogerio knew that at the moment San Germanno agreed with her, but he said nothing of this. "Let me at least prepare our things for travel. It may be we will need them, and with little time to ready ourselves."

"You think we will be exiled?" San Germanno asked, and nodded once in agreement. "Well, it is possible, I suppose, though I expect they will abandon us without food or water if they let us live." He looked down at where Oaxetli lay. "She was a fine woman, fine and brave. She deserved better than this."

"Yes," Rogerio said.

"If she had been willing to . . . to accept what I am . . . and taken my blood . . . " He was unable to finish as the loss of her transfixed him with sorrow. It had been agonizing to lose Acanna Tupac; with Oaxetli dead he was wholly bereft.

"You said yourself she was not. There was nothing you could do to change that, as you could not persuade her to let you prevent her true death." Rogerio glanced over his shoulder and saw villagers approaching carrying torches.

"Yes, I see them, too," San Germanno said as he came to Rogerio's side. "And unless I have lost all sense, there are more guards dispatched into the hills as we speak. Dona Azul has not had her say yet, and she will want it." He went back to Oaxetli's side. "I hope she will pardon me for bringing her here and to her death."

"Why would she not?" Rogerio asked, and wished the words unspoken as he saw the expression on San Germanno's face.

The people of the village were getting closer, close enough for San Germanno to see the men were carrying spears as well as torches. Dona Azul was borne in their midst on her platform chair, a blue chaplet around her head.

"They were waiting for her to die," San Germanno said with certainty. "They knew."

"And you? You knew she was dying," Rogerio reminded him.

"I knew she was being poisoned," San Germanno said. "Whatever they used, however they administered it and whoever used it, the stuff was potent."

Rogerio was about to say something more when the noise of the approaching villagers became too overwhelming for speech. Two of the guards posted at the houses came forward and prostrated themselves before Dona Azul, reciting their verses of adulation together.

"They say she is the promise, or sign of the sky-god, their . . . I think the word is hostage, or prize. She is the link to the sky-god and his will," San Germanno spoke softly to Rogerio, knowing he was being heard.

"Are you certain?" Rogerio asked uneasily. "These are not the verses they've recited before."

"Fairly certain," San Germanno answered.

The villagers made a path for Dona Azul as the men lowered her platform from their shoulders, and those carrying bells shook and struck them with deafening thoroughness.

As Dona Azul approached San Germanno, the people grew silent, watching these unfamiliar developments with intensity and apprehension. When she was an armslength from San Germanno, she said, "The woman died."

San Germanno indicated Oaxetli's body but said nothing.

"She was killed," Dona Azul declared without looking toward Oax-etli. "It was clear from the first."

"She is gone," San Germanno said in Dona Azul's language, his speech deliberately awkward.

Startled to hear him use words she knew, Dona Azul peered narrowly at him. "How much do you understand?"

"I know little," he said, making a gesture of helplessness and choosing the wrong form of little to seem more incapable than he was.

She spat to show derision. "You are nothing but a fool. It is in your face. Foreigners know nothing."

"I know little," San Germanno repeated with the same mistake as before.

Abruptly she signaled to the guards lying prone before her. "Keep them in their house. Do not let them out for any reason until I decide what is to be done with them. And bring that corpse with you. We will have to put it with those who do not worship the sky-god." With that, she swung around and faced the villagers and launched into another harangue. "The woman died because she would not leave the foreigners. We offered her our village as a haven against the outer world where there is nothing but sin. She refused our offer of safety in favor of the foreigners. She was their slave, and her death does nothing to expiate the sins of all of us, for she made petty errors which have little redemption in them."

Three of the bell-ringers let out a volley of noise.

"The women in the bathhouse told her that she would be held accountable for her decision to keep with the foreigners." Dona Azul lifted her hands to the sky in the ritualistic posture San Germanno had come to recognize. "She was given a place among the women, though she could not see, and would have been protected from sins."

"I don't like the implications she is making," whispered Rogerio.

"Nor I," San Germanno agreed in an undervoice.

"This woman has died at the hands of the foreigners. She has suffered the fate of those who serve false leaders." Her voice was loud and nasty.

"I did not—" San Germanno began in the language of the people of the village.

"You did not save her!" Dona Azul cried in triumph. "You cannot save her!"

Rogerio plucked at San Germanno's sleeve. "Keep away from her, my master."

Nodding his compliance, San Germanno took one step back as Dona Azul swung around to face him.

"Your flesh poisoned hers. Your body contaminated hers. When you lay with her, your vileness and sin entered her where she was purified and turned her cleanliness to putrefaction." She did not wait for the bells this time but leaned forward, screaming over the cacophony, "You were the cause of her dying!"

San Germanno studied her closely. He had understood enough of her accusations that he began to suspect what had been done to Oaxetli. "The cloth the women use to bathe. That was how you did it, wasn't it? Yes. Yes." He spoke in Spanish, knowing it would be folly to confront Dona Azul even if he had sufficient command of her language to do it. "You put something in the cloth she used in the bath, didn't you, something deadly. When she rubbed the rough cloth on her skin, and it scratched her, the poison entered her flesh. No wonder there were raw patches on her face and body. No wonder she got worse." He tried to meet Rogerio's eyes, wanting confirmation of his accusation of Dona Azul; finally his manservant looked at him, giving the smallest of nods. "I should have *seen* it when it began. Why did you not suspect this old friend?"

Rogerio stared in increasing astonishment, then turned his horrified gaze on Oaxetli's blanketed body. "Why—"

It was the opportunity Dona Azul had sought. "This man killed this woman; her death is deliberate murder, not an error. He has sinned very much. No wonder his servant has been silent: he fears what will become of him. The stranger, San Germanno, polluted the woman Oaxetli with the venom of serpents, scorpions, and spiders. He anointed her with this when he had his pleasure of her, to keep his seed from growing in her, to ensure her fidelity. It was the callous act of a man who seeks only his own satisfaction. Because he was far away from his own people, he thought he could act with impunity. He came here to keep us from attaining the favor of the sky-god. He has the cardinal crime upon his soul, with the additional crimes of deception and malice." She leveled her hand at San Germanno. "Look at him. He reeks of his wrongs. The body of his harlot accuses him where she lies, newly dead."

Again the bells sounded; the people behind her were becoming frightened and eager at once.

San Germanno wished he had learned more of the language and could use it better, for he wanted to be fully cognizant of the implications of the accusations against him, and to anticipate what Dona Azul was demanding as punishment. He hoped he would be able to reason with her, no matter how grim her sentence might be.

"The sacrifice will bring great redemption to us. He is so much in error, he will produce much expiation. Dona Azul promised that any false man sacrificed would be especially pleasing to the sky-god." She shouted in order to be heard over the bells. "We will be thankful for his sins because the sky-god will show us his favor and grant us redemption when we offer him so much sin. The sacrifice will be worthy of many good things."

"At least I know how she died," San Germanno said to Rogerio as he observed the growing frenzy of the people with Dona Azul; they were moaning, swaying, lifting their hands as Dona Azul had lifted hers, all of them seeking the sky-god through Dona Azul. The bells added their metallic voices to the whole.

"Be glad that we have such a sacrifice!" Dona Azul exulted. "Be grateful that all of you are sure of salvation through his pain!"

As four armed men approached him, San Germanno said to Rogerio in the Latin of Imperial Rome, "I am sorry, old friend. I did not anticipate that we would not have time to leave. I assumed this would happen later. Forgive me for my error. I thought there would be a chance to—"

"Bargain," Rogerio finished for him as he was seized by two of the men. "I know. You did not want to face more death. You have tried to do this before. There have been times you succeeded."

"Yes; though it would seem I am wrong just now," he added ironically as the men shoved him in the direction of his house. He did not resist them; he did not want to give them any excuse to fight with him. Beyond any question, he would need all his strength for whatever was coming.

"See that they are not harmed," Dona Azul commanded. "To be worthy of sacrifice, he must be thanked and honored for his sins, so that he will be pleasing to the sky-god. His sins must be rank so that no punishment of ours will lessen them for the sky-god through suffering."

One of the men struck San Germanno on the shoulder; the blow was deliberately softened. "You will redeem us. You are our contrition."

San Germanno still did not struggle; he called out to Rogerio. "We have endured worse. And night is on our side."

Rogerio's answer was drowned in a crescendo of shouts and clanging bells.

"He will serve the sky-god well with his agony!" Dona Azul screamed. One of the armed men laughed, but the rest were solemn as they forced San Germanno and Rogerio back into the little house that had been provided for them; the shouts and clanging of Dona Azul's followers accompanied them the whole distance and remained, engulfing them in their presence, as the door was closed and barred.

Text of a letter from Lazaro Cerritos to the Harbor Master Don Oviedo Carterez y Atrevido and Don Augustin Murado y Bonsuerte, Presidencia of Acapulco, Audiencia de Mexico, Viceroyalty of Nueva España.

To the most honorable administrators, Don Oviedo Carterez y Atrevido, Harbor Master, and Presidencia Don Augustin Murado y Bonsuerte, the respectful greetings of agent Lazaro Cerritos, regarding the deed of gift shown to me for my evaluation.

I have twice reviewed the deed of gift in question, the one granting the command, possession and revenues of the ships The Golden Empress *and* Queen of the Pacific *along with the use of the staff and residence in Acapulco, currently the property of Francisco Ragoczy, el Conde de San Germanno to Dom Enrique Vilhao, Portuguese hidalgo. Included in this deed of gift are certain sums of money which have already passed into Dom Enrique's hands, and are therefore not the subject of my observations.*

As Don Oviedo is aware, I have served as agent for el Conde de San Germanno for a decade. Most of that time, San Germanno was in the city of Cuzco, the Audiencia de Lima, Viceroyalty of Peru, and he was content at that time to leave the functions of his business dealings in my hands. I have provided him with reports when each of his ships has returned to Acapulco from Manila and other Oriental ports. He, in turn, has sent instructions to me regarding his wishes as they pertain to his property and the voyages of his ships. He has always included a phrase of recognition in his communications to ensure that no false instructions should reach me and cause me to fail to carry out his orders. Although San Germanno left Acapulco some months ago, he left me no instructions regarding any change in how his business is to be done, and I have not received any such notification since.

Such matters in and of themselves would not cause me apprehension as the lack of his countersign on the deed of gift does, for surely he knows you would have to submit this for my review, and it would be appropriate for him to provide the phrase he has used in the past. The lack of it troubles me, and would give me reason enough to withhold my acceptance of its genuineness but there is another, more telling factor in the deed of gift that convinces me it is a forgery: the signature is not San Germanno's. I have many letters written in his own hand, and I am familiar with his style of writing. He does not use the flourishes found in this deed of gift. Indeed, San Germanno's hand is small and neat, the letters precise and clear. I am most certain in the formations of the S and the G, for these elaborate letters are nothing like his.

I regret to tell you, Don Oviedo and Don Augustin, that Dom Enrique Vilhao has presented you with a forgery. It may be that he accepted the deed of gift in good faith, from someone purporting to be San Germanno, and therefore Dom Enrique is as abused as your offices are by this deed of gift. You say Dom Enrique claims acquaintance with San Germanno, and if this is true, it means that Dom Enrique is at the heart of this terrible mischief; it is possible, however, that he has met with a clever imposter who has convinced him of his legitimacy and imposed upon him for reasons of his own. I am not willing to accuse Dom Enrique of knowingly committing a crime, but I do say he has been much abused by a criminal.

It is my own belief that this document accounts in some way for San Germanno's long absence. I now expect a demand of ransom for him by the criminal who has provided Dom Enrique with this deed of gift. Whatever the association of Dom Enrique and this unknown miscreant may be, I recommend that Dom Enrique and his Dutch companion be held for questioning in this regard, and that San Germanno's house be put under constant watch, in case there are thieves seeking to plunder it.

I regret that I cannot render a more favorable opinion in this matter, and I commend my findings to you, Don Oviedo and Don Augustin, for your thoughtful review. May God guide your decisions and bring justice to Dom Enrique as well as San Germanno, whatever that may be.

Lazaro Cerritos
Merchants' agent
By my own hand, the 11th day of March, 1648

10

Not long before dawn they came and stripped him of everything but a single rough cloth tied around his loins; he supposed it was the same kind of cloth that had been used to murder Oaxetli. San Germanno said nothing as Dona Azul supervised the armed men at their tasks.

"Such scars, and so many," she said, touching the pale flesh in a slow caress, and looking speculatively at San Germanno. "These were not from wounds of battle. What crime brought you these?"

"The crime of serving my enemies," said San Germanno in Spanish, recalling the dread he had inspired in the man who had defeated his father when he had turned the tide of battle with his enslaved troops. He added in her language, "No crime."

"Severe punishment for no crime," she said, and indicated the men should take him outside. "You know how we will sacrifice you?"

"I know," he said; over the past two days since Oaxetli's death, he had thought of little else.

"It is as Dona Azul taught us." She was smug with satisfaction. "It is the way of the sky-god."

He spoke to her in her own tongue once more. "Sunlight hurts me." He caught her attention with the force of his speech.

"So. You understand more than you pretend," she said. "You are afraid of the sky-god if you turn away from the sun. That is good, for you will give the sky-god more honor with your fear."

San Germanno had endured the sun without the protection of his native earth in his shoes and each time had left him in horrendous pain and severely weakened. He realized that if Dona Azul suspected any of this, she would relish the knowledge. "One day," he said in her language, "men will come. They will teach what Dona Azul tried to teach you."

"Francisco, the real Francisco, will come again, and we will know him for he will give me a living child." She spat on him. "And the sky-god will ask no more sacrifices and will grant us salvation."

He would not respond to her insult. "My man. What of him?"

"He is nothing," said Dona Azul.

"What will you do to him?" San Germanno insisted. He knew Rogerio lay awake in the other chamber, listening to what was being said. Perhaps he would have enough warning from what he heard to prepare himself.

She sighed and answered as if providing San Germanno a great indulgence. "We will take him away from this valley and we will give him a skin of water. The sky-god will decide if he will live or die."

"In that case, I pray you will give him some time to prepare himself." He hoped Rogerio had overheard as he intended. It was the most he could trust to happen; he was aware of it, and yet it rankled that he could get so little for Rogerio after his centuries of service. He was sorry he could not apologize now. He regarded Dona Azul thoughtfully. "Is this for the sky-god, or are you doing this for your own liking?"

"I do what I am bound to do," she said. "I am Dona Azul."

He was aware she would not admit to her gratification at his ordeal. "And my servant? You have not yet said what you will do."

Her laughter was filled with rancor. "He helped you deceive me. Much worse could be done to him and no one would question it."

San Germanno nodded, and prepared himself as best he could for what was to come. He winced as the door was flung open and the long soft rays of sunrise struck his exposed skin. His guards prodded him forward, out of the little house.

At first the tingling was not unpleasant, hardly more than the shiver brought on by a grue up the spine. But soon he was seized with a headache and a queasiness he had to clamp his jaw against. By the time they reached the earthen platform, moving was an effort and his vision had begun to swim.

The cross was tall, more than twice his height, and there were holes drilled in it for wooden spikes; more guards waited there, two with mallets in their hands. Most of the people of the village stood a short distance from the platform, silently waiting for their sacrifice to be made. It was difficult for San Germanno to focus his eyes on the cross, and as he did he bit back ironic laughter. A wooden cross with wooden spikes. At least it was not a stake through the heart, which would sever his spine and bring him the True Death; after an hour or two, he thought, he might long for the stake, or fire, or decapitation, to end the agony he knew was coming.

He did not waste his strength fighting the armed men; he would need every scrap of it later. As the first wooden spike was hammered through his wrist and into the hole behind, pain radiated up his arm and he pulled against the spike instinctively, only making the pain worse; he kept from crying out, for there was worse to come. The second spike was worse because the guard driving it through him twisted the spike deliberately, tearing skin and sinews. The back of San Germanno's mouth tasted of bile and copper.

"So little bleeding," Dona Azul marveled as the guards went to work on his feet. She stood over him as the work was done, watching the progress critically. "You will last a long time, I think. You will absolve many sins."

There was a reinforced hole dug for the foot of the cross. Using ropes and their own strength the guards lifted the cross up, up, and set it in place, with San Germanno hanging high above them in the morning sky.

Between the sunlight and the strain on his chest and shoulders, San Germanno passed the first hour in strident misery; his breathing was an effort as much because of the hanging weight of his body on his chest as the pulsating agony in his hands and feet. Had he been living as other men lived, his tongue would have swollen and choked him; as it was, he felt a constriction in his throat and mouth that after an hour or so made him pay less attention to the holes through his wrists and arches. Worst of all were the fulgent burns that blistered, peeled, then blistered his skin again before noon.

Below him, the people of the village stood with their hands raised as Dona Azul exhorted them, rejoicing in San Germanno's suffering as the means of their salvation. It was early afternoon before the people returned to their duties, leaving San Germanno to the gathering birds and the molten sky.

By midmorning, Rogerio had escaped his improvised cell and was on his way up the slope behind the village, a compass-point away from the platform where the villagers were engrossed in his master's torture. He carried one of the two chests of native earth from the dwindling supply strapped to his back in an improvised rope net, and the burden slowed him down; a number of tools were thrust through his belt, including a pouch of flint-and-steel to make fires. He paused once to look, and the shock of what he saw all but took his breath away, for although he was not of San Germanno's blood, he had seen often enough what sunlight could do to vampires and he was aware of how terribly San Germanno was being tormented; the burns alone were significantly more painful to him than to living humans, and though their damage was not lasting, the recovery from them was long and harrowing. Resolutely Rogerio set his eyes to the task of finding his master shelter—a cave or a ruin where he could bring San Germanno to recover in safety and darkness. At this time, he knew it would be folly to search out the missionaries, who would ask questions Rogerio would be hard put to answer, assuming he could find any within a day's walk. As he reached the crest of the hill, he looked up to see dark birds hovering in the sky, beginning to circle over the cross below. He would have to hurry if he intended to help San Germanno.

San Germanno could not scream or he would have ruined his voice by late afternoon; his tongue prevented him from making any sound louder than a whisper. His whole body, except for a small portion of his back, was one crusted mass of cracked and blackened skin. His eyes were like lava in his face and the movement of the breeze was atrocious to him. The slightest movement, from breathing to muscle spasms, gave him grinding hurt. Only his swath of scars remained unchanged.

When a buzzard had landed on the wooden cross-arm, San Germanno summoned up all his strength and shouted at the bird, driving it off for a time; it would return, with others, to await the one thing that would not come, no matter how fervently he longed for it. There were so many worse things than death: he had known this before he was sent to the Temple of Imhotep. He had lost track of time and his eyelids were burned closed so his only awareness of the ending of the day was a faint lessening in the ferocity of the sun. He longed for the respite of night, since the mercy of death was denied him.

Through the afternoon Rogerio walked swiftly, taking note of his surroundings so that he could find his way back to where San Germanno was. Often he paused to look backward so that he would recognize the landmarks as he made his way back to the valley. He had caught a rabbit and made a meal of it, knowing he might have long days without sustenance once he got San Germanno down from the cross. He remembered what had happened outside Baghdad and he shuddered, the recollection adding its urgency to his mission.

As the sun's rays grew long, he rounded a hillock and realized it was a partially buried structure, not a hill at all: roughly pyramidal in shape, its bulk was obscured by trees and brush. With the first glimmerings of optimism, Rogerio set about looking for an entrance to the building, and found it a short while later when a tremendous flight of bats emerged from a flank of the ruin into the fading day. Lacking San Germanno's keen eyesight, Rogerio took the time to make a torch before entering where the bats had left.

The passage was steep and narrow, corbel-arched of massive stones; it required ingenuity to fit the chest through the space. The steps down were slick with bat guano and smelled powerfully of excrement. Rogerio, who over the centuries had hidden in far worse places, wrinkled his nose and continued into the ruin, going carefully, marking his progress as he went by breaking off roots that had grown through the structure. As he went he began to hope he had stumbled upon the very sanctuary he sought.

At nightfall the villagers returned to the foot of the cross to listen to Dona Azul once again recite the tale of how Dona Azul had brought them salvation. Rogerio's escape had been discovered, and his theft of the chest; it was supposed he had taken what treasure he could and fled, leaving his master to the fate the sky-god decreed. Three armed men had been sent after him, but without any great determination or haste, for it was supposed the man would die from starvation or misadventure lost in the vast wilderness around them. Dona Azul declared his absence only added to the sacrifice and therefore to the redemption they would receive from the sky-god.

The sounds of the bells jarred San Germanno into semi-wakefulness, a state he did not seek or wish for. He thought fleetingly that it was probably just as well he had no reflection, for what he must look like now would surely be as horrifying to him as it would be to others, so horrendously burned he was. On the edge of delirium, this observation was amusing, and he had to make an effort not to smile and crack his sun-ravaged face further.

Dona Azul ended the celebration with the wish that they might see what the sky-god had done to San Germanno. It was not possible, for it would compromise the sacrifice, but she longed to view the degree of expiation he had provided. "His death," she announced, "is the triumph of us all. We are lifted up as he is, not to suffering but to glory, because all our errors and sins are given to him. When his body is picked clean, we will show reverence to his bones, and thank him for what he has done for us. It will bring us all the salvation he has forfeited with his death, as the son of the sky-god did twenty generations ago in the lands to the east." She began her slow dancing once more. "It is a holy time to die, and it is a holy death for him." Suddenly she stopped. "He was false, saying he was Francisco. Had he given me a living child, he might have brought us to the end of sin."

The bells sounded, but the ringers were tired and the sound faded quickly.

"At first light we return to give thanks to the sky-god for accepting this man as our redemption. It is fitting that we should honor the sacrifice for what he brings to us." She resumed dancing, her blue skirt shining in the torchlight. "Our gratitude will bring other sacrifices to us, so that we may continue our worship until Francisco—the true Francisco—returns to us."

Well before midnight the villagers had gone back to their houses, exhausted by all that had transpired that day. On the cross San Germanno strove to make the most of the ameliorating night, gathering what little strength he could for the ordeal of the day to come, letting the darkness soothe him, ending the worst of the pain from the unforgiving sun. The first day had been hideous, the second would be indescribably worse; a third day on the cross would surely bring madness. With his eyes crusted shut, he could not help but think of Oaxetli, and realized that Rogerio had been right: a blind vampire would be doomed to impossible suffering. It was hardly consoling, but it rid him of his last tatters of guilt.

He thought of all the tales he had heard of holy men and women who had been reputed to be able to separate their souls from their bodies during great travail or ecstasy, and in all his countless years tending to the injured and ill, he had seen many of them in states that made him believe this was a capability accessible to many of humankind. But he had never found that for himself. Perhaps it would only occur when he suffered the True Death, for had he any such ability, this continuing agony ought to have triggered it. Much as he tried, he could not take solace from that thought: that his agony was part of his true nature. Owls and bats competed for mastery of the sky as buzzards and hawks had during the day; he traced their progress by the sounds they made, minute though they were. It was easier than attempting to resign himself to another day in the sun. He dreaded the songs of birds that would mark the coming of dawn, yet he listened for it as obsessively as the devout prayed.

Four leagues away, in the depths of the ruin, Rogerio finally found what he had been searching for: the chamber was large, with fresh air from some place in the ceiling, and little evidence of bats or other creatures. He held his torch high to inspect the place and decided it would do for now. Later, if it were necessary, he could find another refuge for San Germanno. His mind made up, he began to clear away a place for the chest he carried, setting it down gratefully, confident that this place would conceal them safely for as long as San Germanno required to heal. Only then did he permit himself the admission that he was aching in every sinew. He would have to deny himself the long rest he would need to recover from his efforts; he would do that when San Germanno was safe and not now. He reminded himself that there had been many other times he had dealt with deep fatigue, and while it was not pleasant, it was hardly fatal to a ghoul. Making a sconce for his torch with a tree root, he put himself to work clearing the debris from the chamber, determined to have it fairly in order by sunrise.

At least, San Germanno reminded himself as the first, earliest bird-calls shot through him, his muscles were numb and he had only the burning to contend with. It was a small mercy but he received it eagerly. He was going to lose all his hair, as he had outside Baghdad, and his body would be tender for two or three months while the skin regrew, and his hair. His strength would return gradually, even with regular drinking of blood, and with the protection of his native earth. The worst should be over by the middle of summer. That was assuming he would not have to spend a third day up here, he added to himself. If Dona Azul had her way, he would probably remain on the cross until his skeleton fell apart and dropped from the nails, as it would for more mortal men than he. Then the dark beyond his sealed eyes began to be less dense and the morning chorus rose in terrible enthusiasm to mark the coming of the sun. At that moment San Germanno would have infinitely preferred the mournful wail of coyotes or the insanely high trilling of bats; he steeled himself as best he could for the torture to come.

Rogerio found a plant that left a chalky white residue where its stem was rubbed and spent the morning marking the way to the chamber. He found a less difficult entrance to the ruin and made sure the entrance was covered with brush. Satisfied he would be able to find his way late at night, he made another four torches to light the chamber itself. It was a pity, he thought, that he would not be able to take the second chest of earth when he went to get his master that night; perhaps he could retrieve it later. Then he began to make a kind of litter, one he could strap to his back and carry, and resumed his preparations to return to the valley where San Germanno was. His tools were few but sufficient to the task he had set for himself.

As uncomfortable as running water made him, by mid-morning San Germanno yearned for an hour in the stream he could occasionally hear from his place on the cross. Anything that would lessen his sensation that he embraced red-hot metal was welcome, no matter how potentially deadly it might be to him. The one thing occupying his mind was the staunch desire that his pain might end; it did not concern him what the consequences of such relief might be. His time on the cross was the whole of eternity to him now, and no memory could salve him any longer. There were more birds circling, waiting for something that had happened more than three thousand six hundred years ago.

By midafternoon, Rogerio was ready to go back to the valley; he had the litter he had made strapped to his back as he had carried the chest of San Germanno's native earth. A large coil of rope was wound about his waist, and a hatchet was wedged between it and his body. He kept up a good pace, taking care to make note of the landmarks he had memorized the day before. The angle of the sun changed the appearance of a few of them but not so completely that Rogerio lost his way. He felt the urgency of his work as keenly as if a pistol were clapped to his head, and would not permit himself any discouraging thoughts as he continued back along the path he had come, always alert to any guards or spies who might be watching for him. He was careful to watch the progress of the sun down the sky: he did not want to arrive before nightfall.

Dona Azul arrived at the foot of the cross at the end of the day, her people accompanying her. She was still triumphant, and she carried herself as if she wanted nothing more than the satisfaction of seeing her faith vindicated; she could not keep the gloating out of her eyes, and as she walked, she declared that she knew the sky-god would grant much redemption for their sins because San Germanno was taking so long to die. Inwardly she was puzzled that their sacrifice still lived: by all rights he should have collapsed before sundown yesterday, but she supposed they were being shown the power of the sky-god and the strength of his will. The first Dona Azul had taught them that the sky-god lifted up and cast down nations and peoples, that he could raise the dead and make any man bend to his will. This must be a demonstration of that teaching, she thought. With a sudden gesture, she summoned the men who carried all that remained of San Germanno's possessions, indicating they should leave these things at the foot of the cross.

The men complied, their actions heralded by bells.

"Look at the worldly goods of our sacrifice!" she cried aloud. "Look at all he had gathered in the world. What is its worth to him now?" She kicked the chest containing San Germanno's native earth.

High above, San Germanno could sense the pull from the chest below, but the presence was not strong enough to provide any anodyne relief to his anguish. His perception was poignant, wakening longings he had abandoned hours ago—hours that seemed endless as centuries.

"See how the sky-god has blackened his skin, like the cooling lava when it runs from the mouths of the earth. Thus we are reminded that the sacrifices offered to the Black Mirror were false sacrifices. The beating hearts were taken sinfully." She laughed aloud. "The sky-god shows us he is mightier than the Black Mirror, that the hot blood of the earth never burns as hotly as the sun, the right eye of the sky-god, as the moon is his left. Though this foreigner revealed he was one with the Black Mirror when his visage was not seen in the black mirror, he has offered recompense with his death, which is like the death of the Black Mirror himself. It is fitting that the sky-god should vindicate his might in this manner. Look what has come before Dona Azul! Do not think that any god is greater than the sky-god."

The bells rang in San Germanno's throbbing head, magnified by hurt; the deepening twilight was the only relief provided him, and it was no longer as annealing as what he had experienced the night before.

"It is our good fortune to see this proof of our salvation in his suffering." She stared up at the figure on the cross. "I will tell the sky-god we have overcome the Black Mirror at last and will soon welcome the true Francisco back to this valley, and the living child that will be the token of our salvation. The sky-god will make that child his child, so that all the people will worship him." Her dancing was slow, each movement careful and precise. "The sky-god will bring Francisco back to me, as he promised in the name of the sky-god, and the child will thrive."

Some of the villagers were dancing, singing in a monotone as they moved; the eerie sound wound its way up to San Germanno, spiraling into his thoughts and becoming part of his suffering.

"It is right that we await his coming with this sacrifice, so that the sky-god may be certain that we have no reason to turn from him, and that we are willing to receive all he will provide us." Dona Azul lifted her head in the direction of the cross, shouting, "It is this sacrifice that makes us worthy, for all the sins it redeems."

A few of the women brought gourds filled with a raw, potent liquor, which they passed among the other villagers, praising them for drinking.

For San Germanno, the world narrowed down to pain. No sound was anything more than an addition to the hurts heaped upon him; no movement of air gave him succor. He could not feel his hands at all, though he was certain they were swollen and burned, curled like blackened leaves. The festivities beneath him were hardly noticeable, though he was jangled by the disorienting noise. Another day of this and he would need a year at least to recover from it bodily; his mind could well prove more fragile, as the road to Baghdad had taught him.

Gradually the celebration diminished and the villagers wended their ways back to their houses. Only Dona Azul remained at the foot of the cross, in a stupor combined of alcohol and ecstasy.

From his place up the hillside from the platform, Rogerio watched the people of the village as they succumbed to drink and fervor. He waited while they abandoned the platform to Dona Azul, and kept still while Dona Azul danced and drank, drank and danced until she collapsed amid San Germanno's belongings.

This was, he knew, the best opportunity he would have. It was useless to wait another day, in the scant hope that tomorrow night would be safer. He tightened the straps holding the litter to his back and made his way down the hill, pausing from time to time to look about him; there might still be guards posted around the platform and he had no wish to get into a fight now, with his goal so near. Satisfied that any guards were asleep, he finally stepped out into the open. He picked up the Japanese sword as he lowered the litter from his back, taking comfort in its splendid balance. Next he laid out San Germanno's clothes on the litter, then he forced open the chest of San Germanno's native earth and spread a layer of it on top of his garments. He forced himself not to look at the sky so that he would be unaware of the passing time. Finally, knowing he was as ready as he would ever be, he took a length of rope to aid him and began to shinny up the cross. Splinters gouged his skin, and his muscles trembled with fatigue, but he continued upward, his senses alert to any disturbance below. Finally he was near enough to dare to whisper, "My master?"

San Germanno's ears roared with aching, but he heard the whisper and disbelieved it all at once. It was the product of his delirium, or some other illusion conjured by his mind to keep hope alive. He said nothing; his lips were too cracked to move had he made the attempt.

"Sanct' Germain," Rogerio repeated, using the first name he had known the Conde by. "It is Rogerian."

Much as he wanted to open his eyes, San Germanno could not. He made a hissing sound, which was the extent to which he was capable. At the same time he tried to deny what he wanted so desperately to be true.

"It is not so bad as the road to Baghdad," Rogerio assured him, though he could not see well enough to be certain. "You will be well in two or three months." He was high enough to reach the crossbar and hauled himself up the last little distance. "I am going to put a rope around you. It will be painful, but it will let me get you down." He took some time to work the rope from around his waist and loop it over the crossbar. "I am sorry for the pain, my master," he said quietly as he slipped the rope under San Germanno's arm, across his chest and under his other arm.

The thin keening that escaped him was more terrible than a scream would have been. Just the touch of the rope was racking; as its pressure increased, San Germanno was tortured anew with the rasp of the fibers.

"I am going to have to lever the spikes out," Rogerio said, hoping his resolve would not fail him. He used the hatchet blade to wedge the spike out of San Germanno's left hand, moaning in sympathy as his master's crusted arm swung limply as the spike fell away. Closing his mind to the unrelenting agony of his master, he loosened the second spike, then adjusted the rope so that he could use it to lower San Germanno once he was back on the ground. As he began his descent, he stopped to pull the spike out of San Germanno's feet, throwing the thing as far away as he could.

Rogerio's knees were throbbing when he finally reached the ground, but he could not stop his work now. Gingerly he used his rope to lower San Germanno down the cross, taking care to keep his pace as steady as possible. Once a burro brayed and Rogerio halted at once, anticipating discovery. But the village remained silent; no calls or other disturbance followed the burro's complaint.

At the foot of the cross Dona Azul made no response to the noise.

When he was satisfied it was safe to continue, Rogerio lowered San Germanno the rest of the way.

The nearness of his native earth provided San Germanno the first touch of revival he had experienced and he both welcomed and abhorred it, for the process of palingenecy was an arduous one. He hung in the sling and longed for the sensation of earth under his feet—not that his long-numbed feet would register the moment. At last the sling loosened a bit, and Rogerio came to keep San Germanno from falling.

"There is a litter. I am going to strap you to it and tie the lot to my back," Rogerio muttered, afraid that Dona Azul would suddenly wake and summon the village to deal with him and San Germanno. "Do not try to move."

San Germanno made a low noise, not quite a whimper but certainly not a word, that Rogerio took as concurrence. He felt his body moved and his skin continued to crack and crust with blood. Then he was on his back, the revivifying presence of his native earth easing him as he was laid on the litter and fixed in position. Not even the straps holding him in place were as horrible as the sunlight, and he was thankful for them as they pressed his baked and blistered flesh, the white expanse of his scars. The last thing he was aware of before wholly losing consciousness was being hoisted into the air as Rogerio prepared to take him away from the valley.

When dawn came, Rogerio was more than halfway back to the hiding place he had made; he made himself continue to walk, ignoring fatigue and the wretchedness of his master except to rig a makeshift cover for him with his clothes so that he would not be more severely burned than he already was. He yearned for rest, he was hungry, and he was becoming worried at the likelihood of pursuit. It would be reckless and foolish to stop now, when the villagers must be aware of his escape.

Dona Azul was the first to realize the outrage that had been perpetrated in the night. She woke with a monumental headache and the unthinkable revelation that their sacrifice had somehow got away from them during the night. At first she could not believe it, and summoned a number of her guards to search for San Germanno. "He must have fallen from the cross. He could not get far."

One of the villagers suggested that a great bird might have carried him off.

"And leave nothing behind?" Dona Azul scoffed. "How could that be? His hands are gone, and his feet. Surely a bird would have torn the rest of him away from the spikes." She was becoming furious at the villagers for failing to keep their sacrifice where he ought to be. "Is it not possible that one, or more, of you no longer believes in the sky-god, but wants to worship the Black Mirror?"

All of the villagers denied this accusation; a few began to weep.

"If that is not the cause of this catastrophe, what is?" She kicked out at the remaining belongings of San Germanno's Rogerio had left behind. "You cannot tell me that he got down from that cross on his own."

"Perhaps," one of the older women ventured, "the ghost of his woman helped him."

There were murmurs of agreement and dread. A youngster looked uneasily toward the grave of Oaxetli and announced it was undisturbed.

"His woman died through a righteous act. She would not rise after such a death." Dona Azul tossed her head. "The ghosts of those who worship the sky-god can perform great deeds, but those who are not worshippers of the sky-god can only lie in the earth and dream of the punishment to come, when the sky-god will draw the righteous upward and cast the sinners down to the burning realms of the Black Mirror." She put her hands together. "We must ask the sky-god to forgive us for the loss of the sacrifice. There were so many sins in that foreigner that we would have been redeemed through him."

A group of women flung themselves prostrate at once, and a number of men joined them. The leader of the guards was not so willing to accept their failure.

"Dona Azul, it may be that there has been a clever ruse here. It may be that the foreigner has other accomplices whom his servant alerted when he escaped. It may be that they returned to claim his body." He coughed and did his best to look in her eyes.

"Do you want to search for these accomplices?" she jeered. "Do you think you will be less in error if you hunt for these spectres of your mind?"

"I think," said the leader of the guards, "it would be wisest, so that this foreigner does not send others to this valley."

This possibility struck Dona Azul. "I take your meaning," she said, nodding twice slowly. Then, in a more reasonable tone she said, "If you should find any indication of how they got away—and in what direction they fled, report it all to me. Recover the foreigners if you can. And remember that dying in the cause of a sacrifice to the sky-god will redeem you as well as many of us."

The leader of the guards touched his blue headband with his spear and then barked out a number of sharp orders: a dozen men sprang to do his bidding.

"Find them," Dona Azul admonished the leader of the guard. "Find them, or your failure will be sin enough to make you a worthy sacrifice."

The leader of the guards gestured his understanding as he prepared to set off with his men.

By noon, Rogerio was certain they were being followed—not close enough to be in danger, but without doubt trackers were after them. He studied the sky and noticed that a few buzzards were idly circling above them, marking their progress as surely as if they held flags and torches. He reckoned it would be another two hours before he reached the ruin where they could hide. He was not certain that was time enough. Spurred on by urgency and the conviction that he would lose any battle with the guards from the village, Rogerio increased the length of his stride, putting all his attention on reaching their hiding-place and trying to ignore the strain in every joint and muscle of his body. The consequences of failure loomed too heavily over him to permit him to flag when they were so close.

Then he reached the ruin; Rogerio was near to collapsing from exhaustion. Hunger and thirst were forgotten for more than an hour in his determination to find the haven he had prepared before their hunters caught sight of them; arriving without mishap brought a weary smile to his austere features. He made his way into the over-grown pyramid without taking the time to put brush in front of the entrance as he had planned. He felt his way to the chamber where the chest of earth waited, hardly aware of the burden he carried, knowing only the all-pervasive ache that gripped him as a fever would. Against unthinkable odds he had succeeded.

At last Rogerio was able to unfasten the straps and tug San Germanno atop the chest waiting for him, a task that was made more difficult for the terrible burns on San Germanno's body. Rogerio was not quite as tall as San Germanno, and maneuvering his master was awkward, particularly for someone as far gone in fatigue as Rogerio was. Once San Germanno was secure on the chest, Rogerio cast the litter aside, unheeding of where it landed. Food and drink would be obtained later, when he was more himself; and he would bring something for San Germanno to begin the long process of restoration. He checked his master one last time, making sure that San Germanno would receive the full benefit of his native earth. Then, with a long sigh, he sat down next to the chest and fell immediately to sleep.

Text of a letter from Don Ezequias Pannefrio y Modestez, Corregidor of the Audiencia de Lima, at Lima, to Obispo Hernan Guarda at Los Sacramentos in Cuzco, Audiencia de Lima, Viceroyalty of Peru.

To Su Excelencia, Obispo Hernan Guarda at Los Sacramentos in Cuzco, the respectful greetings from Don Ezequias Pannefrio y Modestez at the Residencia in Lima with the prayers that Obispo Guarda will give this missive his kind attention and consider the messages it contains with an open heart.

As you were good enough to point out, I am new to my position and duties, and I suppose it will be some time before I am fully knowledgeable in regard to my office. Certainly my predecessor, Don Vicente, was a man of many accomplishments who is much deserving of his splendid reputation. I will do my utmost to be mindful of his capabilities as I do my best to conduct the office in a manner that will bring glory to España and honor to the Church. It is a consolation to me to know that so many of my associates in Cuzco are praying for me and lending me their advice for my undertaking here.

You tell me that Don Ulixos Llave y Cordillero has disappointed you in his administration as Presidencia. Let me implore you not to judge him too harshly. He has only recently come from España, and he has not yet learned how to accomplish those tasks the office requires of him; as I am a novice Corregidor, so he is a novice Presidencia. But that does not mean he is incapable, for if that were the case he would not have been assigned to so crucial a post as Cuzco. You do him a disservice when you complain that he is unable to grasp the problems of the region. I am confident that this man will do his work well and bring no shame on the city. His tasks will be less an effort, however, if you are willing to let him find his own way. Doubtless you are impatient with his questions and many other manners which are unfamiliar to you, but in time you will come to know him better. He has often been in contact with me, seeking advice from one who has until recently executed the duties of that office, and I have done all that I might to help him to find his way. Your admonitions, most certainly given with the best intentions, are perhaps too stringent for Don Ulixos, and serve only to distress him rather than to support his discharging of his obligations. If you would be willing to mitigate your instruction for a time, it will aid him greatly.

As to the issuing of encomiendas, I must again remind you that your recommendation is only that—a recommendation. Your views are important, but not the only ones I have to consider. I must take many things into account, as must Don Ulixos, and your suggestions form only a portion of the factors that must be considered before such licenses can be granted. It may be that Don Ulixos sees his duty in a different light than you do, as I must regard not only your observations but those of Obispo Puente y Sello before I have adequate intelligence to make a decision. It may be that you are right, and the demands made by others are being given undo weight by Don Ulixos, but I will not reprimand his policies until he has held the position for more than two years. If at that time you are still dissatisfied with Don Ulixos' discharging of his obligations, inform me of particulars and I will include your remarks among those I will consider. Until then, any corrections on my part would be premature, as would requests to the Viceroy to remove me from the post of Corregidor.

Lamentably, there is yet another issue I must address, Su Excelencia, and that is your renewal of the warrant for the arrest of Francisco Ragoczy, Conde de San Germanno. While I cannot fault your zeal, I say again that in the case of this gentleman it is misplaced. I will not be party to any attempt to hold this man for punishment. You have the authority of the Church you may appeal to, of course. I hope you will reconsider your decision and vacate the warrant. There is no reason to think this man deserves the scrutiny of the Secular Arm, or the ordeal of prison; no piece of information provided about San Germanno redounds to his discredit beyond your catalogue of suspected offenses. Your confidence has been abused by greedy and suspicious men who have done all they might to blacken the reputation of San Germanno. Yes, the arm of the Church reaches a long way, and you may seek him everywhere in the New World with the certainty that the Church will do as you command. Yet I implore you to cease this pursuit of a man who did Cuzco great good and very little wrong. If you are determined to keep on this course, one that I must call persecution, I warn you now I will forbid Spanish ships to carry your warrant, and I will request all Corregidores and Presidencias, as well as other administrative officers, not to honor it. It is vengeance you seek, not justice, and as such, I cannot countenance your use of Crown troops to do your bidding. You may still compel the religious to obey you, but they will have to do so without the aid of the Crown, and with my express disagreement as regards the dispute between you and San Germanno. Before you complain to el Rey and Rome, let me remind you that such a complaint would receive a full review, and many of those to whom the matter would be submitted are likely to see the dispute from my perspective rather than yours, and the results may well be ones you do not want. It would be wise to reconsider your warrant in a circumspect posture before you escalate the disagreement beyond its present limits.

May God and your Good Angel guide your meditations, and may you receive the many blessings you have brought upon yourself, Su Excelencia. May God strengthen your faith and your understanding and bring you to bliss. I pray for wisdom daily, and will remember you in all my prayers.

> *Don Ezequias Pannefrio y Modestez*
> *Corregidor of the Audiencia de Lima*
> *Viceroyalty of Peru*
> *By my own hand at Lima, on June 11th, the Feast of San Barnabas,*
> *near mid-winter, 1648*

11

Most of his body had healed but remained tender; that, as much as the meager supply of his native earth remaining, kept San Germanno inside the ruined pyramid during the day. His hair had grown enough to be more than stubble, but it was not long enough to wave. Rogerio had shaved him a few days ago, leaving his face looking polished and fresh in spite of the ancient, parchment-like texture of his skin. He continued to dress in loose clothing, unwilling to chance the discomfort of Spanish fashions.

"Midsummer soon," said Rogerio in the Latin of Imperial Rome as he brought a kid into the pyramid. The young animal was stunned. "When you are finished—"

"I know," San Germanno said mildly. "It is yours." He reached for the goat and pulled it toward him, glad to feel strength in his body once more. Before he took sustenance from the kid, he said, "We will have to leave soon."

"Yes; so I was thinking." Rogerio waited for what else San Germanno would say.

"It would be best to return to Acapulco, where I have gold and ships and chests of my native earth. I can finish my recuperation there."

"And there are women you can visit in dreams," Rogerio added when San Germanno said nothing more.

"Yes," San Germanno agreed. "We will do better moving by night;

it will allow me to use less of my native earth for stamina."

"So I assumed," Rogerio said, and turned away as San Germanno bared the kid's throat. A short while later he heard San Germanno cough diplomatically and he swung around to take the young goat. "This will last a while."

"And the skin can be put to good use," San Germanno said. "We will both need hats, large hats, for during the day when we rest."

"I doubt I'll have time to cure the hide," Rogerio said.

"Ah." San Germanno shook his head once. "A pity to waste it, but—"

Rogerio shrugged. "There have been worse wastes in our travels." He made a decisive gesture. "I will hunt again tomorrow night. That will help us to prepare for the journey, to eat more now."

"True enough," San Germanno responded, although his attention was not wholly on what Rogerio was saying. He was quiet for a short while, then said, "Do you recall how long it was after Baghdad before I could bring myself to walk in the sun?"

"Nearly four years," said Rogerio evenly, doing his best not to remember what those years had been like.

San Germanno nodded slowly. "And this has been little more than three months; I realize the difference in time. This time was not as severe as before. I have been trying to persuade myself to step out into the light. My native earth is in the soles of my boots. I have nothing to fear. But when I tried yesterday, I faltered." This admission filled him with chagrin.

"You are still not fully healed," said Rogerio. "It is not surprising you hesitate going into sunlight after what—"

"So I tell myself," San Germanno interrupted. "But I must be able to travel, and with the best plans, this will mean some time in daylight."

"Would you prefer to wait a while longer?" Rogerio asked, trying not to sound apprehensive.

"No. It would not be wise. If I had another chest of my native earth, I would be tempted, but given our circumstances . . . I will have to manage." He folded his hands tightly together. "I cannot go on living on the blood of goats and fowl forever."

"Shall we wait a week?" Rogerio suggested.

San Germanno thought before he answered. "No; no. Best to go now. In a week I may invent some new reason why we should wait even longer, and that would be folly. I have the determination now; it is wisest to take advantage of it. Tomorrow we prepare and the night after that we start south." He rose and stretched. "Tonight I am going to take another walk around this ruin. My muscles need working before we leave. And the place intrigues me." He chuckled suddenly. "How unfortunate I cannot turn into a bat, as the legends claim, and fly south. Had I been able to change shape, I would have been harder to crucify."

Rogerio's face remained somber. "Just as well that they did not know your true nature, my master."

"Undoubtedly," said San Germanno, an echo of his old urbanity in his demeanor. "Oh, come, Rogerio, laugh a little with me. I cannot weep, so I suppose I must try laughing."

"Pardon me, Conde, if I cannot," said Rogerio with increasing formality.

At that, San Germanno relented. "Very well, old friend. I have too much to be grateful to you for to mock your concerns. It was wicked of me."

"Not wicked," Rogerio countered, "but for me not amusing." He took the kid and started toward the corridor leading to another room inside the pyramid they had taken over.

That night as he walked around the pyramid, San Germanno was once again struck with the extent of the site: once there had been a hundred buildings clustered along the avenue leading to the pyramid. Now they were marked by rectangular heaps of mud bricks and hewn stones. A hundred houses could mean as many as a thousand people living here. Who were they? What had become of them? The last time he had returned to his native earth the ruins of his father's palace were nothing more than a series of low hillocks and an occasional protruding stone. In time this place would be the same. It saddened him to reflect on what had been lost here, and how utterly lost it was.

He was back inside the pyramid well before dawn, and found Rogerio constructing two litters for their backs. "You are doing well. How may I help?"

Rogerio angled his chin in the direction of the coil of rope hung on the wall. "I need two armslengths of that."

San Germanno set about cutting this, using the hatchet. As he handed this to Rogerio, he said, "The chest of earth is mine. I will carry it."

"So I reckoned," said Rogerio, continuing to net the rope about the litter. "I will tend to food and weapons."

"How many of the weapons did you manage to save, other than this hatchet and my katana?" He had made only a cursory survey of their supplies; now he was curious and eager to know what they had. "Have we anything like spears?"

"We have two small knives, your throwing hatchet, the one you wear under your belt along your back, and my short sword." He did his best not to sound discouraged by this recitation.

"Unless we're up against musquets, I suppose it is sufficient," said San Germanno lightly. "Given the aim of most Spanish troops, we are probably safe against musquets as well."

Rogerio gave San Germanno a long, deliberate stare, then resumed working. "I will be back before sunset," he said as he reached for more rope.

The afternoon was drowsy with heat, distorting waves rising from the hard ground. The air seemed to sing with it. Rogerio had the hatchet with him, held loosely in his right hand as he moved quickly from tree to bush, finding shelter and searching out animals dozing through the sweltering hours. Over the last three months he had learned the territory around him fairly well and so he wasted little time reaching the place where he had been most successful on his previous hunts. He reached a stand of scrubby trees where he knew there was a sluggish spring; he had often found game there before, and now he hoped that the rustling he heard meant his quest was over. Swinging his hatchet upward, he slid from cover to grab for the animal drinking.

Two guards from Dona Azul's village looked up sharply, their spears pointed uncompromisingly at Rogerio as he emerged from the brush; their lack of surprise told him they had heard his approach and had waited for him. One of the men shouted, and three more of the guards came running, spears clutched tightly in their hands, their faces hard with satisfaction.

Rogerio struck out with the hatchet and had the pleasure of wounding one of the men badly. In the next moment he staggered as he was bludgeoned into semi-consciousness.

"Tie him up," one of the guards ordered. He went to his companion who was grasping his shoulder and cursing steadily against the pain and fear consuming him. "Is it bad?" he asked, knowing it was.

"Bad enough," the other said through clenched teeth. "That man is as evil as the demon he serves."

"We will get you back home. You will recover," said the first with false sincerity.

"The rot will take me," said the injured man. "Dona Azul will give me in sacrifice."

"The sky-god will honor you," the first assured him, abandoning all pretense of expecting recovery.

"He is secured," announced one of the others. He had tied Rogerio's hands in front of him, pulled his elbows back and shoved a spear through the crook of his elbows. "If he tricks us again, we will catch him. He will not get far trussed up like this."

The youngest of the men looked around uneasily. "Where do you suppose his master is?"

"Long underground," one of the others said with a short laugh. "You saw what he looked like."

"Yes. And he should not have been able to get off the cross, but he did," the young man objected, glancing around warily.

"The sky-god did that," said the first guard. "Dona Azul explained it."

"Because he was a false man, because he was not the true Francisco," said another, touching the blue crosses on his headband to insure protection from the ancient devils who were known to lurk in this part of the country.

Rogerio was vaguely aware of what was being said; his head was ringing and his eyes made the world wobble. Prodded by the butts of spears, Rogerio began to walk, his steps unsteady. Suddenly he lurched and the end of the spear protruding beyond his elbow buried itself in the parched earth. Struggling to stand upright, Rogerio gouged more earth before two of the guards pulled him sharply to his feet and shoved him forward. Rogerio dared not look back at the message he had scratched in the earth for fear the guards would notice it and go back to obliterate it.

When evening came and Rogerio did not return, San Germanno was not concerned. Hunting often took longer than the hunter anticipated; many times it had been well after dark by the time Rogerio had his quarry in hand. He went out again, watching the bats flit off, like flakes of soot against the night sky, and trying to shake off the vague uneasiness that possessed him. He attributed it to his coming walk in the sunlight, and did his best to dismiss it.

But midnight came and went without Rogerio appearing, and San Germanno grew apprehensive. If he had been unable to find game, Rogerio would have been back by now, which meant something had gone wrong. There were wild pigs in this region, quick, vicious beasts with nasty tusks and irascible tempers: a wild pig could do a lot of damage to a hunter. The venom of snakes, insects, and spiders could not kill Rogerio any more than they could kill San Germanno, but they could make him severely ill. Deciding to act, he donned his Spanish clothes, took his katana and his small throwing hatchet, replaced the native earth in the soles and heels of his boots, and set out in search of Rogerio.

Not long before dawn he found the little spring where Rogerio had been surprised. He read the signs on the ground, including the spatters of blood from the wound Rogerio had struck on one of the guards. His night-seeing eyes found the path left by the men, and, at last, the message scratched in the dirt by Rogerio: *DA* ˆ.

The arrow pointed in the direction the men had taken. San Germanno studied the markings for other information and found none. He stood up with a sigh, laid his hand on the hilt of his katana, and began to trudge after Rogerio and his captors, shading his eyes against the advancing light.

Dona Azul met the returning men at the crest of the valley, the bearers of her platform and chair struggling to hold it steady as she rose to her feet. "Fine men you are, going out for a day of hunting, and you return with nothing."

The guard who had been giving most of the orders prostrated himself before Dona Azul. "We found something that should be better than game," he said, his voice shaking in spite of his confident words.

"What is better than game?" she demanded. "You were sent hunting."

"And we have captured something of great worth," the man implored her, daring to look up from his place on the ground. "Bring our prize forward," he said to the others.

With that, Rogerio was thrust in front of the men, his face forced upward in order to show Dona Azul who it was.

Her face went through a number of expressions: disbelief, realization, cunning, and finally hauteur. "So. You did not run as far as we thought." She signaled her bearers to set her down. As soon as she could, she strode off her platform and walked directly up to Rogerio. "Where have you been?"

"Beyond this valley," he said in her language, his pronunciation not quite accurate, but clear enough to be understood.

"If you are searching for your master, we do not have him. The sky-god banished him." She pursed her lips in distaste, as if she were the offended party, not the god she worshipped. "He is not here. You understand me?"

"Yes," he replied to both questions. He knew she was distressed by his presence, and he wondered how she planned to account for it.

"How did you get away?" she demanded, and went on, giving him no time to speak. "You cannot tell me, even if you comprehend the question."

He ducked his head as if to reveal distress as the villagers gathered around him.

"You brought shame on us, shame in the face of the sky-god, and you shame Dona Azul for the faith we have. You and your master were sent to test us and you nearly succeeded in destroying our faith through your evil. It was not enough that the blind woman died, your master disgraced us in sacrifice. You were one who made his vileness possible. You will answer for it."

Rogerio pretended he had not grasped the purpose of her denouncement, and while he did, he began to wonder how he would get free of this place this time. The last time he had been left unguarded while the village celebrated San Germanno's crucifixion, but now they were going to keep watch on him, far more closely than before. "I am tired," he said in Dona Azul's language.

"And hungry and thirsty as well, no doubt," she said smugly. "You will have to wait for anything to eat and drink." She motioned to her bearers as she stepped back onto her platform. "Let us return to the village while I decide what is to be done with you, for the sake of my people and the sky-god."

The leader of the guards called to her again. "One of my men was injured when we captured this devil's servant," he said, and pointed to the man with the gouge in his shoulder.

"It looks to be a deep cut," said Dona Azul with growing interest.

"Too deep to . . . We had to carry him between two men on the way back," the leader said. "He bled a great deal, but it is stopping now."

"He is a worthy sacrifice. He will be offered to the sky-god so that his suffering will alleviate ours." She tapped her foot to put her bearers in motion.

Rogerio was not encouraged by these words, for he knew if the wounded man could expect no mercy from this woman, neither could he. With many dire thoughts racing in his mind, he fell into step with his guards as they made their way down a hill he had hoped never to see again. As he walked, he noticed that the summer had not been kind to the people who lived in the valley. The hillsides were arid, many of the lower bushes already showing signs of drying up. In the pen where goats were kept the number was down from the spring, and there were only two burros instead of the five they had had before. The horses San Germanno had brought were showing ribs through their coats. Most of the children were scrawny and a few were visibly sick.

"Bring a cage. The one we use for coati mundis and coyotes," said Dona Azul, and a number of youths went scurrying toward the storage shed, only to emerge a few moments later with a stout cage with a number of narrow wooden bars. The cage had a wide door and was long enough for Rogerio to sit down in it with his legs extended, but it was not high enough for him to stand up straight.

As the men herded Rogerio into the cage, a few of the children began to sing mocking verses, which Rogerio did not entirely understand, though their intent was plain enough: he was a servant of wrong things and despicable. The door was closed and two stout braces were set in place. Only then was the spear holding his elbows back taken away, though his hands were not untied.

"You have brought much trouble to us, you and your master," said Dona Azul as she came up to the cage where Rogerio sat; she bent down in order to look him directly in the eyes. "You may not be a welcome sacrifice for the sky-god, but you may expunge the shame you and your master have brought upon us."

Rogerio heard this out with increasing foreboding. Beyond the center of the village, he could see a few men preparing a crucifix for the injured guard. "What do you want of me?" he asked, making sure he sounded less knowledgeable in the language than he was. "What must I do?"

"We want to have our revenge on you," Dona Azul said sweetly. "The revenge must be fitting, for your error and for the honor of the sky-god." She raised her voice so the people could hear her. "You will die as men died for the Black Mirror. Thus you will not disgrace the sky-god. You will have the living heart torn from your body in tribute to the old god you serve."

He said nothing, but wondered what they would make of his ghoul's heart which had ceased to beat as living men's hearts did in the Year of the Four Caesars. He could not summon up enough sangfroid to laugh, but he did manage a faint smile. "When?"

"Tomorrow night, I think. When the sky is as black as the Black Mirror, it will be time to offer you." She turned away from him and addressed her people. "This man is to be given to the Black Mirror so that we may be free of the taint left by him and his master. Then the sky-god will honor our sacrifices and give us favor once again. We erred in crucifying San Germanno. We will not make the same mistake with his servant."

A half-hearted cheer went up from the people gathered around her; a few of the guards seemed dubious.

"What if the sky-god punishes us for this as well?" asked the man who had led those who had caught Rogerio at the spring.

"He will not. It is not possible that we would be despised twice." Dona Azul again addressed her people. "In giving this man to the old gods, we show that we have abandoned them for the sky-god. Our sacrifice of this man will deliver us from the curse that has fallen upon us."

If there were villagers who did not agree, not one of them spoke up; Dona Azul had set them on a course and all of them were expected to follow it.

Rogerio did not look at Dona Azul again, but set himself to recalling many of the other scrapes he had had in the centuries since San Germanno restored him to life. He decided he would have to get away late at night, when his guards were sleepiest. If they noticed his escape he would not have time enough to put sufficient distance between this valley and the ruined pyramid to keep from having that hiding-place discovered. He wished he possessed the strange control San Germanno could exercise over animals, for then he would influence the goats to run away; the villagers would then have to chase the goats and he would have an opportunity to flee.

San Germanno followed the tracks and spatters of blood through the dry grass; his dark eyes were grim with intent, and he pressed onward as the weight of the sun bore down on him. Although he was capable of remarkable speed, he made himself walk instead of running, to husband his strength. He felt the protection of his native earth and tried to forget how fragile it could be. Occasionally he would pause to assess his progress, which only served to exasperate him. It would be after sundown that he reached the valley. That was the single advantage of his pace, he thought, and did his best to plan an approach that would put Rogerio in minimal danger. He took comfort in the weight of the katana; that sword had shown its worth many times in the past and he relied on it to do so again.

As preparations for the evening meal began, Rogerio grew hungry again, more from the smell of meat waiting to be cooked than from need. He asked twice for water, but none was given to him and he did not ask a third time. The children who had surrounded his cage earlier now avoided it, as if fearing contamination from his very presence.

Dona Azul, now arrayed in ritual garments of shining blue, came up to his cage. "Tomorrow night at midnight you will return to the Black Mirror who sent you to lure us away from the sky-god. See what he will do to reward you."

Rogerio rubbed his chin. "You will kill me."

"That I will," she said, relishing the prospect. "You will ransom us for the deception of your master." She stared through the bars at him, amusement in her handsome face. "The Black Mirror may not take you back again. The sky-god will not receive you. What will become of you?"

"Dis knows," said Rogerio, referring to the old Roman god of the underworld who had supervision of the dead.

Dona Azul gave a shriek of laughter. "You will not call upon other gods to save you. There are no other gods. The sky-god has banished them all to the torment you will find." She straightened up and twirled around once, humming to herself in satisfaction as the people of the village gathered around her. "We will offer the guard to the sky-god tonight," she declared. "That way, we will have redemption when we send this devil back to the Black Mirror."

There was a mutter of hesitant approval.

At the ridge above the valley, San Germanno surprised a guard who was preoccupied with what was going on around the central village fire-pit. San Germanno was almost upon him when the guard turned sharply and came face-to-face with the Conde. The guard shouted his alarm even as San Germanno struck him a sharp blow, sending him into unconsciousness.

The cry of the guard caused a flurry of activity in the valley: within a matter of minutes two groups of men set out up the hill at a run, and those too old for pursuit gathered the women and children together, Dona Azul in the middle shouting encouragement and threats to her people as they clustered together. Rogerio's cage was outside the ring of protection but not far enough away to enable him to escape during the confusion.

As the men clambered up the hill, San Germanno slipped past them going down their flank and to the platform where the cross was almost complete. Readying himself for a fight, he left the cover of the trees and approached the men drilling the holes for the wooden spikes. He brought his katana out of its scabbard and stepped onto the far end of the cross. "Be careful," he said quietly in their language.

A short distance away the injured man let out a soft cry of distress and tried to push himself onto his elbow.

The two men froze; one of them dropped the bow of his drill, the other could hardly breathe. Neither of them was willing to look at the man who had interrupted their labors. Finally one of them turned slowly, blanching as he caught sight of San Germanno.

"Yes. I have come back." He flicked the katana, indicating they should rise. "Lead the way," he said politely, cocking his head in the direction of the coati mundi cage and Dona Azul beyond it. "If you will be good enough to come with me?" His command of their language alarmed them, as he intended it should.

The two men walked very slowly, as if they trod on shifting ground. They were fairly near the huddled villagers before they were noticed, for the attention of most of the people was on the searchers up the slope.

First to catch sight of the two men and their captor was a boy, no more than seven, who let out a howl and reached for his mother's skirt, pointing, his eyes enormous.

"Stop here," San Germanno said to the two men, who obeyed at once. He waited while the villagers began to realize what had just happened. Then he said, "I have come for my servant."

At the sound of his voice, a number of the people began to weep; Dona Azul glared at them in contempt as she took stock of the situation.

"What are you afraid of?" she exclaimed. "This is nothing but a spectre."

San Germanno bowed slightly to her. "If you think so, test my steel," he offered, flicking the point of the katana in her direction. He gave her a moment to reply, then said, "If one of you will release my servant we will leave you in peace."

She put her hands on her hips, defiance in every inch of her. "Do you suppose we believe you? You?"

"I don't see why you should not," he replied reasonably. "I have no reason to lie."

But Dona Azul was outraged at his calm demeanor. "Do not listen to him! He is not real!" she shouted. "He is an illusion made by the Black Mirror. He is *nothing!*"

The two men standing in front of San Germanno visibly cringed at

Dona Azul's anger; three of the village women forced themselves to dry their eyes.

"Then you will lose nothing by releasing my servant," San Germanno said reasonably. He tapped the men on the shoulder with the flat of his blade; both men knelt promptly.

"If you are going to kill those men, do so now," Dona Azul challenged.

"I would rather not: unless you make it necessary," said San Germanno. Little of his growing apprehension showed in his self-possessed conduct; he was keenly aware that the guards searching the hills were now aware of his presence and might be preparing to attack him.

Dona Azul stepped out from the group and approached San Germanno. Firelight gleamed on her blue garments as she came within two armslengths of him. "There are no burns," she said as she studied San Germanno's face. "And yet you are badly scarred."

"From long ago," said San Germanno steadily.

She made a dancing movement away from him, mocking him. "Should I fear you?"

"It would be prudent," said San Germanno, listening for any sounds that would betray the positions of the guards on the hill behind him.

"The sky-god protects me," she said, almost singing. "I am Dona Azul."

San Germanno glanced in Rogerio's direction and came to a swift decision; it would be a gamble, but it might save them having to battle their way out of the valley. "You say the sky-god protects you," he began, pitching his mellifluous voice loud enough to carry to all those watching them. "Why do you think this is so? If his protection is given to you, why are you not enjoying plenty? Your crops are parched, your livestock is starving and your people—"

He got no further. Dona Azul rounded on him in fury. "My people are going to be redeemed!"

"Are you certain?" He raised his brow skeptically. "You crucified me and—"

"The sky-god would not accept you because you were sent by the Black Mirror. You were no sacrifice—you were an affront." She glared at him, daring him to deny it; her voice was no longer steady. She trembled with ill-concealed rage.

"Then my death should have been doubly triumphant for you and the sky-god," said San Germanno. "Instead you are more miserable than before I came. Your people are being punished, aren't they? Why else should they have to endure such hardships? How is that possible, if my . . . death brought expiation? Then who punishes you? the Black Mirror or the sky-god?" He was glad now that he had listened to her many tirades, for now he could use her own words as she had.

"You are not dead," she accused him, fighting down the cold dread rising in her. "If you had died"—her eyes grew crafty as she moved nearer to him—"we would now be enjoying all the promises of the sky-god. Your sins are great and they would bring us great redemption. But you did not die, and we are made to pay for your living evil with the loss of our crops and our animals."

San Germanno pushed the two men a little nearer to Dona Azul; they shuffled on their knees, afraid to rise. "Listen to me: you show the sky-god no honor in crucifying men. It does not lessen your sins to crucify one you think has sinned more than you."

"The son of the sky-god was crucified, and that brought redemption," she said, and waited for her people gathered behind her to second this assertion. "So we do as the sky-god taught us through Dona Azul: we offer those whose sins are greatest, that our redemption may increase."

"Yes; you said so before." He walked over to Rogerio's cage and laid his hand on top of it in a gesture of protection. "This man has done nothing sinful; he has loyally served his master for nearly half my lifetime."

"And you have served the Black Mirror," Dona Azul exclaimed, glancing at her people to assure herself. "You have given yourself to the Black Mirror, and your servant along with you. He will answer for you both."

"Why?" San Germanno asked, taking care not to look down at Rogerio so that Dona Azul could not claim they were plotting together. "Because you are afraid to try to kill me a second time? You say the sky-god refused me as a sacrifice. What if the sky-god had not power enough to make me one?" He sensed the sudden increase in fascination the people felt, and he pressed on, hoping the enormity of his risk would not prove too extreme. "Perhaps I am not dead because the sky-god has no power over me. Perhaps your lands are barren because the sky-god cannot help you."

"The sky-god is angry with us and withholds his favor because we offered him one unworthy of giving us salvation. Now you try to confuse us, to make our errors greater by twisting the promise of the sky-god into what they are not." She motioned to her people. "There is the cause of your misfortunes. He is the one who has brought all this upon us. He has made the sky-god turn against us."

San Germanno was aware that a number of the guards had returned to the edge of the village, and were listening to this confrontation. Only their awe at his disappearance from the cross kept them from attacking. "You say this, when it was you who chose me for sacrifice? You are given the power to decide who is the most worthy sacrifice. How is it you did not know that the sky-god would find me unworthy? You are the one who is allied with the sky-god. You are the one who preserves his teaching."

Rogerio had not changed his posture, but he was listening closely, prepared to move on the instant San Germanno signaled him.

For the first time Dona Azul's wrath faltered. "You . . . you deceived me."

"And the sky-god as well, it would seem," said San Germanno. "Since you were not warned by him that I was not acceptable. Your sky-god should have let you know I was unfit for your sacrifice." He felt more than saw the questions that were building in the people around her. "And now you are going to offer a mortally wounded man, a man who was injured doing your will. What is his sin, that he will bring you redemption? What if he does not please the sky-god? Are you certain that a dying man has any value in this sacrifice? What sins will his death answer for?" His questions were quick, like sparks from a fire; several people were listening to them attentively.

Dona Azul squared her shoulders and lifted her head. "You are trying to bring these people to sin."

"I am trying to bring them to their senses!" San Germanno said, his dark compelling eyes raking the faces of the people; he paused a moment. "I want to take my servant and go. That is all I want."

"Why is your sword drawn if that is all you want?" Dona Azul asked sharply.

"Because you and your people have already made one attempt on my life. Would you come unarmed to this valley if you had been crucified here?" Out of the tail of his eye he saw one of the guards nod.

"He is right, Dona Azul," said the guard.

"He is *wrong!*" she screamed, and swung around in a circle to address every one of the villagers. "Everything he says is lies. He is here to destroy our worship." She leveled her arm at him, her finger directed at his heart. "You want to end our redemption."

His smile was one-sided and swift. "If it will stop you crucifying people, I do want to end it, for the sake of all those you will decide should die to please the sky-god."

She lunged at him, hands up, fingers hooked. Her followers were too stunned to move. The two men standing with him rushed away, diving away from the firelight, seeking the protection of shadows.

In a single, swift motion, San Germanno tossed his katana atop the coati mundi cage and caught Dona Azul's arms as she reached him. "You cannot make me kill you. I am not like you."

Her face distorted with furious tears. "Sacrilege!" she shouted as she tried to break free of his grip.

"Then why did you try to give me to your sky-god? And why did I fail to die?"

Rogerio took the Japanese sword, cut his bonds with it, and used the flat of the blade to begin levering the heavy brace out of position.

"Make him release me!" she commanded the people of her village.

"Dona Azul," San Germanno said quietly as a number of guards started toward him, "I am going to take my servant and leave. I will fight only if you order your men to try to stop me."

"The sky-god will stop you!" she railed at him, twisting in his grasp. "You will be blasted with lightning before you go ten paces. You will be burned to ashes."

San Germanno glanced up into the clear night sky. "I will take that chance," he said, and released his grip on her arms as he stepped back from her. "You people," he went on to the guards and villagers. "I am not here to bring you harm. I only want my manservant. We will take nothing of yours when we leave."

The oldest of the guards spoke for his men. "We will not stop you if you go at once." He was obviously glad to be rid of San Germanno and all he represented to the village.

"NO!" Dona Azul screamed. *"Kill him!"*

"You've tried that once," he reminded her.

Gingerly, Rogerio got out of the cage, doing his best to ignore his protesting muscles. He kept his hand on San Germanno's sword.

"He is false! Kill *him!*" There was foam at the corners of her mouth and her voice was rough with passion and something more sinister. "He deceives you!"

San Germanno addressed the oldest guard. "We are going to walk away. If you come after us, we will fight until you or we are dead."

The oldest guard held out open hands. "You cannot die. Go. Leave. Do not return."

"You have my Word I will not," San Germanno said somberly.

Rogerio handed the katana back to San Germanno, saying under his breath in Latin, "Do we go back to the ruin?"

"No," said San Germanno with a minute shake of his head, and turned to the road that led out of the village. "Walk slowly," he said in a low voice. "If we run, they will chase us."

"You will not—" shrieked Dona Azul, and rushed toward San Germanno, a stone in her hands. But before she reached him, another stone struck her. She staggered, and looked about, dazed. "Who dares—"

Another rock sailed through the air and landed squarely on her shoulder.

San Germanno stopped, filled with foreboding. "You must—"

But even as San Germanno prepared to try to stop the villagers, Rogerio said, "This is not your battle, my master. They are doing it for their god."

There were more stones in the air, and cries of "Deceiver!" and "Devil!" accompanied the rocks.

"All the more reason to—" He heard more than saw a stone smash into Dona Azul's temple; without a sound she fell to the ground and lay still as the rocks continued to fly.

"Come, my master," Rogerio urged quietly, his hand on San Germanno's shoulder. "There is nothing you can do."

"No; not for any of them," said San Germanno in despair as he resumed walking out of the valley, to the southeast, for as long as the night endured.

Text of a magisterial judgment from Don Augustin Murado y Bonsuerte, Presidencia of Acapulco, Audiencia de Mexico to the Corregidor Don Abrahan Ramierez y Luzadon at Veracruz, Viceroyalty of Nueva España.

To the honorable Corregidor of the Audiencia de Mexico Don Abrahan Ramierez y Luzadon, currently resident in Veracruz, the findings of the official inquiries regarding the activities of Dom Enrique Vilhao, Portuguese hidalgo, and his associate, van Zwolle, a Dutchman and Protestant.

The first accusation against Dom Enrique and van Zwolle was their presentation of a forged deed of gift that purported to give the two miscreants access to two of the ships, the house and household of Francisco Ragoczy, Conde de San Germanno, then absent from Acapulco. The trading agent of said San Germanno determined the deed of gift was a forgery, and supported his statement with several copies of letters in San Germanno's hand that were clearly dissimilar to the one that wrote the deed of gift. The two were imprisoned against the day of their trial. It is fortunate that such a precaution was taken, for I have no doubt but that these men would have fled this Audiencia if they had been released from confinement.

Upon the return of San Germanno after more than a year's absence, he confirmed the deed of gift was not of his making, and further gave testimony in regard to a number of offenses attributed to these men while they and San Germanno were resident in the city of Cuzco, Audiencia de Lima, Viceroyalty of Peru. A review of his affairs has indicated to what extent Dom Enrique and van Zwolle have imposed upon San Germanno here in Acapulco. Their depredations are truly astonishing. The two accused during their time in Cuzco were equally busy if what San Germanno reports is accurate. He contends that at that time they stole many objects of value from various residents of the city, and sold them for their own profit. An inquiry to that city has been sent to ascertain the facts in this regard.

In answer to the assertions of San Germanno, Dom Enrique has made a number of accusations, most of which are probably the result of his own cupidity, and a few of which are preposterous, but which demand inquiry as well, no matter how outrageous they may be. He claims that an Obispo Guarda of Cuzco will support his charges against San Germanno. I will not have it be said that this Presidencia does not examine all factors in a case before making a final disposition, including any accounts this Obispo Guarda wishes to present. Requests for information on this head have been duly dispatched and are expected to be in the hands of this tribunal by the end of the year, the seas and God willing.

Whatever the final outcome of your judgment in this matter, San Germanno is clearly due compensation from Dom Enrique or his family for the misuse and misappropriation of his property. Remuneration will be ordered by me, and I urge you to add your endorsement. It would be fitting for restitution to be made to him, along with suitable apologies in order to diminish the insult this man has suffered, and to maintain the integrity of our laws. To that end, I urge you to grant a writ of restoration for San Germanno so that no claim of Dom Enrique's may be made against San Germanno. It is my opinion that the Conde has had enough to contend with already and ought not to be burdened with the endless formalities of reclamation he would have to undertake without your writ. I ask that you provide this writ as soon as possible so that San Germanno may resume his business dealings without any constraints imposed upon him as a result of Dom Enrique's perfidy.

I most humbly request that Dom Enrique and his associate be returned to España under guard to be tried there for their crimes. I am not sanguine of the outcome if they remain here. I have enclosed true copies of all records concerning this case, which I am convinced give more than enough reasons to treat these criminals in this way. I do not believe that these men will not attempt to bribe their way out of local prisons, and then they have only to sign onto a ship bound for Manila to be beyond the reach of justice for many, many years.

Submitted after appropriate deliberation, with verified copies of all records regarding this dispute, and with the prayers that God will guide you in your decisions, I am your most dedicated

Don Augustin Murado y Bonsuerte
Presidencia of Acapulco
Audiencia de Mexico
Viceroyalty of Nueva España
By the hand of the clerk Isidro Perez, the 21st day of September, 1648

Epilogue

Text of a letter from Sanct' Germain Franciscus in Santa Marta to Atta
Olivia Clemens in Rome, written in Imperial Latin.

*To my most cherished and enduring friend Olivia, Sanct' Germain
sends his greetings to Senza Pari near Rome.*

*So you have left Paris at last. Your letter reached Acapulco a month
after I did, and I apologize for taking until now to write to you. When
I returned to Acapulco, I encountered a mass of difficulties which required considerable time to put to rights. I will tell you the whole of it
when next I see you.*

*I was saddened to hear that you could not escape the consequences
of politics, though I was not entirely surprised. The chaos in France will
need sure hands and many willing helpers to be ended; your Cardinal
Mazarin has enough to occupy a dozen men. I am grateful that he had
the good sense to release you from his embassy at last. However that may
be, I hope your separation from your Gascon Musqueteer is not long-
lasting. You say you are fortunate to have found a lover at last who
knows you for all you are and loves you without reservation. Had I not
sought such love for as long as I have I could find it in my heart to envy
you. But I know that such love is rare and comes not from wishing or
seeking, but from the lover. I am thankful to you for assuring me that
such a love is possible.*

*You were right to chide me for trying to escape wars in the Old World
by coming to the New. If my travels here have reminded me of nothing
else, they have shown me again that people are afraid of different ways
of life; conquest is as much a result of disdain for other ways of life as
it is a striving for military and trading advantage. That all is done in
the name of deities may result in acceptance of the intolerable for many.
For me, it brings only despair, for it convinces me that it is not what we
are but how those of our blood must live that causes humankind to believe us monsters, to hate and fear us.*

As you may have guessed, I am planning to return to Europe within the month. I have sufficient chests of my native earth to cross the ocean with as little discomfort as I can. Perhaps there will be a lull in the fighting that will allow all of us a little peace. At least I will not have to witness the determined destruction I see all around me here. Strange as it may seem, I am homesick, even if coming home means facing terrible circumstances. My affairs here, in all the New World, are all in order, and it only remains to hand the Capitan the money for our passage; our baggage and luggage will be loaded aboard. Before I attend to that, I am bidden to meet tonight with Obispos Trineo y Alfia and Apuesta y Fogon to clear up some misunderstanding they inform me has been brought to their attention. Once that is dealt with, I will give my full attention to readying myself for the ineffable joys of lying in a dark hold for thirty or forty days.

Until I see you once more, this brings you my unfaltering love and my trust that it will find you thriving and safe.

> *Ragoczy Sanct' Germain Franciscus*
> *(his sigil, the eclipse)*
> *By my own hand, the 16th day of April, 1649*